## Praise for *Publish and*

"Like Alison Lurie's *Women and Ghosts, Publis[*
a lot of well-educated Americans long for but
tainment that is sophisticated."

—Janice Harayda, *The Cleveland Plain Dealer*

"Hilarious...an irresistible work of intellectual shenanigans [and] horrific suspense."

—Sandra Chait, *The Seattle Times/Post Intelligencer*

"Three devilish novellas...[A] delightful collection of the ghostly and ghastly."

—Sarah Hepola, *The Austin Chronicle*

"Original, droll, startling...Witty and penetrating:  Hynes creates pungent satires of academic life while at the same time infusing them with genuine suspense and real terror."

—*Kirkus Reviews*

"Cleverly barbed...Hynes's tales are laced with references to Poe, M.R. James and other masters of the macabre, but in this engaging collection he puts his own deft, blackly humorous spin on the genre."

—*Publishers Weekly*

"Dark and delightful...Hynes's satire is effective and as amusing as it is chilling."

—Judyth Rigler, *San Antonio Express News*

"Pure fun, especially for anyone who has ever stomped off to a literature seminar with *The Shining* buried discreetly underneath the great books in her backpack."

—Sharan Gibson, *The Houston Chronicle*

"*Publish and Perish* offers mesmerizing plot, barbed wit and a clear appreciation for the subtle ghost stories of Edgar Allan Poe, Henry James and M.R. James."

—Diane Fisher Johnson, *The Lexington Herald-Leader*

"Pick up a copy of *Publish and Perish* and prepare to laugh and wince as [James Hynes] craftily skewers university life."

—Anne Valentine Martino, *Ann Arbor News*

PUBLISH

and

PERISH

Also by JAMES HYNES

THE WILD COLONIAL BOY

# PUBLISH and PERISH

*Three Tales
of Tenure and Terror*

JAMES HYNES

Picador USA ❧ New York

Picador® USA is a registered trademark and is used by St. Martin's Press under license from Pan Books Limited.

For information on Picador USA Reading Group Guides, as well as ordering, please contact the Trade Marketing department at St. Martin's Press.
Phone: 1-800-221-7945 extension 488
Fax: 212-677-7456
E-mail: trademarketing@stmartins.com

Library of Congress Cataloging-in-Publication Data

Hynes, James.
    Publish and perish : three tales of tenure and terror / James Hynes.
        p. cm.
    Contents: Queen of the jungle—99—Casting the runes.
    ISBN 0-312-18696-7
    1. College teachers—United States—Fiction.  2. College stories, American.  3. Horror tales, American.  4. Satire, American.
    I. Title.
    PS3558.Y55P8  1997
    813'.54—dc21                                    96-53532
                                                         CIP

First Picador USA Paperback Edition: June 1998

10 9 8 7 6 5 4 3 2 1

for MINNIE MAYHEM

# Contents

[The idea of the book] is the encyclopedic protection of theology and of logocentrism against the disruption of writing, against its aphoristic energy, and . . . against difference in general. If I distinguish the text from the book, I shall say that the destruction of the book, as it is now under way in all domains, denudes the surface of the text. That necessary violence responds to a violence that was no less necessary.

—Jacques Derrida, OF GRAMMATOLOGY

O this learning, what a thing it is!
—Shakespeare, THE TAMING OF THE SHREW, ACT I, SCENE ii

QUEEN
of the
JUNGLE

## one

*S*OMETHING WAS WRONG WITH PAUL AND ELIZA-
beth's cat, Charlotte. She was peeing outside of the litter box, and
driving her owners to distraction. Neither of them was certain
what the problem was, but they both thought that it might have
something to do with their complicated domestic arrangement.
Paul lived in Bluff City, Iowa, where he was finishing up a three-
year postdoc in the English department at the State University of
Iowa; Elizabeth lived four days a week in Chicago, where she was
tenure-track at Chicago University. Charlotte, their cat, stayed
with Paul in Iowa. She was an indoor cat, ten years old, with no
front claws. She looked black-and-white at first glance: black across
her back, and over her eyes and ears like a mask, and as white as
ice cream across her chest and jaws and along her forelegs. But in
direct light the black turned out to be blended with fine brown
hairs that spread in faint stripes down her head and back, faintly
ringing her tail like a raccoon's. Her eyes were rimmed in black, as
if by kohl. She was intelligent and high-strung, and she wasn't particularly affectionate, even for a cat, hissing and scratching at
strangers who tried to pick her up. Even when Paul or Elizabeth
lifted her, she would endure it for roughly a count of ten—by
Paul's reckoning—and then scramble out of their grasp with a
petulant croak, only to sit a few feet away with her back to them
and her raccoon tail out straight behind her. Sometimes, though,
on the nights Elizabeth was away, Charlotte would settle in with

Paul, sprawling across his chest as he lay reading on the couch, or nosing her way in under the covers beside him in bed. Lately she had taken to winding slowly between his legs as he sat at his computer, or when he stood in the kitchen preparing a meal. The first couple of times this startled him, but he had gotten used to it. He even looked forward to the warm, silky, gliding pressure against his calves, the little throaty purr.

Within the last couple of months, however, Charlotte had begun to pee where she wasn't supposed to. Paul and Elizabeth lived in a comfortable apartment over an old garage. At first they thought the smell might be coming from raccoons nesting in the junk the landlord stored below, but then Paul stepped barefoot one morning in a wet spot on the carpet. Charlotte began at the top of the stairs that led up from the front door, then she peed on the sofa cushions, on Paul's secondhand easy chair, and finally, by an inevitable progression, in the bed—on the pillows, in the middle of the mattress, among the rumpled sheets in the morning while Paul was still in the shower. The first time it happened, on the stairs, Paul did not tell Elizabeth about it. By time she made it back to Bluff City that particular weekend, Paul had blotted up the stain and the smell with a combination of baking soda and an enzyme he'd bought at a pet store. But the second time, on the sofa, happened on a Thursday night, and when Elizabeth came home on Friday morning, she stopped short inside the door with her bag still slung over her shoulder and wrinkled her nose at the sharp tang of cat pee.

"Oh my God," she said. "Is that what I think it is?"

Paul came away from his desk and nodded. Charlotte was nowhere to be seen.

"Charlotte did *that?*" Elizabeth lowered her bag and looked about for the cat. Her immediate response, Paul could tell, was concern for Charlotte's well-being, with little to spare for her husband's. Though they no longer spoke of her as such, Charlotte had been Elizabeth's cat long before Elizabeth married Paul. She was the offspring, in fact, of an even older cat of Elizabeth's, long deceased, named Emily. Elizabeth loved to tell the story of Charlotte's birth, the whole litter born one icy January day in the back of a closet in her first apartment. The birth had ruined a pair of suede shoes, in honor of which, ever since she was two, Charlotte had worn a green suede collar that matched her eyes.

Now Elizabeth moved through the apartment with her head down, clicking her tongue for the cat, passing the couch without patting the damp spot or even glancing at the stain.

"Are you all right, Charlotte?" she crooned from the bedroom, where Charlotte had a hiding place. "What's wrong, boo-boo?"

"It's not the first time, okay?" Paul raised his voice even though he knew that Elizabeth wasn't listening. She never listened when she was baby-talking to Charlotte.

They took her to the vet, who tested Charlotte for urinary disease and several other things, but there was nothing physically wrong. She put Charlotte on a special diet anyway, to no avail. Every three or four days Paul trod barefoot on a new wet spot in the carpet, or made an unscheduled trip to the laundromat with the bedclothes. Back at the vet's Charlotte glowered up from the examination table as the vet knitted her brow and asked if there had been any recent, sudden changes in household routine—was there a new cat in the house, had they moved the litter box, changed the brand of cat litter? Elizabeth stroked Charlotte's head and glanced at Paul, who shook his head.

"I have to ask," the vet said, crossing her arms. "Are you guys okay? No problems between the two of you?"

"Oh no!" said Elizabeth. "I mean, we're fine."

"Absolutely," said Paul.

So Charlotte got her own prescription sedatives, two tiny pills every day, and the peeing stopped. But her first weekend home after the pills started, Elizabeth saw Charlotte stagger and walk into a wall, and she dumped the rest of the pills down the toilet.

"Did you see her eyes?" Elizabeth said. "She's just a zombie."

"I know," Paul said. "I don't like it either."

On the phone the vet threw up her hands, so to speak.

"I've done everything I can do," she said. "Unless . . ."

"Unless what?" Elizabeth said, as Paul listened in from the phone in the bedroom.

Their veterinarian had a vaguely New Age aspect to her; the

magazines in her waiting room promised spiritual release of a generally nondenominational sort, and the speakers flowed with drifting, tuneless music. Paul and Elizabeth had noted this, and decided to ignore it, because the vet was so good with Charlotte.

"I have a friend," the vet said, "who's had some success at connecting, directly, somehow, with animals."

Paul stood up from the bed and walked to the limit of the phone cord; he caught Elizabeth's eye down the length of the hall as she stood at the phone in the kitchen. Elizabeth was tall—an inch or two taller than Paul, in fact—with sharp features and an open expression that belied her increasing gravity. She had a long, slender neck that Paul had first noted covertly across a seminar room, and now, as she listened to the vet on the phone, she pressed her narrow palm to her throat. Sometime in grad school Elizabeth's hair had gone prematurely gray; Paul had assured her that he found the gray attractive, to which she replied somewhat tartly that she likewise found his receding hairline endearing. In the end, she decided not to color it because it gave her the feeling of being a step up from her grad students, most of whom were only slightly younger than she was. It was that same self-conscious gravity that made Paul certain that she'd scoff—politely—at the vet's suggestion. If anything, Elizabeth had less patience with this sort of New Age occultism than Paul did. It smacked of the sort of essentialist, nurturing, womanist stuff she reviled gleefully and at great length in her own articles on feminist theory. Paul widened his eyes at Elizabeth in incredulity and mouthed the words "A kitty psychic?" But Elizabeth had a sentimental streak where the cat was concerned; she wouldn't be caught dead with *Vogue* or *Glamour*, but now and then Paul glimpsed an issue of *Cat Fancy* in her briefcase. She twisted her long neck and turned away from him, the phone nestled between her shoulder and her sharp chin.

"What's your friend's number?" she said to the vet.

Elizabeth ignored Paul over the next day or two as he joked about swarthy women in colorful head scarves, about crystal balls with one of those suction-cup Garfields clinging to the inside, about "pawreaders" and little kitty tarot cards. Finally, on a bright, frigid February afternoon, the psychic came to talk to the cat. She turned out to be a large woman in a tailored suit and a quilted parka, and mounting the stairs to the apartment, she arrived at the top both breathless and grave. Her name was Andrea, with the emphasis on the second syllable—just Andrea, nothing more, like Roseanne—and she had a deep voice and thick dark hair and a solemn Mediterranean mien which was broken only once by a hearty, throaty laugh. She did not ask to be shown the cat right away—Charlotte had hidden immediately at the sound of a stranger's voice—but instead weighed down one end of the couch and caught her breath and asked questions about what Charlotte did all day and where her favorite places were. Elizabeth sat at the other end of the couch, all elbows and knees, leaning forward and intently answering each question. Paul brought them all tea and sat across the room. The two women looked like a before-and-after picture of some sort, but Paul wasn't sure who was before and who was after. Andrea had a surprisingly pointed chin for someone with such a round face, and she fingered it and looked off into space as Elizabeth nervously answered each question in great detail. Andrea never said much in response, with the result that Elizabeth went on and on to fill the silence, running out of things to say finally and gesturing at the air as if to conjure a sound from the psychic. Then, after an endless pause, Andrea nodded and simply said, "Uh huh." This, and the fact that she scarcely made eye contact with either Paul or Elizabeth, convinced Paul—as if he needed proof—that she was a fraud. He twisted in his seat, trying to catch Elizabeth's eye himself, hoping to lure her into the kitchen for an urgent whispered conference. But then, to his surprise, he felt the silken pressure of Charlotte winding between his calf and the chair, and before he could say a word, Andrea brightened and laughed deep in her throat. She patted the cushion next to her, gazing intently at the cat and clicking her tongue.

"This is Charlotte," Elizabeth said tremulously, as if she were introducing a troubled child.

"I'm surprised she even came out," Paul was about to say, when Charlotte further astounded him by jumping up on the couch next to the psychic, sitting on her haunches with her back to Elizabeth, and looking up at their visitor. She gave a plaintive meow, and Paul and Elizabeth looked across the room at each other in astonishment.

"Could you leave us alone for a few minutes?" Andrea said, the cat and the psychic gazing into each other's eyes with a similar demeanor. After a moment of speechlessness, Paul and Elizabeth retired to the bedroom down the hall.

"How much are we paying this woman?" Paul said, shutting the door.

"Did you see that?" Elizabeth said in a low voice, getting up to reopen the door a crack. "Have you ever seen her do that with a stranger? Just jump right up?"

Paul sat on the bed.

"Okay, well maybe she has an affinity with animals or something," he began, lowering his voice, "but you don't really think she reads their minds, do you?"

They whispered back and forth for several minutes, sitting together on the edge of the bed, glancing down the hall at the doorway to the living room. Elizabeth touched Paul on the arm every few seconds as if she heard something, but there was nothing to hear. Paul started to riff on the idea of doing the Vulcan mind meld with a cat, but he could tell that Elizabeth wasn't listening to him.

"I can't stand it," she hissed finally, and stood, but just then Andrea hove into view, turning out of the living-room door and into the hall with all the solemnity of a minor planet, blocking the afternoon light from the kitchen window at the far end of the apartment. Elizabeth caught her breath and stood in the bedroom door, and Paul looked over her shoulder at Charlotte nestled contentedly between Andrea's arms and her massive bosom. Instinctively, Paul began to count to ten in expectation of Charlotte's petulant growl and leap, but Andrea just kept coming down the hall with the cat in her arms, plucking gently with her short fingers at the back of Charlotte's head. Over the creak of the floorboards under Andrea's feet, Paul could hear Charlotte purring.

"Well, she's upset," said Andrea, stopping just outside the doorway.

"What did she tell you?" Elizabeth said. Paul could tell his wife was serious by the tension in her spine. If he were to touch her backbone just now, she'd twang like a plucked string.

"They don't think in words, dear," said Andrea, still avoiding the gaze of the humans, looking intently at the cat, who gazed serenely out from behind the rampart of Andrea's forearm. "They think in pictures."

"What does she see, then?" Paul said, flashing on the image of mounds of kibble like sand dunes, and Elizabeth, without looking, reached back and gave him a touch which meant "Don't interrupt."

"There's a woman who's always coming and going," Andrea said, "and this coming and going disturbs her somehow."

At this, the psychic at last looked up and met Elizabeth's eye, and Elizabeth pressed her hand to her mouth. Paul felt his heart begin to race.

"Oh my God," Elizabeth said in a small voice, through her fingers. "Is it me?"

"I can't tell," Andrea said. "All I can see is a woman who comes and doesn't stay very long, and who leaves almost as soon as she gets here."

By now Paul's heart was pounding, and he tried to edge into the crowded doorway between his wife, who was white-faced and wide-eyed, and the psychic, who was looking back down at Charlotte, stroking her behind the ears.

"My wife is in Chicago four days a week," he said, licking his lips. "I mean, she comes and goes, you know, all the time . . ."

"Oh Paul, I'll bet that's what it is." Elizabeth gave him a heart-broken glance, and she reached for Charlotte, cooing wordlessly. With the cat in her arms, she sat on the bed and murmured to Charlotte, "Oh boo-boo, Mama's sorry." A moment later, Charlotte leaped out of her arms and scampered through the legs of the humans in the doorway and down the hall. Paul watched her go, with a growing sense of alarm. Andrea plucked at the cat hairs on the lapels of her suit.

"Do you people have a lint brush?" she said.

Elizabeth, biting her lip, followed Charlotte into the living room, and Paul led Andrea into the kitchen, where he helped her rotate into her parka and wrote her a check for seventy-five dollars.

"I could tell you more," Andrea said, buttoning the parka up under her chin, "but I'd have to spend all day with the cat."

Paul's hand trembled a bit as he wrote the check, and he moved so that Andrea couldn't see it.

"It would be a hundred and fifty, for the day," Andrea said in a monotone. "You'd have to be out of the house."

Paul handed her the check without meeting her eye and turned her toward the stairs. He glanced in the living room to see Elizabeth flat on her stomach on the floor, imploring Charlotte to come out from behind the couch.

"Mama's not *angry*," she was saying. "Mama's *sorry.*"

"No, you've been very helpful," Paul said. "I think you've solved our little mystery."

Andrea moved as slowly down the stairs as she'd come up, gripping the rail, bending it under her grasp. On the step behind her, Paul wanted to scream, to give her a push. At the door, Andrea stopped and turned again on her axis, blocking even the freezing February air.

"I'm not sure it's your wife who comes and goes," she said. "It could be somebody else. I'd have to spend the day to be sure."

"We have your number," Paul said, squeezing her out the door and closing it behind her.

In the living room, with Charlotte still behind the couch and Elizabeth perched on the edge of it, Paul and Elizabeth argued.

"We just spent seventy-five dollars," Paul said, still trembling, "to find out that the cat misses you."

"How did Andrea know that I'm not here all the time?" Elizabeth said. She rubbed her knees with long fingers. "I didn't tell her that. How did she know?"

"Look at you," Paul said angrily. "You're practically in tears. Do you mist up when you think about me, all alone here four days a week?"

Elizabeth glared up at him.

"Paul, Charlotte's an animal. I don't expect her to understand about a dual-career situation."

Paul looked at the ceiling.

"You *know* what I think about that," he sighed.

"You overestimate my position, Paul. I don't have that kind of clout." He could hear how weary she was of this argument.

"Lizzie, you're a star." He leveled his gaze at her. "You killed them at the MLA this year. You *killed* them. Walter"—the chair of her department at Chicago—"would do anything for you."

Elizabeth stood, and they faced each other across the coffee table.

"When I have tenure," she said, her voice tight, "I will talk to Walter about offering my husband a position." She marched to the door, and when Paul turned toward her, held up both forefingers, canted her head away from him, and said, "I *don't* want to talk about this now."

Paul waited until he heard the bedroom door shut, and then sagged into his chair, sighing soundlessly with relief at having deflected the argument in a safe direction. His hands were still shaking, though, and whatever satisfaction he felt evaporated as Charlotte pressed herself out from under the couch and jumped up on the coffee table. She stood on all four paws, her tail lashing from side to side, and watched him with her green, kohl-rimmed eyes. Paul sat up, as if preparing to defend himself.

"What have you done?" he whispered to the cat.

two

*I*N FACT, CHARLOTTE, OR THAT FOOLISH FAT WOMAN, had nearly betrayed the fact that Paul was having an affair with a graduate student in another department. This narrowly averted revelation couldn't have come at a worse time. Elizabeth and Paul had graduated from the University of the Midwest in Hamilton Groves, Minnesota, and had gone on the job market the same year. They had married as graduate students in Hamilton Groves, with lots of bold talk from Paul of pulling Elizabeth along in the slipstream of his career. He had made something just short of a promise that a position for her would be almost a requirement for any job he might be offered. Now Paul was finishing a dead-end postdoc at Iowa, and Elizabeth was getting an early-tenure review in a month's time, saying that she would see what she could do with her chair at Chicago. This fall, she had begun to bring Paul the classified pages from the Sunday Chicago papers, with editorial jobs and copywriter positions circled in red felt-tip. She said nothing to him about the pages, but left them on the coffee table, and every week he balled them up and lobbed them overhand into the wastebasket by his desk at the end of the living room. Her compromise, as she saw it, was to make the commute back and forth to Bluff City, rather than have him spend the time and money going to Chicago. She was making nearly twice as much as he was, after all, though they never talked about that, either. When she was in

Chicago, she rented a room in Hyde Park from another member of her department, a friend of hers from grad school whom Paul had never cared for.

In the meantime, Paul had found himself in bed since the beginning of last semester with Kymberly, a first-year master's degree student in communications. He had met her at the start of the fall semester, at the English department picnic. She had come as the date of a doctoral candidate in English, who then ignored her all afternoon as he worked his dissertation committee, moving from picnic table to picnic table in descending order of importance. Since no one in his department was talking to him anymore, either, Paul joined her where she sat alone and introduced himself. She was shy, but remarkably unself-conscious, judging from the cut of her sundress. Paul listened to her attentively—she was from California, she'd just gotten here, she didn't know a soul in Iowa—and reflected that only among ambitious academics would such a stunning and personable young woman sit unattended. In the end he offered her a guided tour of Bluff City and they left the picnic together, unnoticed by anyone else. He'd had no intention of seducing her, at least to begin with, but over the course of a late-summer afternoon, he found her unaffected, charming in her way, and unexpectedly funny. On that first evening, as they sat on a bench beside the river, she had jumped up and demonstrated the patented dancing action of Rock 'n' Roll P.J.—Barbie's Rock 'n' Roll Friend!—who danced when you pressed the button on her pedestal. Kym kept her long legs together and thrashed her shoulders and hair about, and Paul laughed until he cried.

And now, for a man who, professionally, anyway, didn't even believe in the subconscious, let alone the occult, he was uncannily certain that Kym was the woman whose image the psychic had gleaned somehow from Charlotte. The peeing had started just after Kym began to spend the night, starting with the carpet at the top of the stairs where she and Paul had made love for the first time, on the evening after the department picnic. Since then, Charlotte had effectively nuked every site of their lovemaking: the couch, Paul's easy chair in the living room, the bed, the hall carpet, even a corner of the tablecloth on the kitchen table, where they'd done it, thrillingly, during an Indian-summer thunderstorm, with the power out and the kitchen full of crashing white light.

"Will the lightning, like, hit us?" Kym had gasped. She was from Santa Monica, and had an unreasonable fear of Midwestern weather—tornadoes, blizzards, hail the size of golf balls.

"God, I hope so," Paul had said, laughing.

He had managed to keep Kym from learning of Charlotte's little accidents, which wasn't very hard, since Charlotte usually waited until Kym had left in the morning. If Kym noticed the lingering smell, she didn't mention it; she probably assumed that was what a house smelled like with a cat in it. At any rate, he didn't want to spook Kym, who seemed to regard Charlotte as somehow disturbing and unclean. She didn't like the cat hair on her clothes, didn't like the cat watching them when they made love; if there were enough time and foresight, Paul made an effort to put Charlotte out of the room.

But part of Kym's attraction, he realized, was that there was something feral about her. He'd actually given quite a bit of thought to this; he'd never been involved before with anyone quite like her. Unlike Elizabeth, Kym was talkative after sex, and in these intimate moments he learned that her communications degree was part of a well-thought-out plan, that her profoundest ambition was to have her own daytime talk show. This accounted for the extra Y in her name, which she had adopted as an undergraduate, once her calling became clear to her. It separated her from all those other Kimberlys out there, and would look terrific in the opening credits of her show, a script that would write itself across the screen and end in a sparkle, under the sprightly, funky theme music. And like her name, her talk show would be a little bit different, one that wouldn't pander to the audience or feature fat people or stupid people or trash, or, for that matter, fat, stupid, trashy people.

"I'd like to be the next Leeza Gibbons," she'd said, fixing her gaze on the ceiling. Then, without looking at him, she swatted his arm.

"Don't you dare laugh," she said.

In a heroic display of self-control, he didn't, and encouraged her to go on.

"Why does everybody on those shows have to be so unattractive? Even the hosts. Please. I'd only have smart, good-looking people. Intellectual-type people. Like Dan Rather." She rolled on her stomach, kicking her legs. "Anchormen and supermodels," she said. "Next Kymberly."

He buried his face in the hair at the back of her neck to keep from laughing, and she twisted under him and said, "You think that's really stupid, don't you?"

But what he thought was that she walked like a dancer, with her shoulders squared and her back erect and her hips swaying. She had a heart-shaped face and straight blond hair and a way of looking at him, dipping her chin and gazing up from under her bangs, that made him inconsolably restless. And she moved around Charlotte, in fact, the way another cat might move, the two of them circling each other warily. He loved to lie back after sex, on the couch, say, and watch the way Kym jumped up and moved across the room when Charlotte came in to see what all the fuss was; he loved the way Kym's back arched and her hips glided as she edged along the bookcase, away from the cat.

"What you need is a tail," Paul said, reaching up to touch her just at the tip of her spine, in the deep, delicious curve of her back. "Right there."

"I don't think I like cats?" Kym said, with that rising inflection he detested in his students, but found adorable in her. She moved away from his touch, tense and swaying and irresistible, her arms crossed over her breasts, watching Charlotte as Charlotte watched her.

Now Paul wondered what to do about the cat. As long as Kym continued to come over, the peeing wouldn't stop, but at least for now Elizabeth would blame herself. It wasn't that so much, anyway, as that he felt betrayed by Charlotte. Paul prided himself that he was not the sort of husband who had reached an uneasy truce with his wife's beloved pet; he liked Charlotte, and until this awkward turn of events, had really felt that Charlotte liked him. A significant turning point in Elizabeth's regard for him during their courtship had come when Charlotte warmed to him, seeking out his touch, butting her head against his hand as he and Elizabeth lay in bed late at night, watching Letterman.

"She wants you to scratch behind her ears," Elizabeth had said, delighted. "That's level one."

"What's level two?" he said, scratching Charlotte, listening to her purr.

"If she deigns to stand on you," Elizabeth said, reaching across to scratch Charlotte's chest, and within the week, Charlotte was standing on Paul's chest as he lay in bed, kneading him rhythmically with her white paws, purring loudly with a vacant look in her eyes.

"Is there a level three?" he'd said.

"Well," Elizabeth had said, beaming, "if she drools on you, it's love."

By now, a couple of years into their marriage, Charlotte divided her time equally between Elizabeth and Paul, crawling into Paul's lap as often as she crawled into Elizabeth's, drooling on his shirt. When Elizabeth was away, Charlotte shadowed Paul about the apartment, refusing to be picked up, of course, but trotting at his heels whenever he moved from one room to another, and dashing ahead of him whenever he went into the kitchen, watching him wide-eyed, mewling for a treat. When he sat at his computer, she sprawled across the desk at his elbow and watched him write, rousing herself occasionally to nudge his hand as he moved the mouse, or walking across the keyboard, her fur rising with the crackling static from the screen. Alternately amused or annoyed, depending on how much gibberish her paws had created on the keyboard, Paul lifted her to the floor, where she took out her rejection on one of her catnip mousies. As he cleaned up his text, he would hear her on the carpet behind him, leaping at the mousie with her back arched and her legs out stiffly, batting the mousie around between her paws, catching it in her teeth and flinging it into the air to bat at it again. He would turn and watch her and think up an ironic, affectionate nickname for her: Charlotte, the Mighty Huntress. Charlotte, Mousie Terminator. Charlotte, Queen of the Jungle.

Now the queen seemed to be overstepping her authority, claiming priority in matters that were outside her domain. Paul tried bribing Charlotte, bringing her a new cat toy every couple of days—a pink catnip dinosaur, a plastic ball with a bell inside, a handful of furry little mousies. Most of these disappeared under the couch in the first few minutes, so Paul bought a Cat Dancer, a length of wire with twists of cardboard at each end, and he taped one end to the doorway of the living room, so that Charlotte could bat it about at her leisure. But most of the time she ignored it. Only when he brushed past it and set it in motion did she make a few distracted leaps at it. Now and then he would tread on a mousie, padding about the apartment in his bare feet, and Elizabeth asked him once, distractedly, if there didn't seem to be more mousies about the apartment than before.

"Maybe they're breeding," he'd said, and she murmured something and returned to her book.

Now, the night after Andrea's visit, with Elizabeth headed for Chicago the next morning, the echoes of their earlier argument still reverberated, and they went to bed separately, Paul later than his wife. He came into the chill, darkened bedroom, humid already with his wife's steady breathing, and he parted the curtains slightly, to let in a sliver of light from the streetlight so that he could see to undress. As he pulled off his sweater, he saw that the narrow shaft of light fell in a bright strip across Charlotte's back, along the divide between her black and white fur. She lay on his side of the bed like the Sphinx, with her forepaws outstretched and her head lifted, as if she were standing guard over her mistress, who lay on her side in a long lump under the covers, her back to the middle of the bed. Charlotte's head was in the shadow, her pointed ears silhouetted against the pale wall behind her, her round eyes full of a bottomless dark. She watched as Paul lifted one leg and then the other out of his trousers, and he stood there in his briefs for a moment as if she'd caught him at something, his trousers hanging limp from his hand.

"Scoot," he whispered, but she didn't move.

"Charlotte, move," he said, louder, and he swung the trousers slowly at her, dragging a leg across her dark face. But still she didn't flinch. He could feel his skin tightening in the cold of the bedroom.

He turned away and draped his trousers across the chair in the corner, then he twitched the curtains wider, throwing the glare of the streetlight into Charlotte's eyes. This got a reaction. Her whole face flattened and her eyes squeezed into slits, making her look at once devilish and annoyed. Paul felt a shiver which had nothing to do with the cold. This was a look humans weren't meant to see.

"Paul, close the curtains." Elizabeth's voice rose, muffled, out of the dark on the other side of the bed. *"Please."*

Paul turned to close the curtains, and he heard a soft thump against the carpet, and he turned back to see the dim, pixilated flash of Charlotte's white paws moving up the hall, away from him.

# three

IN THE MORNING CHARLOTTE FOLLOWED ELIZA-
beth obsessively, into the bathroom and out again, into the living
room as she filled her briefcase with papers, into the kitchen, where
the cat prowled under foot as Elizabeth and Paul maneuvered back
and forth between the fridge, the counter, and the table. Elizabeth
spoke only to the cat, murmuring baby talk at her that had in it
equal measures of concern and guilt. Once Paul caught his wife
watching him when she thought he wasn't looking, and when he
turned to her, drawing breath to speak, she glanced away and bent
to Charlotte, stroking her firmly from head to tail, and calling her
baby, muffin, boo-boo. Paul left the room to put on his shoes, and
when he came back, jingling his car keys to signal that it was time
to go to the train station, Elizabeth was in her blue coat, stooping
to the cat, still stroking her. At the sound of the keys, Charlotte
started and then scampered away, through Paul's legs, down the
hall, and into the bedroom, out of sight. Elizabeth stood, her face
drained of color, and picked up her bag and her briefcase.

"Lizzie . . ." Paul said, but she marched past him and down the
stairs.

It was so cold in the car they kept their coats buttoned up all the
way to the station. It was a brilliant day, the angled light glaring
off the snow. The car's tires crunched against the snow packed on
the road. He'd forgotten to bring his sunglasses, and he squinted
against the glare all the way down Linn Street. He was aware of

Elizabeth watching him, but he chose not to look at her, taking his attention off the road only to wipe the frost off the windshield with his glove. Finally, as he idled in front of the station, she turned in her seat, wrapped in her coat, and fixed her gaze on him, narrow-eyed and tight-lipped, as if she were sizing him up. She only did this when she was about to make an announcement. She knew how uncomfortable it made him.

"What?" he said at last.

"The tenure thing looks good," she said, her breath a small white cloud. "I don't think I have to worry about it."

"Lizzie, that's what I've been saying."

"I'm going to talk to Walter this week about you," she went on. "I'll talk to him tomorrow."

Paul drew a breath and let it out in a long white stream. Behind them someone honked their horn.

"Okay," he said. "Thank you."

Still narrow-eyed, Elizabeth lifted the corner of her lip in a smile.

"We have to be together, Paul," she said. "Otherwise we won't own a single thing that doesn't smell of cat pee."

"Oh great," Paul said. "Are you doing this for me, or for Charlotte?"

The car horn behind them honked again, twice, and Elizabeth leaned across and kissed him. A moment later she was out of the car, stooping in to yank her bag and her briefcase from behind the seat, and then she was gone, banging the door after her. Paul watched her go, a tall, bright blue blur in the melting frost on the window, and he nearly bounded out of the car after her, he was so relieved. But the car behind him honked again, angrily, and someone shouted something, and Paul put his car in gear and pulled away from the station, rolling down his window to flip the guy the bird in the frigid air.

At home he didn't have time to track down Charlotte and try to make up with her, so he checked her water dish and left her a little dry food, and went down to campus to teach and hold his office hours. In spite of the brutal cold, he felt almost chipper. Elizabeth had finally agreed to go to bat for him, and for the first time in months he went in to work without his stomach clenching up like a fist. In his last term at Iowa, he was becoming a nonperson in the department, undergoing the academic equivalent of being disappeared. People who had been friends of his when he first arrived—people he and Elizabeth had gone to movies with, with whom they had traded dinner invitations—now greeted him offhandedly in the hall and made vague offers of lunch. People who had lunched with him before now merely nodded to him, or ducked out of sight when they saw him coming. And the people who had nodded to him before now looked right through him. Simply stepping into the department office to check his mailbox felt like running a gauntlet, and he would retreat to his office with his heart pounding, as if he'd escaped with his life.

His prospects had looked a good deal brighter three years before. He'd understood from the start that the position was non-tenure-track, but to begin with there had been broad hints that if his dissertation was well published in good time, he'd be on the short list for a position in his speciality that was coming open in the next year or two. Paul had been quietly ecstatic about this. He already had in hand a letter from a major British university press offering to publish his book, subject to favorable reports from the anonymous readers, to certain revisions, etc., etc. Without quite making it public, and without quite saying the book had been accepted, he let this information get about in private, over lunch to a confidant sworn to secrecy and guaranteed to tell, in the quiet corners of cocktail parties to three or four select intimates. Elizabeth, who had followed him without a job to Bluff City, rolled her eyes at this behavior, but he told her that was how the game was played, that nobody else was going to sing his praises, that he had to do it himself, as long as he was discreet about it. And her reaction was three parts jealousy, he reckoned. Her own dissertation had been published, greatly abridged, as a monograph in a series from a small university press in Montana, in a print run of five hundred copies.

Then Paul had had a streak of bad luck. One of the reader's reports on his manuscript came back scathing—a career-destroying masterpiece of condescension and mean-spirited wit—and the major university press withdrew its offer, despite Paul's desperate overseas phone calls offering—begging, actually—to revise the book drastically. Then the permanent job opened up, and he didn't even make the short list; it went to a visiting professor already in the department, a supercilious Brit whose own flashy, overwritten book had won a prize. And finally, worst luck of all, Elizabeth's book won an even bigger prize, and schools that hadn't even wanted to interview her the year before called her up at home and practically offered her jobs sight unseen. In a short time Paul's life turned upside down: Elizabeth had the tenure-track job at Chicago, the British professor had Paul's old office with the view of the river, and Paul was moved into an office off a stairwell with a view of the power plant and a parking lot, sharing the space with a neurotic teaching assistant who left cigarette butts and half-empty diet soda cans all over the desk and an emeritus who came in twice a week to fall asleep in his old easy chair over a split-backed copy of *The Seven Types of Ambiguity.*

Today, however, Paul breezed through the department office feeling giddy as a newlywed. He hummed to himself over the copy machine, and he winked at the secretary. As his students dozed in their overheated classroom, he lectured with his feet up on the desk at the front, twirling a pencil between his fingers and squinting out the window into the light glittering off the snow, thinking of life in Chicago: the ample bookstores, the smoky blues clubs, the Art Institute. Back in his office he found the emeritus in an Empson-induced slumber, his white-haired head hung over his chest, but even that could not derail Paul's good mood. He'd heard once that the old fellow had seen action in Normandy, so Paul leaned over the sleeping man and said, "Hit the dirt!" in an urgent whisper, and the emeritus jolted awake very satisfactorily, wide-eyed and shaking at some private flashback of Omaha Beach.

"Office hours," Paul said, tapping his wristwatch, and after the emeritus had shuffled out, still trembling, Paul locked the door, closed the blinds against the snow glare, and turned out the lights. He pushed aside the cans of Diet Coke and put his feet up on the desk, resuming his dream of Chicago: the cafés, the first-run foreign movies, the Cubs, the Bears, the Bulls. Of course, he could have had all that a year ago, if he'd followed Elizabeth to Chicago as a junior copywriter, but how much better it would be if he could say, oh yes, I teach literature at Chicago. Or Northwestern, that would be just as good. Or even De Paul or La Salle, in a pinch. There was no point in being greedy. He imagined himself in a nicely rumpled suit and a sweeping overcoat, chatting up the sleek but bored trophy wife of some commodities broker in a plush bookstore on the Miracle Mile, and he got a bit excited at the thought of all the untapped *energy* of a woman like that, with nothing to do all day but shop and keep herself fit. He shifted in his chair and took his time over this, closing his eyes and imagining the glances back and forth over the fiction display table, imagining himself and the trophy wife—Helena, no, *Victoria*—thirtyish, with a knowing look in her eye and a British accent—taking themselves across Michigan Avenue for tea in the food court at Neiman-Marcus, then imagining Victoria inviting him to admire the view of the ice on the lake from her penthouse apartment twenty stories up on Lakeshore Drive, where he stood her in the window in the pearly light of a long winter afternoon and peeled off one expensive layer at a time, murmuring to her, "Yes, I'm *tenure-track* at Chicago. . . ."

Someone knocked on the door, and Paul nearly upset himself in his chair. He caught himself but knocked over one of the postdoc's Cokes, and he jumped up, out of the path of a tiny wave of flat soda.

"Come in," he shouted, blotting at warm Coke with a fistful of Kleenex.

It was Kym.

"It's locked," she said, through the door. "Professor," she added, in case there might be someone else in the stairwell. Paul froze and a trickle of Coke hit the floor. Kym was breaking one of their rules—she wasn't supposed to come here. He dropped the Kleenex and hurried to open the door; Kym stood shivering on the landing, wrapped in a huge secondhand coat against the bitter cold outside, the collar pulled up to her ears, her cheeks reddened with her warm Californian blood. He glanced down the stairs behind her, still flushed with his Chicago imaginings. He knew he'd have to give Kym up soon, he'd have to tell her he was leaving for Chicago, but please, dear God, not yet. He pulled her in and locked the door behind her.

"I know I'm not supposed to come here?" she said, but he was already turning her out of the coat, lifting her onto the desk.

"It's okay," he said, slipping his hands under her sweater. "I was just thinking about you."

# four

AT HOME HE FOUND CHARLOTTE CURLED in a ball on the bed with her paws over her head, and as he stood in the bedroom doorway she moved a paw and regarded him with one green eye. They watched each other for a moment, then Paul snapped his fingers and said, "Snack?" Charlotte uncurled instantly and lifted her head.

"Snack snack snackie," Paul sang, walking down the hall toward the kitchen. "Fishy fishy fish snack."

Behind him he heard a thump and then the patter of little feet on the hall carpet. She followed him into the kitchen meowing and looking up at him with round eyes, and he got the fish snacks out of the fridge, nasty, salty, flattened little dried fish as long as his pinkie, their scales and eyes intact. He held one between his thumb and forefinger and waved it slowly from side to side, and Charlotte rubbed up against him, weaving a silky figure eight through his legs. He could feel her purring in his shinbone.

"Now that I have your attention," Paul said, and he sat down cross-legged on the kitchen floor and put the dried fish right in front of him. Charlotte lunged for it, catching it by one end and crunching it between her teeth a millimeter at a time. Paul scratched her behind her ears, and she let him.

"Let's make a deal, Charlotte," he said, digging in the box for another fish, wrinkling his nose at the smell. She nearly leaped for it, so he held it at arm's length over his head.

"If you don't make trouble for the next few months," he said, "I'll give you all the fish snacks you want."

He tossed the snack in the air, and Charlotte leaped and twisted and caught it. Paul laughed and tossed a couple more fish about the kitchen, watching her scramble across the floor, her rear claws clicking against the linoleum. Then he put the box in the fridge behind him and stretched out across the floor, folding his hands over his chest, tipping the back of his head against the cold linoleum. Charlotte came to him, mewing quietly, and peered into his eyes, her nose a few inches from his.

"We're golden, pussycat," he said. "In a few months it'll be you and me and Elizabeth in the Windy City, living happily ever after." He stroked her under her chin and she lifted her head to give him access. "So behave."

And for the next day, things were fine with the cat. She lay on his desk with her chin on her paws as he worked on his book. She crawled into bed with him, purring. But when Kym came over the following night, Charlotte vanished. Paul was certain she was sulking in one of her hidey-holes, but when he went looking for her, she wasn't in any of the usual places—under the bed, in the cabinet under the telephone, behind the rollaway bed in the hall closet. So he left out some food for the cat and took Kym to bed.

But Kym seemed distracted. She was as ardent as ever, but her gaze fixed on the ceiling over his head, her brow knitted as if she were concentrating on something there. He had almost called her that afternoon and told her not to come; he wanted to be alone if Elizabeth called. In fact, he was counting on his wife calling. She must have talked to her chair today, and even though Walter couldn't decide anything on the spot, Paul wanted to know what she'd said to him and what he'd said to her. He lay back in bed, pleasantly sweated, his hands behind his head. Kym was in the bathroom, and he wondered how she'd take it if he told her he'd like to sleep alone tonight. He'd offer to run her home in his car, and if they left soon he could be back before eleven, when Elizabeth usually called.

"Paul, what's going to happen to us?" Kym said. She stood in the bedroom door, wearing his bathrobe, something she'd never done before. Paul blinked up at her.

"I'm sorry?" he said. "What did you say?"

Kym came in and lay across his legs at the end of the bed, propping her head on her hand. She fixed him with the same gaze she had directed at the ceiling a few minutes before.

"I know you don't love me?" she said. "But I know you don't love her either."

Paul stared at her and tried to laugh.

"I hear you talk to her on the phone, okay?" Kym pushed back her hair, a gesture that stirred him even now. "You're so mean to her on the phone. You sound so annoyed when you talk to her."

Paul closed his eyes and sighed.

"Kym," he said in a tone he'd have used with his grad students, if he'd had any, "the way I talk to my wife is none of your business."

"Excuse me?" she said. "You fuck me in her bed the minute she's like, out the door, and she's none of my business?"

Down the length of the bed Paul could feel her tense up. He sat, pulling his legs out from under Kym's arm.

"Well, here's something new under the sun," he said. "Kym stands up on her hind legs."

Kym's eyes widened and her mouth dropped open, and she rapped him hard on the ankle.

"Ow!" Paul jerked his leg away. He was beginning to find this exciting.

"You son of a bitch!" she gasped. "Don't you dare talk to me like that! I'm not one of your little Iowa bimbettes, okay?"

"Then don't act like one, *okay?*" He sighed. "Look, I'll explain this to you one more time." He sighed again. "Marriage has always been more of an economic relationship than anything else. The idea that love has anything to do with it is a fairly recent construction, dating from the Romantic era. Elizabeth and I have a kind of . . . affectionate professional partnership."

"Oh please." Kym rolled her eyes and swung off the bed to her feet. "That's *so* convenient. What would your wife say if she heard you say that?"

Kym stood with her weight canted on one leg, the robe parted nearly to her belly button. He wondered what she'd do if he lunged for her right now.

"I *got* it from her," he said. He started to creep across the bed. "You should read some of her articles, Kym, they're really brilliant. . . ."

She stiffened at that, and he checked his progress across the bed.

"So if she's, like, your business partner," Kym said, "then what am I?"

Paul rose up and hobbled across the bed toward her on his knees, smiling.

"You're *adorable*," he said.

He slid a hand inside the robe, and she twisted away, grasping his wrist tightly and saying, very firmly, *"Don't."*

He had pulled her onto the bed, where she was wrestling with him tight-lipped, when the phone rang. Paul released her and dived for the phone, pausing with his hand on the receiver to glance back at Kym. She stood glowering and breathing hard at the end of the bed, pulling the robe tight around her, jerking a knot in the belt.

"It's probably her," he whispered, and without a word Kym turned and marched out the door. He lifted the phone. It was Elizabeth.

"Paul," she said.

"Lizzie!" he said brightly, rolling onto his back. "Hey!"

"Lizzie! Hi! How *are* you!" Kym's voice, sharp and shrill, piped down the hall, and Paul clapped his hand over the mouthpiece and launched himself off the bed. He hissed down the hall after her, but Kym swung out of sight into the living room, and Paul slammed the bedroom door and pressed his back against it.

"Paul?" said Elizabeth.

"I'm here!" he said. "What's going on?"

"Well, *big* news," Elizabeth said portentously. "I found out something *very* interesting today."

Paul slid down the door to rest on his haunches. His heart was pounding.

"Tell me," he said.

"I was talking to one of my grad students who has a cat," she began.

"A cat?"

"Yes!" Elizabeth sounded excited. "And Carla—that's my student—she was having the same problem with her kitty that we're having with Charlotte."

Paul held the phone away from him and covered the mouthpiece again.

"Shit," he murmured, listening to Elizabeth's miniature voice. Through the door he heard Kym talking in an irritated, high-pitched voice.

"Get *away*," she was saying. "*God*, I hate cats."

Paul lifted the phone to his ear.

". . . it's not a hostile thing," Elizabeth was saying, "it's about security. She feels afraid when I go away, so to make herself safe, she tries to mingle her scent with mine. That's why she doesn't do it when I'm home . . ."

"Get *off!*" Kym cried, distressingly loud. Paul pushed himself to his feet and covered the mouthpiece again.

"She's just trying to protect herself," Elizabeth said. "It's not directed at anybody."

"Did you talk to Walter?" Paul said, taking his hand away from the mouthpiece.

Elizabeth caught her breath.

"Walter?" she said.

"Yes," Paul said, sighing. "Did you talk to Walter?"

There was a shriek from beyond the door, from the living room, loud enough to chill Paul and pull his skin tight from head to toe. He nearly squeezed the phone out of his palm, and he grabbed it with both hands, covering both the mouthpiece and the earpiece.

"Oh my *God!*" Kym was shrieking, over and over, in a pitch several registers higher than Paul had ever heard from a human being before. Dogs were probably hearing it, blocks away. He jumped across the room, away from the door, and ducked into the closet, pulling the door shut against the phone cord.

". . . I haven't had a chance yet," Elizabeth was saying, "Walter's out of town . . ."

"Hey honey, speak of the devil," Paul said in the chilly dark of the closet, hangers jammed up around his ears, his voice trembling. "Charlotte's just knocked something over. Can I call you back?"

"Is she all right?"

"Gosh yes," Paul said. "I'll call you back."

He lunged out of the closet and across the bed, slamming the phone down, then rolled off, threw open the door, and dashed down the hall. Charlotte careened out of the living room and rocketed down the hall. Paul twisted out of her way, lost his balance, and fell hard on his hip just outside the living room. He cursed, rolled over, and looked up. Just before him, a foot or so from the floor, the Cat Dancer he'd taped to the doorway was swinging wildly, the little knot of cardboard trembling on the end of the wire. Beyond that he saw Kym, naked, prancing about on her toes and shrieking wordlessly, dangling his limp bathrobe between her thumb and forefinger. She saw him lying in the doorway and stopped moving, and she looked down the length of her body and gingerly touched her thigh with her free hand, lifting her fingers to her nose and wincing in disgust. Paul pulled himself up in the doorway and reached for her, and she backed away, flinging the bathrobe at him.

"God," she said, holding her hands away from herself. "*God!*" She looked at him, trembling with anger. "Your fucking cat *peed* all over me!"

Paul was holding the robe to his chest with both hands, and at the same moment as Kym spoke he was stung to the back of his nostrils with the ineffable tang of Charlotte's urine. He jerked the robe away from himself, holding it out at arm's length as delicately as the Shroud of Turin. He had just glimpsed the large, dark blotch across the lap of the robe when Kym elbowed him out of the way as forcefully as a linebacker, brushing past the Cat Dancer and setting it swinging again, storming up the hall and into the bathroom, slamming the door behind her.

She stayed in there for twenty minutes, taking the longest shower in Paul's memory, using up every drop of hot water. Meanwhile Paul stalked into the bedroom and dragged Charlotte, snarling and scrabbling, out from under the bed. He lifted her roughly by her green collar and pushed her face into the damp, pungent stain in his bathrobe. She went wild at that, hissing at him and baring her rear claws, drawing scratches across his arm deep enough to release beads of blood. He shouted and dropped her, and she sprang up the hall and out of sight, a black-and-white blur. He balled up the robe and, still naked, stalked up and down the apartment with it, gripped in his hand like a bomb. He stuffed it into the trash in the kitchen and scrubbed his hands in the kitchen sink. Then he thought better of throwing the robe away—Elizabeth might wonder where it had gone to—and he filled up the sink with cold water—cursing Kym under his breath for using up all the hot—poured in some laundry detergent, and plunged the robe into the water, squeezing it with both hands until it was soaked through.

He came back into the bedroom, his hands smelling of liquid Tide, and found Kym completely dressed, pulling her coat on.

"You're leaving?" he said, knowing it was a stupid thing to say. She fixed him with a look and shrugged into the coat, winding her enormous scarf four times around her collar.

"Let me drive you home," he said, casting about for his shorts.

"Oh, please." Kym came around the bed and stopped before him. "Can I get through?"

He stepped aside, fumbling for something to say.

"I'm sorry," he said to her retreating back. "Look, think of it as a topic for your show: Your Married Lover and His Incontinent Cat. Next Kymberly!"

Kym stopped at the head of the stairs and turned.

"You know what the really sad thing is?" she said, looking down the hall at him. "I've been working up my nerve like, all week. Tonight was the night I was going to tell you that I love you."

She turned away and started down the stairs, hitting each step surprisingly hard for such a lithe woman. Paul hesitated, then hurried to the head of the stairs, shouting out, "I'll call you." But the only response was the slam of the front door, followed by a gust of freezing air that shriveled him and sent him scampering for his trousers and a sweater.

He fell back on the bed, unable to think. Then he sat up abruptly when he remembered that he'd promised to call Elizabeth back. He was surprised, in fact, that she hadn't called him back already. He lifted the phone and fingered the speed-dial button for Elizabeth's number, trying to recall what he'd said to her just before he hung up, and when he did he put the phone down without dialing and went into the living room. On top of an antique cabinet that Elizabeth had inherited from her grandmother, at the center of a lace doily, was a blue china vase full of dried flowers, another heirloom from her grandmother. He lifted the vase and dumped the flowers to the carpet, then he hefted the vase for a moment. He let it fall from his hand, and it bounced off the carpet and against the cabinet, knocking only a sliver out of its curved lip. He stooped, picked it up, hefted it again, and then threw it hard against the floor, cracking it into four or five large pieces.

"Charlotte," he said in a loud voice, "you're a very bad girl."

## five

H E LEFT FOOD AND WATER FOR THE cat, but she didn't come out of her hiding place, wherever that was, until Elizabeth came home. Now and then he thought he saw a movement out of the corner of his eye, a black-and-white blur, but when he turned, there was nothing there. It was like living with a ghost.

Elizabeth had been speechless with hurt over the phone when Paul told her about the vase, but by time she returned to Iowa on Friday her face was a map of indecision, over whether to be angry about the vase or concerned for the cat. As soon as she'd dropped her bag and slipped out of her coat, Elizabeth went to the cabinet in the living room where the vase had stood. Paul had made an artful pile of the fragments in the middle of the doily, like a votive offering. He stood at Elizabeth's elbow, rubbing the back of her neck and murmuring to her as she sighed again and again, turning a piece of the vase over in her long fingers. He saw Charlotte come in before Elizabeth did, and the cat gave him a brief, unreadable glance, then jumped up onto the end of the couch, where she gave a little chirrup to get Elizabeth's attention. Elizabeth sighed again and dropped to her knees next to the couch, tugging hard on the cat's ears.

"Charlotte, you are such a *bad girl*," she said, but there was a tender intonation to it, and Charlotte shook her ears free and rubbed her head against Elizabeth's hand, purring madly.

"Give her a break," Paul said. "She's just a cat."

Overnight, Paul had weighed the possibilities. There was no getting rid of Charlotte, Elizabeth wouldn't stand for that, and he knew she'd never forgive him if anything accidentally happened to the cat while she was gone. He had thought of suggesting that Charlotte move to Chicago and stay with Rebecca, the friend with whom Elizabeth stayed in Hyde Park, but he knew Rebecca was allergic to cats. Lying in bed alone after Kym had left, his hands behind his head, his bare arm stinging where Charlotte had clawed him, he had smiled to himself, finally appreciating the irony of the situation. Charlotte was in fact his greatest ally. The last thing he should do was make her happy. The more the cat acted up, the quicker he'd have a job in Chicago. He nearly took down the Cat Dancer, but Elizabeth would have noticed the change and made him put it back up, and at any rate, Charlotte mostly ignored it. He did get down on his stomach and pull the pink dinosaur and a handful of mousies out from under the couch, stashing them in his desk drawer, out of Charlotte's reach. Now, watching Elizabeth stroke the back of Charlotte's head with the tips of her fingers, Paul nearly said aloud, "The sooner we're all together, the happier she'll be." But he held his tongue. He knew from the way Elizabeth knitted her brow and sighed that she was thinking just that already. He reached out to stroke Charlotte's head himself, and the cat twisted away and walked, tail erect, to the other end of the couch, where she flopped over on her side and began to lick her private parts, ignoring them both.

"She's mad at you," Elizabeth said, scooting down the couch to the cat.

"I'm not surprised," Paul said. "You should have heard me when she broke the vase." He thought of rolling up his sleeve to show her the scars, but he knew she wouldn't look.

"Oh Charlotte," Elizabeth said, sighing again.

He knew better than to mention Walter again, though he was dying to know. After a moment, Elizabeth pushed herself up and went into the kitchen, leaving Paul and Charlotte to regard each other.

"Where are the fish snacks?" Elizabeth said from the kitchen, her head in the refrigerator.

Paul lunged silently at Charlotte, his hands out like claws, and the cat started violently, as if she'd been given an electric shock. Then he turned, smiling, and followed his wife into the kitchen.

"Behind the cottage cheese," he said.

He said nothing about Walter all weekend, waiting until Elizabeth brought it up herself, when they were in the bookstore downtown. They were in the pet section on the second floor, the two of them sitting in their coats and paging through guides to cat behavior with titles like *No Bad Kitty!* and *How to Make Your Cat Do What You Want*, when Elizabeth spoke without looking up from her book.

"Walter's in Ireland till next week," she said, "giving a paper."

Paul nearly looked up from the book across his knees—a coffee-table book open to a glossy picture of a Persian cat riding a surfboard—but he checked himself.

"Hm?" he said.

"I made an appointment with his secretary, though," Elizabeth said.

"That's good," Paul said. He held up the book. "Look. Surfin' kitties."

Elizabeth looked up and smiled, and behind her Paul saw Kym coming up the stairs. Her face wore a blank expression, but it brightened when she saw him. Their eyes met, and Kym started to smile. But then she saw Elizabeth sitting there, and she twisted away and went back down the stairs.

"I'm not supposed to know, of course," Elizabeth was saying, "but Rebecca told me."

"I'm sorry," Paul said. "Rebecca told you what?"

"Tenure," Elizabeth said, looking back down at her book. She smiled to herself. " 'Sure thing' was the phrase she used."

"It's what I've been saying."

"I know."

He turned the page of his book to see a cat in a fedora, à la Al Capone, posed in front of the Chicago Stock Exchange.

"Listen." He closed the book. "I'm going downstairs."

Elizabeth turned a page without looking at him. "Did you hear what I said about Walter?" she said.

"Yeah. I'll be downstairs."

He couldn't find Kym on the ground floor, so he stepped out onto the street and saw her moving away up the street. He started after her, glancing about, trying to look as if he weren't hurrying. The rule was no public recognition of each other; he couldn't even visit her apartment, since the neurotic teaching assistant, his officemate, lived in the same building. Finally he caught up to her, bundled up against the windchill in her enormous coat and scarf, only her eyes visible. He caught her by the arm and pulled her into an alley. She said something, but it was muffled by the scarf wrapped across her mouth.

"I'm sorry about the other night," Paul said, holding her by the shoulders.

Kym tugged down the scarf to free her mouth, but she didn't say anything. She looked away down the alley.

"And not just about my cat's incontinence," he said. "About her peeing on you, I mean."

Kym leveled her eyes at him.

"I know what 'incontinent' means," she said. "My gramma is incontinent."

"You're right, I'm sorry, what I mean is, I'm also sorry about, you know, not taking you seriously."

He paused, but she was waiting to hear more. He cleared his throat.

"You had something important that you wanted to say to me, and I wouldn't listen. I was . . . well, I was afraid, Kym. I was afraid, so I tried to make a joke out of it, and I'm sorry."

"You were afraid of me," she said flatly.

"Of course," he said, moving closer. He lifted his hand to stroke her reddened cheek, and hesitated. "Kym, I want you so much it terrifies me." He brushed her cheek with his knuckle and pulled away.

Kym looked away down the alley and sighed heavily.

"God, was I really screechy the other night?" she said.

"Well, you had a very good reason to be." Paul touched her face again, and she closed her eyes.

"Kym, there's a good chance I'll be getting a position in Chicago."

Her eyes popped open and she withdrew a fraction, away from his touch.

"And I want you to come with me."

Her eyes widened, and Paul stepped back.

"Come over Monday, after Elizabeth's gone."

"What are you saying to me?" she said, her breath wisping away in a little white cloud.

"Come over Monday," he said. "We'll talk." He trotted away down the alley, back to the bookstore.

## six

FTER ELIZABETH LEFT FOR CHICAGO ON Monday morning, Paul expected Charlotte to disappear again, but instead she followed him around the apartment, at a distance, eyeing him, but flinching away if he tried to come near her. The more he thought about this, the happier it made him. The trick, he realized, was to make the cat unhappy with the situation, but not with him. He decided not to try to buy her favor with fish snacks, to see if she would come to him, and sooner than he expected, she did, winding between his legs as he stood at the kitchen counter making a sandwich. He knew it was the tuna fish which lured her, but he was sufficiently moved by her willingness to come close to him that he let her lick a little tuna salad off a spoon. After lunch, though, when he was getting ready to go down to campus for class and office hours, she was nowhere to be found.

In the evening, Kym came over in jeans and a bulky sweater, and she sat in Paul's chair and refused at first even to take off her boots. Instead she sat with her feet together and her arms crossed, and she listened expressionlessly to his avowal of affection for her. He was very careful never to use the word "love." He and Elizabeth had agreed long ago not to use it with each other, as an intervention against hegemonic practice, but he was avoiding it with Kym for altogether different reasons.

"You know I have feelings for you, Kym" was as close as he allowed himself to come. Mainly he was trying to persuade her to leave the communications program at Iowa and follow him to Chicago. This idea had only come to him on the spur of the moment in the alley a couple of days ago, and the possibilities of it had been the central fixture of his fantasy life since. Right now he thought he was doing a pretty convincing job of persuading her that he'd actually given it some thought. He started out sitting across the room on the couch, protesting that she meant a great deal to him. Then he jumped up as if he were agitated and began to pace, wondering aloud if he shouldn't forswear this wonderful career opportunity in Chicago in order to stay in Bluff City with her, even if it meant teaching comp at the community college.

That got a reaction, and she began to unkink her sharp angles, leaning forward in her chair, her eyes glistening as she protested that she would never ask him to give up his *career*. Then, in a move that he thought would have earned Elizabeth's grudging admiration if she'd witnessed it, he found himself kneeling at Kym's feet with his hands folded on her knee like an ardent suitor from a Victorian melodrama—Professor What's-his-name from *Little Women*, say—protesting that he was too old and dried-up for a sweet, intelligent young woman like her with all the prospects in the world.

The moment was nearly spoiled by a blurred movement across the room, a flash of black and white between the couch and the antique cabinet. Kym flinched away from Paul's touch and nearly folded herself into the chair again, saying, "Omigod, it's that cat." But Paul took her hands in his and made her look into his eyes, telling her with a smile not to worry, that Charlotte was scared to death of him. After that she let him take her boots off, and sliding his hands up her jeans to the tender spot behind her knees, he slowly pulled her out of the chair.

Afterward, he lay back in bed with his hands behind his head, warming himself in her pinkish glow, and spun out reasons at the ceiling why a communications degree in Iowa was a waste of time for a woman of her talent and ambition, that big-city television stations didn't give a damn for a master's degree, that it was up to her to take the Chicago market by storm, with her charm and wit.

"Like Shelley Long," she said, pressing herself suddenly against his chest. "Don't laugh," she added.

He pinched off a smile and put his arms around her.

"And you'll be like my kept man," she said.

He spun her onto her back and said with surprising fervor, "I'll be your lover," a pronouncement that was perilously close to the word he had no intention of using, but he knew it was the right thing to say. It was a word evocative of her girlish ideas of sophistication, of thrilling, grown-up wickedness. At any rate, it had the desired effect, and in the morning she left promising to say nothing to her adviser just yet, not until he had the job in Chicago sewn up.

In the meantime Charlotte was either a movement at the edge of his peripheral vision or completely invisible. It was a bit unnerving to turn suddenly at a motion just out of sight only to see nothing. Indeed, there were times when the silence of the apartment in the afternoon was electric with her unseen presence, but he decided not to press it, since she seemed to have declared a truce. He noticed the absence of catnip mousies lately. He parceled them out one at a time from his desk drawer, but they disappeared faster than usual, never to be seen again, as Charlotte hoarded them for some feline reason of her own. He began to concoct new nicknames for her—the Phantom Kitty, the Cat Who Wasn't There—using them on those rare occasions, usually his mealtime or hers, when he got a good look at her. Otherwise she kept out of sight, and he accepted it as a tacit part of their truce that he would not try to find her hiding place. She only came out again when she heard Elizabeth's familiar step on the stair, rocketing down the hall through his legs to stand mewling and wide-eyed at the top of the steps, her tail erect, waiting for Elizabeth to drop her bag and scoop her up.

"Oh, did boo-boo miss me?" Elizabeth cried, lifting Charlotte in her arms. To Paul's surprise, the cat showed no sign of wanting to jump free of Elizabeth's embrace.

"She did," Paul said, putting his arm around his wife as she cuddled the cat. "We both did."

Indeed, he was waiting at the top of the stairs for much the same reason—his tail would have been erect, too—but he managed to wait a decent interval before asking the latest about tenure and her approach to Walter on his behalf. She volunteered that her imminent tenuring was virtually accepted by everyone in her department, and that there had been informal discussions already about where her office would be, her salary, and so on. But she said nothing about talking to Walter on Paul's behalf. Elizabeth did not have much of a flair for the dramatic, but Paul could tell she was trying to build suspense. She did have a knack for being coy at the most inappropriate times, though, and finally, after dinner, when Paul was about to cast dignity to the winds and ask her, she said at last that she and Walter had spoken.

"And?" Paul said, his heart hammering.

"He'd like to see a couple of chapters from your book." She had lowered herself onto the couch, folding her long legs under her. Charlotte appeared from nowhere and jumped up into Elizabeth's lap, and Elizabeth sat stroking the cat, at the same time avoiding Paul's blunt gaze from the doorway. The plunge of his book into professional purgatory, at the same time as hers ascended to paradise, was an almost unmentionable topic between them. Ever since his book had been dropped by his press, he'd been unable to face the manuscript for more than an hour or two at a time, once a week or so. The revisions he told everyone he was working on were a series of feeble and quickly abandoned false starts. At the moment the book was in pieces. The very thought of trying to reassemble it into a coherent whole again wearied him beyond despair.

Now Paul stood in the doorway, unable to enter, unable to flee. Elizabeth sat with her head bowed, peering at Charlotte, but the cat watched him in the doorway with a flat, unreadable gaze, her head dipping with each pass of Elizabeth's hand.

"What did you tell him about it?" he finally managed to say.

"That it needs some work, but that the argument is fundamentally sound."

Still she did not look up at him, tugging instead at Charlotte's ears. Paul stood trembling across the room, clutching the sides of the doorway in a white-knuckled grip, struggling to speak. A tiny, dispassionate part of his brain wondered if this was what a stroke felt like. But he was practically blinded by an image of himself crushing his wife's head between his hands, and he was deafened by the ringing, rolling, rhythmic cadence of a bell, in the timbre of his wife's voice, tolling the same phrase over and over, "fundamentally sound, fundamentally sound." The only real thing he could see through his murderous fury was Charlotte's gaze watching him from across the room, and all he could hear over the tolling of the bell was the little motor of Charlotte's purr.

"Look, hon, I had to tell Walter the truth."

Somehow Elizabeth was standing next to Paul now, holding Charlotte against her chest. When had she gotten up? When had she crossed the room?

"Your book has some real problems," she was saying, "and there's no point in lying to Walter about it. In fact, you know what I think?"

"No," Paul heard himself say.

"I think this is just the kick in the butt you need to get back to work on the manuscript."

She kissed him on the cheek and slid around him in the doorway. As she passed, Charlotte's tail lashed across his face.

They spent the rest of the evening, and indeed most of the weekend, at separate ends of the apartment. Elizabeth pointedly left him alone to struggle with his book, which only made him angrier; she would not even allow him the dignity to shut her out himself. Still, after she went to bed that night he sat dutifully in his niche at one end of the living room with the lights out, bathed in the chilly glow of his computer screen. The first night he didn't even call up any of the files of his book. He stared for an hour at the Program Manager screen while thinking of different metaphors for the way the rules of his professional life had been changed: the goalposts had moved, the track had lengthened, the carrot was dangled a little higher, Walter and Elizabeth were tossing a job back and forth over his head in a vicious game of Monkey in the Middle. He surfed the Net for a while, calling up online lingerie catalogs and downloading the pictures. He checked his e-mail three or four times. He played SimCity for two hours, building up a city from scratch, crowding the little digital landscape with roads and factories and colorful office buildings, filling in all the blank spaces with trees. Then he clicked on the Disasters menu and set the city on fire, letting it burn while he sat glassy-eyed in the electronically crackling glow of the little orange flames.

At last he went to sleep, sharing the bed with Elizabeth for only a couple of hours before she rose. When he got up, around noon, she mothered him silently, bringing him tea and making him sandwiches. This only made it worse, but he let her do it. After lunch she came to where he sat scrolling through his book on the screen, laid a hand on his shoulder, and said, "The chapter on Kafka and *jouissance*. I think Walter would be really impressed." Then she brushed his hair with her hand and left him alone in the apartment all afternoon. After she had left he called up the chapter she'd suggested—it was the one chapter he could face without rage at his own intellectual impotence—but he spent the entire afternoon playing with it, running the spell-check program, trying out different fonts and type sizes and margins, transforming the entire chapter into 48-point Gothic. He got up and paced the apartment from end to end in his socks, surprising Charlotte at one point as she lay in a square of winter sunlight on the kitchen tile. He stooped toward her, intending to give her a playful tug of the ears, but she jumped up and scampered away as soon as he approached, so he swung a kick at her instead, just missing her with the toe of his stocking foot.

It was already dusk when Elizabeth came back, and as soon as he heard the car in the drive, he switched off the computer and hurried into the bedroom for his shoes and his coat. He passed her coming up the stairs and said he was going out for a walk. He ended up sneaking up Kym's fire escape in the dark, tiptoeing through the snow past the kitchen window of the neurotic teaching assistant, where he glimpsed her weeping at her kitchen table. Peering in Kym's kitchen window on the floor above, he saw her sitting at her table in a T-shirt and sweatpants, reading *Sassy* and eating corn chips out of the bag. He was surprised to see her wearing glasses— he hadn't known she wore glasses—but he tapped on the window anyway, startling her so much that she nearly choked on a Dorito. She came to the window still coughing, and he climbed in, taking off her glasses and pulling her to him.

"Oh baby," he heard himself say, "I need you. I need you so bad."

By time he got home the apartment was dark, and he tiptoed into the bedroom and hung up his coat. Elizabeth's breathing was slow and steady, but he was certain she was faking it, so he tiptoed out again and went back to his computer. The chapter had been restored to its original typeface, and there was a yellow Post-it note on the screen in Elizabeth's angular hand, saying, "I know you can do it." He wanted to weep. He lowered his forehead to the keyboard and sighed heavily two or three times while the computer beeped at him steadily. When he looked up again he saw the screen full of line after line of gibberish. Sitting in the glow of the screen, with all the lights out behind him, he shook himself all over, whinnying out loud like a horse.

Then he laid his hand on the mouse, selected the gibberish, and deleted it. He began to type, convinced that this moment right here, right now, was the end of his career. So he just began spewing, churning out a farrago of wild speculations and categorical statements utterly unsupported by any evidence or argument. It didn't matter what he said, the words meant nothing to him, what he enjoyed was the glow of the screen on his skin, giving his hands the pallor of a corpse. He liked the cool, dry feel of the keys under his fingertips. He liked the way the brittle rattle of the keys seemed to amplify the silence behind him. Indeed, he felt the pressure of the silence mount, as if he were filling up the room with words. His hands flew, the keyboard clattered, and he filled the screen with dirty limericks, multilingual puns, the lyrics of TV theme songs. He pulled his chair closer to the keyboard, hooking his legs back behind him, stiffening his backbone. Finally he started to laugh as he typed, and he pinched his lips together to keep it from coming out. His stomach heaved with it, and it burst out through his nose in little chugging hisses.

Sometime in the middle of the night he started awake in the chair before the computer, his heart pounding. His back ached from the way he'd been sitting, and he had no idea how long he'd been asleep, but he found he was afraid to move. His skin was chilled with a cold sweat, and he saw that his *Jurassic Park* screen saver was running. A little Jeep was being chased back and forth across the darkened screen by a *Tyrannosaurus rex*, only this time it wasn't a dinosaur chasing the Jeep, but a huge black-and-white cat. As Paul watched, the giant kitty actually caught the Jeep, fetching it a nasty swipe with its giant paw and sending the riders sprawling. The cat on the screen lunged for one of the tiny people, its eyes full of murderous glee, its jagged teeth bared wide, and Paul jolted violently in his chair, nearly upsetting himself, throwing himself forward and gripping the desk with both hands. He blinked at the screen and saw it restored to its old self, the birdlike *T. rex* silently chasing the little sport vehicle, never catching it. But Paul was still afraid to turn around. His hair rose on the back of his neck. He was certain someone was watching him. He sat up and drew a deep breath, and slowly swiveled around in the chair to see Charlotte sitting in the middle of the living-room floor, just beyond the pale glow of the screen, her dilated pupils wide enough and dark enough to swallow him whole.

Paul snatched a book up off his desk, lined two fingers along the edge of it, and flung it spinning as hard as he could at the cat. Charlotte vanished like a phantom, the book slid across the carpet to the far side of the room, and Paul jumped up from the chair. Now the cat crouched in the door of the living room, silhouetted in the streetlight from the window at the top of the stairs. She pressed herself as low to the floor as a lizard, her legs splayed, her tail curled around her, her ears flat against her head, and she hissed at him, a long, harsh, inhuman sound that chilled him through to his spine like a gust of winter wind. He stepped back and blinked, and she was gone, the patch of streetlight as empty as if she'd never been there at all.

# seven

E WOKE ON THE COUCH AT MID-morning; Elizabeth had spread a comforter over him. He sat up, feeling dizzy. The computer was off, but there was another Post-it on the screen.

"I've made a disk of your revised chapter," it read. "I'll print it out in Chicago and show it to Walter. XO, Lizzie."

"Oh my God," Paul said aloud, his hair sticking up in spikes, his mouth cottony with sleep. "Oh my God, no."

"Lizzie?" he called out, stalking through the apartment, but she had left already, having gotten herself to the train station on her own. He sagged onto the bed and picked up the phone, pressing the speed-dial button for Elizabeth's number in Chicago. He knew she wouldn't be there, but he left a long, nearly hysterical message on Rebecca's machine, begging her not to show Walter the chapter, even begging her not to read it herself.

"It, it, it's rough, Lizzie, it's just a, just a draft, okay? Please don't show it to anybody. Please." He disconnected, and sat there with the phone in his hand. He felt a tingle along the back of his neck again, and he turned to see Charlotte crouched on the far corner of the bed, watching him.

"Get out," he said. When she didn't move, he lunged for her, pulling the phone off the nightstand with a clatter, and she jumped lightly away from him and trotted up the hall.

He called Elizabeth again from his office, once before class, and three times during his office hours, hanging up each time without leaving a message. At home he couldn't face reading what he'd written the night before, so he lay on the couch with the remote control and channel-surfed for the rest of the afternoon, talk shows full of screaming white trash, cooking shows featuring hyperkinetic hosts with funny accents, Seventies sitcoms with people in wide bell-bottoms and bad hair. He watched only one program straight through, a Filipino beach movie in which the characters danced and lip-synced to Tagalog versions of Elvis Presley songs.

After that he lay there through dusk and into the early evening, without even getting up to turn on the lights, watching nature programs, infomercials, fishing shows, and an episode of a golfing show devoted to getting out of sand traps. When Kym arrived at nine o'clock, he went down and opened the door, and he stood in the doorway and stared blankly at her as if he'd never seen her before in his life. But she didn't even notice, squeezing past him and chattering breathlessly all the way up the stairs about how cold it was outside. He followed her to the top of the stairs, where she handed him her coat and said, "You know, Paul, I think I should have a key to your place? So I could let myself in?"

He stared at her, holding her bulky coat in his arms. It was as if she were speaking another language.

"I mean," she went on, throwing her arms loosely about his neck, "I know you don't like to talk about emotions, but when a man crawls in my kitchen window and practically *ravishes* me, it's got to mean something, right?" She kissed him and turned away, followed the sound of the TV into the living room. Her skin was ghostly in the TV light as she peered at the screen.

"Omigod!" she cried. "You're watching *Melrose!*"

He let her stay, too weary to make her go. When she fell asleep finally, wrapped about him in bed like a squid around its prey, he stared at the ceiling, contemplating the ruin of his life. Elizabeth had not called, and he wasn't surprised. She had no doubt read his chapter by now. And having read it, she wouldn't show it to Walter. His career was over and probably his marriage as well. She would cast him overboard like ballast, and soar into the academic empyrean, while he would fall and fall, to land from a great height at some state school in North Dakota, or at a community college teaching comp at a thousand dollars a semester. He'd end up owning a used-book shop in some rustbelt city. He'd be a clerk in a video store, working alongside eighteen-year-old Tarantino wanna-bees for the rest of his life.

In the morning, while Kym was in the shower, he found a dried little cat turd in her shoe, and he nearly laughed. He dumped the turd into the litter box, saying aloud to the cat, wherever she was, "Pretty feeble, Charlotte. You'll have to do better than that." He wondered what Charlotte could be worried about anyway. Chances were she'd end up in Chicago long before he ever would.

Still Elizabeth didn't call, and he mooned about the apartment for another useless day, reading magazines without ever finishing an article, shooting free throws into the wastebasket with crumpled pages from the original draft of his book, thumbing the television remote as he reclined on the couch in his underwear. He imagined himself sitting slumped in one of the chairs on the set of a daytime talk show, overweight, balding, and bearded, while Kymberly stalked the aisles of the audience in four-inch heels and a power suit with a very short skirt, her hair teased to an impossible height, wielding a microphone like a weapon. She thrusts it into the face of a large, middle-aged black woman, who glowers at him across the bright studio and says, "You had it all handed to you on a platter, Paul."

The women around her in the audience nod vigorously in agreement.

"You're a white man with a college education."

Murmurs of assent from the audience. Kym knits her brow thoughtfully.

"How could you let it all slip away?"

People are crying out now, "Tell him, sister!" and "Amen!"

"Man," says the black woman, "I got *no* sympathy with you at *all.*"

The audience bursts into applause, some of them rising to their feet to shake their fists at him, and the camera cuts to Paul, hollow-eyed and pallid from a steady diet of frozen dinners, pizza, and macaroni and cheese. Below his face a caption reads, *Paul: Failed Academic*, and as he stammers feebly Kymberly cuts him off and says, "We have Paul's ex-wife via satellite—Elizabeth is a two-time, I'm sorry, *three*-time winner of the National Book Award, the first woman chancellor of Harvard, and the president of the Modern Language Association—hello, Elizabeth, are you there?"

The phone had been ringing for some time before Paul pushed himself up from the couch and padded into the bedroom. He fell back on the bed and let his hand hover over the receiver for a moment before he picked it up. He thought he could still hear the talk-show version of his life from the other room—"When did you first realize that your husband was a loser?" Kymberly was saying—and he picked up the phone to hear Elizabeth's voice.

"Paul!" she said breathlessly. "I was about to hang up."

"I'm here," Paul said, staring at the ceiling.

"I can only talk a minute—I've got class—but I wanted to let you know that Walter was very impressed with the chapter."

Paul blinked and sat up slowly, swinging his feet to the floor.

"I have to admit I was surprised," Elizabeth was saying. "Frankly, it was a little too Andrew Ross for me, but Walter loved it, called it *very* cutting-edge."

Paul cleared his throat and said, "He *liked* it?"

"Hell yes!" Elizabeth said heartily. "Especially the linkage you made between 'The Metamorphosis' and *My Mother the Car*."

Paul stood up, pulling the phone with him. His heart was pounding.

"What did he, I mean, did he say . . ."

"He wants to see another chapter, Paul," Elizabeth said. "Can you have another one ready by next week?" Paul stammered something, but Elizabeth kept talking in a torrent. "Look, I'm going to stay here through the weekend, Rebecca's having a party, I wish you could be here, but I know you'll want to get to work on that chapter so we can show it to Walter the week after next, that'll give you ten days alone to work on it, and I know you work better if I'm not . . ." She paused to draw a breath. "I love you, Paul."

That brought them both up short. She'd never said it before—at least not since the second year of grad school—and neither of them knew what to say next. Paul stood very still with the phone to his ear, and finally Elizabeth said, "I knew you could do it, darling. I'll call you tonight."

# eight

LIZABETH'S ABSENCE COINCIDED WITH IOWA'S spring break, and when Kymberly found out, she cashed in her plane ticket to South Padre Island and moved in with Paul for the duration.

"I have to work, you know," Paul protested, but she arrived on Friday afternoon with spring-break supplies she'd bought with the money from her plane ticket.

"We're going to have a beach party," she announced, "whether you like it or not."

She set up a bright red tent in a corner of the living room. She brought a plastic ice chest full of wine coolers and Zima. She made stars and a crescent moon out of silvery construction paper and hung them from the ceiling. She walked around the apartment all day in an assortment of brightly colored bikinis. She brought a box of tapes and a boom box, preferring the sound to Paul's stereo.

"Don't mind me," she said, but he found himself typing to the thunder of Dick Dale, King of the Surf Guitar, and every time he turned around he discovered Kym stretched out topless on a beach blanket in the middle of the living room, reclining against an inflatable pillow under a portable sunlamp and reading a Pat Booth novel, the smell of Coppertone rising off her like musk. By Saturday afternoon he had only written six pages. Instead, he found himself dancing in his own living room, twisting to "Fun, Fun, Fun" in his swimming trunks and sunglasses, and, as the pale Iowa sun went down outside, slow-dancing by candlelight to "Surfer Girl" three times in a row. By now Paul was into the spirit of things, and they spent the night on the beach, so to speak, making love all slippery with sunblock in the humid little tent, lying awake afterward on the carpet and looking up at the construction-paper stars and listening to a New Age tape of crashing surf. In the morning they played volleyball with a Nerf ball over a net of clothesline; and by Sunday evening Paul had dug out his Harry Belafonte tape and they limboed, taking turns holding the broomstick. Sunday night they lay awake under the stars again, holding hands and concocting silly lovers' arguments, such as whether Kym was too young to really appreciate Jan & Dean.

"Oh please." She struck a pose, mock-outraged. "They're part of my ethnic heritage! They are the colorful folk songs of my people!"

By Monday afternoon, Kym was a little bored, and she left for a few hours to go back to her own apartment and check her mail and messages. Paul found himself energized, though, and he sat at his computer in his swim trunks and a Hawaiian shirt, eager to begin work finally on his book—now called *My (M)other the Car: Difference and Memory in the Matriarchal Narrative*—hammering out the outlines of a new chapter linking the Surfaris and Eric Hobsbawm, arguing for surf guitar as an invented tradition, the constructed ethnic heritage of Anglo-Californian immigrants, the folk music of the newly mobile white suburban middle class. That went so well that ideas began to pour out of him, and he popped one of Kym's tapes into his stereo and listened to thunderous guitar instrumentals as he concocted a whole new outline for his book, chapter after chapter: "The Sitcom at the End of the New Frontier: *The Brady Bunch* and *The Wild Bunch* in Contrapuntal Perspective." "Slouching Toward Minneapolis: William Butler Yeats, Mary Tyler Moore, and the Millennium." And, in honor of his beach-party weekend, "A French Bikini on a Wild Island Girl: *The Tempest, Gilligan's Island,* and the Social Construction of the Narrative of Abandonment."

During all of this Charlotte had become an outcast. Out of her beach bag, Kym had produced a brand-new plastic squirt gun in the shape of an Eastwood-sized revolver, and the first time the cat slunk into the living room—as Kym sat cross-legged cutting stars out of construction paper—Charlotte was blasted with a practiced long-range stream of water. At the yowl of the cat, Paul jumped out of his chair and tried to wrestle the gun away from Kym, but she held it behind her back, out of his reach, and when she leveled it at him he relented, throwing up his hands and shouting, "Not toward the computer!" After that, in between dancing and volley-ball, Kym in her bikini stalked the cat about the apartment, wielding the squirt gun in a two-fisted grip that would have done Mrs. Peel proud, surprising Charlotte as she sunned herself on the kitchen floor, or as she crouched in the bedroom window watching the birds in the tree outside. Each time she was doused, Charlotte became a little more frantic, her snarls rising into wild screeches. The last time Paul saw Charlotte was as the cat rocketed past the living-room door, her ears flat against her head, her tail out straight behind her, her eyes wild with fear. A moment later Kym stood in the doorway in a heart-stopping pose, hip canted and gun held across her chest, James Bond regendered by way of the *Sports Illustrated* swimsuit edition.

"You know what's wrong with your cat?" she said.

"Um, no," Paul said, torn between lust and the sudden idea for a new chapter.

"She can dish it out," Kym had said, pausing to blow across the barrel of the gun like a gunfighter, "but she can't take it."

Now, waiting for his lover to come back, Paul labored eagerly through dusk and into the early evening. The surf-guitar tape ran out, and he typed in the glow of the screen, the apartment unlit behind him, the only sounds the clatter of the keyboard and his own laughter, under his breath. He wrote so quickly that he didn't bother to read over what he'd written; even the brief interruption of the computer's automatic save feature every ten minutes annoyed him, so he shut it off. He was jazzed now, his mind throwing off ideas like a Catherine wheel—the new chapter was "A Gun of One's Own: Mrs. Dalloway vs. The Girl from U.N.C.L.E."—and he found himself thinking of Chicago again, of life among the tough-minded glitterati of the Windy City. Maybe it really was a good idea for Kym to join him there; maybe in the sophisticated urban context he could persuade Elizabeth to take a more European view of their marriage. Maybe Lizzie and Kym could even become friends, and a refrain from one of Kym's beach-party songs circled in his brain, and he began to murmur it aloud as he typed, mimicking the high, innocent tenor of the original, *two girls for every boy.*

He was distracted only by the sudden advent of Charlotte. She hadn't come near him in several days, and he was startled by the unexpected but still familiar pressure of her winding between his legs as he typed. She slid around his calves two or three times in a warm, silky figure eight, looking up at him forlornly and even mewling a bit. The black-brown fur along her flank was still matted with water from Kym's squirt gun, chilling the skin of Paul's calf as she passed. He looked down between his knees at her. In the ghostly light from the screen, all he could see was her white chest and legs moving dimly in the dark under the desk and, when she lifted her face to him, her white muzzle and the dark holes of her dilated pupils. He made no move to pick her up or stroke her, and for a moment he said nothing. She disappeared beneath his chair, and then reappeared a moment later on the desk at his elbow, her white breast glowing in the light from the screen, standing on all four legs and meowing loudly at him, glaring at him with her wide, dark eyes. The sight of her like this, in this half-light, chilled him a bit, and finally he said, "I don't know what you want, Charlotte. I can't help you."

She meowed again, splitting her jaws wide open, her teeth catching the glow from the screen, and she stepped closer to Paul. He jerked back from her involuntarily.

"I'd give you a mousie to play with, Charlotte," he said, "but you've hidden them all."

She stepped up to the edge of the desk, crying and baring her jagged teeth, her eyes as wide as olive pits, and Paul stiffened in his chair, thinking of his bare legs and arms, his loins covered only by the thin cotton of his swim trunks.

"Easy, Charlotte," he said, and he would have sworn that in the half-light she was tensed and ready to spring. Then he heard the front door slam, and Kym's voice coming up the stairs in a chipper singsong. "Hi honey, I'm home!"

"You'd better hide, cat," he said, twisting out of his chair, and he slid away into the dark, hearing a cat-sized thump against the carpet behind him. He caught a glimpse of her as she dashed out of the living room through the streetlight at the top of the stairs, and then down the hall. The thin wire of the Cat Dancer trembled against the pool of light. A moment later Kym stepped into the light in her coat, carrying a grocery bag full of supplies—corn chips, salsa, more Zima. She stopped, breathless and red-cheeked from the cold outside, and said, "Why are all the lights out?"

"I've been working," he said, "waiting for you." He kissed her and took the groceries into the kitchen. When he came back into the living room, she had taken off her coat and sweater and T-shirt, and she stood before his computer pulling off her shoes and stripping off her jeans down to the swimwear underneath.

"Would this interest me?" she said, peering at the screen.

He came up behind and slid his arms around her, nuzzling his chin in her hair and kissing her throat.

"Only because," he said, "it's going to get us to Chicago."

He picked her up suddenly and slung her over his shoulder, and she shrieked with laughter, struggling with him, tugging on his Hawaiian shirt, pleading with him to put her down. He did finally, in a pleasant tangle of limbs, more or less in the center of the beach blanket in the middle of the living-room floor, and he pulled off his shirt and his trunks and began to undo the knots of her swimsuit.

"Let's put on some music," she said, reaching behind her for the boom box.

"Uh-uh." He pulled her arm back and kissed the inside of her wrist. "All I want to hear is us." He tossed aside the halves of her suit and slid his fingertips down the backs of her thighs, gently spreading her knees. He glanced over his shoulder at the glowing square of the computer screen and said, "I want to make love to you by moonlight."

They moved slowly together for a while, and he watched her solemnly as she searched his face with her gaze, her lower lip trembling. The unnatural light of the screen was not quite constant; it strobed at a rate a fraction too fast for the eye to calibrate, but if he turned his head a little and watched out of the corner of his eye, Kym's skin had a bluish, electric glow, and her movements a rapid, vibrating stutter that excited him. He began to move faster, pulling her legs tighter around his waist, driving deeper. She turned her head to follow his gaze, trying to catch it in her own, and when she began to call out that she loved him, he closed his eyes and slipped his fingers into her mouth, wincing with the sharp pleasure as she bit down, bringing him to climax.

He rolled onto his back, his eyes still shut, and listened to the pounding of his heart. He felt Kym turning onto her side next to him, caressing his face, kissing his chest.

"I want you all to myself," she said, and he opened his eyes to the dark ceiling.

"Aren't you going to say anything?" she said after a moment.

He turned to her and looked at her shadowy face, silhouetted against the glow from the streetlight that fell just outside the living-room door. Her pupils were dilated, round and dark like Charlotte's, ready to swallow him whole.

"Not before Chicago," he said, still a little breathless. "I need Elizabeth to get me . . . to get us to Chicago."

"And then?" She laid her warm palm along his cheek, so that he couldn't turn his face away.

He blinked at her in the dark, unable to make out her expression clearly. The blue, stuttering light was gone.

"What happened to the light?" he said sharply, snatching her hand from his cheek.

She glanced over him toward the computer and said, "I guess the moon went behind a cloud."

Paul sat up abruptly, pushing her hands away. The computer was nearly invisible in its niche at the end of the living room; the screen was dark, not with the dark blue glow of his screen saver, but dead, powerless, an unblinking gray eye.

"Oh no," Paul said, jumping up. "Oh shit."

He crossed the room in the dark, ignoring Kym's protest behind him. The little green power light was out on the CPU itself, and he pressed the power switch back and forth several times. Nothing happened, so he pushed back his chair and dropped to his knees, crouching on the carpet to peer under the desk. As far as he could see in the blackness under the desk, everything was plugged in—the computer into the surge suppressor, the surge suppressor into the wall—and he thought immediately of the fuse box in the pantry. He lifted his head too quickly, banging his head on the underside of the desk. He cursed and called out to Kym without looking at her, saying, "Turn on a light."

"Are you okay?" she said. "What's wrong?"

"Will you turn on the fucking light?" he shouted, and she jumped up, crossing to the doorway and turning on the overhead light. His head throbbing, Paul peered under the desk again, and in the yellow glare of the overhead, among the tangle of wires and cords and clots of cat hair, he saw that the fat black wall plug of the surge suppressor was nearly pulled out of the socket, hanging only by the tips of its three prongs. He let out a long, deflating sigh and pushed it in again, and immediately heard the computer clicking and buzzing to life above him. He got up and sat in the chair, both hands pressed to the back of his head, watching the start-up cycle of the computer, the rapid crawl of white letters up the black screen. He wanted to moan, but he was too stunned. He felt Kym's hand on his shoulder, and he stiffened.

"Omigod, did I do that?" she said.

"What do you mean?" he said. He couldn't bring himself to look at her.

"I mean, when you picked me up?" she said, her hand trembling on his bare shoulder. "Maybe I kicked it or something."

"No," he said. "It was on when we were making love."

"Was the file really important?" she said. "I mean, you backed it up, right?"

Paul shot up from the chair, pushing it back, forcing Kym to stumble back, and he brushed past her into the living room, holding the top of his head in both hands as if afraid that it would fly off.

"You *didn't* back it up?" she said, with all the incredulity of a generation that had grown up with computers, that had heard the injunction to back up files as often as Paul had been told to brush after every meal and look both ways before crossing the street.

"No," he said numbly. "I didn't back it up."

"Well," Kym said, as soothingly as a kindergarten teacher, "most programs automatically save the file every ten minutes."

He turned to her, the two of them naked in the harsh overhead light, pale despite two days of the sunlamp, their skin cooling from their exertions of a few minutes before.

"I disabled it." Paul's head throbbed with pain. "I turned off the automatic save."

He sagged onto the couch, and Kym perched at the edge of the cushion next to him. She tried to pull his hands away from his head, saying, "Let me see," but he flinched away from her, waving his hands in the air.

"Don't do that!" he said. He sighed. "Look, Kym." He clutched her lightly by the wrists and looked into her eyes, his head pounding. "Listen to me."

The light went out of her eyes, but she did not pull away from his grasp.

"The stuff I lost," he said as evenly as he could manage, "is our ticket to Chicago. It's gone. I have to start from scratch. Elizabeth'll be back in . . ." He had to think. ". . . in three days, and I have to have something to show her. If I don't, then I'm not going to Chicago, you're not going to Chicago, nobody's going to Chicago. Do you understand?"

"I'm not an idiot," she said, pulling free, looking right through him, and Paul mustered enough tenderness to take her face in his hands.

"I'm not angry with you," he said, "I'm angry with myself, okay? I wish you could stay, I want you to stay, but I have to get to work now. I have to be alone now, all right?"

Her gaze flickered, trying not to look at him.

"Kym, I'm doing this for us," he said, and her expression softened, though she said nothing. "Now go get dressed, and we'll clean up all this stuff."

Kym gathered up her clothes and went into the bathroom to dress, closing the door. Paul pulled on his swim trunks and started stuffing things into Kym's beach bag, rolling up the tent, yanking the paper moon and stars from the ceiling and wadding them up, dumping the half-melted ice from the cooler into the kitchen sink. He stalked about the apartment looking for any telltale sign of Kym's presence, keeping an eye out all the while for Charlotte.

An unpleasant suspicion had begun to grow in the back of his brain, an awful suspicion, which played itself out as a little horror-movie sequence shot with the Cat-Cam, INT. NIGHT. CHARLOTTE'S POV, as Charlotte pads silently into the living room, cruising behind the easy chair, slinking along the wall, pausing to watch, with her terrible feline rage, the two humans rutting in the eerie electric light from the video screen, then creeping through the viny rain-forest tangle of wires and connectors under the desk, stepping over the red glow of the surge-suppressor light, and, while the humans gasp and cry out offscreen, taking the thick black cord of the surge suppressor in her wide, jagged jaws and giving it a little tug. Paul's career FADES TO BLACK.

Kym came out of the bathroom already in her coat, and Paul handed her the cooler and beach bag full of stuff. He told her he couldn't see her for at least a week, that he'd call her after Elizabeth's next visit home. Kym listened without looking at him.

"I kept a couple of the tapes," he said. "For inspiration."

Kym nodded and then threw her arms around him, holding him tight and sighing heavily.

"I know you can do it?" she said. She looked up at him. "I love you."

"I know," he said, and she started down the stairs. The swing of her hair against her coat collar stung him suddenly with desire.

"Kym!" he said, starting after her in his bare feet, chilled in the open stairwell in his swimsuit. She stopped and looked up at him. "We'll be together," he said. "You'll see." She blew him a kiss and passed out the door.

He put on his bathrobe against the sudden chill. He'd kept one other thing besides the tapes from Kym's beach-party gear, and that was the large, dangerous-looking squirt gun. He filled it at the kitchen sink and then placed himself in the kitchen doorway where he could see down the length of the dark apartment, standing with his legs apart and the gun hanging loose in his hand at arm's length. He flexed his grip on the gun, then suddenly dropped to a crouch, swinging the gun up and firing a long stream of water down the length of the hall, peppering the bedspread with the drops at the far end of the stream. Then he stood up, relaxed his grip, and did it again, Paul as Chow Yun Fat, the stylish hit man in one of John Woo's gunfire ballets, blowing away a whole warehouse full of homicidal kitties.

He sighed and put the squirt gun in his bathrobe pocket, and he went in to his computer, turning out the overhead lamp so that he could work again only by the light of the screen. The screen was glowing with the dirty white of his word processor's document window, and by the light of it he cued up one of Kym's tapes and hit play, keeping the volume low. He approached the screen feeling a little enervated, but loose; all he'd lost was notes, really, outlines, and he remembered most of it, some of the wilder connections might be lost, but that's why he was playing surf guitar in the background, trying to get back to the beach, so to speak. But as he pulled the chair back to sit down, he froze. In the subliminally strobing, brutal glare of the screen, there was something round and dark placed neatly in the middle of the keyboard. He hesitated to touch it, bending down to look at it carefully first, to sniff it. The whiff of catnip rattled him, ruining his mood, setting his nerves on edge like fingernails down a blackboard. It was one of Charlotte's carefully hoarded little mousies, placed dead center on his keyboard like a fish on his doorstep, and he picked it up and flung it away into the darkness.

"You little bitch," he murmured, and he sat down to the keyboard, his hands trembling a bit. He took the squirt gun out of his pocket and set it on the desk at his right hand, then he started to type.

E CALLED ELIZABETH ON TUESDAY
night from the phone in the bedroom, pressing her speed-dial
number. He'd been up all night, and he sat on the edge of the bed,
unshaven and unwashed, still in his swim trunks and bathrobe.

"The tenure committee meets Thursday," she said. "I think we'll
have something to celebrate this Friday."

"That's good," he said. The squirt gun lay on the bedspread next
to him. He took it with him everywhere now.

"So," she said, pausing. "I almost hate to ask, but how's your
work coming?"

"Well, we had a little accident here," he said.

"An accident?"

Paul laid his hand on the squirt gun, looking around for the cat.

"Charlotte unplugged my computer," he said. "I lost everything
I did over the weekend."

"Oh my God, is she all right?"

Paul leaped off the bed and stood shouting into the phone, waving the squirt gun about in his other hand.

"What about me, goddammit? Why is it always about the fucking cat?" He knew he sounded shrill and petulant, and he caught
himself.

"What about me?" he added feebly.

There was a long, awful pause, and Paul was on the verge of
stammering an apology when Elizabeth said, as if she were speak-

ing to a child, "Paul, I'm sorry. But you should have backed up the file. Right?"

He said nothing, and she persisted. "Am I right?"

"Yes, yes, yes," he muttered, but Elizabeth was already speaking again. He sat heavily on the bed again, dangling the gun between his knees.

"She's just an animal, Paul," Elizabeth was saying. "She doesn't know about plugs, for God's sake. It was an accident. Why would a cat try to sabotage your work?"

Paul drew in his breath sharply and let it out in a long sigh. He lifted the gun and fired a long stream of water against the windowpane, watching the water roll down the glass.

"You're right," he said. "You're right, you're right."

"Look, I'm sorry, but I'm really tired, and a little wound up. I know how the vote's going to turn out, but it's still hard, you know, waiting."

Tell me about it, he thought, but he said, "Listen, Lizzie, don't worry about me." He flopped back on the bed. "I can, you know, reconstruct what I lost."

"I know. I'm sorry I . . ." She sighed in the phone. "I love you, Paul."

He lifted the gun and fired straight up, so that the water fell in fat drops on his face, making him squint and blink.

"Love you too," he said.

"And don't be too mean to Charlotte, okay?" she added, affecting a meek voice.

"All I did was shout at her. She's hiding. I don't even know where she is."

Elizabeth hung up, and he pushed himself up off the bed and wiped his face with his hand. He turned to see Charlotte crouching tensely in the doorway, and instantly he jumped up on the bed, firing with both hands, pelting her head-on with a thick spray of water. She yowled and leaped straight up, twisting in the air. Paul bounced off the bed and charged after her up the hall, firing burst after burst of water, speechless with anger. In the kitchen she skidded to a stop and turned to watch him come. He was thrilled to see her terrified, ears back, eyes wide, scrabbling for purchase on the smooth kitchen floor. He laughed, charging forward, but at the last minute she found her grip and bolted toward him, right between his legs. He twisted and fell hard on the kitchen floor with a loud thump, howling in pain. He sat up and blindly fired down the hall, bellowing. He stopped and sat breathing hard, peering around the gun. Charlotte was nowhere to be seen, and the walls of the hallway were streaked with water. He lowered the gun and stood painfully, rubbing his bruised hip. Against the wall at his feet he saw Charlotte's food and water dish; she still had some water, and there was even a little dry food left over from yesterday. Paul stooped and dumped the dish into the sink, washing the pellets of food down the drain and through the garbage disposal. Then he topped up the squirt gun and went back to his computer. He left Charlotte's empty dish in the sink.

He sat at the keyboard for hours at a time, eating oyster crackers out of the box and drinking the leftover wine coolers, the empty bottles lined up along the windowsill next to him or rolling underfoot. The words were coming, he filled up screen after screen, but he couldn't reproduce the *jouissance* of the weekend's output, not starting cold, not from a standing start. For the first day he played Kym's tapes over and over, but the high spirits of the music had curdled and turned sinister, and finally he jumped up and shut off the Surfaris in mid-wipeout. He'd have to sweat it this time, he was back into dissertation mode, making the words come out of sheer willpower, pushing himself like grim death. He was the bespectacled dork swotting it out at his keyboard while all the other kids were motoring toward the beach in their hot rods and woodies, surfboards thrust out the windows like fins; he pictured some smoothly muscled kid in red-and-blue doggers and Ray-Bans, with Kym on one arm and Shelley Fabares on the other, taunting him, saying, "Back down, dude, you haven't got what it takes. You're always a half second behind the curl." Together they walked off down the beach, the girls shaking their hair back and singing "Two girls for every boy" in a sneering, minor-key falsetto, a beach movie with music by Kurt Weill.

"Fuck off," he murmured aloud. Hadn't he done this the first time out of desperation? Wasn't he desperate now? He hadn't bathed since he didn't know when, and he could smell himself. He sat in a miasma of sweat and fear. His hair stuck up in oily spikes, his stubble itched. He thought about calling Kym and asking her to come back, but what good would that do? She called once and left a message on his machine, and he stood in the kitchen doorway listening to her. As soon as it was over, he rewound the tape and erased it, playing back over the erasure to make sure he'd gotten every trace of it. Then he went back to the computer. He made himself write the way he had written over the weekend, not revising, not even reading what he wrote. But there was an extra step now. His self-consciousness was like the two-second delay in an international phone call, screwing up the rhythm of the conversation, the sentences piling on top of each other or lurching to an awkward silence.

He could feel Charlotte's presence, he knew she was watching him somehow, and he saved what he wrote every paragraph or so. Now and then he felt a tingle along the back of his neck, and he'd snatch up the squirt gun from the desk and whirl around in his chair. But she was never there, and he never saw her directly, only a blur in his peripheral vision that might have been lack of sleep, or the Cat Dancer swaying in the doorway as if under its own energy.

He worked until his eyes started to slide shut and he sagged in his chair, and then he would save the file, switch off the machine, and throw himself onto the couch, where he was unconscious in a matter of moments. He would start awake later on, wildly disoriented, sometimes to pitch-blackness, sometimes to sunlight streaming through the windows across his bare legs. Once he woke up to see Charlotte in the middle of the living-room floor, her head thrust into the box of oyster crackers, and he twisted violently about on the couch, slapping about in vain for the squirt gun. His movement startled the cat, and she jerked back out of the box, watching him with narrow eyes. Both of them froze for a moment, holding their breath, not moving a hair. Then Paul lunged for her, diving off the couch and bursting the cracker box, bringing his hands together on her tail as she whisked it out of his grasp and vanished up the hall.

After that he kept the squirt gun in the pocket of his robe, where its steady drip soaked the fabric, chilling his thigh. He saw her again—the same day? a day later?—as he staggered into the bathroom, catching her as she drank from the toilet, and he tore at the pocket of his robe, pulling the robe open, the plastic gun hooked in the fabric. Charlotte hunkered down low, her haunches pressed tight, ready to spring, her tail curled around her, her front paws splayed. She feinted right, she feinted left, her tail lashing across the floor like a snake, trying to find a way past him in the narrow doorway, and he matched her feint for feint, waving the gun at her in both hands. She hunkered even lower, noticeably thinner, her limbs trembling, and she opened her jagged jaws and gave him a long, guttural, evil hiss. Paul shuddered and closed the front of his robe, clutching it tight over his waist.

"All right," he said, and he backed slowly out of the bathroom, holding up the squirt gun with two fingers and stooping slowly to lay it on the hall carpet. Then he backed down the carpet into the living room and waited till he heard the patter of her feet on the carpet. When he went into the bathroom, he found he was unable to pee.

He was awakened again by the sound of his wife's voice on the answering machine by the kitchen phone. He was lying on top of the squirt gun, his face pressed into the crack at the back of the couch, his bare legs sticking into the air over one end. He lifted his head and shifted painfully, groaning at the stiffness of his limbs, and the lump of squirt gun under his thigh.

"Paul, are you there?" said a tinny voice from the kitchen. "Pick up the phone."

He shifted and felt a clammy dampness under his groin, and he pushed himself up roughly from the couch, patting at a wide damp stain on the cushion and peeling his soaked bathrobe away from his skin. He sniffed at his fingers, terrified that he'd pissed himself, but it was only water. He had crushed the squirt gun under him as he'd slept.

"Paul, I'm at the station. Where are you?" There was a long, hissing pause from the machine, and he staggered up from the couch, tripping on the belt of the robe and landing full-length with a crash that rattled the bookcases.

"Well, look," Elizabeth said, "I'll get a cab. I hope you're home. I've got great news."

He hauled himself around the doorway into the kitchen, limping, and snatched up the phone just as she hung up. He stood in the sunlight pouring through the kitchen window, blinking and trying to get his brain going, rubbing his various bruises with both hands, the top of his head, his thigh. The wall clock over the table read 11:21; it was Friday. Elizabeth had just gotten off the train from Chicago; she'd be here in ten minutes, maybe even five. He spun about and stopped, wondering if there was anything he needed to take care of before she got home. He plucked the pieces of squirt gun out of his pocket and wedged them into the trash under the sink, where the empty bottles of wine cooler and Zima reminded him of the other empties stacked in the window by his desk, so he dashed into the living room, wincing with pain, and snatched up the rest of them, holding his robe up like an apron and piling them in. There wasn't room in the kitchen trash, so he dumped them into a new trash bag, and he twirled and tied both bags to take them down to the garbage can. He stopped halfway across the kitchen, the bags swinging from his hands, at the sight of the bare spot along the wall where Charlotte's food dish had been, and he dropped the bags, retrieved the dish from the sink, and set it out brimming with water and a mound of dry cat food.

"Come and get it, Charlotte," he called, snatching up the bags and trotting down the stairs in his bare feet. "Damn you."

He braced himself for the cold outside, but somehow spring had broken in Bluff City without his noticing it, and he stepped out onto the driveway into fifty-degree weather, the blinding snow reduced to dirty white archipelagoes against the brown, matted grass, meltwater coursing in a steady stream down the drive, the sky the delicate blue of a robin's egg. As if on cue his heart leaped at the bright sunlight, the warm breeze, the smell of mud, and he pranced along the walkway to the garbage can, heedless of the rough concrete and the freezing water and the pebbles stinging his bare feet, chanting to himself in his best grad-student Middle English, "Whan that Aprill with his shoures soote . . ."

He stuffed the trash bags into the can, leaning on the lid to make it shut, chanting Chaucer aloud with gusto, and as he came to "So priketh hem nature in hir corages" he turned to see Elizabeth standing on a dry patch of the drive, with her bag at her feet and the cab pulling away behind her. She watched him wide-eyed and open-mouthed, and Paul's heart fairly stopped. And then she smiled and tossed her head back and started to laugh, walking toward him beaming, with that certain glow that only tenure gives a woman.

"Oh you poor boy," she laughed, and she lifted her hands to his stubbled cheeks and gave him the tenderest kiss of their marriage. He was afraid to touch her, afraid that if he didn't he might fall down, and he touched her elbows lightly with trembling hands.

"Oh," she said, pulling back a moment, "you smell awful," and she kissed him again, pulling him closer with her long, cool fingers across the back of his neck. Then she held him at arm's length, their eyes brimming, both of them, and she glanced past him at the open front door.

"What's it like up there?" she said. "I mean, is it even safe to go in there?"

He knuckled the mist out of his eyes and gestured feebly.

"I was trying to clean up," he stammered. "I was asleep when you called."

She turned him by his elbows and gently pushed him toward the door.

"Go inside, darling, you'll catch your death."

As she came up the stairs behind him with her bag, they heard a heartbreaking yowl down the stairwell, and Elizabeth gasped and pushed past Paul, thrusting the bag into his arms.

"Oh baby!" she cried. "Mama's home! Oh sweetie!"

At the top of the stairs Charlotte stood as if on tiptoe, her tail standing straight as a flagpole, her eyes wide, wailing like a siren. She leaped for Elizabeth even before she'd reached the top, springing into her mistress's arms, writhing in feline ecstasy.

"Oh, *Paul*," Elizabeth said, cuddling the cat, rubbing cheeks with her. "She's so *thin*. Haven't you been feeding her?"

Paul stopped at the top of the stairs and dropped the bag. He sighed and rubbed his head.

"I've been preoccupied," he said. "Neither of us has been eating very well."

"Poor sweetie," Elizabeth said, stepping into the kitchen to glance at Charlotte's dish. She fixed Paul with a knowing smile and said, "You just put that out, didn't you?"

Paul sighed again and shrugged. He was speechless.

"Poor, poor sweetie." Elizabeth nuzzled the cat in her arms, and Charlotte purred like a Harley. "Everything's going to be fine from now on. Mama's going to take care of both of her poor souls."

Paul stepped toward her, his heart hammering. He swallowed and forced himself to speak.

"So?" was all he could manage.

"I'm tenured." Elizabeth smiled, her head cocked, her face pressed against the cat.

Paul closed his eyes and clutched the side of the doorway, afraid his knees might buckle.

"And you?" Elizabeth said. "Have we got something I can take to Walter?"

Paul opened his eyes and nodded.

"I don't know," he began. "I mean, I'm not sure how good it is."

"Don't worry," Elizabeth said. "You're ninety percent there. Whatever you show him next doesn't have to be as, um, kinetic as that first sample. He just wants to see that you've been working steadily."

"Oh, that's me," Paul said. "I'm a steady worker."

"Are you," Elizabeth said, pursing her lips and looking him up and down in his damp bathrobe and swim trunks. She pulled him forward by his lapels and kissed him.

"Why don't you," she said, "go take a shower."

"Right now?" he said.

"Yeah, I think you should take a shower. And brush your teeth." She put her hand on his bare chest and gave him a little shove. He started down the hall, turning to say, "Should I shave?"

"Uh-uh," she said, "I like it. Makes you look like Andrew Ross."

As he brushed his teeth he heard her moving about the apartment, opening windows, calling out to him, "God, Paul, this place is *toxic*. It smells like spring break in here."

In the shower all he could hear was the hiss of the water, and he pressed his hands against the tiles and leaned into the blessed, muscle-loosening sting of the spray, the heat washing over his skin like sleep. In fact, he had almost dozed off standing there when he heard the rustle of the shower curtain and felt a chill, and Elizabeth stepped into the shower with him, long-legged and smooth-skinned and angular, pressing up against him between his arms and tipping her head back into the water. She slipped her hands around the small of his back and said, "Lover, this morning I feel *empowered*."

At last they fell asleep in each other's arms in the middle of the afternoon, but when Paul awoke, after dark, they had separated somehow. Paul started awake, his eyes opening to the beam of streetlight falling through the crack in the curtains and into his eyes. He shifted, feeling chilled. Elizabeth lay with her back to him, having pulled all the covers onto her side of the bed. He heard a noise, a steady, low thrumming like a lawn mower far away, and he sat up suddenly, making the bed shake. Elizabeth stirred but did not wake. She lay cocooned in the covers, but she had left one arm free, and it was curled lovingly around Charlotte, who lay pressed to Elizabeth's chest, purring. Charlotte lifted her chin and looked across her mistress at Paul, her eyes black. There was something between her paws, close to Elizabeth's face, something pale and smooth and papery. A white spike like the point of a star stuck up between Charlotte's paws, and Elizabeth's steady, contented breathing blew it back and forth. Paul sucked in his breath. It *was* a star, one of Kym's construction-paper cutouts from the beach party.

He let his breath out very slowly, and leaned carefully across the bed, peering at Elizabeth as he tried to reach for the star without touching her. Charlotte watched him, though, and actually growled at him as his hand descended, baring her teeth, her little cat gums white in the dim light from the streetlamp. Paul snatched his hand back and cursed at her silently. His heart was pounding; what else did she have stashed away? He propped himself over Elizabeth on his elbow, his butt and the backs of his thighs clammy in the draft from the window. He and Charlotte glared at each other, and then Charlotte began to mew softly, kneading the star between her paws, sliding it slowly toward Elizabeth. The scratchy tip of the point began to scrape against Elizabeth's nose, and she stirred, smiling.

"Stop that," she murmured, but playfully, and suddenly Paul slid his arm forcefully under the blankets around her back, sliding his hand up across her waist and cupping her breast, and he rolled her over, insinuating himself inside the blanket and pulling her against him. Charlotte was forced back onto her haunches. She snarled.

"You stole all the blankets, Lizzie," Paul said, "and I'm freezing."

He nuzzled her neck and watched Charlotte; the cat was on all fours, trying to find a way between them, the star clutched in her teeth. Elizabeth, meanwhile, squealed girlishly—a sound that chilled Paul's blood—but he twisted his legs around hers and pulled her closer, nibbling on her shoulder, watching Charlotte.

"Paul, ow!" Elizabeth said, and she ducked her head under the covers. At the same time he wrapped his whole hand across Charlotte's face and squeezed, plucking the star from between her teeth as she released it. The cat bit him, very hard, in the web of skin between his thumb and forefinger, at the same time as Elizabeth pinched the loose flesh at his waist with both hands, and he gasped aloud. Elizabeth shoved her head out from under the covers and peered down at him from an inch away, biting her lip, her eyes bright.

"There," she said. "How do *you* like it?"

Paul kissed her hard and rolled her over, away from the cat. Just before he pulled the covers over their heads, he shoved the crumpled paper star into the crack between the mattress and the box spring.

THE NEXT DAY PAUL'S HAND STILL STUNG
from where Charlotte had bitten him. She hadn't broken the skin,
but there were deep red dents that matched her canines. He wel-
comed the pain, though, for it kept him alert; he knew he'd have
to watch Charlotte for the next few days, at least until Elizabeth
went back to Chicago. After that he could tear the place apart and
look for her hidden cache of incriminating evidence, but for now
he stayed close to his wife, sitting awake in bed next to her on Saturday morning as she slept in, rubbing his aching hand and keeping watch. Charlotte came no closer than the doorway, but she
crouched there and watched Paul steadily, until her gaze became
uncomfortable and he had to look away.

After lunch, he went into the living room to print out what he
had written, so that Elizabeth could take a look at it before they
showed it to Walter. He had to leave her alone to run the printer—
she stayed in the kitchen to read the newspaper—but Charlotte was
nowhere to be seen. Once he had called up the file and gotten the
printer buzzing, chucking out a page every minute or so, he
stepped out of the living room into the hall to peek into the
kitchen. And saw Charlotte sitting on her haunches in the bright
spring sunlight at Elizabeth's feet, one of Kym's bikini bottoms
dangling from her jaws. Elizabeth wasn't looking, though; she was
reading the paper, one hand curled around her cup of coffee. Charlotte reared up and put her front paws on Elizabeth's leg, one long

red thong of Kym's bikini draped over the cotton of Elizabeth's jeans.

"Hey boo-boo," Elizabeth said absently, without looking at the cat. She let go of her coffee cup and lowered her hand toward Charlotte's head.

"Charlotte!" roared Paul, and everybody jumped. Elizabeth jerked back, knocking over her coffee, wide-eyed with fright. Charlotte dived under the kitchen table with the bikini. And Paul charged forward, dropping to his hip and sliding under the table as aggressively as Ty Cobb, spikes first.

"Paul! My God!" Elizabeth cried, holding her arm up, dripping with hot coffee.

Paul cornered Charlotte under the table, and she dropped the bikini. She crouched with teeth bared and ears back, ready to hiss.

"Charlotte, *no!*" barked Paul, snatching up the bikini and stuffing it in his pocket. "You're a very *very* bad girl!"

He gritted his teeth and grabbed the cat roughly by her collar and slung her out from under the table, howling and writhing.

"What the hell are you doing?" Elizabeth cried, bending over in her chair to peer under the table.

"Take her, Lizzie!" Paul yelled. "Just take her!"

Elizabeth reached out and caught Charlotte under her front legs, and Paul let go of her. As Elizabeth cradled Charlotte in her lap and murmured to her, Paul crawled out from under the table and stood up. He was trembling, his heart pounded, his breath came short.

"What has gotten into you?" Elizabeth looked at him, wide-eyed and incredulous.

"She was about to pee all over the floor, Lizzie," he said, breathless.

"What?"

"Lizzie, she was doing the squat, she was assuming the position."

"That's ridiculous, Paul."

Elizabeth's hands were busy stroking the cat. Charlotte had curled into a very active ball, kneading Elizabeth's thigh with her paws, trying to burrow her head into Elizabeth's sweater. Elizabeth cooed at her and looked up at Paul again.

"She hasn't peed anywhere in weeks," she said.

"Yes she has. I just haven't told you about it." Paul rested his hand against his pocket, feeling the soft lump of bikini. "She's walked right up to me several times, sat at my feet, looked me in the eye, and peed all over the floor."

Elizabeth goggled at him, silently.

"Last week," he went on, "she jumped right up in my lap and peed all over my trousers."

"*Paul,*" she said, but the word held a mixture of emotions— disbelief, anxiety for Charlotte, even, he thought, a modicum of sympathy for his suffering in silence.

"Lizzie, I think I should take her to the vet this afternoon," he said.

Elizabeth sighed. She was stroking Charlotte with long, firm, rhythmic passes now. Charlotte's head was buried under Elizabeth's sweater.

"I know what the problem is, Paul." She looked up at Paul, her eyes pleading. "I think there are some abandonment issues we have to deal with."

"Lizzie." Paul knelt in front of his wife and put his hands on her knees. "She's a cat. She has a brain the size of my thumb. She doesn't have issues."

Elizabeth looked away.

"This isn't your problem." He squeezed her knees. "This is between me and Charlotte. She needs to see that I'm as much her . . . caregiver as you are." He made himself smile. "Charlotte and I need to spend some quality time together."

"Oh Paul," Elizabeth said. She was starting to cry. "Oh my poor boo-boo."

"Anyway, I need you to stay here and read my new chapter." He stood and looked down at his wife and her cat. "Help me get her into the cat carrier."

# eleven

LIZABETH CARRIED CHARLOTTE DOWN THE
stairs in her blue plastic cat carrier and put her in the car on the
front passenger seat, with the door of the carrier facing the
driver's side, so that she could see Paul and wouldn't be scared.
Charlotte cried all the way down the stairs and into the car, but as
soon as Paul had pulled away, Elizabeth watching them go from
the bedroom window, Charlotte stopped crying and lay watching
him through the stiff wire mesh of the door. Paul pulled the bikini
bottom out of his pocket and pressed it against the mesh.

"I ought to shove this down your fucking throat," he said, but a
couple of blocks from home, he tossed the bikini out the window.

The afternoon was even warmer than the day before. Tight little buds were beginning to swell on the trees, and there was a
warm wind blowing through Paul's open window. The bicyclists
were out in their spandex suits and helmets, and joggers ran along
the sidewalks, weaving and leaping to avoid the puddles and running streams of melting snow. He pulled into a convenience store
and parked; he stepped up to the pay phone outside, digging in his
wallet for the number of Andrea, the cat psychic the vet had rec-
ommended to them. She was home, thank God, but at first she
wouldn't agree to see him, said that it was no use bringing Charlotte out to her house, that she had to see the animal in its own setting. But Paul insisted, saying, "It's an emergency. I'll pay you anything you want."

With a heavy sigh, she agreed, and gave him directions. She lived outside of town, in the hills north of Bluff City. Usually Charlotte cried when she was made to ride in the car, but all the way out to Andrea's house she didn't make a sound. After a few minutes of glaring at Paul, in fact, she turned around in the cat carrier and laid her chin on her paws in the back of it, presenting Paul with only a view of her rump. Finally Paul arrived at a huge old Victorian farmhouse situated picturesquely on a hilltop. It was beautifully maintained, painted pink with white trim. There was a white gazebo on the front lawn, with neatly trimmed bushes all around and a sign out front lettered in elaborate calligraphy, saying "Fresh Farm Eggs." There was a little circle driveway before the pink two-car garage, and Paul parked and got Charlotte out of the car, lifting the carrier by the handle and pointing the door away from him so he didn't have to look at her. Andrea came out of the side porch before he had made it across the driveway, and she approached him purposefully. She wore slacks and a blouse, but managed somehow to look every bit as imperious as she had in the suit she'd worn to their apartment. She met Paul halfway across the drive and without saying a word held out her hand for the handle to the carrier. The unspoken formality of it reminded Paul of a midnight exchange of spies in the middle of a bridge in some cold-war thriller.

"You wait here," she said, and turned and sailed back toward the house, lifting the carrier like a suitcase and throwing out her other arm for balance. At the porch steps she paused, and looking back she spoke to him, slightly more personably.

"Look around if you want," she said. "Make yourself at home."

The back of the house had a very pleasant southern exposure, and the lawn there was dry, the snow on the hillside already melted away. Paul stood just by the corner of the house and admired the view, hills against hills in bluish silhouette against the pale, whitish glare of the spring sky. Down the slope behind the garage he saw a pond swollen beyond its banks by the spring melt, and between the garage and the pond a low white shed that he decided was the chicken coop. Something white moved against the matted grass between the pond and the shed. He thought it might be a chicken, but then he saw it was a cat with long white fur, crouched low, step-

ping deliberately over the clumps of brown grass, stalking something. Then he felt a warm pressure against his leg and he started,
nearly exclaiming aloud. Another cat, an orange tabby, brushed his
leg again and mewed up at him. He felt himself stiffen involuntarily,
and he gritted his teeth and gave the cat a shove with the side of
his foot.

"Get away," he said, and at the same moment he heard a dry,
rasping cry, followed by a string of words in a foreign language in
the same rasping voice. He peered around the edge of the house
and saw a wide redwood deck, water-stained, with a stack of plastic patio chairs under a tarp. Near a glass door that let into the
house, a tiny old woman sat in a lawn chair in the weak spring sunlight, wrapped in a shawl, a blanket around her legs, an aluminum
cane with four feet like a claw standing alone just within her reach.
Something was moving in her lap, and she hissed and cursed it in
her harsh tongue, pushing at it with her gnarled hands. A small gray
Siamese turned around and around in her lap, trying to curl itself
there. As Paul came around the house, peering up through the railing of the deck, the old woman pushed the cat right out of her lap,
but it jumped up onto her again, provoking her to another torrent
of Mediterranean curses. He had no idea what the language was,
but he knew it wasn't Spanish, French, or Italian. Then the old
woman saw Paul and stopped talking, looking down at him with
piercing eyes, her witch's hands pinching the ears of the Siamese.

"Hey you," she said. "You wanna cat?"

"No thanks," Paul said. "I have one already."

The old woman hissed dismissively; she was practically bald, with
tight, papery skin. She was nearly lost in the shawl and blanket, and
Paul marveled to think that Andrea might have descended from
her, even at a generation's remove; he reckoned that it might take
five or six of the old woman to equal one of the psychic.

"Too many goddamn cats," she said.

"I agree."

"This one blind." She plucked at the Siamese, which was purring
and kneading the blanket, cloyingly affectionate. "Stupid, too."

"Is it bothering you?" Paul said. "You want me to take it away?"
He put his foot on the bottom step of the deck.

"Son of a bitch," the old woman said, and she lifted the cat suddenly with both hands, by its tail and the back of its neck, and with surprising force flung it away from her as if she were passing a basketball. The cat soared off the deck, over the steps, and landed halfway down the hill, rolling to a stop in the brown grass. It righted itself, stood, fell over, stood again, and walked off, toward the chicken coop. As it did, the woman made some sort of simple but emphatic gesture at it, and spoke again, vehemently, in her indecipherable tongue. It came to him suddenly that the language might be Romany, and he thought, My God, I'm having my cat's mind read by gypsies. He backed away from the deck, instinctively feeling for his wallet in his back pocket.

"Hey mister!"

He wheeled and looked back toward the driveway. The psychic waited in the same place where she'd taken the cat from him. The blue cat carrier rested at her feet.

The feeling of an exchange between enemies was even stronger this time. As he met her in the middle of the driveway, Paul could see that Andrea was agitated, breathing heavily, working her mouth.

"So what is it?" Paul said. "What do you see?"

She said nothing for a moment, refusing to meet his eye, breathing hard through her nose.

"I saw . . ." she began, and paused. Paul glanced at the carrier. Charlotte was curled in the back of it, her tail toward him.

"I saw her eating you," Andrea said, and she lifted her gaze to his, glaring at him.

"Eating me?"

"Yes."

Paul laughed feebly and said, "C'mon."

"You're real small," Andrea said, her voice shaking with anger, "and she's chasing you around, batting you between her paws like a mouse."

Paul stopped laughing. His mouth was very dry.

"Then she bites your head off."

There was a long moment of silence as Andrea seemed to search Paul's face, and he blinked and stepped back, wondering if she was trying to read him as she read an animal. A blur flashed at the edge of his vision and startled him, and he whirled to see nothing but the tremble of a bush at the edge of the drive.

"Take her." Andrea lifted the carrier off the concrete with a scrape. "She's your cat. There's nothing I can do about that."

Paul took the carrier. It seemed even heavier than before.

"What do I owe you?" Paul said.

"I don't want your goddamn money, mister," the psychic said. "Get the hell out of here and don't ever come back."

Andrea spun gravely, rotating like a planet, and started across the drive, and Paul slung Charlotte into the backseat of the car, where he didn't have to look at her. He fumbled at the key in the ignition and put the car in gear, but when he looked up through the windshield he saw Andrea standing immovably in his path, just before his front bumper. He hit the brake pedal and the car lurched to a stop, but Andrea didn't flinch. Instead she laid her hand on the hood of the car and walked around to Paul's window, pushing with her hand against the car as if to keep it from going anywhere. Paul rolled down his window, and she laid her beefy hands on the sill.

"If I had any proof, I'd get the Humane Society on your ass," she said, her voice beginning to lose its control. "I don't know what you've done to that cat, but you keep doing it and you'll be really, really sorry."

Paul looked away from her through the windshield and noisily shifted through all the gears. Still she held on to the car, and he had the awful feeling that if he put the car in gear and stepped on the gas the car wouldn't budge an inch until she let go. Then she pushed away from the window, and the car lurched forward, turning around the driveway and out onto the narrow road, spraying a little gravel. Paul glanced up and was shocked to see Andrea in his rearview mirror. With preternatural speed she had somehow made it already to the end of her drive, walking slowly, and as he descended the hill he saw her sink out of sight behind him, standing implacably in the road, watching him go.

# twelve

$\mathcal{S}$HE NEEDS TO FEEL SAFE," PAUL SAID TO ELIZ-abeth when he got home. He let Charlotte out of the carrier in the living room, and she jumped up on Elizabeth's lap, displacing the loose pages of his chapter.

"The vet says," he went on, "we need to restrict her movement around the apartment until Charlotte and I make the move to Chicago."

"Which means?" Elizabeth asked, stroking the cat, who was burrowing into her mistress again.

"When you're not here, locking her in the bathroom."

"Is that necessary?"

"Vet says she'll feel safer with a smaller territory to patrol." He sat across from Elizabeth, the carrier on the floor between his feet. "And it's just until I move to Chicago." He gestured at the pages of his chapter, spread across the couch. "Which will be shortly, right?"

"Well," Elizabeth said, switching emotional gears and picking up the pages. From across the room, Paul could see that she'd marked them up, and for the next ten minutes he endured it while she spoke to him as if he were one of her grad students, reading his own prose back to him in a derisive tone with her pen in her mouth, making him wait as she pawed through the pages looking for a passage she wanted to point out to him. He clasped his hands together and squeezed them tight in an attempt to keep his equanimity, saying "uh huh, uh huh" over and over again to let her know he was listening, while not really hearing a word. In the meantime Charlotte purred in Elizabeth's lap, her head buried in the folds of her mistress's sweater.

Finally Paul held up his hands, which were numb from being squeezed so hard, and said, "What about Walter? Will he like them?"

"Oh, Walter." Elizabeth waved her hand. "He'll love it. I mean, you're practically tenure-track as far as he's concerned. I doubt he'll even read this," she said, gesturing at the unruly heap of papers on the sofa.

She went on, and Paul's heart leaped, but he let himself settle back in his chair, his hands loose in his lap.

At Elizabeth's insistence, they let Charlotte have the run of the place that night, and Paul got up Sunday morning before Elizabeth to make sure that the cat had left nothing incriminating about the place. All he found was one of her mousies on the kitchen table, and he flushed it down the toilet. That afternoon, Paul and Elizabeth went for a drive, and Paul locked Charlotte in the bathroom with her litter box and a water dish. He lifted Charlotte straight out of Elizabeth's lap just before they left, and the cat fought him, snarling and trying to scratch him with her rear claws. While Elizabeth was watching, he laughed and said, "Charlotte, Charlotte, Charlotte," but as soon as he was out of Elizabeth's sight in the hall, he rattled the cat so hard that she went stiff with fright. Then he dropped her from shoulder height into the bathtub and shut the door.

The day was another warm one, and they followed winding two-lane roads through the hills, the car hissing through streams of snowmelt or grinding sclerotically up steep grades.

"Let's get a new car when we get to Chicago," Paul said, and to his surprise Elizabeth said, "Yeah. I want a Miata."

In fact, Elizabeth was as affectionate and playful as he had ever seen her. She sang snatches of song. She played with the hair at the back of his neck as he drove. She dug around in the shoe box of tapes in the backseat and exclaimed with delight when she came up with Katrina and the Waves. The tape had been the soundtrack to their courtship in grad school, and now they rolled down the windows to the warm, windy spring air and sang along to "Walking on Sunshine," Elizabeth rapping the dashboard to the beat with her long fingers.

"Tenure becomes you, my dear," Paul said, and she gave a long, musical laugh. It occurred to him that perhaps he wouldn't need Kym in Chicago after all, that she was merely the pastime of his blue period, his exile in the provinces, and that what tasted like caviar in Bluff City, Iowa, might be meat and potatoes on the Miracle Mile.

"You need to come to Chicago, Paul," Elizabeth said at one point, shouting over the wind through the windows of the car. "Meet the members of my department."

"Our department," he shouted back, and she gave him a smile.

"In fact, why don't you board Charlotte next weekend," Elizabeth said, "and come? I think we'll have something more to celebrate."

Paul cocked an eye at her.

"Show me a good time?" he said.

"Hey, sailor." She snapped out of her seat belt and lunged across the small car to kiss him full on the lips, nearly driving them off the road.

Back home he raced up the stairs ahead of her, just to make sure that Charlotte hadn't gotten out and left a surprise for them. He opened the door to the bathroom, but she wouldn't come out while he stood in the doorway, wouldn't come out in fact until she heard Elizabeth's voice coming up the stairs. Then she bolted past Paul and followed Elizabeth into the bedroom, perching next to her as Elizabeth sat on the edge of the bed and picked up the phone from its cradle. Paul stood in the doorway behind them.

"Paul," she called out, not realizing he was so close, "what's my number in Chicago? I never call it."

Charlotte looked back at Paul in the doorway, and Paul grimaced at her, widening his eyes and baring his teeth, and he hooked his hand into a claw and made a vicious swipe in the air. Charlotte plunged under Elizabeth's arm as Elizabeth held the phone in her lap.

"It's a speed-dial number," he said. "Just press one."

Elizabeth held the phone away from Charlotte, saying, "Watch it, sweetie, don't step on the phone."

She hit the button and wedged the receiver between her chin and shoulder, looking back at Paul.

"I'm calling Rebecca to let her know you'll be coming next week," she said. "You have to promise to be nice."

"I'm always nice," he said.

He cleaned up his chapter that night, incorporating as many of Elizabeth's suggestions as he could stand, then he ran off a clean copy and left it in her briefcase. He came into bed still fuming at her presumption, and found Elizabeth and Charlotte curled up together like spoons. Elizabeth slept on, but Charlotte cracked her eyelid and fixed Paul where he stood in the doorway. He glared back at the cat, enduring her watchful eye, listening to the steady breathing of his tenured wife, and wished he had a pillow big enough to smother them both.

In the morning, they slept too late and had to rush around a bit to get Elizabeth to the train on time. At the station she collected her briefcase and her bag into her lap and opened her door, but she didn't get out. Instead she turned to Paul and beamed.

"We did it, Paul," she said. "We *did* it."

Paul kissed her, and she held on to him for a moment, then pulled away and bustled out of the car. Before she closed the door she said, "I'm showing your pages to Walter this afternoon. Stay by the phone tonight, darling."

HAT DAY PAUL COULD SCARCELY CONCEN-
trate on teaching. It was the first day of class after spring break,
and his students shuffled in looking even wearier than they had before their vacation. He stood for a moment looking at their brutal, expensive tans from South Padre Island and Cancún, and then
announced that it was too nice a day to stay indoors, and he took
them on what he called a field trip, leading them along the swollen
river and declaiming to them from *Beowulf* and *The Canterbury Tales*
in Old and Middle English, respectively, drawing links between the
former and Arnold Schwarzenegger movies, and between the latter and *Tales from the Crypt*. Meanwhile his students followed behind him, clutching their notebooks and book bags, trailing their
coats, and exchanging bemused glances. Some of them peeled off
when Paul wasn't looking, but he led the remaining hardy few up-
town and bought them ice cream.

After class, he pulled into his driveway to find Kym sitting on
the concrete step before his front door, her knees up against her
chest, her arms wrapped around her knees. She watched him as he
parked the car and sauntered up to the door.

"Hi," she said uncertainly. "I know I'm not supposed to just
show up."

Paul stood with his foot up on the step, swinging his car keys
around his index finger, gazing down at her, biting his lip.

"I missed you, okay?" She hugged her knees. "You couldn't like call, or anything?"

Paul swooped down and pulled her up, and he hustled her into the house and up the stairs, while she laughed nervously and asked him what was going on. At the top of the stairs he slipped one hand around her waist and held her palm up with the other and started to dance her in a circle.

"Paul!" she said, laughing more easily. "What are you doing?"

He stopped and pulled his head back and gazed at her open-mouthed until she began to blush.

"What?" she said.

Paul began to sing wordlessly to the tune of "Surfer Girl." He danced Kym slowly down the hall, crooning aggressively in her ear, a syrupy catch in his throat. In the bedroom he fell back on the bed and pulled her squealing on top of him. She laughed and tugged at him, and he lay on his back and struck poses, still singing.

"Did you get good news?" she said, writhing ticklishly as he pulled at her sweater. "Are you going to Chicago?"

He kicked off his shoes and tugged at the button of her jeans. She grabbed his wrists and shook them, saying, "Paul, are you going to Chicago?"

Paul lunged up off the bed and took her face in his hands.

"No," he said. "*We* are going to Chicago."

Kym threw back her head and screamed, and she stripped off her sweater and started to dance on the bed in her bra, straddling Paul on her knees. Paul howled too, and the two of them began stripping off articles of clothing, thrashing about on the bed, flinging shoes and trousers and underwear into all four corners of the room. They jumped up and down on the bed like children, naked as sprites celebrating spring. Suddenly Kym froze, still bouncing, and crossed her arms over her chest.

"What about that cat?" she said.

"Aw, she's coming with us," said Paul happily. Then, shouting, "Come out, come out, wherever you are, Charlotte! All is forgiven!"

With that he swept Kym off her feet into his arms, then kicked his own legs out from under him, and the two of them crashed squealing with laughter onto the bed, which groaned and creaked wildly under them, until it began to creak in a steadier, more urgent rhythm, which stopped and commenced again several times until late afternoon, when Paul and Kym lay back in a lubricious tangle, panting and sweaty, their skin cooling.

Kym got up to go to the bathroom, and Paul got up and padded loosely down the hall, his limbs aching pleasantly. The low afternoon sun threw a golden light through the kitchen window down the length of the apartment, gilding Paul's skin, making him squint. The whole apartment seemed humid from their lovemaking, so he opened the kitchen window, looking out on the backyard at the matted grass through the rusty old screen. He drank a glass of water and walked back into the bedroom to open the window there and get a breeze going, and he found Kym sitting cross-legged in the middle of the bed with the phone to her ear, listening.

"Who you calling?" he said, lifting the bedroom window.

"Nobody." She cupped her hand over the mouthpiece. "It was off the hook."

Paul sat down on the edge of the bed.

"What do you mean, it was off the hook?"

"It's weird," she said, keeping her hand on the phone. "It wasn't beeping or anything like it does when I leave my phone off the hook?" She lowered her voice. "It almost sounds like someone's there."

Paul took the phone from her and listened. She started to talk, and he held his finger up. All he could hear was a sort of hollow hiss, like a blank tape. He licked his lips, glanced at Kym, and said, "Hello? Is anybody there?"

"Paul, what is it?" Kym whispered.

His heart was beginning to pound. He hit the cutoff button and heard a dial tone.

"How did you find it?" he said. "Exactly."

"It was lying on the nightstand, right there, next to the bottom part. Paul, what's wrong?"

"Did you touch it while we were fucking?"

"No," she protested, laughing.

Paul stood up, shaking, his skin pulling tight all over in the spring breeze flowing through the apartment.

"Oh my God," he murmured. "Oh my dear God."

"Paul, you're scaring me." Kym plucked up a pillow and pressed it against her chest.

Paul drew a deep breath and pressed Elizabeth's speed-dial number. It rang once and then the machine picked up, the signal that there was a message. It was Rebecca's machine, but it was Elizabeth's level voice on the tape, reading her utilitarian greeting from a card she'd written out beforehand. Paul knew the code to play back her messages, and he punched it in, but he didn't know anything else: how to rewind the tape, how to erase it. He heard the high-speed, chipmunk gibberish of the rewind, and it went on and on and on. He squeezed his eyes shut, his knees beginning to wobble. After what seemed like forever he heard a beep and a woman's voice, some grad student breaking a coffee date with Rebecca, and he sucked in his breath, hoping uselessly that there was nothing more, but then the tape beeped again and he heard his own voice, tinny and pathetic, with an adenoidal whine that shriveled him to hear, crying out in passion, "You fucking whore! You tight bitch!"

Paul groaned wordlessly and sagged to the floor below the window. The phone trembled in his hand, and on the answering-machine tape he heard Kym gasping and saying slyly, between grunts, "So Paul . . . does your wife . . . let you . . . do this?"

Paul flung the phone away, and it struck the pillow across Kym's chest. She picked it up and listened, and she clapped her hand over her mouth and widened her eyes.

"Omigod?" she said, her voice rising into the range of a dog whistle. "Whose machine is this? What number did you dial?"

"Elizabeth's," he whispered.

"Omigod?" She listened for a moment, trying hard not to smile. "Omigod, this is so funny. Why aren't I laughing?"

"Because I'm screwed!" Paul roared, launching himself from the floor, his fists clenched. "Because somebody just fucked me up the ass!"

Kym shrugged and said, "Well, actually, it was the other way around."

Paul slapped the phone out of her hand, then grabbed it and grabbed its cradle and yanked the cord out of the wall, swinging the phone and the cradle violently around his head like a bolo, knocking over the lamp, thudding against the walls. Kym shrieked and rolled off the bed on the other side, dragging the bedclothes on top of her. With a shout, Paul hurled the phone all the way down the hall. It skidded to a stop on the kitchen tile. Paul fell to his knees on the bed, trembling and breathless.

"I didn't do it," Kym said from under the blanket, on the far side of the bed.

"I know," Paul said hoarsely.

"I mean," she said, poking her head out, "I don't even know your wife's number."

"I know." Paul pushed himself off the bed and stooped to pick up his shorts. He pulled them on.

"You have to go now," he said.

"Look, maybe it's for the best." Kym sat with the covers pulled up to her neck. "I mean, she has to find out sooner or later."

"You just don't get it, do you?" Paul said sharply, wheeling on her, his trousers limp in his hands. "Lemme put it *simply* for you. Let me put it in words you can *understand*. My position in Chicago depends on Elizabeth. They're only hiring me because of her. If she turns me loose, then I'm teaching composition for a thousand dollars a semester at some community college *for the rest of my fucking life.*"

Kym blinked back at him, and he turned away, pulling on his trousers with shaking hands.

"I'm fucked," he said, "you're fucked, we're all fucked."

"Well, at least we got it on tape," Kym said, and Paul lunged for her, stripping the bedclothes away from her, pushing her shouting into the hall, and throwing her clothes after her, pelting her with her jeans, her sweater, her shoes. He stormed out after her, but suddenly she spun about with a cry and hooked his legs out from under him with her heel, knocking him onto his back. She pressed the sole of her foot with a thump on his chest, just this side of a kick. She was poised over him in some sort of martial-arts stance.

"Don't you ever put your hands on me like that again," she said, in a voice he'd never heard her use before. He moved to speak, and she shoved him back with her foot. "Do you hear me? Don't you *ever* put your hands on me like that *again.*"

She turned and scooped up her clothes and went into the bathroom, slamming the door and locking it. Paul lay back on the floor of the hall, the cool spring air flowing over his bare chest, blowing from the kitchen, through the hall, and out the bedroom window. He thought he could pick smells out of it, mud, of course, but also flowers and the smell of garbage from the alley behind the house, the smell of pine trees and of sap rising. "Whan that Aprill with his shoures soote" came to him, and he shuddered. He stared up at the ceiling and saw the golden sunlight glancing along the plaster, picking out every little bump and ridge like mountains on the moon.

Kym came out of the bathroom and stepped over him without a word. He heard the creak of the bed as she sat and pulled on her running shoes. He heard the rustle of her jacket, heard her zip it up. Then the floor creaked just behind the top of his head as she knelt and leaned over him, her face upside down in his field of view, her blond hair hanging down. She laid her palms along the side of his head and adjusted his head to look up at her more directly.

"I forgive you for hitting me," she said, and when he tried to speak she touched his lips.

"I bet if you calm down?" she said. "You can think of something. Do you know anyone in Chicago who can go get the tape before she gets home?"

"Everyone I know there is a friend of hers," he said. He nearly sobbed. "What would I say? Take the tape out of Elizabeth's machine because you can hear me . . . ?"

She touched his lips again and hushed him.

"You know the playback code," she said. "Maybe you know how to rewind it. Then you could call and leave a really long message and tape over it."

"It's not her machine," he said. "It's her flatmate's. I just know how to . . ."

"Shhhh." She touched him again. She leaned forward and kissed him on the forehead, her hair brushing along his cheeks and ears. She stood up.

"You do what you have to do," she said, stepping over him and walking to the head of the stairs. He lifted his head to watch her go. She stopped, her hands in the pockets of her jacket, and said, "I love you, Paul, but I have to go now."

He lay there until dusk, feeling ill, afraid that if he tried to stand he'd throw up or faint. He thought of where Elizabeth was right now, what she was doing, who she was talking to, the way she walked home, what she did when she stepped in the door, how she'd look as she hit the playback button on Rebecca's machine, knitting her brow in puzzlement as the tape rewound and rewound and rewound. This terrified him, and he sat up sharply into the stream of even cooler air blowing through the apartment, chilling the skin on his bare chest. He stood up, careful not to make himself pass out, and picked up his sweater and pulled it on. In the kitchen, in the twilight, he looked at his own answering machine, and with a rather distant emotion noted that the red light was blinking. He had a message. He cocked his head one way and then the other, looking at it. He'd shut off the bell on the kitchen phone and turned down the volume on the machine when he'd been working long hours at his computer last week, and now he had a message. Someone had called him, sometime in the last, oh, six hours, and left him a message. He reached out and patted the dusty top of the machine, and then, as an afterthought, hit the replay button and listened to it rewind for quite a long time, not as long as Elizabeth's machine, but long enough. The machine clicked, the light flashed, and at the last minute he remembered to slide up the volume. Someone was breathing heavily on the tape, and he thought, Isn't that ironic, under the circumstances. A breather.

Then a low voice began to speak, a sort of growl, full of obscenities and curses, rising in pitch and volume until it resolved itself into the voice of his wife. At first he thought she was speaking to him in a foreign language, Romany, maybe, he couldn't understand a word she was saying. She didn't sound angry, exactly. Oh, he'd heard her angry *plenty* of times, and this didn't sound like that.

When she was angry there were long silences, taut as a wire, and short, clipped phrases, but this was fluent, florid, almost poetic in its cadences and meter. It was a hoarse aria of rage, Maria Callas doing Medea crossed with Ezra Pound chanting the *Cantos* on a scratchy vinyl disk. He tried to think of a word to describe it. She sounded . . . furious? No. She sounded . . . insane? No, insane people sounded calmer than this. She sounded—what *was* the word?—rabid. Yes, that nailed it. Elizabeth sounded rabid over the phone. He half expected to see foam boiling up out of the little holes of the speaker.

Now words and whole phrases began to make sense, like little bits of high school Spanish coming back to him. Colloquial expressions denoting emasculation figured prominently. Slurs against his ancestry were featured, in terms of which he knew Elizabeth usually disapproved, on ideological grounds. For the duration of this recorded message, sisterhood was temporarily in abeyance, as Kymberly—the name of which little fucking slut Elizabeth declared that she would very much like to know—was described in colorful turns of phrase, variants of utterances which Paul had used himself in a rather different context only an hour or two before. Indeed, Paul thought he detected a kind of postmodern eclecticism at work, as certain phrases and endearments of his erotic usage were repeated to him over the answering machine in a sort of collage, an ironic reconstruction of his phallogocentric passion, a playfully intertextual inversion of *jouissance*, orgasm rendered joyless and bitter. He was glad to hear she could keep her sense of humor about it.

Then her voice stopped, and he thought she'd hung up. But the machine did not beep, and he heard more heavy breathing, sobs perhaps, and then Elizabeth returned, sounding much more like her usual self, the newly tenured Dr. Jekyll taking over the phone from Ms. Hyde. This was the Elizabeth he knew and once had loved, thinking about what she was going to say over the phone before she said it, practicing it first, reading it from an index card if she felt particularly nervous.

"I could kill you with my bare hands, Paul," she said, her voice shaking only a little bit. "I could gouge out your eyes. I could rip your fucking throat out. If I knew how to go about it, I'd go over to Cabrini Green *right now* and hire some crack-crazed gang-banger and give him the bus fare to Bluff City to come and slit you open like a trout. Except I'd like to be there when he does it. Except I'd like to do it myself."

A pause for a long intake of breath and a monumental sigh.

"Listen carefully, Paul. You hear that gurgling sound? That's the sound of your career going down the drain. I'm going to make it my personal crusade to ensure you never set foot in a classroom again, unless you're pushing a fucking broom. Kiss it goodbye, pal. You're dead. Screw you. Goodbye."

She hung up, and the answering machine clicked and whirred, rewinding the tape. When it stopped, and the red light stopped blinking, Paul hit the replay button and listened to the whole tape again, lowering himself to sit cross-legged in the middle of the kitchen floor in the near dark. The breeze from the window ruffled his hair and chilled his cheek, and he turned toward it, opening his eyes, letting the wind rouse him a bit, letting Elizabeth's aria of rage wash over him. Below the window, up against the wall, he saw the bedroom phone, lying in a tangle of cords and wire, the plastic housing cracked. Something small lay on top of the broken phone, like the cherry on top of a sundae, and in the last of the daylight Paul blinked and leaned forward into the breeze to look at it more closely. It was one of Charlotte's catnip mousies, placed carefully at the center of the phone's keypad. Paul closed his eyes and pictured another tour de force with the Cat-Cam, CHARLOTTE'S POV, as she pads silently into the bedroom, out of sight of the two humans otherwise engaged, slinking around the bed and then leaping silently to the nightstand, pausing to watch the activity on the bed with the barely contained contempt of the neutered, and Paul hears, as if in voice-over, Elizabeth's voice saying, "Watch it, sweetie, don't step on the phone," but of course Charlotte wouldn't step on it, she'd lower her head and nudge the phone out of its cradle with her cold, wet, pink nose, calmly watch the frantic couple on the bed for a moment longer, then lower her nose to touch Elizabeth's button, the key in the upper left corner, even a cat could recognize it. Just press one.

Paul rose to his feet in the dark and turned around. The answering-machine tape had run its course again, the machine had gone through its cycle. It was very quiet in the apartment, and all the lights were out, but Paul's eyes were adjusted and he could see in the dark now perfectly. Like a cat. He stalked the length of the hall into the bedroom and started with the bed, heaving it up with a grunt, box springs and all, and letting it drop with a crash when he saw nothing but dust bunnies and a pencil. He wrenched open the door to the bedroom closet and plunged headfirst into the tangle of boxes and shoes and fallen hangers at the bottom of it, pawing like an animal, heaving stuff behind him as if he were digging a pit. He found cat hair and a cache of her mousies, and he smelled her where she'd made a nest for herself across an old sweater, but he didn't find Charlotte. He stood and cleared the shelf along the top of the closet with a sweep of his arm, but she wasn't there either.

In spite of the chill breeze blowing through the apartment, he was beginning to sweat, and he went into the living room, his heart beating hard. He pulled all the cushions off the couch, he kicked over the stack of magazines in the corner, he heaved the couch aside the way he'd heaved the bed, crying out as he let it drop at an angle to the wall. He found more mousies and a white sock that might have been Kym's, but Charlotte wasn't here either. He moved to the bathroom, breathing hard, still in the dark, pawing in the cabinet under the sink, yanking back the shower curtain. No Charlotte, not a sign of her.

"You little bitch," he said breathlessly. "Where are you?"

He stepped carefully into the hallway, looking both ways, and stood panting in front of the sliding door of the hall closet. He pushed up his sleeves, he drew a deep breath as quietly as he could. Then he wrenched the door aside, lunged inside, and yanked the rollaway bed out of the closet by main force, dragging the vacuum cleaner with it, tipping the broom and a mop into the hall, pulling coats off the rack to fall in a heap. He thrust himself into the closet and swept all this aside with his arm, groping above him for the chain to the light. It came into his fingers, he jerked it, and squinted in the harsh yellow glare. In the rectangular square of carpet where the rollaway had stood he found the mother lode: half a dozen mousies, three wine-cooler bottle caps, an earring, Kym's paper moon, a litter of oyster-cracker crumbs.

Something stirred over his head, and he glanced up to see the cat carrier on the top shelf shift ever so slightly. He jumped up and heaved it out of the closet so that it banged against the wall behind him, and he plunged his arm into the dark corner of the shelf. But Charlotte was ready for him, curled in a ball with her rear legs toward him, and she slashed at him with her claws, scoring his arm and making him scream. She screamed as well, hurling herself off the shelf at his face, and he threw up his arms and fell back into the tangle of junk, snapping the handles of the broom and mop as he fell. Charlotte rocketed over him into the doorway of the living room, and Paul scrambled up out of the heap in the hall and crashed into the doorway after her, just in time to see her dash behind the couch. The couch was halfway into the middle of the room, and he bounded onto it, lunging over the back at Charlotte, tipping it over with his weight. Charlotte shrieked and scrambled back, slipping free as the couch crashed onto its back, tipping Paul into the wall. But he was up again in an instant, diving for her, landing on his chest with a tuft of her hair in his fingers as she skidded into the kitchen.

"*Charlotte!*" he roared, drawing it out like a battle cry, and he scrambled on all fours into the kitchen after her, into the cold wind from the window. Charlotte crouched on her haunches in the open window, scrabbling furiously at the rusty screen with her front paws. She had no front claws anymore, but the screen was old and nearly eaten through in places, and she was making progress, widening a couple of holes with her frantic pressure, bloodying her paws. At the squeak of Paul's bare feet on the tile, she looked back—her teeth bared, her eyes wild, her ears flat against her head—and saw him coming, and she pawed even faster, her paws a white blur. With a little thrum like a plucked string, the mesh of the screen parted, and Charlotte thrust her head and paw through the hole, but at the same moment Paul hooked four fingers through her collar and jerked her back, swinging her high over his head, away from his face. She screamed and flailed wildly, twisting about in his hand and clutching his wrist with her front paws, slashing his arm furiously with her rear feet. But he didn't let go, and averting his face, he carried her over his head into the hall, shaking her hard, shouting wordlessly with pain.

He kicked the cat carrier with his toe, and he bent and groped for it. Charlotte was hissing and spitting now, biting his knuckles and still slashing at his arm, and he could feel his own warm blood pouring down into the sleeve of his sweater. He fumbled with the carrier, tipping it up on end, propping the door open. Then he swung the cat into it, bringing her down by the collar headfirst, overhand, and he banged the door shut. In the yellow glare of the closet light he saw her tumbling about in the carrier, trying to right herself, and he swung it up by the handle, and stepped over the junk in the hall and into the bathroom. She was crying now, a rising and falling siren like a baby wailing. He put the carrier in the bathtub with the wire door away from him, and he plugged the drain and turned on both taps, full-blast. The water was immediately stained with his blood, and he jerked his arm out of the tub, cursing.

Holding his arm away from himself, he went to the sink and turned on the light, squinting at himself in the mirror; he tipped his face from side to side. He was pale and sweating, and his chest heaved, but his face was unmarked. His arm, however, was dripping blood from a web of long scratches, and he opened the medicine cabinet and began to pull things out, disinfectant, cotton balls, gauze pads, an Ace bandage. He carried them out to the kitchen and dropped them on the table, then he went back to the bathroom and stood over the tub, where the water crashed in at full force, splashing drops onto the floor and the wall opposite. The tub was a quarter full; the carrier shuddered from side to side. Charlotte howled. He stooped and turned off the hot water, and he turned the cold water down to a thin stream. Then he turned off the light, shut the door, and went into the living room, where he punched play on the tape player and turned it up all the way, one of Kym's tapes roaring the Beach Boys at a volume to make the walls vibrate. He hardly heard it, though, cradling his stinging arm against his sweater, heedless of the blood by now. In the kitchen he turned on the light, yanked the roll of paper towels off its rack, and spread a newspaper on the tablecloth. He sat in the cold stream of air from the window beside him, in the bright light of the overhead lamp, the stereo blasting, and he began to blot the blood off his arm with a paper towel, folded in two.

# fourteen

OR DAYS AFTERWARD, HE THOUGHT HE SAW Charlotte everywhere, but always just a blur at the edge of his vision. Preparing a meal he'd imagine he heard the click of her rear claws against the kitchen floor, or lying in bed he'd start awake out of a restless sleep and imagine he saw the outline of her head against the drapes, her little sharp ears pointing up in sharp silhouette, her eyes full of darkness. But of course there was no trace of her left in the apartment. He had gathered up everything that last evening, stalking around the apartment with a black trash bag in his hand, tossing in a handful of mousies, a pink catnip dinosaur, a plastic ball with a bell inside. He had ripped the Cat Dancer out of the living-room doorway, he had emptied the food dish down the kitchen sink and tossed that in the bag as well. Then he'd driven to the nearest supermarket, where he pulled around into the dimly lit drive behind the building and carried the contents of his backseat across the greasy pavement there, treading on slick, flattened boxes and rotten lettuce leaves. He had lifted the shrieking lid of the supermarket's rusty Dumpster and slung in the trash bag full of cat toys, the litter box, litter and all, and the cat carrier, its contents sliding around as he tipped it in with a fat, wet sound like soaking laundry.

One afternoon he found a mousie he had missed, in the cushions of his chair, and that provoked him to another frenzy of exploration, but he found no more of them, only blurry clots and shreds of cat hair under the bed and the sofa and in the corners of every room. So he went back to the same supermarket and rented a shop vacuum and a carpet-cleaning machine, and he spent all of a warm spring afternoon hoovering every crevice of the apartment, deafening himself with the roar of the shop vac. Then he cleaned the carpets in the hall, the living room, and the bedroom, the black water churning like bile in the plastic bubble atop the cleaner. He had to throw open every window in the place to keep from being overwhelmed by the smell of the detergent.

Turning off the carpet cleaner, he heard Elizabeth's tight, halting voice on the answering machine, and he followed the sound into the kitchen, where he stood and listened for a moment without picking up the phone. She sounded as if she were reading from a card again, giving him the name and number of her lawyer, telling him that he could keep the car for now.

"There's one thing that is nonnegotiable," she said, the heat rising from her voice even out of the machine's little speaker, "and that is Charlotte. I want you to put her in her carrier and send her to Chicago on the train . . ."

"Hello?" Paul picked up the phone. "Lizzie?"

There was an electric silence on the other end.

"Lizzie, how are you?"

"Don't," she said, lowering her voice. "Don't you say a word to me."

"I was outside," he said. "Searching the neighborhood for Charlotte. I was calling her name, over and over again. I didn't hear the phone ring. 'Charlotte,' I said, 'Charlotte, where are you?' "

"You were what?" Her voice was even lower.

"She got out, Lizzie. She broke through that rotten screen in the kitchen window. I came home and found a Charlotte-sized hole in the screen, darn the luck. I told you we should have got it fixed. Naturally, I blame myself."

"You son of a bitch." Her voice was guttural and electric, the voice of the woman from the answering tape a few days before. "You did this deliberately, you heartless conniving bastard, I'll fucking kill you, there was a chance just a chance that we could have worked this out but now you've gone too far, I hope your little slut can buy you a good lawyer because I'm going to crucify you, do you hear me you useless piece of shit I'm going to . . ."

He hung up on her at that point. He knew he shouldn't, but he started to laugh, and although there was no one to hear him, he pinched his lips together to try to keep it in, and he ended up doubled over with his hands on his knees, his shoulders shaking, the laughter hissing out his nose.

On a hot day at the end of the term he emptied out his office down on campus; he only needed one box, which he carried home on his shoulder like a stevedore, sweating in the heat. Kym had his car; she was moving in with him today, shuttling her stuff over one carload at a time—whole cubic yards of clothes, scrapbooks of head shots for her portfolio, tapes of Oprah and Ricki Lake for detailed analysis. He didn't really want her to move in—didn't really care if he ever saw her again, frankly—but without Elizabeth he couldn't afford the rent on his apartment. And Kym insisted, lifting the car keys out of his pocket and leaving him with a girlish kiss on the lips to dance down the stairs in her shorts and T-shirt, her ponytail bouncing, her sunglasses tipped up into her hair. When he got home, she was carrying colorful plastic milk crates full of stuffed animals up the stairs. He followed her up, watching the sway of her hips and the taut curve of her back as she carried the milk crates, smelling her sweat. He searched himself for some sort of erotic response and found nothing. At the top of the stairs he dropped his own box and booted it into the living room. He rolled his shoulders and peeled his sweaty T-shirt away from his back. Kym breezed by him down the stairs, and a moment later she came back up carrying a large purple dinosaur, nearly three feet high.

"You have a Barney," he said.

"Yes, I have a Barney," she said definitively. She stopped at the top of the stairs, her arms around the dinosaur. "But don't worry. I don't really like him." And she let go of the dinosaur and executed a perfect drop kick, booting Barney down the hall and onto the bed with all the other cartoon characters. Then she turned and put her arms across his shoulders, touching his chin to make him look at her.

"I know you're feeling down, sweetheart," she said, "but it can only get better, okay?"

He looked at her dully and said, "Well, it can't get any worse."

"That's the spirit!" she said, kissing him. Then she stepped back and put her hands on her hips, blowing her bangs up in the air.

"That's the last load, no thanks to you. I have to go back and clean up the old place, but let's plan on making dinner here, okay?"

"Sure," Paul said. "Why not."

She started down the stairs, then stopped and reached into the pocket of her shorts.

"Paul, I thought you got rid of all that cat stuff."

"I did."

"Well, you missed something." She held a catnip mousie by its little felt tail, and she flipped it up the stairs at him. He caught it and closed his hand around it. "I found that in the middle of the bedspread." She started down the stairs again, tipping her sunglasses onto her nose, calling out, "It's not funny anymore, Paul."

He stood at the top of the stairs with the furry cat toy curled in his fist, afraid to look at it. He heard his car start and pull away up the street, Kym heedlessly grinding the gears. At last he stepped into the kitchen and opened his hand and looked at the little gray mousie lying in his palm. He thought he saw something move, a black-and-white blur at the edge of his vision, and he started and glanced about, clenching the mousie in his fist. Despite the sun pounding in the kitchen window, despite the heat, he felt very cold suddenly, as if he stood in the doorway of a freezer. He turned slowly, his sweat freezing on his skin, the air rasping like February at the back of his throat. There was nothing to see, of course, nothing at all, but he heard, very distinctly, the click of claws against the kitchen floor and a little throaty purr. Then, standing completely still in his freezing kitchen, he felt the unmistakable, silky, sidelong brush of a cat, winding between his legs.

99

WOULD YOU LIKE TO HEAR AN AMERICAN joke?" Martin said, over drinks. He and Gregory were in a smoky pub around the corner from the BBC. "Perhaps it'll do you good."

He spoke in that same British singsong with which he always said, at the end of a day's shooting, "Fancy a pint?"

"Will it make me laugh?" said Gregory, an American. He lifted his sharp chin and tossed his hair back, not meeting Martin's eye, but watching himself in the mirror behind the bar.

"Well, it pertains to your present situation," Martin said.

That got Gregory's attention, and he swung his gaze back to his producer. Early in the project, Martin had made a pass at Gregory, who found it understandable but not especially welcome, and deflected it politely. I have no *theoretical* problem with it, he began, but . . . Martin simply shrugged and said, if you ever change your mind. Now he was smiling, with a puckish I-told-you-so look in his eye, amused at Gregory's pain.

"Do you want to hear it?" Martin said. "The joke, I mean."

Now it was Gregory's turn to shrug. Martin wouldn't rest until he had told it.

"Right." Martin leaned forward, folding his hands. "A man is jumping up and down on a manhole cover. As he jumps, he's shouting, 'Ninety-eight, ninety-eight, ninety-eight . . .' "

Martin moved his shoulders up and down to simulate jumping.

"Now, another chap comes along and says, 'What on earth are you doing?'

"The first man keeps jumping up and down on the manhole cover, and he says, 'Ninety-eight . . . it's wonderful fun . . . ninety-eight . . . you really should try it . . . ninety-eight . . .'

"So the second man says, 'Really? What's fun about it?'

"And the first man says, 'Ninety-eight . . . try it and see . . . ninety-eight . . .'

" 'All right then,' says the second man, 'step aside.'

"So the first man jumps aside, and the second chap steps onto the manhole cover and starts jumping up and down, shouting out, 'Ninety-eight, ninety-eight, ninety-eight . . .' "

"I get the picture," Gregory said. Martin had little sense of pacing, an unfortunate lack in a documentary producer.

"Of course you do." Martin smiled. "So the first man says, 'Jump higher.'

" 'Like this?' says the second man, crying, 'Ninety-eight, ninety-eight, ninety-eight,' and jumping as high he can. And as he jumps higher, the first man reaches under him, pulls away the manhole cover, and down falls the second chap into the hole. Then the first fellow puts the manhole cover back over the hole, and starts jumping up and down and saying, 'Ninety-nine, ninety-nine . . .' "

Martin dissolved into a sort of wheezing laugh, but Gregory had to force a smile. He pushed his hair back from his forehead and looked away. It was like hearing a joke in another language.

"How exactly does this pertain to me?"

"You Americans are so thick sometimes." Martin lifted his pint.

Gregory sighed. He wondered if his British friends would ever stop marking his foreignness in every conversation. He'd known Martin for a year now, and it was still right-hand drive versus left, warm beer versus cold, pram versus baby buggy. Gregory hated being identified as an American. He flattered himself that he looked the part of the European guerrilla intellectual, at least from a distance, with his distressed leather jacket, his wool trousers by Helmut Lang, and the goatee he'd grown to blunt the sharpness of his face.

"Your teeth give you away," Martin had said, when Gregory

complained. "The relentless and all-pervasive dental hygiene of North America." Not to mention, he went on, still trying, your height, your blue eyes, and your pixieish smile.

"Let me make it easy for you," Martin was saying now. He put down his pint and licked his lips. "Fiona is the chap jumping up and down and counting her victims."

"And I'm number ninety-nine."

"Precisely. Clever lad."

Gregory felt that odd, acid bubbling in his stomach again. He could never decide if it was rage or pain, or both. He peered at Martin through the haze of cigarette smoke.

"Did you know this about her before?"

"Of course. A number of blokes have fallen down that hole."

"But not you."

"Well," said Martin, trying not to smile at the foolishness of heterosexual passion. "I've fallen down others."

"Thanks for warning me." Gregory lifted his drink and glared at Martin over the rim. He even indulged in a bit of paranoia, wondering if Martin had pushed him in the direction of Fiona as revenge for Gregory's brush-off early in the shoot.

"Don't give me that look." Martin crossed his arms, giving Gregory a superior smile. "You told me yourself you were happy to get out of the States because of—"

"Yes, yes, yes," Gregory said, cutting Martin off.

In his other life, when he wasn't the on-camera host of a BBC series, Gregory Eyck was an anthropologist at the University of the Midwest in Hamilton Groves, Minnesota. He was an apostate child of Holland, Michigan, the ambitious son of an ambitious father, Greg Sr., a successful minister in the Dutch Reformed Church. After an adolescence alternating between blowing away his classmates in Bible Study with his encyclopedic knowledge of scripture and raising the amount of hell required of a preacher's kid, Greg Jr. walked away from the church and out from under the immense shadow of his father to find his own spectacular success in secular scholarship. Greg Jr., PK, became Gregory, the critical theorist. But even he admitted, at least to himself, that his upbringing had stood him in good stead for a postmodern life. He had come away with two invaluable gifts from his father and the DRC: a cheerful ruthlessness in the practice of institutional politics, and a capacity for intellectual rigor within a closed theoretical system. Thus he saw no sin against the Holy Ghost—and certainly no sin against Foucault, quite the opposite—in happily twisting the knife in his enemies, who were, after all, mere backsliders and reactionaries. And parsing Derrida line by line on the difference between *différence* and *différance* was a piece of cake after a youth spent parsing Calvin, line by line, on justification by faith.

In the secular academy, Gregory only rose and rose. The year before, he had been poised to ascend to the peak of his profession. He was already the de facto chairperson of his department (though not the actual chair, since that involved a level of responsibility that Gregory found tedious): his grad students got the most grant money, junior faculty were tenured only with his say-so, the final decision on new hires was usually up to him. Already a national figure in the discipline, he now had an opportunity to make himself an international one: in the running debate over the meaning of the death of Captain Cook at the hands of the Hawaiian Islanders in 1779, the two most important figures were friends of Gregory Eyck. One was Joe Brody, his grad school mentor from Wisconsin State, a stubborn old Irishman who argued that the Hawaiians murdered Cook because they mistook him for the god Lono. The other was Gregory's old grad school friend Stanley Tulafale, a massive, soft-spoken Samoan who bristled eloquently on behalf of Third Worlders everywhere at the imputation that level-headed Hawaiians could mistake a bad-tempered Yorkshireman for their god of renewal. The debate had been born in a bag-lunch talk, escalated to an exchange of letters in the *New York Review of Books*, and erupted at last into a full-blown, intercontinental, multiple-warhead exchange of dueling monographs, while the predoctoral and the untenured cowered among the bouncing rubble and looked on in awe.

Gregory conceived of a conference at which the two of them could hash it out in public, head to head, knowing that most of the important anthropologists in the world would want to be there when they did. He took care of all the details himself, from ensuring that the two combatants had equally plush accommodations to providing a touch of theater. The debate over Cook was pretty prosaic in itself, focusing on the mere facts of his fatal misunderstanding with the Hawaiian chief Kalaniopu'u, so Gregory added some dramatic touches. Since the controversy hinged on the coincidence of Cook's arrival in the islands with the start of the Makahiki festival, which in turn was heralded by the appearance of the Pleiades on the horizon at sunset in mid-November, Gregory scheduled the conference in mid-November. And since Cook's fate was reputedly sealed by the further coincidence that he had sailed around Hawaii with the land to his right at the same time as the god Lono made his annual right-hand circuit of the island, Gregory arranged that each successive seminar was to take place in a different building, in a right-hand circuit of the campus. Finally, Gregory called the conference " 'Captains' and 'Cannibals': The Cultural Constructions of the Death of Captain Cook." The poster, which Gregory designed, featured an imperial-era engraving of a brutish Hawaiian chieftain wielding a nasty-looking wooden club, juxtaposed with a modern black-and-white photograph of a skull. Purely in the interest of evenhandedness, Gregory awarded himself the privilege of giving the keynote address, a witty and cogent intervention which he called "Eat Me: Captain Cook and the Ingestion of the Other." He stopped shaving three days before the opening of the conference to give himself a more glamorous look, cultivating just the right amount of postmodern stubble.

But he never had a chance to deliver the paper. At the opening session, just as Gregory was at the podium lubricating his throat with a glass of water, a graduate student in his own department, a woman of Third World ancestry, stood up in the audience and denounced the conference poster as racist.

"Why is the Pacific Islander represented as a brute," she declared loudly, "and the European captain as a starkly beautiful white skull?"

Gregory was nothing if not savvy, and he realized instantly that the irony he'd intended by the poster was lost on this crowd. His chief regret, of course, was that he hadn't thought of this earlier. He was forced to abandon his paper and stammer an impromptu reply to the woman in front of the assembled conference. In the end, none of the scheduled papers was presented; the conference became a two-and-a-half-day shouting match over the conference poster. The conference started on a Friday, and by Saturday afternoon Gregory was aware of the gleeful whispers that followed him down the hall, of the embarrassed silence that greeted him every time he walked into a room. He could feel his professional reputation fluttering after him like a shredded flag. Neither Brody nor Tulafale got a chance to speak, and by Sunday, neither was speaking any longer to Gregory. It came back to him, in fact, that Stanley Tulafale had been heard to say that *pace* Cook, Gregory ought to be beaten to death by his graduate students, for mistaking himself for a god.

What made it worse was that he happened to have been sleeping with the graduate student who had raised the question in the first place, a lovely if lugubrious young woman from Sri Lanka named Catherine. Later, in a more private setting, he asked her plaintively why she hadn't mentioned the poster to him long before the conference.

"It's not my job," Catherine declared, "to explain the world to ignorant white men."

"That's grossly unfair," protested Gregory, his political vanity stung.

"You guys are all alike," she said. "You think that if you fuck a dark girl, it takes the juju off your white skin. Like, you're absolved of guilt. Weil, Cook thought he understood the natives, too, and he ended up as just another roast pig at the luau."

Worst of all, Gregory's presumptive fiancée, a brilliant crusading feminist lawyer—who was, personally and professionally, the most suspicious person Gregory had ever met—had sniffed a lover's spat the instant Catherine stood up, even before she opened her mouth. It was only a matter of hours before her suspicion became public, and by the following day some wit had retitled the conference "Captain Cook, the Chief, Greg Eyck, and His Lover." Almost overnight his grad students stopped coming around to see him, his colleagues "forgot" to tell him about departmental meetings, and his imprimatur was no longer sought for hiring decisions.

And for months afterward Gregory awoke shuddering from a nightmare of being barbecued alive like a pig, with Catherine turning one end of the spit and the lawyer turning the other. In the dream, the famous British explorer himself stood by, basting Gregory with a bottle of Open Pit, and wearing over his naval uniform an apron that read, in big black letters, "Kiss the Cook."

Luckily, one of the other participants at the conference had been Martin Close, a documentary producer for the BBC, and when he idly suggested over drinks on Saturday evening that Gregory might be interested in hosting a series Martin was doing on the cultural uses of archaeology, Gregory decided on the spur of the moment that a sabbatical overseas might be a wonderful thing.

"And what about that dusky young woman of yours?" Martin was saying now, in the pub. "What was her name?"

"C-Catherine," Gregory said, pretending to choke on his olive.

"There you go. You told me in the taxi from Heathrow that you were here to cut a swathe through the women of London. Your words, Gregory. I want to be a loose cannon for a while, you said, mixing your metaphors."

"I never mix my metaphors," Gregory said, with some heat. He prided himself on the elegance of his prose. His first book had been called "lucid" by Edward Said.

Martin shrugged.

"Whatever you say. I simply thought you'd settle for a dirty weekend with Fiona. I didn't expect you to fall in love with her."

"Well, *love*," protested Gregory.

"Oh, of course, I forgot. Love is a bourgeois affectation, isn't it?"

"No," said Gregory, "but it is a bourgeois affectation to reduce a complicated ideological position to that sort of epithet."

"Save it for your graduate students," Martin snapped, and there was a moment of awkward silence, as each man regretted letting the conversation come to this pass. Gregory considered apologizing, and decided to wait for Martin to apologize first. Which he did: Martin was a television producer, after all, and practiced in degrees of servility to which an academic could only aspire.

"Look, I feel the tiniest bit responsible," he said, "though I shouldn't. So I'll make it up to you."

"You've been a lot of help so far."

"I have, actually, so I'll ignore that remark. Get out of town is my advice. Go see bloody Stonehenge or walk across the moors or whatever it is you Americans like to do. We don't really need you anymore, quite frankly. We're well into postproduction, and the last thing we need is the lovelorn host mooning about and tripping over the cables."

"Maybe next week," Gregory said, a little panicked at the thought of his own company, even for a few days. He was a man who needed onlookers, even if he chose to ignore them.

"No. Right now. Drink up." Martin stood and lifted his coat off the back of his chair. "We'll go get you packed, and I'll drive you to the station tomorrow."

He moved behind Gregory and lifted his leather jacket from the chair so that Gregory was forced to stand and push his arms through the sleeves.

"There's some wiggle room in the budget," Martin added, murmuring seductively into Gregory's ear. "We'll call it 'research.' "

At this Gregory turned abruptly; nothing catches the attention of an academic like the prospect of a free trip.

"I thought you said we were down to the bone on the budget," he said, instantly relishing the thought of going nearly anywhere at the BBC's expense.

"My dear," Martin said, taking his arm as they stepped into the evening air, "there's always wiggle room in a budget. Especially when it comes to coddling our star performer."

Gregory smiled and said nothing and let Martin keep his hand in the creaking leather of his elbow.

"Now aren't you ashamed of yourself," Martin said, "for being beastly to me?"

two

ERY EARLY IN THE MORNING, GREGORY FOUND himself in the vast, bright, dank space of Victoria Station, as Martin put him on the train. There was a familiar feel to the leave-taking. It was just like similar occasions during the shoot—in the Mideast, in Africa, in Southeast Asia—when Martin had carried Gregory's glamorously worn leather bag and handed him his ticket and sent him on his first-class way to the next location, while the crew followed on a cheaper, charter flight. This time, of course, he was only going as far as Salisbury, and no one was coming with him. Martin really was sending him to Wiltshire to walk among the standing stones and Neolithic tumuli, but at least Gregory wasn't paying for it. "You'll thank me later," were Martin's parting words. But sitting in his first-class seat, nursing a Styrofoam cup of bad British Rail coffee, gazing into the window of the car at his own reflection, Gregory was distressed to find that with nowhere particular to go, and nothing particular to do when he got there, his mind wandered irresistibly into painful areas.

The production of the series had begun promisingly enough. Martin's project was not about the world's great ruins *qua* ruins, but about their cultural uses. Which was why Martin required an anthropologist, not some working archaeologist whose vision was obscured by too many years in the dirt with a whisk broom. Gregory was tailor-made for the job, since he came from a generation of anthropologists who had forsworn fieldwork as colonialist, essentialist, and racist, just another tool of cultural imperialism. No longer need a grad student lose weight and risk disease for three years in some muddy, malarial village; instead he or she could research his or her dissertation without leaving North America or Western Europe. This had been a godsend to Gregory during the writing of his own dissertation: having spent his youth in the fanatically detailed exegesis of the Word, now he could devote his young manhood to attacking logocentrism from his carrel in the graduate library. There he found the unpublished papers of one of the founders of the field, a district officer in colonial Kenya who had written one of the "classic" ethnographic texts of East Africa. With all the pastoral glee of Greg Sr. publicly exposing one of his flock as an adulterer, Gregory exposed the great ethnographer as a brutal drunk who beat his informants, fathered children (whom he later disavowed) on the local women, and, worst of all, filled his private diaries with the worst racial epithets imaginable. But it wasn't enough, of course, to simply expose this bad behavior. One had to explain its theoretical significance, to propose a paradigm shift that put one's own work in the vanguard of cultural studies, to show how these revelations yanked the rug out from under the entire history of anthropology . . . up until Gregory Eyck. Which Gregory did, in a brilliantly epigrammatic conclusion that made his career.

" 'The proper study of mankind is man' is a bankrupt formulation," he wrote, "the worst kind of Enlightenment arrogance. We must live by a more rigorous, more honest standard: the proper study of anthropology is anthropologists."

So, after his disaster at the conference back in Hamilton Groves, there was nothing so restorative to Gregory as the idea of himself posed before the Parthenon, Angkor Wat, and Machu Picchu, deftly deconstructing the various meanings that these great archaeological monuments held for different generations of Europeans. This was fieldwork, as far as Gregory was concerned: world travel in first-class seats to four-star accommodations in exotic and striking locales, entirely funded by the television-viewing public of a faded colonial power. Best of all to his wounded self-esteem, though, was the reconstruction of himself as PBS matinee idol, as each segment featured Gregory in various seductive poses: Gregory as boulevardier, sipping strong, muddy coffee from an enormous cup in a sidewalk café in Athens, with a tiny spotlit Parthenon in the background. Gregory as hearty explorer with a careful growth of stubble at Machu Picchu, looking as if he'd walked three days through the mountains to get there, even though Martin had chartered a helicopter to take them every morning from the roof of the Cuzco Sheraton and back again at night. Gregory as sweaty sensualist, posed before Angkor Wat with his shirt open to the middle of his chest and a strand or two of hair plastered suggestively to his forehead in the Cambodian heat, as he ran his long, sensitive fingers over the writhing bodies carved in stone.

He was sensible enough not to bow to temptation on location, where he might pick up a disease, but he had returned to London afterward for postproduction with his sexual batteries recharged, every cell topped up, so to speak, with erotic energy. Here he had gotten involved, if that was the phrase, with Fiona, a production assistant on the film, a cool, pale, sharp-tongued young Englishwoman who combined the youthful vigor of Gregory's Sri Lankan lover with the neurotic avidity of the crusading lawyer. Now, rocked nearly to sleep by the rhythm of the train, Gregory closed his eyes against the weak light filtering through the mist along the tracks and discovered that there was nothing so exciting and so deliciously painful as the mental image of his own pale limbs tightly twined with Fiona's, their respective manes tossed back, their muscles taut as ropes under strain. He could still smell the musky New Age soap she affected. After their lovemaking, stretched pleasantly beside her in the rumpled sheets, only touching her at a few points, he had often clasped his hands behind his head and silently considered various titles for the series: *The Seven Wonders of the World: A Personal View by Gregory Eyck. The Archaeological Imagination: A Personal View by Gregory Eyck. The Construction of the Ruined: A Personal View by Gregory Eyck.*

In Salisbury he was collected at the station by a yawning cabbie, who drove him through whitewashed neighborhoods to a bed-

and-breakfast Martin had arranged, which was run by a gentle but slightly befuddled old woman named Mrs. Speedwell. She seemed a little put out at the sight of an unshaven Gregory in his leather jacket and designer trousers, and she stood immovably in her doorway, blocking the way and looking him up and down.

"Oh dear, you're very tall, aren't you?" she said. "I'm not sure the bed's long enough, you see."

She made him leave his bag on the front walk and then take off his shoes, come upstairs, and lie down on the bed before she'd let the cab go away. She actually stood across the bedroom while he lay on the narrow bed with his arms at his sides, holding out her hands and shutting one eye as if measuring him to make sure.

"That'll do, then," she said, leaving him in his stocking feet while she went down to fetch his bag and send the taxi away.

He'd packed his hiking boots, exotically well worn with the dust of the Andes—or at least the Cuzco Sheraton—worked into them, but for the first day he left them in his room and walked about the cathedral close in Salisbury under a sky of pale November blue, looking up at the vast gray bulk squatting uncomfortably on its splayed buttresses. Inside the cathedral he paid the extra pound and took the tour of the roof, where the tower was bound with iron bands to keep from splitting under the unanticipated weight of the spire. Leave it to the British, he decided, to turn an architectural disaster into a tourist attraction. In the evening he drank tea with his hostess in her parlor and watched soccer on the telly with the sound turned low. She warmed to him when he told her he was a writer, confiding in him that after Martin's phone call and his own appearance on her doorstep, she'd suspected that he was an aging rock star come to sweat out his heroin addiction in her back bedroom. He smiled, feeling foolishly flattered, wondering just which rock star she thought he looked like, and he decided not to take the time to explain "cultural anthropologist" to her. It had a prosaic professionalism about it: cultural anthropologists graded papers, held office hours, and sat through tenure meetings. They didn't pose bare-chested in front of Angkor Wat.

"Oh, I'm a terrific reader," said Mrs. Speedwell, leaning forward a bit in her massively upholstered chair. "Have you written anything I'm liable to have read?"

"Actually, I'm a screenwriter," he decided on the spur of the moment. "I'm writing a series for the BBC."

"Oh my goodness," said Mrs. Speedwell, gratifyingly impressed. Then her eyes narrowed. "It isn't another one of those Thomas Hardy novels, is it?"

"Actually, it's a documentary series," he said, adding after a moment of consideration, "About the archaeological imagination."

"Ah. So you're here to see Stonehenge." Mrs. Speedwell settled back and returned her gaze to the telly. "That makes more sense, you see. I didn't think they'd bring in an American to do Thomas Hardy."

Gregory was swallowing a mouthful of tea at the moment, and he wasn't able to protest that he was here for pleasure, or that the series was rather more sophisticated than that. He was also, truth be told, a little stung at the return of Mrs. Speedwell's attention to the soccer game. Perhaps he'd be forced to explain cultural anthropology to her after all.

"It's rather a disappointment, you see," Mrs. Speedwell continued, before Gregory could recover himself. "Stonehenge, I mean. A lot of tour buses and noisy school groups. If you like standing stones, you ought to go up to Silbury. It's much more impressive, in my opinion."

She said all this without diverting her gaze from the television, and Gregory dabbed at his lips with the little napkin and said, "Silbury?"

He had a vague memory of the name, and his anthropological imagination began to tick over. Maybe a sequence at some British standing stones might not be such a bad idea. He pictured himself posed in his leather jacket against some gloomy sarsen with a windy sky in the background. He saw himself squinting against the wind, and heard himself saying, "I'm standing at Stonehenge, arguably the most famous archaeological site in the world. . . ."

"Oh yes," Mrs. Speedwell said. "It's much more mysterious than Stonehenge. If you like that sort of thing. Older, too, I should think. The village is right inside the stone circle. Hardly anyone goes there. I tell you, this time of year, you'd have the place to yourself."

But why do Stonehenge? Gregory was thinking. Everybody did Stonehenge. Silbury might be virgin ground, cinematically speaking. He lifted his chin and tossed back his hair as if he were about to begin his stand-up commentary, and he caught Mrs. Speedwell looking at him, catching him in the act. He was amazed when she spoke as if answering his thoughts.

"You could put it in your television program," she said. "You see Stonehenge every time you turn around, of course, but I've never seen Silbury on the telly."

As if seconding the notion, the crowd on the television roared at a goal that both Gregory and Mrs. Speedwell had missed. She leaned forward for the teapot.

"Shall I warm you up?" she said.

# three

I N THE MORNING GREGORY LACED UP HIS BOOTS and caught the bus to Silbury. It was an old double-decker, overheated and humid, with bench seats and a scuffed floor of colorless linoleum. For a while, it looked as if Gregory might be the only passenger, but just before the bus left the station, a pair of pale, scrawny teenagers in tattered denim got on and sat a few seats ahead of him. They sat quietly as the bus rumbled through the empty early-morning streets, but as soon as it passed into the countryside, they began to nuzzle and grope each other, their mouths locked together in a series of deep, probing kisses, each one longer than the last.

Unexpectedly, Gregory felt his cheeks burn as if he'd been slapped. He jumped up from his seat and climbed the narrow stair of the bus and sat furiously alone on the upper deck, his temple against the cold glass, watching the bleak expanse of Salisbury Plain roll by below while his stomach churned acidly. He had considered bringing Fiona back to the States with him, finding her a place at the university, maybe even setting her up as his research assistant. She'd told him once, in an intimate moment, that she had a first from Oxford in . . . well, he didn't remember what exactly, but certainly a first in anything at Oxford would get her past a hiring committee at Midwestern. He still had enough clout for that; he'd even begun to make a few transatlantic phone calls. Then, of course, he'd arrived one afternoon at the flat Martin had rented for him in Mayfair to find Fiona stuffing her things into one of his bags.

"I'm off to Tahiti, darling," she said brightly. Another lover of hers had got her a job on his film about Polynesian navigation. She kissed Gregory, left him standing in his own doorway with all the blood drained out of his face, and told him to keep in touch, trilling "Tirra!" after herself as her heels clicked down the stairs.

Now the whole outing to Silbury seemed pointless all of a sudden; he knew he wouldn't enjoy the day. In the market square of Marlborough he nearly boarded the next bus back, but then he'd either have to spend another day wandering about Salisbury or, unthinkably, go back to London. So he boarded the little local bus to Silbury and sat near the back to wait, feeling like an idiot all over again. The storefronts of Marlborough just beyond the window blurred over, and he lifted his fingers to his cheek and found it damp.

"Damn," he whispered, angrily knuckling away the tears, hoping the driver up front wouldn't notice. This had to happen on the bus, of all places: Martin had refused to spring for a rental car, and paying for one himself was out of the question. It wasn't as if he'd never had a woman walk out on him before, but on previous occasions *she* had always been the angry one, while he'd watched her go with a mixture of rue and relief. That Fiona turned out to be as much of a player as he was, was only a further indication of how far he'd let his standards slip. Just this once he allowed himself an unreconstructed moment of bile on the subject of women, particularly the Graduate Student and the Production Assistant. One had nearly blown up his reputation, while the other was only an aftershock of that, but he was bitter nevertheless. The next woman I meet, he decided, might as well stab me in the heart and get it over with.

Luckily, no one else boarded until just before departure, and he managed to dry his eyes by the time an elderly couple got on, carrying their shopping in plastic carrier bags. They were old but hearty in tweed trousers and running shoes; the woman wore a bright orange anorak and the man an old olive-green bush jacket covered with buttoned pockets. They both had white hair and bright eyes and complexions like hammered bronze, which Gregory concluded was probably from years under the tropical sun someplace, in some colonial capacity. The man paid the driver as the woman carried the plastic bags up the aisle and picked a seat. Gregory glimpsed the name on one of the bags—Trevor's Art Supply—and as the woman distributed the bags on the floor and the seat across the aisle she fixed Gregory with a sharp glance, twisting her head to keep her gaze on him even as she sat down. Gregory feigned looking at something in his lap; were his eyes so red she could see them down the length of the bus? She looked away finally when the man sat next to her, but a moment later she whispered to her husband, and the man turned without any attempt at discretion and looked back at Gregory. Gregory nodded at him, and the man smiled and turned back to his wife.

The bus started up then, and Gregory looked away out the window, watching the shopfronts glide by. In a few minutes the bus was grinding through open country along a narrow road. Gregory swayed numbly from side to side in his seat as the bus wound along a wide river valley, the broad brown slopes of the downs rising on either side, the stubble of mown fields picked out in the slanting November light. The peerless blue of yesterday's sky was mottled by massive gray-bottomed clouds today, dragging their shadows after them down the slopes of the downs and along the length of the valley, so that the silver of the river below was alternately glittering and dull.

Up ahead, the elderly colonials continued to whisper to each other, punctuating their conversation with glances back at Gregory. Finally, just as Gregory was about to say something, the man in the bush jacket turned laboriously around, hooking his elbow over the seatback.

"I say," he began in a loud voice, apparently unsurprised to find Gregory looking at him, "are you on your way to see the stone circle at Silbury?"

"Yes I am," Gregory said, suddenly dreading an intrusive invitation of some kind. Some awful luncheon with Mr. and Mrs. District Officer, Ret., listening to loud and tedious stories of life in the bush and the colorful stupidity of Africans, with corrections by the missus.

"Splendid day for it!" cried the old colonial. "Very brisk!"

He didn't say anything else, but only smiled back at Gregory, who was not happy to find himself struggling under the obligation to fill the silence. An invitation to lunch was inevitable and, judging from the bag of art supplies, would conclude with a slow-motion display of appalling amateur landscapes.

The woman, who was watching Gregory over her husband's shoulder, nudged the man and said in a loud whisper, "He's very *tall.*"

The old man nodded to Gregory with a wince of a smile, then faced forward again, entering into another whispered conversation with his wife.

Gregory shrugged it off, and looked out the window to find that the landscape had changed. The valley had broadened out into a wide delta of rolling ground, with the downs looming up all around on three sides. It was very striking, and Gregory pressed his temple to the window. To the right of the road, Gregory saw an ancient barrow against the ragged sky along the top of a plowed ridge. It was a grassy, semieroded burial mound, as long as a boxcar but only half as high, with tall gray stones erected at one end like bared teeth. He looked across the bus to the left side of the road and saw ahead, through the glare of the windshield, some sort of artificial hill, a nearly perfect cone of grassy earth with a flattened top, two or three stories tall.

"I say," the old man began again, as if he were shouting across a field. "I say there."

Gregory looked away from the window and saw the man turned about in his seat again.

"I beg your pardon," he declared, "but if you don't mind my asking, just how tall a chap are you?"

"How *tall* am I?" Gregory said, blinking.

"Yes, that's right," said the old colonial. "Over six feet, I should say, though of course you're sitting down."

"Six-two," Gregory said, biting his lip to keep from laughing.

"Jolly good!" cried the old man. "Well, carry on. Have a splendid day!"

The old man faced forward again, and he and the old woman engaged in another whispered conference. The bus was slowing now, and Gregory peered out the window at the barrow on the hilltop, lowering his head to manage the steep angle. The clouds parted just at that moment, and any detail Gregory might have made out on the mound was lost in the glare; it was only a silhouette against the pale blue sky, a sagging loaf of bread.

Just before the artificial hill, the bus turned off the main road and followed an even narrower road south into the village, between fields of stubble on either side. The road rose and fell across gentle swells of earth, obscuring the village ahead, while two lines of broken standing stones marched in the field alongside the road like stumpy pillars. As the bus breasted the next swell of land, Gregory saw a remarkably situated village laid out across the road ahead: a huge, foreshortened circular embankment covered with grass, within which stood another circle of large, irregular standing stones, while at the center of the site the square little houses of the village sprawled at a slant across the bull's-eye of the crossroads. The bus passed through a gap in the embankment and between two immense, wrinkled stones standing taller than the bus itself, and Gregory saw a National Trust sign announcing that this was Silbury.

The old colonial shot a glance back at Gregory, and the bus hissed to a stop right at the crossroads. Gregory stood, stooping under the low ceiling of the bus, and waited for the elderly couple to descend to the pavement before he stepped out into the wet, windy air. The bus grumbled away up the road and plunged through another gap in the embankment. Mrs. Speedwell had been right about the place. Unlike Stonehenge, there were no tour buses full of teenagers, no ice cream vendors, no park guards. Indeed, he and the elderly couple were the only people in sight, standing in the middle of the road, buttoning and zipping up against the damp chill. The old colonials weren't moving, and Gregory turned away from them, his leather jacket creaking. He was hoping to avoid an invitation, but he turned back too soon and found the man lifting his chin and peering down his nose at Gregory. The old woman was a step or two behind him, a plastic bag hanging from each hand. She was clearly hoping to move her husband along, but he didn't budge, looking Gregory up and down.

"Knew a black fellow in the back country once," he said, "who was quite a bit taller than this one." It was unclear to Gregory just to whom the man was speaking.

"Come along, Ross," the woman said. "You know you're not used to the damp."

The old man grunted, and turned laboriously.

"Right you are, Margaret," he said, following with a stiff-backed walk as his wife set a brisk pace away from the crossroads.

Gregory watched them go with relief, and he pulled up his collar and turned slowly, surveying the village. The village was an unlovely mix of whitewashed cottages and two-story redbrick houses, with a provisional, temporary look against the incomparably older site all around them. But even so, he could see that Silbury was much more striking and mysterious than crowded, touristy Stonehenge. Across the wide reach of cropped grass between the houses he saw the huge, irregular sarsen stones, as gray and wrinkled as elephant hide, standing at even intervals all around the inside of the embankment. A stout man in blue coveralls, balancing a rake on his shoulder, walked a track that ran along the line of sarsens, and they were easily twice as high as he was, higher even than the prongs of the rake. Just beyond the ring of sarsens the grass dipped into a deep ditch, then climbed sharply to the embankment itself, which was much blunted by the centuries, no doubt, but still stood taller than most of the houses. Only the bare, wintry branches of trees and a couple of TV aerials stood higher, against the humped back of the downland all around. The clouds had massed together finally and cut off the sun, and Gregory could see the little bumps of tumuli and burial mounds along the rim of the downs, silhouetted against the ragged, gray underside of the overcast. It was a long way from the bright, lubricious pleasures of London, and Gregory allowed himself a pleasurable little shiver that was not entirely an effect of the cold. Even a postmodernist could take pleasure in the eerie charm of standing stones.

Just for a moment, in fact, he craved the company of the old colonial couple, thinking that a friendly pint might not have been such an imposition. But they were gone, and he felt another, less pleasurable chill at the way they had disappeared so quickly and completely. The man with the rake had vanished, as well, and the houses were perfectly still, except for the coal smoke rising from the chimneys and whisked away by the wind. It might have been his imagination, but he thought he saw out of the corner of his eye the twitch of curtains here and there, and he was somewhat reassured. At least someone was taking note of him.

He started toward the pub, a two-story whitewashed building just up the road, with a picturesque lean to it and a sign swinging silently over the door. "The Seven Sisters," read the sign, and it showed seven bright stars against an irregular patch of dark blue sky. It was the Pleiades, and for the first time in months Gregory recalled the conference on Cook; the coincidence of Cook's arrival in Hawaii and the Makahiki festival were heralded by the appearance of the Pleiades on the horizon at sunset. Just this time of year, in fact: it was almost exactly a year since the disastrous conference. Gregory shivered, as if it were the members of his department watching him from behind the twitching curtains. He could use a beer, he decided. A little lunch might warm him up.

Inside the pub he was almost relieved to find the old colonial couple standing at the bar, engaged in an earnest conversation with the barman, a broad-shouldered man in his thirties with a sandy beard and a pushed-in face. Ross and the barman were leaning against the bar on their elbows, their faces close together, while Margaret leaned on one elbow and looked from one to the other. The plastic bags sat on the floor at her feet; a brand-new paintbrush stuck up at an angle from the art supply bag, its virgin brush a perfect inverted comma.

As Gregory stepped into the doorway, the conversation stopped, and all three turned to look at him. He hesitated with his hand on the latch, then smiled and came in, making a point of huffing and puffing and rubbing his hands against the cold outside. The two men at the bar stood up straight, exchanging one last glance, and Margaret stooped to lift the carrier bags, handing the art supplies to her husband. They started toward the door, and Gregory ostentatiously held it for them, exchanging a nod with the old man as he passed.

"Cheerio," said Ross, letting his wife pass through first. "Enjoy your day."

"Thanks," said Gregory, "I will."

Then, to Gregory's surprise, the old man gave him a wink and a brisk thumbs-up, and passed through the door. Gregory let the door shut after them, and he approached the bar, where the barman waited solemnly, his hands on the bartop.

"Don't tell me," Gregory said, feigning a bit of breathlessness after the chill outside. "I'm very tall."

There was the slightest loosening around the corners of the barman's mouth, and his eyes brightened.

"Well," said the barman, in a broad, country accent, "Captain Orr gets an idea in his head, it's hard to shake it loose."

"Not from around here, I'm guessing," Gregory said, undoing the catches of his jacket around his neck.

"Not true, sir," said the barman, blinking back at him. "My family's lived here for centuries."

"No, no," said Gregory. He unzipped his jacket, shook back his hair, and gave the barman his narrow, pixieish smile. "I meant . . ." He gestured after the old colonials.

"Ah." Now the barman did smile, professionally. "And what can I do for you, sir?"

Gregory drew a breath, seeing that his question wasn't going to be answered. He lifted his gaze to a chalkboard behind the bar advertising a ploughman's lunch, the English meal that had been made up out of whole cloth by an advertising man on behalf of the British tourist board. Talk about your invented tradition.

"Ploughman's lunch, sir?" said the barman.

"And a pint," Gregory said. This was to be the tenor, then, of his holiday in Wiltshire, letting the locals assume he was a tourist, and make all his decisions for him. And why not? he thought, as the barman disappeared through a doorway at the end of the bar. It was their prerogative as locals—as "natives," as it were—to construct the discourse of their interaction with the Other. Gregory took off his jacket and draped it over a chair at a table near the bar. There was no one else in the pub, and he walked along the wall, surveying the usual kitschy paraphernalia: engravings of hunting scenes, old-timey photographs, nameless farm implements coated with rust. In a corner away from the door, with the tables pushed back to form a lane, a well-pocked dartboard was mounted on the wall. A chalkboard hung from the wall at right angles to it, the scores erased, only blunt, English country names listed in a row: Mick, Ted, Jack. There were no darts to be seen, and Gregory turned to the bar, looking for the barman. But he had not returned, and Gregory caught his reflection in a mirror behind the bar. He pushed his hands back through his hair and turned his face from side to side, gauging his profile. I *am* tall, he thought.

On his way back to the table he noticed an odd dogleg to the room, and he stepped around the corner. In a little nook out of sight from the bar, the wall was covered with neatly ordered rows of photographs. They seemed to be placed in chronological order, starting with older, black-and-white photos on the upper left, nearly at the ceiling, and moving into newer, color photographs on the lower right, not far from the floor. Gregory stepped up and peered at them more closely. All the photos were dated with little typed labels, one photo per year, starting in the 1890s and apparently coming down to the present. Some of the same people, Gregory noticed, reappeared from photo to photo, though the further he went along in time, the more the faces changed. Each picture, however, showed the same pose: it was always a flash photo, taken outside at night apparently, of a row of men and women facing the camera, their faces bleached in the light of the flash. They seemed to be country people or villagers, their dress changing over the years, some of the repeated faces growing older over time, but essentially the same, ruddy, broad-faced people: Mick, Ted, and Jack.

There was a more remarkable feature, however, which caused Gregory to catch his breath and step closer: at the center of each photo, at the middle of the row of villagers, either standing with his arms around the men on either side or being supported by them, was a naked man. Not only naked, in fact, but a *painted* naked man. In each photo the man was covered with dark lines and whorls that made him look almost like a tattooed Polynesian warrior from an old engraving. And while the other, fully dressed people in the photo either smiled or stared poker-faced into the lens, in every picture the naked man was wearing a broad, woozy, drunken grin.

"Your lunch, sir."

Gregory gasped and jerked back from the wall of photos. The barman stood in the archway of the nook, holding a plate of bread and cheese and tomato in one hand and a dripping pint in the other. His eyes flickered over the photos, and then, adding to Gregory's surprise, he blushed a deep red.

"Oh them," the barman said. "A load of rubbish, if you ask me."

He turned and walked back into the main room, so that Gregory had no choice but to follow.

"Some sort of festival?" Gregory said, thinking of the maypoles some British villages danced around for tourists every year.

The barman set the plate and the pint on the table where Gregory had left his jacket, and he started back to the bar.

"Well," he said, his back to Gregory as he walked away, "if you call it a festival to get some daft geezer drunk and stand him up in his skin in front of a camera, then I suppose it is."

He rounded the end of the bar and disappeared through the doorway again. Gregory picked up the plate and carried it back into the nook. He ate his lunch in quick bites as he surveyed the photos, looking now as an anthropologist, his imagination abuzz with notions of invented tradition, of "ancient" rituals created out of whole cloth like the ploughman's lunch, as an attempt to preserve some idea of community, or out of a desire for tourist dollars, or, perhaps, just for something to do. Though some of the faces of the clothed people were the same from year to year, the naked man was always different. Especially in a small village like this, Gregory reckoned, you posed for a photo like that only once, even drunk. He swallowed the last of the cheese and popped the cherry tomatoes into his mouth one by one, stooping slowly to follow the narrative of the most recent photos. He was looking for the barman, on the assumption that his embarrassment came from his own naked image somewhere on this wall, but the photos did not seem to show him at all, clothed or naked. He studied the faces of the last five photographs, and discovered the old colonial and his wife, Ross buttoned up in his bush jacket, Margaret in her orange anorak, grinning handsomely at the end of the row of people.

Gregory went back into the other room, pressing breadcrumbs against the plate and then sucking them off his thumb. He lifted the pint and drank off half of it, wiping the foam off his mustache with the paper napkin. He wished the barman hadn't been so coy about the photos; he'd have loved to ask him about them, perhaps even mention the documentary he had written. A sequence here might be even better than the druids at Stonehenge. It would certainly be something that had never appeared on the BBC or American public television: the villagers of Silbury, or one of them, anyway, cavorting naked among the standing stones. Gregory thought of juxtaposing footage of that with stock footage of naked New Guinea highlanders, to show that even Europeans stripped off their clothes from time to time in the interest of ceremony.

He finished his beer in another massive gulp, and went looking for the barman, leaning far forward over the bar and peering into the doorway. But the passage beyond the door took a sharp turn, and Gregory could see nothing. He coughed loudly, and even called out "Hallo" in the British fashion two or three times, but there was no answer. He glanced at the chalkboard for the price of his lunch, added a few pounds for the beer and a tip, and left it on the bar. He put on his jacket and looked at himself in the mirror again, pushing his fingers back through his hair. He would pop in again later in the afternoon and charm the barman or some other villager into telling him more. It was surprising what the initials BBC would drag out of a person.

# four

O N THE CROSSROADS A FINE, PIERCING DRIZZLE
had begun to sift between the houses. Gregory zipped his jacket
and turned up the collar. People in this village had an annoying way
of disappearing just when he wanted to talk to them. He brushed
his hand over his head and shook off the rainwater, wishing he had
a hat, hating the way the wet damped down his hair. If Martin were
here, he'd be darting about looking for angles, holding up his
palms with his thumbs touching like a silent movie director, telling
Gregory to hit his mark, or to hold still while the camera assistant
measured the distance between the lens and Gregory's nose. But
no one can see me, Gregory thought, and then, with another shiver,
No one in the world even knows where I am. Mrs. Speedwell knew
he was here, but then of course she couldn't be *sure* he'd gone to
Silbury; she really had no idea where he was. Nobody knows where
I am, he thought, and nobody cares.

Water was beading on his leather jacket, and he brushed it off,
flinging the drops away from the ends of his fingers. He looked at
his watch; the return bus wasn't coming for another three hours.
He could sit in the pub and get pleasantly drunk, assuming the barman ever came back, but that would only make him feel worse. And
the site was interesting, after all; Martin would be pleased if he
came back to London with a fresh idea for a new sequence. There
was also a good deal to see outside the village—the artificial hill,
for instance, and the long barrow on the hilltop—and his jacket

would keep him dry as long as it didn't actually pour down rain. He'd need a guidebook, though, if he was going to look around, so he followed the little wooden signs to the National Trust gift shop.

The shop was in a trim little restored cottage with mullioned windows, whitewashed walls, and a thatched roof, and as he came up the neat gravel walk Gregory was surprised to see the barman from the pub coming out. The two men stopped, Gregory on the walk, the barman with his hand on the door latch.

"Well," Gregory said. "I wondered where you'd gone."

The barman blushed again, averting his eyes, and he pulled the door shut behind him. In his other hand he held a brand-new roll of film in a little bright green box, and he stuffed it quickly into his breast pocket.

"Everything all right?" he said, still not meeting Gregory's eye.

"It was fine," Gregory said, assuming he'd meant the ploughman's lunch. "I left you some money on the bar."

The barman nodded, and there was an awkward little side-to-side shuffle as he and Gregory negotiated the right-of-way on the walk. But as the barman passed, he glanced at Gregory and gave him a surprisingly brisk thumbs-up, and, astonishingly, winked at him. He hurried away, the gravel crunching under his thick-soled shoes, and Gregory, silently amused, turned to watch him jogging away up the lane toward the pub, hands wedged into the pockets of his jeans, head down against the drizzle.

A bell tinkled as Gregory came into the shop, and a rather gaunt woman in a cable-knit sweater and a long print skirt looked around the edge of the doorway from the next room, glanced up and down at Gregory, and then retreated before he could smile at her. When he was sure she wasn't looking he checked himself in the glass of the door; his hair was a bit damp, but it wasn't matted. He brushed his palm over his mustache and goatee, then he turned from his reflection and looked about the shop. The main room was bright, with whitewashed walls and low roofbeams; wind chimes and dangly New Age pendants hung from the beams, fringy things with crystals and metal medallions stamped in odd circular designs. The shop was unusually warm for a British place of business, and there was an almost overpowering mingling of New Age fragrances, of perfumed soaps, candles, and incense. For a moment he thought he recognized one of them, but in the massed assault of sweet odors, he lost it again.

Gregory glanced through the doorway at the woman, who sat on a stool with her knees up behind a counter, reading a paperback book in her lap and ignoring him. He unzipped his jacket, careful not to drip on the souvenirs. On an unpainted wooden shelf underneath the front window were several stacks of a journal called *Circular Studies*, each issue featuring on its cover a different aerial photo of a crop circle. Gregory picked up the most recent issue and flipped through it. The pages had soaked in the fragrances of the shop, and he winced at the musk that blew up into his face, a sort of New Age scratch-and-sniff that set the mood for the journal's content, mostly faux-scholarly articles about crop circles, with long, sober titles and extensive footnotes and archaeological-style line drawings showing placement, layout, and scale. Gregory turned and looked again at the pendants dangling from the roofbeams: they were all crop circle designs. Still carrying the journal, he moved among the shelves in the middle of the room: there were crop circle pins, crop circle earrings, and crop circle necklaces; there were crop circle bath soaps and scented crop circle candles; there were neat stacks of T-shirts and sweatshirts showing various popular crop circle designs. His interest piqued, Gregory recalled why he'd heard of Silbury before: the village had been the center of the crop circle mania the summer before last, until a television news crew had revealed that most of the circles were the work of a pair of con men.

Gregory felt his enthusiasm mounting. This was even better than hooded druids at Stonehenge; it was certainly a good deal more *au courant*. He found himself trying out phrases in his head: Silbury as New Age mecca, sarsens as literal touchstones for the zeitgeist, the archaeological reconfigured as the mystical. Add in some footage of a naked, painted Englishman dancing among the megaliths and, as Martin might say, you'd have yourself some killer television.

Still carrying the fragrant journal, he stepped up into the next room, pausing in the doorway with the top of his head brushing the lintel. The woman looked up from her book and surveyed him up and down. Gregory gave her a smile.

"I'm the tall American you've heard so much about."

The woman let her eyelids droop fetchingly, and she smiled.

"It's true," she said, keeping her place in the book with a long finger. "Your reputation precedes you."

He ducked through the low doorway into the room, where he saw a rack of Silbury postcards and guidebooks, and a display of red-and-green Ordnance Survey maps. This was the only display that featured Silbury as a historical site, as opposed to some sort of spiritual nexus. The woman watched him from her stool behind the counter.

"May I ask a crass American question?" Gregory said, turning to her.

The woman raised an eyebrow.

"Do you sell a lot of that crop circle stuff in there?"

The woman pursed her lips as if she might actually smile, and Gregory decided that she was pretty in a sharp-nosed, angular-cheek-boned sort of way. She knew it, too, meeting his gaze frankly with her green eyes.

"Well, we did," she said, shifting her hands around her book. "We were the center of it, you know. Most of them were within a fifteen-mile radius of here. It was quite exciting for a time."

Gregory nodded, flipping through the journal, braving the little scented wind. He caught the word "Gaia" in passing.

"At least," she went on, "until it turned out that most of them were made by a couple of yobbos from Swindon. They'd have a few pints, tramp around some poor farmer's field in the middle of the night, and hey presto. Next day we'd have camera crews out, and a mob of very strange people all over the village." She smiled. "And quite a few of them in here, buying maps and the like."

"And now?" Gregory said.

"I don't suppose you could use fifteen back numbers of *Circular Studies?*"

Gregory looked up from the magazine. He decided not to tell her that he might be back with his own camera crew. It probably wouldn't impress her.

"Didn't the circles interest you?" he said.

"Not my cup of tea, frankly." She shook back her hair. "Just between you and me and the lamppost, of course."

Gregory smiled at her. She really was quite pretty, in a tight-skinned, English way. He imagined the pressure of her hipbones against his.

"I suppose there aren't any circles left for me to look at," he said.

"Hm," said the woman, looking off into the middle distance, considering.

"Within walking distance, perhaps."

"Dear me, I don't think so. It's much too late in the year, you see—all the fields have been harvested. You sometimes see the outline of one in the frost, where the grain was tramped down, but it's much too damp today for that." She gestured offhandedly at the rack of maps and guidebooks. "There is the *stone* circle to look at, of course."

Gregory laughed and rolled the journal tightly in his hands. He wouldn't tell her, of course, but the stone circle was only interesting to him now because of the exotic use to which it had been put recently. Silbury would make a really appealing addition to the series, if not the opening segment. All he had to do was persuade Martin.

"Can you recommend a guidebook?" he said, and the woman rose, setting her paperback facedown next to the cash register. She came around the counter, her long skirt swinging. She was tall—not as tall as he, of course, but he didn't have the advantage of peering down at her as he often did with women. She stood close to him and helped him pick out a guide to the circle, then turned and swayed back behind the counter, where she played the keyboard of the cash register with her long fingers. As he reached inside his coat for his wallet, he glanced at her facedown book on the counter, an old, orange-backed Penguin, and read the title upside down: *The Cask of Amontillado and Other Stories*, by Edgar Allan Poe. He resisted a smile.

She handed him his receipt and his change, and he stuck the book inside his jacket and carried the copy of *Circular Studies* back to its shelf in the other room. He peered out the window over the shelf to see if it was still raining.

"If you really want to see a crop circle . . ."

Gregory turned. The woman was leaning in the doorway, her head nearly brushing the lintel, her arms crossed, her hip canted.

". . . then you might go up to the long barrow, north of the village. You can get the best view across the downs from up there."

Gregory smiled. He could stop back here afterward, he thought, perhaps get himself invited into the back of the shop for a cup of tea.

"But I'd have a look round the circle first," she went on, turning her head to indicate the stones all around them. "You've got the place to yourself this afternoon."

"I'll do that," Gregory said, stepping back down the walk. He almost gave her a wink, but he decided against it.

# five

THE RAIN HAD STOPPED. A SHAFT OF CLEAR light had pierced the clouds, and it glided like a searchlight across the village, making the road gleam and the stones of the giant circle glitter. The wind gusted, the light came and went, sometimes pearly, sometimes gray, and Gregory started across the grass toward the ditch around the inside of the embankment. He came to the track that ran between the stones and the lip of ditch, and he turned left. The Seven Sisters and the Englishmen painted up like Maoris on the wall of the pub had put him in mind of his conference, and he was damned if he was going to walk a right-hand circuit of anything. But as he started up the track, someone stepped out from behind one of the immense standing stones, a half-dozen paces in front of Gregory. It was the man with the rake Gregory had glimpsed earlier, a stout, balding fellow with a green National Trust oak leaf stitched to the front of his blue coveralls. With a self-conscious glance at Gregory, he swung his rake to the ground and began to drag at the damp grass, blocking Gregory's way.

"Pardon me," said Gregory, and another shuffle ensued, with the National Trust man muttering his apology, darting glances at Gregory, and blocking his way with each sidestep.

Gregory sighed and spread his hands, giving the man an exasperated smile. This was the utterly typical and perfectly dotty British behavior: a worker raking where there was nothing to rake, and standing in Gregory's way. He'd gotten his fill of it shooting the series. On a really miserable day on Easter Island, rain pouring down as they waited to pose Gregory in front of the statue quarry at Rano Raraku, at last the rain had stopped, the clouds had slid away, and the sun had shone down. At that moment the crew, tapping their watches and clearing their throats, had taken a break. When Gregory protested, Martin had shrugged and walked off with the crew, saying, "Teatime, mate."

"Walking the ring, are you, squire?" said the National Trust man now, tearing up grass with his rake.

"I'd like to," said Gregory, urging the man aside with his hands.

"Well, sir, if you're following your guidebook," the man said, pausing in his excavation of the lawn, "you're going the wrong way."

"My guidebook?" Gregory instinctively put his hand against the guidebook inside his jacket.

The man glanced to either side; Gregory was afraid he was going to wink.

"I seen you coming out of the shop, didn't I?" he said in a confiding whisper. "If it was me," he continued in a louder voice, starting up the rake again, "I'd go the right way round. See, the numbers in the guide go this way," he said, circling the end of the rake clockwise, "and if you was to go t'other way," circling counterclockwise, "why, you wouldn't get the full effect. If you don't mind my saying."

Gregory was speechless at this Wodehouse rustic. Had he really called Gregory "squire"? Gregory could hardly tell him why he'd gone left around the circle rather than right; it would seem, and indeed was, foolishly superstitious. And after all, he was a tenured professor. It wasn't his job to explain things to some drone with a gardening implement.

"Of course not," Gregory said, turning. "Thanks for the tip."

Now the man did wink at him, and gave him a hearty thumbs-up.

"That's the way, squire," he said. "You'll thank me later."

Gregory marched briskly up the well-worn track, doing a right-hand circuit of the stones. The day was chillier than he'd expected and he had come without gloves, so he kept his hands in his pockets. He felt the edge of the guidebook inside his coat, but he was irritated now, and he didn't want to give the worker the satisfaction of pulling it out. About a quarter of the way around the circle he stopped before one of the giant sarsen stones and lifted a hand to its cold, grainy surface, glancing back casually across the site. But the National Trust worker had disappeared again. Gregory sighed and gave the immense stone a little shove, and in spite of his irritation he felt a childish thrill that it might actually shift under his touch. Even the odd little exchange just now couldn't spoil the power of the site. Silbury really would make a good opening segment to the series, particularly if contrasted with Stonehenge a few miles away: Stonehenge, the ancient focus of spiritual power reified as national monument and tourist destination, with Silbury constructed as the "purer" and less adulterated site, a place where one might come to see the "real" neolithic. Or perhaps "the neolithic real."

"Here at Silbury," he imagined himself saying, in voice-over, "only a few miles from world-famous Stonehenge, this lonely and picturesque site reifies for the modern visitor what I call 'the Neolithic real.' . . ."

Without warning he was overwhelmed by the memory of sitting in a tiny sound booth at the BBC, recording his voice-over as he sat thigh to thigh with Fiona, struggling to keep his voice steady as she ran her sharp nails along the inside of his thigh. He jerked his hand away from the sarsen, as if he had received an electric charge from the stone itself. He closed his eyes. Martin's silly joke nagged at him, though he still didn't see the humor in it. Behind his eyelids he saw Fiona, naked, jumping in slow motion on top of a manhole cover, singing "Ninety-nine, ninety-nine, ninety-nine." An unfortunate name, that: *manhole*. What made it an American joke, anyway?

He opened his eyes to see the stone spotlit in a silvery beam of November light playing through the clouds. Pulling his collar tight against the wind, he turned away and followed the road across the ditch and through the embankment, stopping just beyond it to unzip his coat and pull out his guidebook. Even the guide had become permeated with the smell of the gift shop, and opening to the map of the region around the village, Gregory caught the whiff of the New Age again. But he ignored it, and plotted his walk. He reckoned to end up at the barrow atop the downs, where the gift-shop woman had said he could see a crop circle, but decided to head northwest first, toward the conical hill with the flattened top he had seen from the bus. He mounted a stile over a wire fence, then followed a path that ran alongside a clear little stream running through the cropped turf of a pasture. It was good to stretch his legs and work the city kinks out, and he marched along the path as if he were rolling the earth itself under the tread of his boots.

Now he was thinking that a segment here might not be enough, that he might have to talk Martin into a whole new episode. He could get an article out of it as well, maybe even a little book, something to help revive his flagging reputation in the discipline. Something witty and playful on the modern uses of an ancient site.

"There is, of course, more than one Silbury," he said aloud as he walked, trying out the sound of it, whether for the camera or the lectern he wasn't sure. A title came to him: *The Uses of "Silbury."* Or, better still, *On the Uses of "Silbury"*—which had more of an Eco to it, combining eighteenth-century eloquence with the postmodern.

He smiled to himself, treading the path under his stiff soles. The track was slick from the drizzling rain earlier, but already hard with frost underneath. Up ahead it climbed to the embankment of the Marlborough road, and to the left of the path, in a reach of sunlight, Gregory saw the flattened top of the hill rising green and shining in the silvery light. He heard a buzz from the direction of the hill that reminded him of a lawn mower, an incongruously American sound, and he looked above the hill for the darting speck of one of those annoyingly insectoid model planes. But he saw only the clouds rushing by, and he fumbled in his jacket for the guidebook and pulled it out, flipping to the page about the hill as he walked. That naggingly familiar fragrance he'd noted in the gift shop rose from the pages, bringing him to the cusp of some memory. He came to the page on Stukely Hill, as it was called, and read that it was artificially constructed, that it was as old as the stone circle, and that the top had been flattened by some sort of ceremony that had survived until the eighteenth century.

Then the sun went behind the clouds again, and the light faded to gray, and the distant buzzing sputtered and started up again. Lowering the book, Gregory saw that there really was something mysterious about this landscape, a mystery that had nothing to do with the tumuli and barrows and standing stones. The ground looked so rolling and easy when seen from a bus window, but now that he was right down in it, among the folds and hollows, he couldn't see the village or the downs; the ground itself cut off his view in nearly every direction. The lay of the land reminded him of the faces of some English women he knew: deceptively pretty and smooth and clear of skin, but ridged underneath with secrets and deceit. . . .

Suddenly Gregory's heart was pounding, his knees trembling; the scent from the book had penetrated to the back of his nostrils. He was flashing again on a moment with Fiona, as they made love on the couch of his flat on an overcast afternoon while the traffic buzzed around Hyde Park four stories below, and he saw her breasts, round and alabaster and damp in the same gray light he was walking in now. The fragrance of her soap steamed off her with her sweat, and it was the same scent as some perfume in the Silbury gift shop, the same New Age musk. He clapped the book shut and thrust it inside his jacket. His stomach churned, and he felt chilled.

He charged breathlessly up the short bank onto the Marlborough road and turned left toward Stukely Hill, taking long strides, his boots crunching against the macadam. He breathed deeply to calm himself. The clouds were an unbroken, shifting mass rushing overhead. Up ahead he saw a grassy track winding in a spiral down the hill, and he heard the buzzing rising in pitch, growing louder. A moment later he saw a riding lawn mower putter around the side of the hill, coming down the track with a large man astride it, his knees up like Sancho Panza on his mule. A ditch and a fence ran around the base of the hill, and Gregory came down the embankment toward the open gate, his boots thudding against the ground.

The man on the riding mower saw Gregory coming and veered down through the ditch and up toward the gate. He was a large fellow in huge black Wellington boots, faded jeans, and a barrel-chested red sweater, with a leather cap pulled low over his blunt, florid face. He stopped the mower—a John Deere, oddly enough—yanked on the brake, and switched off the motor, which farted loudly and died. As Gregory approached, the man waved him back and said loudly, "Can you read, mister?"

The man's face was familiar, and Gregory thought the man might have been one of the villagers in the photographs on the wall of the pub.

"Sorry?" Gregory said.

"The sign on the gate," the man said, still loud, as if shouting over the engine of the lawn mower. "Can you read it?"

Gregory stopped just outside the fence and saw a National Trust sign that announced NOT OPEN TO THE PUBLIC. Scanning the fine print below it, Gregory caught the word "erosion."

"I couldn't just pop up to the top?" Gregory said, mustering his pixie smile.

The man shook his head as he walked the gate closed, the brim of his cap slicing the air. He fumbled in his pocket and brought out a big steel padlock. Gregory looked past him up the hill.

"I'm surprised you don't use goats to keep the grass trim," he said, smiling.

The man hooked the hasp of the lock through the latch, but he didn't close it.

"Seems to me," Gregory went on, "that goats would be more in keeping with the construction of the hill as a Neolithic site."

The man blinked at Gregory.

"It would be more traditional," Gregory said, trying to explain in language the man could understand.

"Goats," the man said, his face as flat and hard as stone.

"Something less . . . mechanical, surely."

The man lifted his cap and glanced back up the hill, then resettled the cap over his matted hair.

"What, and leave little turds for folks to step in?" The man laughed, unmusically. "I don't think so, sir. Old ways in't always the best ways."

"What difference would it make," Gregory insisted, smiling more aggressively, "if the public aren't allowed up?"

The man's smile stiffened, and he looked away from Gregory, lifting his cap again.

"Ah, well, couple times a year, folks're allowed up," he said after thinking it over. "On special occasions, like."

"And today's not one of them," Gregory said.

The man settled his cap with both hands and leveled his eyes at Gregory. He shook his head slowly.

"I understand," Gregory said, turning away.

Halfway up the embankment, the man called after him.

"There's the long barrow, up top of the hill," the man said, leaning on the gate, lifting a hand to gesture up the Marlborough road. "You can get into that, if you like."

Gregory threw the man a wave and started up the road the way he'd come, his hands in his jacket pockets. At least he didn't wink at me, Gregory thought. The wind was cold and damp, and he was sweating a bit inside his leather jacket; no wonder he felt feverish. He was tired of riding Fiona's roller coaster. Perhaps the thing to do was just go back to the pub and get drunk until the bus came back.

A sudden gust blew his hair forward over his eyes, and pushing it back with both hands he saw someone coming on foot toward him down the road. The down rose along the road to his left, divided into fields, some stubbled, some plowed, and at the foot of the slope ahead, beside the road, a small two-story house stood within a square of hedge. The woman coming toward him had just come out of a gate in the hedge and was walking in his direction; it was hard to tell at this distance, but he thought she was looking at him. Then he recognized the long print skirt, and saw that it was the woman from the gift shop, hurrying along in running shoes, her skirt pressed against her thin legs, her hands tucked up in the sleeves of her sweater. Just like the barman, Gregory thought, trotting around in this weather without a coat on. No doubt these people were hardened to the climate, like Peruvians with increased lung capacity from living high in the Andes.

He pursed his lips, admiring the way the gift-shop woman's English skin was burnished by the wind, the way her cheeks and nose were reddened by the cold. He thought she said something as they approached each other, but she was downwind and he couldn't be sure. He picked up his pace along the road, his pixie smile forming, his eyes twinkling. He started to think of what to say, something bantering and flirtatious.

Suddenly she veered off the road and, her running shoes flashing, trotted quickly down the slope onto the path that led back to the village. Gregory stopped, disappointed, and as if she had heard him say something she paused and looked back at him. She pressed her hair back out of the wind and called out something which he couldn't hear.

"Sorry?" Gregory said, hesitating at the top of the slope. It would be nice to walk back to the village with her, perhaps get invited in for a cup of tea.

"Going up to the barrow?" she called up to him, gesturing up the hill.

Gregory turned, and there was the long barrow he'd seen coming in on the bus, silhouetted very dramatically against the wild gray sky. A tractor was moving along the side of the hill below it, pulling a flatbed trailer, throwing up windblown puffs of exhaust, silent at this distance.

"Well, I . . ." he called down to her.

"Jolly good!" she said, and she gave him a wink, and, poking one hand free of her sweater, a hearty thumbs-up. Then before he could say anything else, she hurried down the path toward the village, her skirt wrapped around her legs.

Gregory sighed, and, dutifully, trudged up the road toward the long barrow. Walking a little faster, he crossed the road and approached the house below the barrow. The hedge around the house wasn't quite bare yet, but all the leaves were brown and dead, and they rattled at him in the wind as he passed, bristling at him like spearpoints. He just glimpsed the house when he passed the little gate in the hedge; it was neither old nor picturesque, but redbrick and square and waterstained, with plain gray windows and a gray slate roof that gleamed dully in the wet. It was a bit dingy, in fact, and he glanced away.

The hedge stopped abruptly, and a wire fence continued along the road, up to a gate at the foot of a track that led up the slope to the barrow. The tractor he had seen from a distance was coming down the track toward the gate; Gregory heard its engine chugging at the same moment he saw it, now that it was no longer downwind. The driver was a dark-bearded young man in a denim jacket, while on the trailer behind him, three more men in stained coveralls sat on the edge of the trailer's bed, their boots dangling. There were a bulging canvas sack, a dented metal bucket, and a toolbox on the trailer behind them. One of the men, a curly-haired fellow, clutched a huge iron crowbar across his knees.

The tractor driver vigorously shifted the tractor's gears and yanked on the brake, so that it skidded to a stop just uphill from the gate. The three men on the trailer swayed together, and one of them called out in mock anger to the driver. Gregory thought he recognized a couple of them from the pub photographs, but he couldn't be certain. The curly-haired man handed the crowbar to the man next to him, then jumped off the trailer and started down the track to open the gate, splashing through the mud in his boots.

"I got it," Gregory called out, and he jogged forward and fumbled at the latch. Curly Hair hesitated until he saw that Gregory had managed the latch, then he trotted back to the trailer and hoisted himself up. Gregory walked the gate to one side and held it, the bearded driver ground his gears, and the tractor rumbled through, throwing up big fantails of mud from its enormous tires. It slowed as it negotiated the turn onto the road, and the trailer nearly came to a stop before Gregory.

"Is the barrow open to the public?" he called out.

The three men on the tractor, all ruddy-faced and thick-haired, looked at each other and laughed.

"Oh, aye," said Curly Hair. "That'd be one way to put it."

The tractor heaved the trailer up onto the road, and the three men rocked together, grinning at each other. It was only a moment in passing, with the other three men literally in motion, but even so, Gregory felt the electric field of contempt and fear that automatically forms between men who work with their hands and men who don't. He'd hated moments like this, ever since his youth in western Michigan. Their upper-body strength aside, he was probably more aerobically fit than all three of them put together, and given their wretched English diet and vast consumption of beer, he had no doubt who had the least to worry about, stripped to the waist.

Now they were taking their leave of him. The one with the crowbar waggled it in the air at Gregory, the other man winked, and Curly Hair gave Gregory a thumbs-up.

"Enjoy your stay!" he called out, and all three men laughed again. The tractor picked up speed on the road, pressing wide tracks of mud into the pavement.

Gregory walked the gate forward again, contemplating Marx on the idiocy of rural life.

"Hallo there! Excuse me!"

Gregory paused, the big wooden gate wobbling under his hands, and he turned to see a woman calling him from the yard of the red-brick house. The hedge was not a square at all, but only ran around two sides of the house, the windward side and along the road, while the side and rear of the house were open to the field and the downland above. Beyond a barbed-wire fence along the edge of the field a short woman in a red nylon jacket, woolen trousers, and black Wellingtons waved at him and approached the wire, smiling.

"Hello there! Could I trouble you to give me a hand?"

Gregory lifted his hand to her and pushed the gate shut, then walked to the fence between the field and the yard. The woman was round-faced, with bright yellow shoulder-length hair cut in bangs across her forehead; she seemed a little out of breath, and even in this wind some of her hair was stuck to her forehead with perspiration.

"Hello," Gregory said. I'm the tall one, he nearly added, recalling that the gift-shop woman had just come out of this woman's gate.

"I'm sorry," she said, pausing to put her hand to her throat. "I've got a goat loose, and I was wondering if you could give me a hand with him."

Behind her Gregory saw a dirty gray goat wandering slowly about the backyard of the house, stopping to yank up tufts of grass with its enormous square teeth.

"He's gotten out, you see," the woman went on breathlessly, but brightly, "and I can't lift him. I've been picking potatoes all day, and my back . . ."

Gregory glanced down the road at the receding trailer. There went three men in muddy coveralls who could have done her this favor just as easily as he could. But he turned his smile on her.

"No problem," Gregory said, and he placed his hands on the wire between the barbs, considering how to get over.

"Oh, don't," the woman said, lightly touching his hand. "You'll cut yourself. Come to the front gate."

She started off around the house, and Gregory let himself out of the field, carefully latching the gate behind him, and came up the road again to the gate in the hedge, where she let him in with a broad smile and led him back around to the garden in the rear. She stumped along ahead of him in her rubber boots, her nylon jacket crackling, her hair swinging now that she was behind the house and out of the wind. The jacket seemed too big for her, its cuffs rolled back, but then so did all of her clothes, the baggy trousers, the boots nearly up over her knees. She glanced back at him, smiling, and he blinked, as if she'd caught him at something.

"Just this way," she said.

In the backyard the goat looked up and regarded them both with a dark eye, then turned away and stooped to a tuft of grass, pulling it up with an audible tearing sound that set Gregory's nerves on edge. The small woman stopped and stood with her fists on her hips.

"Right," she said, sighing. "I'm such a silly woman, you see, that I left the gate open when I went into his pen. And he won't be coaxed or led back in, will he, so we'll just have to lift him. Do you mind?"

She cocked an eye at him, and Gregory smiled.

"Tell me what you want me to do," he said.

"I'll just step into the pen, and you lift him over the fence."

The woman marched across the yard and into a little square of chicken wire with a wooden gate, and Gregory started slowly across the grass toward the goat, with his palms down, as if he were approaching a wary dog. He glanced over at the woman, and she smiled and waved him on.

"He's quite used to people," she called to him. "Go right up to him and lift him up, like this."

She stuck her forearms out stiffly from the waist, and Gregory nodded and walked up to the goat, bending at the knees.

"Easy there," he said to the goat, which was ignoring him stiffly. "I come in peace."

He put a forearm each under the goat's chest and rear end, and the animal began to struggle a bit, bleating harshly, a surprisingly loud sound heard so close up. Gregory hesitated, thinking of those teeth and the animal's nether end pressed up against his expensive leather jacket. He thought again, with a flash of anger, of the men on the trailer, and their filthy coveralls.

"Ah, I don't have to worry about either end of him, do I?" he called out.

"Not if you bring him quickly."

Gregory lifted the goat and carried it wriggling across the yard to the pen, where he lifted it over the fence into the arms of the woman, stooping to get it down to her. She held the goat just long enough to let its spindly legs touch the ground, then it scampered away, its dignity wounded, and stood in the corner with its tail toward them, twitching.

"There," she said, slapping her hands together. "Thank you so much."

She offered him her hand, which was cold from working outdoors, but she gave him a good, firm shake.

"You're American, aren't you?" she said.

"Yes, and I'm very tall," Gregory said, watching for her reaction.

The woman laughed politely, and came out of the pen, latching it firmly behind her.

"On your way up to the barrow?" she said.

"Yes. I'm hitting all the high points today." Gregory reckoned that, unlike the brittle women of London, English country women liked nothing more than a breezy, jaunty American, a Yank at Oxford.

The woman looked up the hill at the barrow and thrust her hands in her pockets, and she gave a theatrical shudder.

"I see it every day, of course, but it still spooks me a bit."

"Really?" Gregory turned shoulder to shoulder with her, looking up the hill at the long, low mound silhouetted against the ragged sky. It dipped in the middle, like a fallen cake.

"Oh, not because of *that*," she said, and Gregory wondered what *that* was. "They took the old bones out of it years ago. It's just that you get all sorts of strange folk around here. Sometimes I see people going up there at night with torches, and I can hardly sleep afterward, wondering what they must be up to. You wouldn't get me up there after dark, for all the money in the world."

Gregory wondered if she was telling the truth, or if she was trying to spook an innocent Yank, until he remembered that "torch" was just Brit for "flashlight," and his kitschy image of hooded, fire-bearing druids winked out.

"The woman at the gift shop said I could see a crop circle from up there," he said.

"Oh dear, you're not a croppy, are you?"

Gregory widened his eyes, but she was teasing him.

"Croppies, we call them. Circle gits. Servants of Gaia," she added dramatically.

"I hear they were quite a nuisance for a time."

She grunted and rolled her eyes.

"A lot of longhairs from the cities. Squatters and mystics and university dropouts with too much time on their hands." She nudged Gregory with her elbow. "Listen, if the earth goddess wants to send me a message, she lets my goat out of its pen."

"And I helped you put it back in," he said, angling for an invitation to tea. "She'll be angry at me."

"Then you'd better go on up the hill and pay your respects, hadn't you? Come on, I'll show you a short cut."

She started briskly toward the back of the yard, and Gregory followed, disappointed, and she motioned him up a rough stile over the fence and into the field.

"Listen, thanks again, so much," she said from the other side of her fence. She smiled brightly at him, clearly putting an end to their visit. Just like every other woman in this chilly country: so nice to have made your acquaintance, now piss off. Gregory gave her a tight smile, and started up the hill.

six

H E FOUND THE LONG BARROW RE-
storative, though. He paused on the gravel forecourt of the mound,
peering past the tall standing stones at the entrance into the shadowy chambers beyond, and he felt again the pleasant, adolescent
thrill of the mysterious he'd felt down in the village. But before he
went in he wanted to see his crop circle, so he climbed up onto the
back of the barrow and hunched against the wind. The gift-shop
woman was right, the view was good: the whole triangular expanse
of country between the downlands was on display from here. He
could see the village and the embankment around it in one glance,
the bare trees like a mist among the houses, and the sarsen stones
themselves like little gray teeth set in a circle. The wind cut through
to his cheekbones, and he turned to look across the downs, over
the bare, treeless fields. There he saw, perhaps half a mile distant,
the faint shadow of a crop circle in a field against the side of a
hill. The field had been harvested but not plowed under yet, and
the circle was limned in mud and yellowish grain where hundreds
of feet had tramped it down. At first glance it looked like the as-
trological symbol for the male, but then he saw that the lines sticking out of the main circle led not to a spike but to a series of smaller
circles. Gregory felt a chill at the sight of it, but not because of the
supernatural. He knew that even in August, this damned country
could be awfully damp and unpleasant, especially at night, and he
shivered at the thought of those two con men from Swindon, even

warmed from drink, tramping around in the dark for a couple of hours in these high, chilly downs. He almost respected them for it. They were literally inscribing their own text on the landscape, constructing an alternative paradigm to the logocentric "history" or "prehistory" of the Neolithic real, reifying the spiritual in a field of wheat, making a palimpsest of the archaeological text. That the two con men might not see it quite this way did not trouble Gregory; until his Sri Lankan lover stood up at the Cook conference and yanked his professional feet out from under him, he'd always appreciated that a kind of prankishness lay at the heart of the postmodern.

He trotted down from the top of the barrow, still thinking about this idea of inscription. The naked man of the village's annual festival was inscribed with designs and symbols that were certainly no more "authentic" than the circular designs in the field of wheat. Gregory crunched across the gravel forecourt and ducked past the standing stones into the chamber within the barrow, as much to get out of the wind as anything else. The burial chamber was made up of massive stones stacked atop one another, and it was dank and cold and dark inside, with the vaguely urinous smell of a public toilet. A central aisle of white sand ran down the middle, while low archways of cantilevered slabs led to circular chambers on either side. The ceiling was not quite high enough for Gregory to stand erect—Because I'm so tall, he thought—and he hunched over, touching the cold stone over his head with the palm of his hand.

He stepped into one of the side chambers, but there was nothing to see in the gray light but stone stacked on stone. There had been a plaque out front which he hadn't bothered to read, and in here it was too dim to look at the guidebook. The slabs were stacked surprisingly tight, especially for a culture that had lacked metal tools, but even so, it wasn't the precision stonework Gregory had seen at Machu Picchu, where Martin had filmed him unsuccessfully trying to slip a knife blade between two blocks.

He went up the aisle to the large chamber at the far end, where the stones were stacked more tightly and the ceiling was a little higher. Again the chamber was empty, and he stood with his hands in his jacket pockets and the top of his head just brushing the ceiling. Here, however, there was some work in progress: a rectangular slab about three feet across stood on edge in the sand, leaning against the wall below a hole of the same size and shape. This was what the three workmen on the trailer had been up to, evidently; a pair of trowels and a bucket of mortar, still wet, rested in the sand next to the slab. Gregory peered into the square hole and saw nothing but darkness; he stuck his hand in and felt the rough, gritty floor of the niche.

This was clear proof, as if he needed it, that everything in the barrow, and in the entire village, in fact, was reconstructed and museum-perfect, no more "real" than a diorama or the two-thirds-scale castle at Disneyland. Indeed, Silbury was a sort of theme park, incorporating notions of "history" and "national identity," but where one could "ride" the Neolithic the way one rode the Pirates of the Caribbean. A whole new sequence was shaping itself in Gregory's imagination: a speeded-up Steadicam shot accompanied on the soundtrack by the rumble, roar, and squeals of a roller coaster, a shot that raced through the standing stones and past the artificial hill and up into the long barrow, plunging finally into the darkness of the burial niche. He wondered if he could talk Martin into a shot of himself at the entrance to the tomb in a straw hat and neckerchief like a carnival barker, calling out, "Ladies and gentlemen! Step right up!"

His eye was caught by a corner of something sticking out of the sand at his feet, and he stooped and pulled it out. Though it was too dark to read the brand name, it was clearly a condom wrapper, and Gregory recalled the woman at the bottom of the hill talking about the people coming up here at night by torchlight. The idiocy of rural life? Gregory thought. The sheer boredom, was more like it, the plight of English country teenagers looking for a place to do it, boys daring girls, or the other way around, to come up into the dank of an ancient tomb and have it off. In the interest of future archaeologists, Gregory dropped the condom wrapper back to the sand and buried it with his toe. The Neolithic-burial-chamber-as-no-tell-motel was yet another of the uses of Silbury. And the condom in the main chamber raised the whole issue of phallicity, as did the crop circle almost signifying the male, and the standing stones thrusting erect out of the earth. Then of course there was the chambered, uterine interior of the barrow, with its tight, vaginal entrance, the mound itself recumbent at the apex of the triangular valley. . . .

Gregory dipped his head and withdrew up the narrow passage to the bared teeth of the standing stones at the mouth of the barrow, and he sat on a small stone behind one of the larger sarsens, as much out of the wind as possible. He took out the guidebook, opened it to the inside cover, and pulled out his pen to jot down ideas for a pitch to his producer—the long barrow as tunnel of love! Sex and death and amusement-park rides!—but before a word was inscribed he hesitated, the tip of his pen trembling over the blank page. He'd done this sort of playful intervention many times before. Indeed, it was just this sort of postmodern prankishness that had brought him to disaster at the Cook conference. What he needed was a way back into the discipline that was completely original and totally unexpected. He needed to come out of nowhere, and what place better fit that description than Silbury? He could extend his sabbatical until the spring and *move* here, getting to know the villagers, learning their customs and traditions, invented or otherwise. In time, he'd become part of the community himself: the barman would stop blushing and explain the pictures on his wall. The man with the leather cap would let him through the gate to Stukely Hill with a wink and a smile. The three workmen would stand him drinks at the pub, where, after a suitable, modest interval, he'd beat Mick, Ted, and Jack—whoever they were—at darts night after night, while the gift-shop woman looked on with a saucy smile for the winner. Why not? Gregory had reversed the direction of anthropological theory once before, and he could do it again. He'd astonish them all, Joe Brody and Stanley Tulafale and Catherine and Martin and everyone in between. He would do something he'd never done before, something brilliant, outrageous, transgressive. He'd move to Silbury and do . . . fieldwork. Gregory Eyck would reinvent himself as an ethnographer.

It was beginning to rain again, and Gregory stood. But he was too excited to step back into the barrow, out of the wet. No doubt the pub did bed and breakfast, and he could make some sort of long-term arrangement with the barman, but that would be too close to the life of the village, too intrusive. Darts every night would get tedious. He needed someplace quieter to stay, someplace a bit removed, more intimate, and naturally he thought of the gift-shop woman. Now *there* was an informant, with long limbs and tight skin and a wry take on Silbury's New Age tourist trade. The gift shop couldn't provide much of a living; no doubt she'd be happy to take in a lodger, and grateful for the money. But he'd seen her coming out of the farmhouse at the foot of the hill; what if she didn't live alone, but shared the house with the shapeless woman in the red jacket? That could be awkward—Gregory felt little con-nection with the farm wife—but for the moment he managed to exclude her from his little fieldwork fantasy. This was something out of D. H. Lawrence, rustic and erotic, Gregory helping the gift-shop woman reach a tin on the top shelf of her narrow pantry, Gre-gory lifting heavy things for her and building up his upper-body strength, Gregory digging in the garden and getting dirt under his fingernails, Gregory washing himself at the pump behind the house, bare-chested, while the woman—Ursula, perhaps, or Gwynneth—stood in the doorway in her flannel nightshirt, her eyes on fire. . . .

The rain began to pelt down, and Gregory cursed, shoving the guidebook and pen into his coat as large drops spattered into the gravel all around him. The wind blew the rain into his face, and he backed into the barrow, zipping up his jacket and glancing at his watch. It was later than he thought; the bus was due in twenty minutes, just enough time to get down the hill and back to the vil-lage. He glanced through the doorway up at the pelting sky, dark-ening already into twilight.

"Shit," he said, and he pulled up his collar, tucked his hands up his sleeves, and dashed out into the rain.

And stopped short at the top of the hill. In the gloom below, the bus was already grinding up the lane from the village toward the junction with the main road.

"Hey!" Gregory shouted, and he plunged recklessly down the

track at full speed, his boots slipping and throwing up great splashes of mud, the rain beating through his hair to his scalp. He waved his arms and shouted, but he could see that it was already too late: the bus leaned around the corner and lurched up the road toward Marlborough, grinding into higher and higher gears until the red taillights glided out of sight around one of the forepaws of the downs. Gregory skidded to a stop halfway down the hill and just barely caught himself from falling full-length into the muck. His breath misted before him in the chilly air, and he was splashed up to his knees in mud. He glanced back up the hill at the mound, just a long, black shadow now in the fading light, and for some reason thought of Martin's silly joke: ninety-nine, ninety-nine, ninety-nine. He looked away down the hill through the gray rain, listening to the last, dwindling grumble of the bus, and he cursed long and hard and imaginatively.

The light was fading fast. He'd have to hurry if he wanted to see his way up the path to the village. Already he could scarcely make out the circular embankment or the standing stones; all he could see of the village was a couple of amber streetlights burning through the thickening twilight, and here and there the tiny bright square of a lit window. The rain was slackening to a drizzle again, but now his throat was raw from his exertion, and he was sweaty under his jacket and chilled without. He started down the slope again, his boots slapping forlornly in the mud.

At the bottom of the hill, Gregory glanced over the fence into the yard behind the house. The goat in its pen was just a darker patch of gray in the twilight, but the red of the woman's coat was still just visible as she worked in her garden, bent at the waist and vigorously patting something down with a spade. He could hear her breathing hard, and without thinking he stepped up to the fence and called out to her. She looked up, her face pale in the gloom, her eyes wide.

"I'm sorry to bother you," Gregory said over the fence.

"It's no bother." She stood up straight and brushed back her bangs with her sleeve. He thought she smiled at him, but he couldn't be sure.

"Hey," he said brightly, trying to muster the Yank at Oxford, "tell me that wasn't the last bus to Marlborough just now."

She looked away into the gloom with the back of her hand at her cheek.

"Oh dear," she said. "I'm afraid it was."

"Oh dear," Gregory echoed. Their gazes met, and then they both looked away.

"There's a bus to Devizes later in the evening," she said, looking down the road, "but I don't know if you can get a connection back to Marlborough."

"Well, actually, I'm trying to get back to Salisbury," he said, adding a little grunt of a laugh.

"Oh dear." A pause. "That's a poser."

Gregory blew out a sigh and said, "Well, there must be somebody in the village with a car. I'd be glad to pay them to drive me back."

An image came and went, of himself sitting on the edge of the trailer with his feet dangling, riding all the way back to Salisbury behind the tractor.

The woman leaned on her spade.

"*I* don't have a car, I'm afraid," she began.

"That's a pity."

"And tonight's Seven Sisters, you see. It's a good two hours to Salisbury and back, and I don't think anyone can spare the time."

Gregory's heart leaped at the reference to the Pleiades.

"Seven Sisters?" he said.

The woman caught her breath and stammered a bit, which only heightened Gregory's interest. He thought immediately of the photographs in the pub.

"It's the, um, annual darts competition," the woman said. "Down the pub."

The woman shifted in the dark, and Gregory sensed a reluctance in her demeanor.

"Really," he said, suddenly seeing the missed bus not as an inconvenience but as an opportunity. He thought of the naked guy in each photo, all painted up like a tattooed man. He thought of the man in the leather cap, mowing the grass on top of Stukely Hill. Folks were allowed up a couple of times a year, he'd said. It was impossible to tell just where the photos had been taken, but the artificial hill seemed a good guess. Perhaps every year the winner of the darts competition had to pose in the nude. Or the loser.

"A sort of festival, is it?" he said.

"Oh, hardly." The woman lifted the spade a foot or two and jabbed weakly at the ground. "More a sort of . . . loud party, really. Downright obnoxious, in fact. If you ask me." She sounded sorry that she'd mentioned it.

"Well, in that case, is there anybody in the village who does bed and breakfast?" He smiled at her through the gloom. "I'm a . . . I'm interested in local festivals and that sort of thing. I'd like to see it."

"No you wouldn't," said the woman, quickly. Then, "Really, it's dreadful dull. And noisy. You wouldn't get a wink of sleep."

"Maybe I'll enter," Gregory said, smiling. "I'm a fair hand at darts."

"Oh, well," sighed the woman, "I'm afraid it's not open to visitors. It's locals only, you see." She was watching him, her expression not readable in the fading light. "The only place that could put you up in the village would be the pub," she went on, "and he's full up with locals during Seven Sisters."

"I'm sorry to hear it," said Gregory, already forming a pitch to the barman in his head. "Well," he said, stepping away from the fence, "thanks for your help."

He turned away and stepped up to the gate, and had begun to fumble with the latch when the woman called out to him again.

"Actually," she said, and he turned to see her coming up to the fence, the spade at shoulder arms, "I do a bit of bed and breakfast from time to time. I could put you up."

Gregory hesitated at the gate.

"I'm afraid I don't have a telly," she went on, "but I do have the empty room. And I could do you a nice supper."

There was something sort of sweet about the invitation, Gregory thought. She actually sounded shy, as if she were imposing upon him in some way. There was none of the brass he heard in the voices of London women, with that hint that behind their bright eyes they were laughing at you already.

"Aren't you going down to . . . the festival, or whatever it is?" Gregory said.

"Oh, no," sighed the woman in a singsong. "It isn't really my place, you see."

Gregory drew a breath to ask her why not—was it a male-only event? But there were women in the photographs. Was she excluded for some other reason? But then his brand-new field-worker's caution checked his tongue, and it occurred to him that he might learn more about the local festival from someone who felt excluded than he would from a bunch of sullen villagers who didn't want him around. There was no point in going back to the village only to find out he'd have to walk all the way back here. And, as it happened, he did need a place to stay. He stepped up to the fence so that the woman could see him smile.

"All right then," he said. "I'm yours."

*S*HE DIRECTED HIM OVER THE STILE IN THE back, and then led him through the dark toward the house. She stepped around a dark, lumpish mound in the middle of the yard and glanced at him over her shoulder.

"Mind the potatoes," she said.

Inside the house, where he could see her face, she was brisk, even breezy. The moment of shyness had passed, evidently. She led him into a mudroom at the back of the house, where, in the dim glow of a bare yellow bulb, they sat shoulder to shoulder on a wooden bench while she took off her Wellingtons and he took off his hiking boots. She hung up her red coat on a wooden peg, then turned to him for his leather jacket. He hung on to it and caught his breath, but she smiled and said, "That's a very nice jacket. I suppose you ought to bring it into the kitchen, where it's dry."

"Thank you," he said.

"I could loan you a pair of trousers," she said, "and we could toss that pair in the wash."

Gregory peered down at his muddy legs. Helmut Lang did not engineer his trousers for fieldwork. They were ruined anyway, so whatever harsh treatment she might deal them couldn't make them worse.

"That would be wonderful," he said, "but do you have anything, well, long enough?"

She surveyed him with her hands on her hips.

"Well, you are awfully tall," she said, "but I think I can accommodate you."

"If it's no trouble," he said.

"No bother," she declared, padding off into the house in her stocking feet. She went up a narrow hall and started up a staircase, then leaned back over the banister and smiled.

"My name's Gillian, by the by."

"Gregory," he said. "Thank you so much for putting me up on such short notice."

She gave him a sweet smile and said, "Hang on a tick, Gregory," and stepped lightly up the stairs.

He waited in the inner doorway of the mudroom and peered into her kitchen. It was old, with bare pipes and a small gas cooker and an old tin hot-water tank over the sink, but it was clean and orderly, a bright floral cloth on the square table, the shelves lined with glass jars of homemade preserves. It was chilly, too, not that much warmer than outside. He heard her step on the staircase, and he turned back to the outside door, pretending to squint out into the yard.

"You might want to keep your sweater on," she said, handing him a pair of woolen trousers, much like the ones she was wearing. "I don't have central heat, I'm afraid, and it'll take me a while to get a fire going in the parlor."

"Thanks."

She marched up the hall again, and he watched her go, brisk and compact, her hair swinging against her shoulders, her bulky sweater and oversize trousers cinched way in by a leather belt at her waist. He changed into the wool trousers, which were a bit big around the waist, but more than long enough. He left his own trousers draped over a kitchen chair, carefully hanging his leather jacket over another chair away from the stove. Then he followed Gillian up the hall, stooping through the doorway and poking his head forward until he came into her parlor. His hostess knelt on a faded carpet in front of a small fireplace, packing coal into it with her bare hands. She glanced up at him in the doorway, then lit a twist of newspaper that stuck out of the little pyramid of coal.

"Pardon the clutter," she said. "I go a bit slack when I don't have a regular clientele."

"Oh, please," Gregory said, waving his hand. The parlor was small and, like the kitchen, not new, but comfortable. In the yellow light of a floor lamp were an old, rounded easy chair, the upholstery shiny in the seat, and a sofa with tea towels draped over the bald spots on its arms. Where a coffee table might have been was a low, black trunk, and the only sign of clutter was a dirty teacup in its saucer and some glossy magazines in a heap.

Gillian stood, holding her blackened palms away from herself. Gregory noticed that her hands were small, and the backs of them were rough and red from working outside.

"There," she said, blowing her bangs away from her eyes and glancing about the room. "That will warm up presently." She turned and looked up at him, lifting her eyebrows. "Make yourself at home. There're some magazines in here, and some books in the room across the hall."

"I'll be fine," Gregory said.

She cocked her head at him and smiled.

"Of course you will." Then, briskly again, "Now I don't have a separate dining room, I'm sorry to say, so you'll have to eat in the kitchen."

"That's fine."

"Good! I'll get to it then."

She edged past him into the hall, and Gregory spun and touched her lightly on the arm.

"Gillian, hey."

She gave a little start, her hands held closer to her in the narrow hall.

"I'm not interrupting your dinner, am I?"

"Of course not," she said, a little too heartily. "I'll eat with you, if you don't mind."

"That would be lovely," Gregory said. He smiled. "I lifted your goat, after all. We sort of know each other, now."

"Right," said Gillian, turning away. He thought she might be blushing, but he couldn't tell in the dingy light. "I'll get started," she said. "Don't mind me banging about."

Gregory stepped into the parlor and thrust his hands into the deep pockets of the wool trousers. He looked down at his legs; the trousers were large even on him, and he trod on the cuffs when he walked. He sat down and flipped through the magazines—*Radio Times*, a women's magazine, a two-year-old copy of *Country Life*—and when he began to feel the dry heat from the fireplace, he stood and shifted the coals around a bit with the poker. He glanced around the parlor and wondered if he could look at this dingy floral wallpaper for six months without going crazy, and he decided he'd rather live in a mud hut. From the kitchen he heard water running, pots being shifted about, a woman's voice reading the news on the radio. He stepped into the hall, but he could only see the end of the table and the door to the mudroom. Gillian had turned out to be a more pleasant informant than he'd given her credit for at first; at the very least he might be able to draw her out a bit and get a read on the situation in the village. He thought about joining her in the kitchen, under the pretext of listening to the radio, but he didn't want to push too hard just yet; he wanted to get her talking naturally, over dinner.

So instead he went into the room across the hall, where she'd said there were books. The door was ajar, and he stepped into darkness, stumbling across a slippery rug and along a bed until he found a lamp on a table. It was the guest room, apparently, for there were no personal touches, only a bed with a white metal bedstead, a little table, a chair, and a wardrobe. Just inside the door was a small handmade bookcase full of used paperbacks—romance novels, a couple of Penguins, some historical fiction, an old Bible. He picked up a water-stained old paperback—by Balzac, of all people—something he'd never heard of called *La Grande Bretèche*; its pages were swollen with damp, and he put it back again. On top of the bookcase, not surprisingly, were several neatly stacked issues of *Circular Studies*. Gregory turned off the light and took a couple of the magazines back into the parlor, settling into the sofa under the light of the floor lamp.

But the magazines did not prove to be as entertaining as he'd hoped: every article he started was a dull conflation of pseudoscientific jargon and utter credulousness, full of unconvincing prose about ionization levels and traces of gamma radiation. Only at the end of the most recent issue did he find something juicier, an article about the distress of the Earth Mother at humankind's failed stewardship of the planet, by a writer who called herself simply Grainne. She was listed as the director of something called the Institute for Druidic Studies in Milton Keynes, and her article was just goofy enough to hold Gregory's interest, until he was distracted finally by the smell of boiling potatoes and frying sausages. The radio had been switched off, he noticed, so he got up and padded into the kitchen, taking the magazine with him.

There were two places set on the floral tablecloth. Gillian stood at the cooker with the sleeves of her sweater pushed back, and she poked a fork at a pair of fat sausages sizzling in a skillet.

"Oh dear, you're not a vegan, are you?" she said. "I should have asked."

Gregory shook his head. "They smell wonderful. Mind if I come in?"

"Of course!" She smiled brightly. "It's almost ready. You can wash up at the sink, if you like."

The tap rattled and the water was numbingly cold, and Gregory caught Gillian glancing at the magazine he'd left on the table. She noticed him noticing her, and this time he was certain she was blushing.

"Are you . . . ?" he began, rubbing the feeling back into his hands with a thin towel. "Do you . . . ?" he began again, and he realized his hesitation gave away the question: Do you believe in that nonsense? Are you a kook?

"The circles?" Gillian said, giving the word a brisk, singsong lilt that tweaked his heart, momentarily reminding him of Fiona. She wrinkled her nose. "I was a bit mystified at first, I'll admit. But I only keep those around," she said, pointing behind her with her elbow, "for the clientele. Do you want your potatoes mashed?"

She set out two plates with sausages and potatoes and carrots, and after a moment's hesitation she sat at right angles to him, instead of across the table. They ate in silence for a moment, and Gregory discovered that he was really hungry. She watched him eat, her brow knitted.

"So how did you find the barrow?" she said.

He swallowed, and said, "Turned left at the crop circle, and there it was."

"I beg your pardon?" She peered at him, then realized he was making a joke and smiled to herself. "Oh."

"Sorry."

"That's quite all right. It's just that I'm alone a good deal of the time. I don't hear many jokes."

Gregory nearly said that he had a good one about a man jumping on a manhole cover, but instead he glanced at the magazine on the table and said, "The barrow was actually rather intriguing."

"Really? How so?"

"Well, I found a . . ." He caught himself, and she looked at him with her eyebrows politely raised, chewing demurely. "Well, let's just say I found out what people do up there at night."

"Really?"

"Teenagers with their hormones raging, no place to go . . ."

"Oh yes." She smiled down at her plate. "Of course. Silly me. You mean they're shagging up there."

"I beg your pardon?"

"*Shagging,*" she said again, giving the word extra emphasis. She looked away, wondering how to explain.

"Oh yes, *shagging!*" Gregory said, a little too loudly. "Shagging, that's just what I meant."

They both smiled, Gillian at her plate, Gregory at the magazine on the tablecloth.

"I'm sorry," he said. "I've embarrassed you."

She gave him a sharp look and said, "Oh, for pity's sake, I'm a farm wife. I've seen every sort of shagging there is."

"Really," Gregory said, seeing an opportunity to change the subject. "Was that your husband on the tractor?"

Gillian caught her breath, her utensils poised over her plate.

"On the tractor?"

"The fellow I let through the gate. Just before I helped you with the goat."

She prodded at her last bit of sausage.

"Well, no, actually," she said.

"Ah," said Gregory, as it dawned on him uncomfortably that his pleasant dinner with the pretty farm wife might be interrupted at any moment by the return home of one of the loud, grubby men on the trailer. Curly Hair, say, the Stanley Kowalski of Wiltshire, who'd stand bare-chested at the kitchen sink and soap his armpits.

"That's Bill on the tractor," Gillian said. "He lives up the road. I live here, but he owns the land. Farm *widow*, I suppose I should have said. Technically."

"I'm so sorry." Thank God, Gregory thought. "It's none of my business."

"It's all right. My husband was taken from me three years ago."

"I'm very sorry. So he . . ."

"Was taken from me." She contemplated the piece of sausage pinned between her knife and fork. "I'm alone now. I've quite gotten used to it."

They continued in silence for a moment, both of them nearly finished eating. It came to Gregory that he was probably wearing a dead man's trousers, and he pushed the thought away. Gillian laid down her knife and fork and patted her lips with her napkin.

"You see," she said, "after he was taken, I sold the land, except for the bit around the house itself. And while I was deciding what to do, the circle business started up, and before I knew it, I had all sorts of people knocking at my door every day, asking if they could set up a tent in my garden, or whatever." She looked at Gregory as if wondering if he'd understand. "You'll think me very mercenary, but I realized I could make a tidy living right here, doing this." She spread her hands to include him, and he raised his eyebrows.

"Bed and breakfast," she added.

"Ah yes," Gregory said.

"It was jolly profitable for a while, too," she went on. "More often than not, I had to turn people away. Until the BBC proved it was all a hoax."

"The two yobbos from Swindon," Gregory said, enjoying the sound of the word.

"The very same." She lowered her chin and smiled at him, enjoying herself now. "Then, of course, business rather dropped off.

People stopped coming. Except for the real loonies, of course, and they don't want a nice bed-and-breakfast, they just strip off their clothes and sleep right in the field."

Gregory smiled, and Gillian stood and took her plate to the sink.

"The woman in the gift shop said the same thing," he said, lifting his own napkin to his lips. "About the business dropping off."

"Did she?" Gillian said absently, from the sink.

Gregory folded his hands and considered how to proceed. Gillian's back stiffened a little, as if she knew he was watching her. Since the BBC had indirectly spoiled her business, he didn't want to blurt right out that he was working on a series himself. She'd probably had more than one camera crew passing through during the circle frenzy, banging around her house with their metal cases, talking too loudly in her kitchen over breakfast, coming back drunk from the pub. Not only would she not be impressed, she might even be downright hostile, and he needed the place to stay tonight. And he had to be careful about telling her he was an anthropologist; either it would take all night to explain what he did, or she'd already have had it up to here with university types poking around the area.

"Did it ever occur to anyone in the village," Gregory went on, "to salt the mine?" He mustered his pixie smile, hoping she'd turn around. "Drum up a little business."

Gillian turned and looked at him.

"Why not," Gregory said deliberately, "sneak out at night and make a few crop circles yourselves? Bring the tourists back."

Gillian looked startled and then started to laugh. It was a charming laugh, Gregory thought, low and musical. Gregory leaned back in his chair, and Gillian went on laughing in little gusts, hugging herself and pressing her hand to her chest, bursting out again every time the laughter faded.

"Come on," Gregory scolded her playfully, "don't tell me you haven't thought of it."

Gillian shrugged, her shoulders still shaking, her face turning red. She pressed her hand to her mouth and glanced at him, and Gregory smiled; it was the first time he'd gotten a genuine response out of her.

"Well," she said breathlessly. "Are you finished? Shall we have some tea in the parlor?"

In the dry heat of the coal fire she seemed to withdraw again, setting the tray with the tea things on the black trunk, then tucking her legs under her in the easy chair and letting him pour, as if he were waiting on her. She closed her hands around the cup he offered and sat back in her chair. There was a long silence during which they both simply sipped their tea; Gregory was tempted to say something, but decided to endure the awkwardness in order to provoke her to fill the silence, an old teaching trick. When she did speak, at last, it was a polite question: where did he come from in the States? After he'd told her, she smiled and retreated again into the contemplation of her cup. A moment later, she asked him what he did, and seemed marginally more interested when he told her he was a professor.

"A professor of what?" she said, watching him over her cup.

"Anthropology, actually," he said.

"Really?"

"It's an interesting coincidence, in fact," he said, deciding that this might be his only chance to draw her out. "Just about a year ago, I organized a conference at my university, about the death of Captain Cook."

He paused to gauge her reaction; her eyes had begun to glaze over as he spoke, only to brighten a bit at the mention of Cook.

"The sea captain?" she said.

"That's right, the explorer." He paused. "You see, there's a theory that the Hawaiian Islanders killed him because his visit to their island coincided with a festival of theirs called the Makahiki."

"That's very interesting," said Gillian, stifling a yawn.

"The beginning of the Makahiki festival," Gregory went on, watching her, "is announced by the appearance on the horizon, just about this time of year, in fact, of the star cluster called the Pleiades." He paused for effect. "Also known as the Seven Sisters."

Gillian blinked at him.

"So I'm wondering if there's any sort of synchronicity between the Hawaiian festival and your Seven Sisters event here in Silbury."

He took a sip of tea then, watching her over his cup. Gillian sighed and looked away and acted as if she was thinking about it.

"Oh, I rather doubt it," she said after a moment, picking at a thread on the arm of the chair. "I don't think anyone here's ever been to Hawaii."

"Well, that's not what I meant," said Gregory, smiling. "I'm not saying there's a cause-and-effect connection, but rather a sort of metaphorical parallelism...." He paused; Gillian was looking restless. "Have you ever read *The Golden Bough?*"

"I don't think so," she said. "Is it any good?"

There was a bovine look to her eyes now, and Gregory realized that if there had been a clock in the room, she'd have been glancing at it. He didn't answer her question because it was clear she wasn't really interested in the answer. He decided to take a more direct approach.

"When I was in the pub this afternoon," he said, "I saw a display of photographs on the wall...."

"Oh that," she said, stiffening a bit in her chair. "That's a load of old nonsense."

"That's what the barman said."

"Did he?" She bristled a bit.

"Or words to that effect."

"Well, he's got a nerve." She gazed into her teacup. "He's lucky he's not posing for one of those photos."

Gregory peered at his hostess, but she wouldn't meet his eye. He decided to push a little harder, and risk everything.

"Is your husband in one of them?"

She looked up abruptly at him, wide-eyed.

"As, well, the guest of honor?" Gregory said gently, meaning was her husband one of the naked, painted men on the wall of the Seven Sisters.

To his dismay, Gillian's eyes filled with tears, and her pert mouth twisted with her struggle not to show any emotion. Gregory cursed silently. This meant he wasn't going to get anything more out of her.

"I'm so sorry." He put down his cup and slid to the end of the couch. He laid his hand on Gillian's wrist. "I didn't mean to . . ."

"It's the last photo there is of my David," she said, her voice trembling. "And it's on the wall of that bloody pub."

"I'm very sorry," Gregory said, squeezing her wrist. "I shouldn't have said anything. It's really none of my business."

"It's all right," she said, handing him her cup and knuckling away the tears. "It's not your fault."

He meant to protest that of course it was his fault, but she gently tugged her wrist away from his grasp and stood, yawning and stretching her arms.

"Yes, well, it's that time," she said. "You must be tired." She smiled weakly at him. "I'll show you to your room."

Gregory looked up at her with his mouth open. Without looking at his watch he knew it couldn't be any later than seven. But if he was going to be a fieldworker, he'd have to learn to go to sleep when the natives did. He stood and walked ahead of her out of the parlor, pausing at the door of the bedroom across the hall, to let her pass. She blinked at him.

"That's my bedroom," she said briskly. "You're upstairs."

Gregory opened his mouth, surprised at the thought of her sleeping in a bare room with no photographs or knickknacks in it, but she was already starting up the stairs, treading on her toes and swinging her hips.

"Um, Gillian." Gregory paused with his stocking foot on the first step.

She turned with her hand on the rail and looked down at him from the shadows. He could not see her eyes.

"I was hoping to use your phone before I turn in. I ought to call my landlady in Salisbury. She'll be wondering about me."

Gillian drew her breath in sharply.

"Well," she said, letting it out again, "I don't have a phone, I'm afraid."

"Ah."

"And even if I did, actually, I'd rather you didn't call." Gillian came partway down the stairs, bringing her face into the light. Her eyes were dry, with no trace of redness. "You see, I'm not licensed to do this, actually, and I could . . ."

"No problem." Gregory waved his hands. "No big deal."

"... the Inland Revenue, you see ..."

"Really, forget I asked."

Gillian nodded briskly—that's that, then—and started back up the stairs, Gregory following.

"I just didn't want her to worry," he said.

At the top of the stairs Gillian paused and turned just enough, her hair swinging, for him to see the curve of her cheek in the dark.

"You'll just have to charm her, won't you?" she said. "When you get back."

As he came up the stairs behind her she stepped away and opened a door into a shadowy room, saying "The loo" in a sepulchral voice and promising to put out a towel for him. Then she turned and squeezed past him and led him into a corner bedroom, where another bare, yellowish bulb revealed an old white metal bed with a large blue duvet across it, a wooden bedside table, and a chair under a window. The window was covered with a faded blue curtain.

"There's no heat, I'm afraid," she said, turning back the duvet, "but I can bring you another blanket."

Gregory stepped to the other side of the bed and fingered the duvet; below it were a couple of blankets already.

"I'll be fine," he said. "I like a cold room when I'm sleeping."

"All right then." Gillian nodded with her hands on her hips, and looked about the room with pursed lips.

"Gillian," he said gently, "I'm sorry about ..."

But she waved it away and came around the bed to the door, where she paused, turning back without quite looking at him.

"I hope you don't mind the quiet," she said. "It's very quiet here."

Gregory sat on the bed, and the springs whined under him. He gripped his knees.

"Quiet's just what I need," he said.

"Good night, then." She pulled the door shut, and Gregory heard the creak of her step moving along the hall, then down the stairs.

# eight

THE ROOM WAS VERY COLD, BUT BEFORE HE got into bed, Gregory put out the light and pulled the curtain aside and peered out the window into the dark. It was the sort of night a city dweller alternately longed for and feared. There were no lights, and for a while he couldn't see anything at all. Then, as his eyes adjusted, he saw that the clouds were beginning to break, ragged white wisps rushing past one of the darkest skies he had ever seen, full of vivid November stars. There was no moon. The dark mass of the downland above the house rose to a sharp silhouette against the stars, while below the house the road, still damp, actually gleamed a bit in the starlight. He could hear the wind rustling the dead leaves in the hedge below and whistling around the corner of the house. Although the window itself did not rattle, Gregory could feel the pressure of the wind against the pane.

He wondered what Gillian would say if he went back downstairs and announced that he was going down to the village to watch the Seven Sisters festivities, to have a look at the "darts competition" in the pub. She could hardly object; he was a paying customer, after all, not a schoolboy with a curfew. But he was more tired than he had thought, having walked longer and farther today than he was used to. His feet were sore, his knees and his calves ached, and the thought of lacing up his heavy boots again to go out into the windy night just made him sleepy. Unless Gillian had a flashlight—a torch—he could borrow, he'd have to walk down to the village and back in the dark. Flashlight or no flashlight, it would be cold and windy out, and he could easily get turned around in the rolling folds of earth between here and the village.

And anyway, he was already in the perfect position to witness the most interesting part of the ceremony, assuming he was right about when the annual photograph was taken. Peering out the window, he saw beyond the road the dark, blunted silhouette of Stukely Hill; no doubt it would be best, from an ethnographical point of view, to be present at the ceremony itself, but barring that, he had a sort of box seat for whatever the natives got up to on top of the hill, whether it was picture-taking or simply colorful traditional dances by starlight, clothed or unclothed.

He stepped out to use the toilet, the floorboards creaking loudly even though he trod carefully past the head of the stair; he could hear water running in the kitchen. Then he went back into the bedroom, quickly stripped down to his shorts, and sat on the edge of the bed. He had no idea when, or even if, anything was going to happen on the hill tonight, but he set the alarm on his watch anyway, for midnight, and placed the watch on the bedside table. Then, without pausing to brace himself, he plunged feet first into the bed. He gasped out loud at the shock; the sheets were so cold and so stiff that for a horrible instant he thought they were actually frozen. He curled up into a ball, uncomfortably awake, and pulled the blankets tight around him until it began to warm up under the covers. Then slowly he stretched himself out, reclaiming the bed inch by inch until he lay full length with his head pressed into the thick pillow and the duvet pulled up to his nose. His eyelids were heavy, and he felt every aching muscle in his legs from walking all day. He turned his head to look out the window, where he'd left the curtain open, and the sight of pale clouds racing through the warp of the windowpane chilled him even more than the icy sheets. His eyes drifted shut, and he shivered and went to sleep like a child in his little warm cocoon of bedclothes, thinking, I'm safe where I am.

And woke again, startled and dizzy, unsure for a panicky instant just where he was or how long he'd been asleep. Had the alarm on his watch gone off? Something gleamed in the window, and he turned and saw a pale light moving in the reflection. Gregory squeezed his eyes shut, afraid to look. It wasn't his watch that had startled him; it would still be beeping if it had. But just before he'd awoken, the bedroom door had opened and closed, he was sure of it, and now, with the covers pulled nearly over his head, he heard the faintest pad of a footstep. Something was in the room, and he summoned up the nerve to twist slowly around in bed and open his eyes. A dim, wavering light played on the walls and the duvet, and he peered over the edge of his covers to see a pale figure in white, with something dark about its shoulders, bearing a candle with a trembling flame. Gregory was unable to breathe. He clenched the duvet in his fists.

"Gregory?" said the figure gently, and he groaned aloud and released his hold on the covers.

"Oh my God, Gillian," he said, his voice trembling. "You scared me half to death."

"I'm sorry." She moved silently to the side of the bed, holding the candle at shoulder height, watching him with wide eyes that seemed to wax and wane in the wavering light. In the freezing room, she was barefoot and wore a thin white nightgown that fell to her ankles. Over the nightgown she wore his leather jacket, hanging open to reveal the rise and fall of her breasts. Gregory pushed himself up a bit in bed, but kept the covers pulled up to his collarbone.

"What are you doing?" he said.

"I thought you might want your jacket," Gillian said in a small voice, almost as if she were pleading with him.

Gregory gasped and blinked at her, and without taking her wide-eyed gaze off of him, she set the candle on the bedside table and slowly took off the jacket, the candlelight gleaming in its folds. Her shoulders and arms were bare without the jacket, the nightgown held up only by thin straps, and she held the jacket by the collar, folded it neatly back upon itself, and laid it gently across the end of Gregory's bed. She sat on the edge of the bed, leaning across Gregory like a mother, propped up on her arm, but with her eyes wide and pleading unlike a mother's, her skin pale as parchment.

"Are you warm enough?" she said.

Gregory opened his mouth but said nothing. His heart was pounding.

"I came to keep you warm," Gillian said, and she slid off the bed to her feet, then with one smooth motion lifted the nightgown off with both hands. Gregory gasped; he could not look away; he could feel himself hardening already. She held the nightgown up by the straps and folded it carefully, like his jacket, laying it with the jacket across the end of the bed. She was compact and rounded, with full white breasts and a round little belly and strong-looking thighs that met in a dark triangle. She looked at him gravely and pulled back the covers with one hand, tugging them out of his grip, and she crawled onto the bed and straddled him with the duvet draped around her hips like a bustle. The freezing air of the room flooded in and tightened the skin of Gregory's chest. She leaned forward, her breasts brushing his nipples. The weight of her against him was exquisite, and Gregory sighed in spite of himself. Still he kept his hands away from her, reaching back and grasping the bars of the bedstead behind him.

"Gillian," he said, swallowing. "Oh my God."

Gillian touched her lips, then touched his with the same finger. She lifted herself on her knees and whisked off his shorts, then reached down and put him inside her. Gregory closed his eyes and gasped.

"Gillian," he made himself say, afraid to look at her, "I don't think this is a good idea."

She laid her warm, roughened palm along the side of his face, and he opened his eyes to see her bending forward, her breasts swinging, her hair falling past her cheeks. She kissed him.

"Sh," she said into his ear, and began to move.

Gregory's heart was racing, and the tight warmth of her was wonderful, but the cold and his astonishment conspired to distract him and make him self-conscious. He closed his eyes and tried to think about what he should do, what he should say, but his mind held on to nothing, and opening his eyes to see her swaying up and down above him, her mouth working wordlessly and her wide, bright gaze fixed on his face, he was both thrilled and terrified. She finished before him, suddenly, with a piercing cry, and she rolled onto her back and rolled him on top of her, pulling the covers over them both, clamping him tight with her thighs. She kept him going in the humid dark under the blankets, not speaking, kneading his shoulders with her powerful hands, her hot breath rasping in his face, the bedsprings groaning. He could hardly see her under the blanket, and he drove ahead faster in a panic, chasing his own elusive pleasure. Then she cried out again and nearly squeezed the breath out of him with her thighs, and he sobbed as he came, shuddering and rattling the bedstead against the wall. Everything seemed to empty out of him—his fatigue, his fear, his rage at Fiona, his professional humiliation—and he collapsed on his back next to her, his heart hammering, his throat raw with the cold air. Gillian pushed herself up and straddled him again in the cold with her breasts rising and falling, sweat glistening in the candlelight. She closed her eyes and pushed back her hair with both hands, pressing her lips together and flaring her nostrils. It almost looked as if she were praying. Gregory gazed up at her in slack-jawed amazement, spent, breathing hard, his skin tightening in the cold. He lifted his hands to her thighs, her belly, her breasts. He was quite certain that he had never been so grateful in his life.

"Thank you," he said breathlessly.

She opened her eyes and ran her fingers up his arms, pressing his hands against her warm breasts.

"I want to tell you something," she said.

Gregory lifted his gaze to her face. Her eyes were shining in the candlelight.

"I love you," she said.

Gregory stared up at Gillian. He opened his mouth to speak and closed it again. He blinked at her. He wanted to say something to her, but his mind was completely blank, every convolution in his brain smoothed out by the massive release of pleasure. At last he started to laugh, and he pulled a hand free from her breast to press it against his mouth.

"I'm sorry," he mumbled, squeezing his mouth, but he couldn't stop. The laughter poured out of him endlessly, the way his troubles had just a moment before. He laughed so hard the bed shook under him.

Gillian lifted the corner of her lips and reached down to pull his hand away from his mouth. Gregory bit his lip to try to make himself stop, but he was still inside her and the laughter was making him hard again.

She leaned forward, squeezing him deliciously and making him groan, and she pressed her cheek against his, her hair falling over his eyes.

"It's all right, my darling," she whispered. "It's good to laugh. It *is* funny."

She squeezed him again, and Gregory laughed all the way up from his gut, deep, wrenching laughter that rocked the bed and drove him deeper into her. She rode him, propped up on her arms, looking down at him wide-eyed.

"I love you," she cried. "It's *true.*"

"I know," Gregory said, weeping with laughter.

He came again and cried out, and she stopped and lay down across him. He could feel her heart beating, her breath pounding in his ear. Her sweat was chilling his skin, and he tried to reach past her for the covers.

"Gillian," he said.

"Mmpf," she said, her face pressed into his neck.

"Gillian," he said again, giggling. "Could we pull up the covers? I'm freezing."

She pushed herself up and looked at him seriously.

"Roll over," she said.

"Could we pull the covers up, Gillian? It's freezing in here."

She smiled at him, playful and girlish all of a sudden.

"Roll over first." She tugged at him.

Gregory started to laugh again.

"I want to do something nice for you," she said.

"Something *more?*" Gregory felt loose, he didn't want to move. "You do anything nicer than this, Gillian, and you'll kill me."

"I know," Gillian said, laughing herself now. "Roll over."

She lifted herself over him and practically picked him up and turned him onto his belly. He clutched the pillow with both arms, his cheek pressed deep into it, and with one eye he could see the window. The clouds were gone, leaving nothing but stars and the bright, trembling reflection of the candle. He hadn't known it until just now, but this was what he needed more than anything else, this was the uncomplicated pleasure he had told Martin he was after the day he arrived. And where was the harm in it? He'd brought a little joy to the life of a lonely farm widow, and God knew he'd gotten what he needed. The village's silly, anachronistic little "festival" seemed remote and useless to him now. Screw fieldwork. They could play darts until hell froze over, they could dance all night on the freezing hilltop, they could ring the standing stones with conga lines of naked men, as long as he could spend a week or two in Gillian's arms, shagging himself into oblivion. Leaving her might turn out to be a bit awkward, under the circumstances, but then again it might play out with a sort of sweet *tristesse*, the anthropologist's version of *Madame Butterfly.* . . .

Gillian straddled the small of his back, clamping him tight. He felt her lean across the bed, heard the bedside table rattle behind him.

"Now what?" he mumbled into the pillow, smiling.

"You'll love this," she said. "It'll be wonderful."

"Mmm," Gregory murmured, squeezing the pillow and settling himself into the creaking mattress.

"Hold still," Gillian said, pressing him firmly with her palm between his shoulder blades, and Gregory felt a sharp prick in the back of his neck. A blinding pain entered his spine, and he jolted from head to toe as if by electric shock and sucked his breath in. It was the worst thing he'd ever felt in his life, and he howled. He tried to rear up, but she held him down between her thighs, her hand pinning him between the shoulders. The pain drove deeper, accompanied by a blinding light, and then, unexpectedly, it stopped, replaced by a spreading bliss and a slow darkness. He couldn't speak. He tried to swing his arm at her, but he couldn't do more than raise his elbow off the mattress and let it fall. Gillian turned him onto his back. He knew he was being moved, because he felt his center of gravity turning, but he could no longer feel her hands. As he was turned he glimpsed an old-fashioned syringe with curving brass finger grips on the bedside table in the warm light of the candle.

Gillian leaned over him, her eyes brimming with tears. They were falling against his face and he couldn't feel them. He could scarcely see her now.

"Dear, dear Gregory," she was saying as she faded from sight. "My dearest, dearest love."

# nine

REGORY AWOKE AGAIN TO STARLIGHT, OPEN-
ing his eyes to a vivid sky full of stars. He had never seen stars like
this, so bright and so hard. The light seemed to penetrate him, the
stars like brilliant, diamantine spearpoints, pointed directly into his
eyes. He wondered if he was dead and this was some sort of passage, but the stars didn't seem to be moving. And at any rate, he
didn't believe in an afterlife. If he was seeing stars, then he was still
alive.

Then he began to hear the wind, as if someone were turning up
the volume slowly, and then the murmur of voices, somewhere out
of sight. He wanted to look toward the voices, but he found he
couldn't turn his head. All he could do, in fact, was blink, and when
he closed his eyes the sky appeared in negative, hard black points
in a vast sea of white. He opened them again.

His powers of concentration were returning, and he was able to
separate the voices he heard into two separate groups. One was
nearby, a pair of voices, male and female, engaged in some sort of
project, the woman commenting to the man, who replied in mono-
syllables. At first he couldn't make out exactly what they were saying; he could hear the words clearly enough, but he didn't know
what they meant. Then a shadow moved against the stars he saw
above him and stayed there, the outline of a head.

"Look here, Ross," said the woman's voice. "You've missed a
spot."

The outline of the head turned and another head joined it, blotting out more of the sky.

"Where?" said the man.

"Just there," said the woman, pointing.

The man grunted and stooped out of Gregory's sight, and he recognized the voices at last. It was the old colonial couple from the bus, Ross and Margaret.

"How's that, then?" he heard Ross say.

"Well, I don't know," said Margaret skeptically. Gregory could begin to make out her features in the starlight.

"Blast this wretched brush," Ross said. "I shall have to give Trevor a piece of my mind."

"It's a poor workman," said Margaret, "who blames his tools."

"Perhaps you'd care to take a hand, my dear," Ross said, with just a modicum of irritation in his voice. He moved into view, holding up something long and thin. A paintbrush.

"Oh Ross, really," said Margaret.

The sound of the other set of voices rose behind them, and Gregory shifted his attention there. An argument was going on among several people, out of his sight, some of their words carried away by the moaning wind. Everyone was talking at once, and then an angry male voice rose out of the racket, silencing everyone.

"Look," the man said firmly. "Is it the night of the Seven Sisters or is it not?"

"Yes it is, but . . ." said a woman, who might have been Gillian.

"And did he walk a right-hand circuit of the stones?" Gregory thought it might be the voice of the man on the riding mower, the one with the leather cap.

"Yes," said another woman firmly. "This afternoon." A pause. "Didn't he? Ted?"

"Oh, aye," said a voice, which Gregory recognized immediately as the man with the rake. "Right the way round, yes he did."

"And did he lift the goat?" said Leather Cap.

"Yes he did, but . . ." said the first woman's voice, rising into a sort of cry, the words themselves lost on the wind. A moment later Gregory heard Leather Cap declaiming loudly.

"Look, there's no bloody argument," he said. "It's him. He belongs to Her. Let's get on with it. It's bloody cold out here."

Gregory tried to sit up, but he couldn't do that either. In fact, apart from his eyelids, he couldn't move at all. It came to him then that he couldn't feel anything either; he could see and hear, evidently, but nothing else. It was the oddest sensation, not at all the cottony pressure of Novocain at the dentist, but simply no feeling at all. He knew he must be breathing, but he couldn't even feel the cool rush of air through his nostrils, he couldn't smell. He felt neither hot nor cold; it was as if he were just a pair of eyes and ears, immobile in a starry void.

A black shape loomed over him, blotting out the stars, and Gregory could just make out the face of Margaret.

"Ross?" she said. "Come look."

"What is it now?" Ross grumbled, out of sight.

"His eyes are open."

Gregory was aware of her peering closely at him, from only a foot or two away. Then she was moved to one side, and he made out the face of Ross, the old district officer, blinking down at him, his bronzed face unusually pale in the starlight.

"Oh bugger," Ross said. "He's awake."

That started a commotion that ended the distant argument, and Gregory was aware of shapes and faces moving all around him, towering over him against the stars.

"His eyes are open," said Ted, and then a painfully bright light shone directly into Gregory's eyes. Gregory closed his eyes against the light, as several voices, male and female, called out at once.

"Bloody hell!"

"Turn it off, you idiot!"

The pressure of the light on his eyelids vanished, and Gregory blinked up again. A bright blob of afterimage floated against the blackness, but he could make out the shapes of several people standing over him now.

"How much did you give him?" asked the second woman from the argument, briskly. It sounded like the woman from the gift shop.

"The whole syringe?" Gillian's voice sounded small and querulous out here in the wind.

"Maybe we should give him another," said Leather Cap.

"I could give him a clout," said Ted. "With the torch, like."

"No!" cried Gillian, suddenly fierce. One of the figures standing over him moved vehemently. "What a wicked thing to say!"

There were murmurs and movement, and the brisk voice of the gift-shop woman silenced them, nasal and authoritative.

"Gillian's right," she said. "We can't risk killing him. She wouldn't like that."

There were more murmurs, and as the afterimage of the flashlight faded, Gregory could begin to make out faces. One of the men standing over him wore a dark beard; indeed, from this angle, it nearly obscured his face. Gregory wondered if he was the man on the tractor, and from below he watched the beard point in one direction and then the other as the man followed the debate. At last the gift-shop woman cut it off again.

"Let's not argue," she said firmly. "Captain Orr, are you finished with the decoration?"

The old gentleman hemmed and hawed, and at last his wife spoke up.

"He's finished," said Margaret.

"Right," said the gift-shop woman. "It's time to move on to the barrow, then."

In the starlight Gregory could see the sharp angle of her cheekbone, her hair blown back from her tight forehead.

"Bill," she said, turning to the bearded man, "bring the tractor round." She turned and spoke to people Gregory couldn't see. "The rest of you, lift him carefully and bring him down the hill."

The figures looming over Gregory all moved away, revealing the stars, leaving only the gift-shop woman. She knelt down next to Gregory, her sharp, pale face hanging close to his, peering into his eyes as if looking for something there.

"This is a very great honor for you," the gift-shop woman said, as if speaking to herself. "I hope you're up to it."

Several figures loomed in, and Gregory was lifted. Again, it was an odd sensation, because he couldn't feel the hands on him, could not even feel his center of gravity shifting. As he rose, his head lolled back and he saw the world upside down, the dark mass of the horizon above, the glittering sky below. The inverted horizon tilted from side to side as his head wobbled, and he heard a choking sound. The sky began to darken, the stars to fade, and Gregory realized that he was passing out, that the choking sound was coming from him, as his windpipe was pinched off.

"Be careful!" someone cried. "He can't breathe!"

His head was lifted and the choking stopped, and Gregory saw Gillian clearly for the first time since he'd woken, her round face looming over him upside down, her hair whipping in the wind past her eyes and mouth. It was hard to read her expression, but her eyes were wide and glistened with tears. She sniffed and moved a hand near his face, and Gregory wondered if she was caressing him.

"It won't be long now, my darling," she said, in a tight voice. "You'll be with Her soon."

She lifted his head higher and Gregory could see himself from the chest down. He was naked, his arms crossed at his waist and tied at the wrists, and his pale skin was marked all over with dark stripes and circles and slashes, a sort of complicated hieroglyphic.

I'm the text, he thought, then, No, that's not right, I'm only the ground. The text is inscribed *on* me.

Between the dark figures of the people carrying him he caught glimpses of the starlit landscape all around, and realized that he was being carried feet first down the spiral track that ran around the artificial hill. The people carrying him held him lightly, jerking him this way and that, watching where they were going and not him. They bit their lips, their hair tugged at by the wind.

"Very nice job on the hilltop this year, Mick," said Ted, a bit breathlessly, from his position at Gregory's ankle.

"Thanks," grunted Leather Cap, from Gregory's thigh.

"I appreciate a well-tended lawn," said Ted.

Someone stumbled, and Gregory's head flipped back, showing him the track behind him, upside down.

"Please slow down!" cried Gillian, nearly in tears. Gregory's head was pushed up again.

Gregory, in his deadened state, was beginning to feel alarm for the first time. It's me, he thought. I'll be the one in this year's photograph. I'll be on the wall of the pub.

A couple of sharp reports like gunfire cut through the sound of the wind and the shuffle of his escort's feet, and then Gregory heard the steady, violent chugging of the tractor. He caught a glimpse of it, squatting on the road with its lights out and the flatbed trailer hooked up behind, then he was turned around and handed up to another group of people on the trailer. Here he was propped up in a sitting position, between the gift-shop woman and the barman, and he watched as Gillian started up onto the trailer, only to be held back by several people.

"Now, now, dear," said Margaret, catching her firmly but gently around the shoulders.

"No!" she cried, struggling. "I have to ride with him!"

Margaret looked up onto the trailer.

"Why shouldn't she walk with the rest of us?" she said, a bit petulantly.

"Let her come," said the gift-shop woman. "It's her right."

Gillian shook off Margaret's grasp, rather haughtily, and pulled herself up onto the trailer with her chin lifted. She waited until the barman gave up his position, then knelt down next to Gregory, out of his sight. The trailer lurched forward, and Gregory watched the little knot of people, fifteen or twenty of them, fall away very slowly behind, following on foot, the road glittering ever so faintly beneath their feet in the starlight.

Gregory's view of this tilted from side to side, and he realized that Gillian was rocking him; he could hear her sobbing and murmuring wordlessly in his ear. He tried to make himself think, tried to remember what he could from the wall of photographs in the pub. Apart from simply not being able to move, Gregory felt a good deal of frustration in not being able to talk. If he could, he might have explained to them his deep fascination, even his profound sympathy, with what they were doing. If they'd asked him, he might even have agreed to participate willingly, out of a sense of play, or at least out of a willingness to transgress his own hegemonic status as an academic observer of local folkways. There was no need to drug him and truss him up like a pig—unless, of course, that was a necessary part of the construction of the ritual, in which case he might still have agreed to participate, out of his respect for the fundamental moral authority of indigenous peoples, and he supposed that these villagers were indigenous peoples of a sort. . . .

Then Gregory thought, But that's crazy. He closed his eyes. The motion of the trailer and Gillian's rocking of his head were unsettling to him. He was all alone, floating in blackness, trying to find some shred of hope in this situation. But no one was expecting him: Martin had told him not to come back for a week, and Mrs. Speedwell, his landlady in Salisbury, would probably do nothing for a day or two. Of course, by then he might have recovered from whatever ordeal they were going to inflict on him, but as the tractor rumbled behind him and Gillian wetly murmured his name over and over in his ear, he was beginning to doubt it.

The wind grew louder, rising in pitch, thumping and whistling. When he opened his eyes again, he saw, beyond the end of the trailer, the view from the barrow: the villagers coming up the track in the dark, Gillian's darkened house at the bottom of the hill, the black ribbon of road, a handful of lights shining out of the darkness of the village within the embankment. Between the dark symbols on his belly and legs, his skin was ghostly pale; he looked like a corpse. It occurred to him that he ought to panic, but then he realized that panic didn't seem to mean anything in this state, when he couldn't move or speak, when he couldn't even feel his heartbeat or his breath. He had an odd longing for his notebook, wishing he could write down this insight, that panic was largely a physiological thing. Then he heard the tires of the tractor and the trailer crunching over gravel, and the forecourt of the long barrow edged into his peripheral vision: the white gravel, the tall, gray sarsens at the entrance, the long, black bulk of the mound itself.

Oh no, Gregory thought. Oh no. Not that.

The tractor stopped, and the villagers collected in a semicircle behind the trailer. The gift-shop woman rose to her feet and stood looking down at them, her back to Gregory, her hair flying in the wind, her skirt pressed against her legs.

"We all know why we're here," she said, shouting into the wind. "Let's get on with it."

She stepped aside as a man climbed up onto the back of the trailer—Curly Hair from the trailer this afternoon, in fact, looking self-consciously solemn in a nice pair of slacks, a sweater, and a tie, a workingman in church. He was wearing his boots, though. As he approached, Gillian leaped up, and Gregory fell back; he heard the thunk of his head against the wooden floor of the trailer, but he felt nothing. All he could see was stars again.

"Wait!" Gillian cried.

If he swiveled his eyes down to the bottom of their sockets, Gregory could just make out the back of her head, and the face of the gift-shop woman.

"Why does She get them all?" Gillian declared, her voice trembling, near tears. "Why can't I have one? Why do I always have to lose them?"

She was met with a general groan, and a chorus of voices.

"Every bloody year . . ."

"Oh Christ, not *again*, Gillian . . ."

"Let's bury *her* next time."

"Silly bitch."

Everyone was silenced by the crack of a loud slap, and Gregory could see Gillian's head snapping away from a hard blow. The gift-shop woman lowered her hand and grabbed Gillian by the shoulders, rattling her.

"Silly woman," she said, acidly. "*Stupid* woman. This is the work of *centuries*, do you understand? Who are you to stand in its way? Hey? *Who . . . are . . . you?*"

Gillian looked at the woman, her shoulders trembling, then she buried her face in the gift-shop woman's shoulder, and the woman put her arms around Gillian, stroking her hair as she wept. Looking sharply over Gillian's head, the woman nodded, and Curly Hair loomed into Gregory's view, stooping and lifting Gregory up over his shoulder in a fireman's carry.

Then everything went black for Gregory. He could see nothing even with his eyes open, his face pressed up against the man's back. He heard the thump of boots on the wooden bed of the trailer, then the jolt of boots on the ground, and their steady crunch over the gravel. Then they stopped, and he heard other feet shuffling over the gravel, and the murmur of voices. There was even a little laughter, and suddenly he was able to see again, as he was propped upright and turned around, the world reeling past his eyes: the white gravel, the mound, the sky, then, at last, a wide view of the horizon from his usual eye level. He was aware that he was looking down the side of the hill across the downlands toward the crop circle he had seen that day; tonight it gleamed with frost in the starlight. Hanging in the sky above the crop circle, Gregory saw the Pleiades, the Seven Sisters, like a bright necklace carelessly laid against velvet.

Gregory was suspended between two men, one of whom apparently held his head up from behind. He could hear them breathing.

"Tell us the truth, Ted," whispered the one on his left. It was Curly Hair. "Did he really do the whole circuit this afternoon?"

No! Gregory cried silently. I only went part of the way around the stone circle!

"Well, it's like this, Jackie," said Ted, on Gregory's right, in a conspiratorial murmur. "It was near enough for government work."

The two men chuckled quietly and hiked Gregory up a little higher. About ten feet away the barman was lifting a camera to his eye with one hand, and gesturing this way and that with the other. Gregory could not turn his head, but just out of the corner of his eye he was aware of a line of people on either side of him. A few people trotted quickly in front, finding their places, and one of them, an elderly woman, paused to peer at him. It was Mrs. Speedwell, in fact, his hostess from Salisbury, and she looked him up and down very critically, as if he weren't quite measuring up. If he could, Gregory would have screamed. Then Mrs. Speedwell looked off to Gregory's right and said, "A very nice job this year, Captain Orr."

As she waddled off to find her place, there were murmurs of assent from the assembly:

"Yes indeed."

"Even better than last year."

"You're a real *artiste*, Captain Orr."

"Thank you very much indeed, Mrs. Speedwell," said the captain. His voice trembled with foolish pride.

"All right, everybody," called out the barman from behind his viewfinder.

The shuffling of feet and the crunching of gravel subsided to windy silence.

"Say cheese," said the barman, and there was a click and then nothing.

"Bugger," said the barman.

"What's happening?" said someone.

"Flash didn't go off," said Leather Cap, off to the left.

"It's a new camera," said the barman sheepishly, holding it away from him and peering at it in the starlight. There was a general letting out of breath and more restless shuffling. On either side of Gregory, Ted and Curly Hair let him sag a bit.

"Here," someone said, and a man trotted out from the line to join the barman. Gregory blinked; there was something familiar about the figure as he and the barman put their heads together.

"Did you put the battery in?" said Martin Close.

Gregory felt the closest thing to a physical sensation that he was capable of, something like nausea. It rose in him and he recognized it as rage. He willed himself to cry out, but of course, nothing happened.

"It's brand-new," protested the barman. "I had to drive all the way to bloody Swindon for it."

"Hm," said Martin, and he lifted the camera to his eye and clicked something.

"There," he said. "Try that."

The barman nodded, and Martin trotted back into line without a glance at Gregory.

"All right, we've got it sorted out," said the barman in a loud voice. "Sorry, everybody."

The shuffling stopped, breaths were drawn in, and Gregory was hiked up a few inches higher.

"Look this way, everyone," called the barman. "Smile."

A little red light blinked on the camera, and Gregory was blinded by a flash. Then everything was in motion again: people talking as if at a party, the crunch of gravel. Gregory himself was dragged between the two men into the barrow, his feet trailing in the sand. He heard other feet shuffling after them into the inner chamber. In the enclosed space, out of the wind, coughs and sniffles and whispers reverberated sibilantly in the dead air. Then he was lifted up, and in the stabbing glare of flashlights—torches, he thought desperately—he was folded into the fetal position and his knees lashed together. The room spun all around Gregory, but he was aware of being lifted and slid on his side into the stone niche he'd seen that afternoon. But he evidently wouldn't go in all the way, for they pulled him out and tried again, cursing and grunting under the weight of him. At last they set him down, curled up like an infant, on the sandy floor of the chamber, where in the shifting torchlight he saw several pairs of feet gathered in a quick conference: a pair of loafers, work boots, Martin's motorcycle boots.

"Did anybody think to measure him?" said Leather Cap. "He's too tall."

Somebody sighed, and Gregory recognized the sound of his producer trying to think his way out of an impossible situation.

"I suppose you think this is *my* fault," Martin said.

"Surely we could *make* him fit?" said Captain Orr, taking the middle ground.

"Could we break his ankles?" said Curly Hair. "Is that allowed?"

"No," said the gift-shop woman definitively, from somewhere down the passage, her voice reverberating off the stone. "It is most certainly *not* allowed. He has to be undamaged. She won't take him otherwise."

There was more weary murmuring, like that of men stuck with the wrong part, and finally Gregory was lifted again, turned around, and slid into the niche a different way, his chin forced down nearly to his chest.

"That'll do," said the barman, blowing out a sigh, and then someone propped a flashlight inside the niche, illuminating the gritty stone surface before Gregory's face. Peering past his knees, Gregory saw people step up one at a time into the narrow opening, their starkly lit faces tilted at ninety degrees. Each of them laid some small object on the stone. Gregory could only wonder at the significance of each object, if it meant something to them all or was purely personal. Leather Cap left something folded in a piece of cloth, one woman left a cheese grater, and the barman left a ploughman's lunch—a cherry tomato, a small loaf of bread, a wedge of Stilton. One by one they all shuffled in and out of the glare, their steps reverberating, until Martin's face appeared in the slanting light. He placed a small plastic toy in the niche, a wind-up gorilla that did flips on its knuckles. It was blessedly unwound, though, and just sat there as Martin met Gregory's eyes.

"Accommodations all right, Gregory?" he said. "Everything to your satisfaction?"

"You mustn't address him so." The gift-shop woman spoke out of the dark behind him, scolding. "He is going to Her."

"I'm sorry," Martin said, dropping his eyes, genuinely contrite. "I beg Her forgiveness."

He stepped away, and the gift-shop woman appeared. Without really looking at Gregory she left a pair of crop circle earrings, and stepped back. For a moment Gregory saw nothing beyond the glare of the flashlight and the clutter of offerings, but he heard dragging footsteps in the sand, whispering, a sob. Then Gillian came forward, held upright by someone's arm around her shoulder. She was clutching to her breast Gregory's folded leather jacket, and she stood for what seemed like a very long time, sobbing, until the person holding her up gently tugged the jacket out of her grasp and helped Gillian place it inside the niche. Gregory caught a glimpse of the other person's face. It was Fiona. She wore a pale, demure headscarf tied under her sharp chin, her face gravely arranged into a look of self-conscious piety, like some fifties starlet in a biblical epic. Her arms loosely around Gillian's shoulders, she gazed on Gillian as if the farm widow were the Virgin Mary. Gregory felt a violent urge to burst out of the niche and grab her by the throat. It was an utterly useless feeling in his state of paralysis, though, and rather distant as well, as if somebody else had suggested it to him.

Meanwhile, Gillian's lips trembled and her eyes welled over, and

Fiona folded her arms about her, kissing her gently on the forehead.

"I know, darling, I know," she murmured, lifting her eyes to the ceiling. "Her love is terrible."

Gillian sobbed and stepped forward. Then she hesitated, looking back out of the glare, over her shoulder. In the shadows behind her the gift-shop woman nodded, and Gillian leaned in and kissed Gregory wetly on his forehead.

"Goodbye, my dearest," she whispered hoarsely. "I'll love you forever."

She kissed him again, and clung to him until Fiona and the gift-shop woman pulled her away.

"I love him!" Gillian cried feebly, a restless, petulant child. "He's mine! I love him!"

Fiona stepped out of sight, her head bowed. The barman came out of the shadows and wrapped his arms around Gillian, and the gift-shop woman trapped her face between her hands.

"Which is why you have to give him up, dear," she said, gently but firmly. "Don't you see? It won't work otherwise."

Then the barman and the gift-shop woman escorted Gillian away, and Gregory heard her screaming all the way down the length of the chamber, "I'll love you forever, my darling! I'll love you forever!"

The screams stopped abruptly, and there was no sound at all for a few moments. Gregory heard footsteps in the sand, and a man's brawny arm reached in and snatched away the flashlight. Gregory saw black; he heard the ring of stone against stone, and heavy breathing, and men's voices, cursing.

"Christ, it gets heavier every year, dunnit."

"Fuck."

"Move your foot, will you?"

Then a final scrape, and a definitive thump. Gregory heard men's voices, dimly.

"Seal it proper, Mick," someone said. "We don't want a repeat of last year."

"Phew," said someone else, and something scraped for a few moments at the outside of the stone—a trowel, perhaps—and then there was nothing.

Gregory was aware of the rhythmic hiss of his own breathing. Otherwise it was perfectly dark and perfectly silent. He felt a tingling along his limbs, and to his horror he realized that his sense of touch was coming back. Not now, Gregory thought, pleading to the God he no longer believed in, please, dear Lord, not now. What's the point? He could feel his tongue in his mouth now, and he tried to pray—The Lord is my shepherd, I shall not want—but it was a horrible sound, thick and guttural and spastic, and he stopped. Don't do that again, he told himself. It was only a matter of time before his air gave out and he lost consciousness, and he could only hope it would be soon. In the meantime his mind spun uselessly, a rat on a treadmill, a car grinding its tires in the mud, and part of him watched these efforts from a distance, as if they were the efforts of someone else. This can't be happening to me, he thought. I've got tenure.

He felt a final, useless flash of rage at all of them—Mrs. Speedwell, Martin, Fiona, even Catherine and Captain Cook—and before he could stop it, Martin's joke came to him one last time. His lips and tongue were looser now, and if he wanted to, he could almost have said it aloud: Ninety-nine, ninety-nine, ninety-nine. But Gregory felt a sound stirring in his gut, working its way up his throat, and this time he let it go. At last the joke made perfect sense to him, and Gregory Eyck began to laugh and laugh and laugh.

CASTING
the
RUNES

{with apologies to M. R. James}

"THIS. IS *RUBBISH,*" SAID VICTOR KARSWELL, enunciating clearly. For emphasis, he slapped the desktop with Virginia's paper, rolled tightly in his pale little fist. In spite of herself, Virginia Dunning flinched, and she couldn't help but notice the tremor of satisfaction that crossed Karswell's lips. Watching her, he grasped the paper between both hands and rolled it tighter, and he swatted the desk again, making the various gleaming implements upon it—his sleek fountain pen, his silvery letter opener, the sharp spike on which he impaled departmental memos and student papers—seem to tremble in fear of him, like animate kitchenware in a cartoon.

"Rubbish, rubbish, rubbish!" he cried, in his high, thin voice. He twisted the paper between his hands and turned slightly away from her in his silent, well-oiled office chair, as if he were speechless with disappointment, looking through the blinds into the angled Texas glare.

Virginia took this respite from his gaze to shift slightly on the little footstool. She was furious at him, furious at herself for letting him get to her, and furious that she had nowhere to put her anger just now. At the moment, in fact, it was difficult enough just figuring out what to do with her knees. There were only two places to sit in Karswell's office. One was the massive, padded, custom-made oaken chair behind his desk, modeled after the chairs in the *old* British Library and not, God forbid, after the chairs in the new one, a postmodern monstrosity. The other was a low footstool on the other side of Karswell's desk, where his visitors were invited to sit. Usually, when she knew she was going to see him, Virginia wore trousers or a skirt that fell to her ankles. But today she had worn a sundress that came to just above her knees, and Karswell had caught her in the history department office, checking her mailbox.

Now she sat a bare ten inches off the floor, forced into one of two possible postures on the stool, both of them offensively coy. She could sit with her knees pressed together in front of her and her hands linked around them, like a pinup girl circa 1943, in which case her skirt slid back into her lap. She decided on the second choice, sitting sidesaddle, as it were, twisting her knees together to one side with her spine erect and her hands folded at her hip, a Gal Friday pose, Virginia thought, from some thirties screwball comedy. (Take a letter, Miss Smith, barks Claude Rains, and Jean Arthur marches briskly into his paneled office, steno pad pressed to her pert bosom, pausing only to straighten her seams.) Either way, Virginia revealed rather more thigh to Professor Karswell than he had any right to see. She could stand, of course, but that would be interpreted as insolence, and Jean Arthur, after all, never lipped off to Claude Rains, at least not until the final reel. Note to myself, she thought: Never wear a short skirt on campus, under any circumstances.

"I had hoped," Karswell continued, his voice the very model of pained disappointment, "that of all my junior colleagues, you might have remained professionally chaste. Your dissertation, while deficient in certain crucial respects, was admirably reasonable for someone your age." He gazed sorrowfully through the blinds, tapping her rolled-up paper against his palm. His face was in shadow, but strips of light fell across his waistcoat and his bow tie.

"But I see that you are, or have become," he went on, "intellectually promiscuous, giving yourself wantonly, like the rest of your thrill-seeking generation, to the vulgar pleasures of postmodernism."

He turned silently in his chair to level his gaze at her like a bright light. By any reasonable measure, this was harassment. The fact that he never touched her, never touched anyone, by all accounts, shouldn't matter; at the moment he might as well have had his hand up her skirt. She unclasped her fingers and put her hands firmly on the edges of the footstool, as if to push herself up, to stand and march out of his office. But she didn't. It wasn't that no one would believe her—hundreds would; it was well known that Karswell liked to *watch*—but she had no way to prove it. It was his word against hers, and at the moment her professional future literally lay between the palms of his hands. Close your eyes, she told herself, and think of tenure.

"And what is the result of your promiscuity, my dear Virginia?"

Karswell seemed to be waiting for an answer, but she would deny him that at least. After an awful moment, he lifted her paper by a corner between his thumb and forefinger, letting it uncurl like a shriveled flower.

"The result," he said sharply, "is that you have become infected with the French disease."

He pursed his lips.

"If I were feeling more forbearing this morning," he said, dangling the pages of her paper between his fingers, "I might ask you what the Franciscan fathers had to do with 'constructing' women on Easter Island."

Everything, she thought, and it's Rapanui, jerk, not Easter Island. But don't even try to answer, she told herself, he doesn't want an answer.

"But the truth is," he went on, his lips twitching with amusement, a schoolyard bully who had just thought of something funny to say, "when I hear the phrase 'gender, race, and class,' I reach for my revolver."

He let the paper sag from his fingers and splay across his desk with a soft hiss. He's been saving that one up, she thought, he wants me to repeat it, to add to his legend. She puckered her lips to keep from saying anything, and thought, Count your blessings, it could have been worse. Karswell had been known to skewer the seminar papers of his graduate students, before their eyes, on the office spike he kept on his desk. Vic the Impaler, they called him, among other things.

"Of course, it goes without saying," Karswell said briskly, "that

I cannot allow this to appear in the festschrift volume." He pressed the tips of his fingers together and leaned back in his chair; how he managed it, she could not tell. Karswell was such a short little guy he must have been pushing with the very tips of his toes.

Virginia shifted on the footstool. She wanted to stand, she *ought* to stand, but she clutched the edges of the stool as if to keep herself from ricocheting off the ceiling. The moment had come for her to speak, and she had to judge her words carefully.

"The publications committee has already accepted it, Victor," she heard herself say. "You can't unilaterally refuse it."

"*Can't* I?" Karswell's eyes popped wide. "My dear, I *must*. I have no choice. Professor Blackwood is a very old man, with a weak heart. If he were to see this, this, this—" Karswell gestured at her paper in dishabille on his desktop, unable to bring himself to name it. "If he were to see *this* in his festschrift volume, the poor dear man's heart would seize up and kill him." Karswell smiled again, and she fought the urge to shudder. "Though perhaps that is your intent."

Professor Blackwood, she wanted to say, had slept through his retirement dinner, from the soup course through the testimonials. He probably hadn't read a book in his field straight through since 1975.

"Victor," she said, drawing a breath, licking her lips, "the volume is already at the press—"

"From where I may remove it, with a simple phone call." Karswell's fingertips sprang apart, and he let his small hand hover over the phone on his desk. Then he closed his hand into a fist with an almost audible snap, and said, "Which is the heart of my dilemma. You've left me with a terrible choice, professor, a *terrible* choice. Do I postpone the volume, at great expense to the press—and at great inconvenience to the other authors, I might add—or do I proceed with the volume as it is, knowing that there is this *rot*, this *corruption*, at the very heart of it?"

Virginia twisted on the stool. She planted her feet firmly on the floor, her knees together, the skirt be damned. She felt her face get hot.

"I'm not rewriting it, Victor," she said. "For one thing, there isn't time . . ." For another, she wanted to say, it's the best fucking paper in the book.

"I blame myself," said Karswell, cutting her off with a gesture. "In the press of my other responsibilities, I did not catch up with your paper in as timely a fashion as I ought. *Mea culpa*, my dear Virginia. And since," he continued, lifting his finger to forestall her further protest, "and since I freely acknowledge my own dereliction in this matter, I am prepared to propose a solution which will, I think, allow us to proceed on schedule, and preserve, or at the very least protect, the reputation of everyone involved."

Virginia closed her mouth and turned her knees to the side again, tugging down her skirt. She crossed her arms.

Karswell leaned silently forward in his chair and gathered up the sheets of her paper, shaking them between his hands against the desk until they were even. His eyes gleamed as though he had his hands around her throat. Virginia fought the urge to flee the room. Then Karswell reached into his vest pocket, and to her astonishment brought out his notorious pince-nez, delicately squeezing the little lenses onto the bridge of his nose.

"I am prepared," he said, peering at her through the pince-nez, "to shoulder my share of responsibility for this debacle by offering to list myself as the primary author of the paper."

For the first time in this encounter, Virginia was grateful that she wasn't standing. If she had been, she'd have passed out for sure, toppled over from the shock like a redwood. As it was, all the blood drained out of her face and her jaw went slack. Karswell said nothing, but simply blinked at her calmly from behind his round lenses, waiting for her to compose herself. She could not think for a moment, let alone speak, and the only thought that came to her was, *Of course, I should have seen this coming. This is what he wanted all along.*

"You have a long and productive career ahead of you, Professor Dunning," Karswell said finally, when she could not muster the words to reply, "and I trust you will be guided in this matter by my own long experience."

Virginia found herself rising to her feet, and at first she knew it only because Karswell lifted his face to follow her progress; it was as if she were being lifted by wires. All she could think of to say was clichés from some nighttime soap, herself as Amanda on *Melrose*, bristling with fury in a tight skirt, tossing back a wild mane of blond hair, and saying, Not until hell freezes over. I'll see you dead first, you little bastard. I'll get you if it's the last thing I do.

"I think that's a little . . . irregular, Victor," was what she did say, however. This was Victor Karswell, after all, not Courtney Thorne-Smith.

"I'm offering to protect you, my dear," Karswell said, attempting warmth and chilling Virginia to the bone. "I am offering, at no little risk to myself, to encompass you within the cloak of my reputation."

The image this conjured made it hard for Virginia to breathe. She plucked at her hands to keep them from shaking. I'm not your dear, she wanted to say. Call me that again and I'll have you up before the dean. Call me that again, you little eunuch, and I'll drive that spike through your heart. Then suddenly the anger was replaced by a strange light-headedness, and she wondered if this was what dying felt like: with a rising, rushing whoosh like the wind in the trees, her whole life rewound before her eyes, past the deceptions of lovers, the betrayals of friends, the lies of parents and teachers, until, the windy rush rising to an unbearable pitch, her little highlight reel came to rest in junior high, at that moment when book reports had been handed back by her English teacher, when Virginia had read every word of *Moby-Dick* and gotten a B+, and Jessica Lindenmeyer had read the Classics Comics version and gotten an A. The problem, then as now, was that Virginia's paper had been too good. With a windy crescendo like the last chord of *Sgt. Pepper*, she saw Mrs. Altenburg's precise handwriting across the page: "Virginia: Is this your own work?"

"Yes it is," she murmured, blinking in the gloom of Karswell's office.

"I beg your pardon," Karswell said, widening his eyes behind the pince-nez.

"No," she said more forcefully, straightening her shoulders. "It's my work, Victor. You may not put your name on it."

There was a long silence in which Virginia was half afraid that Karswell could hear her heart beating.

"Think about what you're saying, my dear," he said quietly, his eyes oddly dark behind the little lenses.

Her throat was nearly too dry to speak, but she swallowed and managed to say, "I know what I'm doing, Victor."

"I see," Karswell said.

Against the thin strips of glare between the blinds, his face was suddenly hard to make out; he was working his mouth somehow, and it looked to Virginia as though he was trying to keep from smiling. Then he set his face, and rapped the edge of her paper against the desk.

"Is that your final decision?" he said.

"Yes," Virginia said. "Yes, it is."

"Very well." He laid the paper on his desk, reached for his fountain pen, lifted a few pages, and wrote something quickly and definitively near the end of the manuscript. He blew on the ink, capped the pen and put it aside, and held Virginia's paper out at arm's length.

"Then may I give you this, professor," he said. "I believe it is yours."

Virginia, her heart pounding, stepped across the carpet.

"Yes," she said, "it certainly is."

As she took the manuscript, she felt a chill run up her arm and down her spine, as if the paper itself had just come out of a deep freeze. As soon as she had it, Karswell snapped his hand away. Virginia rolled it between her palms and rubbed it up and down, as if to warm the paper, and she turned on her heel and walked toward the door, her shoulders stiff, Karswell's gaze like a spear pointed at her back. As she turned to slip out the door, he was still watching her, his eyes dark behind his pince-nez.

"Goodbye, my dear," he said, and Virginia closed the door.

IRGINIA DUNNING WAS A TALL, PALE DAUGH-
ter of small-town Minnesota, and had lived the first twenty-eight
winters of her life under the protocols of the upper Midwest—
handknit sweaters and thermal underwear, long wool stockings
and boots with rubber soles like tractor treads, six-foot scarves
that came up over her nose, and wool hats that came down to her
eyebrows. The worst thing that could happen to you, said her
genes and her mother, was exposure, so you showed as little of
yourself as possible, layering your clothes and keeping your opin-
ions to yourself.

She had been a quiet, bookish girl in high school, proceeding
dutifully to academic stardom at a small liberal arts college in the
town where the flamboyant outlaw Cole Younger had been shot
to death by tight-lipped Minnesotans. From there she went straight
on to the prestigious University of the Midwest in Hamilton
Groves, where she had been an improbable star of the history department. As shy as she was gifted, Virginia scarcely said a word in
public for the first two years of graduate school. Even if she had,
she certainly did not intend to tell anyone at Midwestern that her
favorite book as a girl, and the seed of her interest in history, had
been *Hawaii* by James Michener, or that she'd devoted a good deal
of her early adolescence to imagining herself in the place of Julie
Andrews, who'd played a missionary's wife in the film version. Re-
garding herself in the mirror after yet another viewing of the video,

the young Virginia had even thought that she glimpsed a Juliesque paleness in her complexion, a similar astringent sharpness to her cheekbones. Hence, years later, her dissertation topic: a feminist history of Christian women missionaries in the Hawaiian Islands, modestly written but rigorous, and widely regarded as an important intervention in the study of the European encounter in the South Pacific.

But even as her confidence grew and she allowed herself to speak in the presence of her professors and the other graduate students, Virginia kept covered up. She wore her hair to her shoulders like a blond helmet, with bangs to her eyebrows and huge glasses like Gloria Steinem's, and she tiptoed through graduate school with a tall girl's stoop, hunching her shoulders and wringing her long-fingered hands. Even in the mild Minnesota summer, she wore a long-sleeved T-shirt, a skirt to her ankles, socks with her Birkenstocks, and a big hat to keep the pale Midwestern sun off her head.

Upon graduating, she received offers from several admirable institutions, including an Ivy, but she astonished everyone by accepting a tenure-track position at Longhorn State University in Lamar, Texas. From the cocoon of their progressive, Yankee rectitude, Texas seemed like a foreign country to her friends in Hamilton Groves, a semi-imaginary land made up in equal measure of old John Wayne movies, episodes of *Dallas*, and the last scene of *Easy Rider.* What about the heat? they all cried, recoiling from the thought of cool, pale Virginia shriveling up like a pepper under the wide Texas sky, as if she were some rancher's mail-order Norwegian bride. What about the scorpion in your shoe in the morning? The fire ants in the kitchen, the snake in the brushpile, the black widow in the grass? What about the tight-jeaned, potbellied bubbas in their pickups, shotguns in the rack behind the seat, cruising the backroads, flattening armadillos, flinging beer cans out the window, and looking for hippies to kill? What about the big-haired women with gaudy, expensive designer suits and matching nails and lipstick, who cruised the eight-lane freeways in pink Cadillac convertibles with a pair of longhorns for a hood ornament, on their way to spend Daddy's oil money on black sable at Neiman-Marcus? And what about the heat?

Virginia went anyway. Her graduate department at Midwestern had been a vipers' nest of big egos, empire builders, and campus politicians, a neo-Jacobean play in which the only thing that didn't run down the halls was actual human blood. Longhorn State was a step or two down the academic food chain from Midwestern, better known for its powerhouse football team than for its scholarship, but the history department was a young one, a lot of ambitious assistant professors with reputations to make. Maybe it wasn't the pinnacle of her profession at the moment, but given half a chance she could help put it on the map. And contrary to her friends' expectations, Lamar itself was one of the grooviest addresses in the nation these days, a slacker theme park staffed by long-haired singer-songwriters, buzz-cut cowboy novelists, video clerks turned indie filmmakers, skinhead neopunks, and the latest twenty-five-year-old billionaire software designer.

Indeed, the moment she arrived in Lamar, stepping out of the air-conditioned cab of her little yellow rental truck into the basting heat and whitish glare of a July afternoon in central Texas, she knew she'd made the right choice. In a matter of seconds the heat soaked through to her bones and melted twenty-eight years of ice, and almost overnight she blossomed like a Texas bluebonnet. Lamar was a great place to be young, and Virginia wasn't even thirty yet. She straightened up and threw her shoulders back, she discovered sandals and tank tops and miniskirts, she learned to walk in long strides like a rancher. She gave away her assorted records by lugubrious Canadian folksingers and bought the Butthole Surfers and Bob Wills and the Texas Playboys on compact disc. She ate brisket with her fingers, she bought a tortilla warmer, she made her own fajita marinade. With her first paycheck from the university, she traded in her rusty, salt-eaten Dodge Colt and put a down payment on a little cherry-red pickup—Japanese, but enough of a truck to warrant the coveted "Texas Truck" license plate. Pulling out of the dealer's lot, she set the radio to a Tejano station, bopping behind the wheel to accordion music all the way home.

Without a trace of regret she ended by phone her moribund long-distance relationship with her patronizing, alcoholic British boyfriend, and took a new lover, Chip, a tall, wry native Texan like the young Clint Eastwood who worked in a hip video store by night and wrote television pilots on spec by day. She cut her hair into a pageboy and slicked it down on a Texas Saturday night, when she wore a little red dress and cowboy boots and went clubhopping with Chip till dawn down on Sixth Street. She spent weekends in her pickup cruising the yellow grass and dusty green cedars of the Hill Country, opening the windows to the hot blast of air at seventy-five miles an hour as she dodged the armadillos in the road and drove with a cool, sweating, nonreturnable bottle of Shiner Bock between her legs. She wanted to stay at Longhorn State for the rest of her life; she wanted to grow old under the hot Texas sun; she wanted her skin to bronze and thicken and crease up like an old boot, so she could age into a tough ol' Texas gal like Molly Ivins or Ann Richards, and say what she wanted and do as she pleased, a lover of good times and a sworn enemy of bullshit.

She and Chip moved in together, sharing a little Texas bungalow on the side of a hill, with a fireplace they never used. Neither of them could have afforded it on their own, but it had a wonderful view of the campus and of Lamar's burgeoning skyline of bluntly angular pomo skyscrapers. She often came home in the afternoon to find him acting out scenes from his TV scripts, pointing a squirt gun in a two-handed grip at their dim-witted cat and shouting "Freeze! Police!" or performing aggressive CPR on a sofa cushion, saying "Breathe, dammit!" through gritted teeth. So far, his ideas for TV pilots—a vampire detective, a musical emergency room, a sitcom about four lovable kids and their foster father, a killer android from the future—had been a half-step behind the zeitgeist. But this summer, Chip had come up with a surefire script, an hour-long drama about a pair of married private investigators in L.A. He's T. K. Moore, a black ex-cop who served time for a crime he didn't commit! She's Verandah, a white supermodel with a degree in parapsychology! Together they live in L.A.'s hippest beachside community and investigate alien abductions while they look for the real killers of the ex-cop's ex-wife! Chip was pitching it as a cross between *MacMillan and Wife*, *The X-Files*, and *Baywatch*. He called it *The Moores of Venice*.

So at the moment Chip was making the rounds in L.A., renting a room from his friend Mel in Las Feliz, and, over the phone, acting awfully vague about when or even if he would return to Texas. Meanwhile, Virginia was barely meeting the rent on her own, gazing every night at the neon angles of Lamar's skyline and wondering if she had a boyfriend or not. Worse still, she was approaching her third-year tenure review, and not long after Chip had left, the department chair, Professor LeFanu, took her for margaritas at a tamale house down by the river and gave her an avuncular talking-to, after his fashion. LeFanu was a courtly Southerner in his late middle age, a poor woman's Shelby Foote, gentlemanly to the point of cowardice. Every time he spoke, Virginia thought she heard mournful fiddle music. His only concession to the Texas heat was to go without a tie, and sitting at a rough trestle table overlooking the river, he was careful not to rest the arms of his linen jacket in the sticky beer rings on the tabletop. Virginia knew why she was there; she picked at the crust of salt around the rim of her glass. For the longest time they chatted lightly about nothing, for all the world like a visiting uncle and his favorite niece, but at last the chairman drew himself up, looked out across the river, and put his hands on the tabletop as if he were about to get up and leave.

"Everybody likes you, Ginny," Professor LeFanu said in a soft Tennessee drawl, squinting into the glare off the water, "don't get me wrong. But your publication record is weak. I'll admit your book was treated a little unfairly, but it didn't do well, and there it is. Your recent work is solid, but the other junior faculty have all had two or three articles published by now. Richard even has another book coming out. Lamar's a great place to live, Ginny, it's why I've stayed on here for twenty-five years, but maybe, just maybe, you've been having a little bit too much fun."

With this, he had swung his sad, dignified, disappointed gaze off the river and brought it to bear on her. She said nothing. There was nothing to say. He was right. The published version of her dissertation had not lived up to its early reception; the old-school scholars who wrote for the journals, and who were congenitally skeptical of the young and the testosterone-deficient, gave the book tepid reviews. Virginia's career hadn't entirely recovered from this setback, and despite the freer, hipper atmosphere at Longhorn

State, where she was emboldened to do tougher work with more of a theoretical edge to it, she hadn't, as LeFanu noted, put her nose to the grindstone. She ran the risk of being the academic equivalent of a one-hit wonder, doomed to playing oldies at community colleges for the rest of her life.

"You need at least one paper in print by the end of the school year," LeFanu had said at the tamale house, "or you're not going to pass your review."

That very evening she called up on the screen of her laptop a chapter from her new book on the Franciscan mission to Rapanui, aka Easter Island. In spite of the reception of her first book, Virginia was trying to be bolder with the second, subverting the dominant discourse on the European encounter in the Pacific, attacking the old myths that Polynesian women were easy, that they worshiped white men as gods, and that the Rapanui ended up eating each other. She stayed up nearly till dawn, trimming and focusing the chapter and making it reasonably self-contained. Then, as the skyline neon flickered out and the sun began to slant through her living-room window, she printed the paper out and put her head in her hands and wept, because her only chance of getting it published before the chairman's deadline was Victor Karswell.

In a department divided roughly between comfortably settled, professionally melancholy middle-aged white men and a much more diverse, energetic, and ambitious cadre of junior faculty, Karswell was *sui generis*. He was simultaneously the biggest name in the department and the one whose star had fallen the farthest. For twenty years he had been an Ivy League professor, a leading member of Providence University's history department, the name to reckon with in the history of European exploration in the Pacific, the new Beaglehole. He was also ferociously ambitious, having very nearly ascended to the chairmanship of his former department. Somehow, in the rarefied and cutthroat environment of the Ivy League, rivals who were every bit as driven and ruthless as Karswell had a strange way of backing down or falling by the wayside, allowing Karswell a steady ascent to the top.

But then there had been a scandal. Providence had hushed it up, but even so there were rumors of a troubled manuscript, plagiarism, and the suicide of one of Karswell's graduate students. Karswell was suddenly on the market, within the reach of schools which otherwise would never have had a chance at a scholar of his stature. Longhorn State was thrilled to get him, but the feeling was not mutual. While most of his colleagues in Texas were resigned to a comfortable exile in a semiprovincial setting, Karswell was bitterly aware that he had washed up at a second-rate school. He did not participate at all in the life of the department, making it clear that the chairmanship was not worth his time. He attracted few graduate students, and kept none. Even his Anglophilia made no concession to the Texas climate: in the summer heat, when it was ninety degrees before ten in the morning, he could be seen every day mincing across the plaza in a tweed suit complete with waistcoat and bow tie and little cloth cap. His clothing ought to have been drenched with perspiration, and he at least should have arrived at his office red-faced and sweating, but he walked up the hall every morning as cool and pale and dapper as if he'd just had a brisk walk around the water meadows at Oxford.

To someone outside of the academy—to Virginia's mother, for instance—Karswell might have seemed to be the perfect mentor for Virginia. But even before he left Providence, Karswell, perhaps feeling the hot, theoretical breath of the younger generation on the back of his neck, had largely abandoned the study of the European encounter and had taken up a more obscure topic, the study of the occult in early modern Europe. His generous deal at Longhorn State, where they were using oil money to buy Nobel Prize winners and other name-brand professors by the gross, allowed him to amass at the university's expense an extensive collection of antique books and rare manuscripts on magic, witchcraft, and alchemy by the likes of Bruno, Ficino, and John Dee. Tenured and endowed, he taught very little, and published nothing. He certainly did not mingle with the junior faculty. Making him even less appealing was the fact that, for all Virginia knew, he might very well have been one of the anonymous Old Guard reviewers who had yanked the rug out from under her first book. So far she had managed to avoid him.

Virginia's initial interview with Karswell had been nearly as creepy as her last turned out to be, though she had come prepared that first time. Having been warned by another woman professor, she had resurrected her graduate-school look and worn to Karswell's office a bulky sweater and an ankle-length skirt. Even so, he looked her up and down through his pince-nez and said, to her surprise, "I have had my eye on you for some time, my dear." Then, with a bone-chilling smile, he invited her to be seated. He watched, his lips twitching, as she cast about unsuccessfully for another chair. Then at last she saw the footstool and sank to it slowly, her heart sinking even lower.

"Now what can I do for you, professor?" he had said, and Virginia, pulling her skirt tight and clasping her hands over her knees, had thought, I'm going to regret this.

## three

NDEED, SHE HAD NO IDEA HOW MUCH. NOW SHE hurried down the pastel hall of the history department away from Karswell's office, her manuscript rolled tightly in her hand, and she nearly ran down the echoing stairwell, her shoulders hunched against the uncanny feeling that she was being followed. Outside, she hurried beneath the gaze of the statues of Texas heroes that stood at regular intervals around the sunny plaza at the center of campus, everyone from Colonel Travis to Lyndon Johnson. She had developed a bemused affection for these eight Dead White Men, cast in bronze in various ridiculous poses, but today each one seemed to be giving her the same predatory look as Karswell. The sun beat down on her arms, and she ought to have felt the skin-loosening embrace of the heat, but somehow the dank, Forever England chill of Karswell's office had followed her out of the building; it was as if something ill defined and impalpable had stepped between her and the sun. She hugged her elbows and shivered. For the first time since she'd come to Texas, she wished she'd worn a sweater. Her sunglasses and the mail she'd come to pick up were still on the desk in her office, but she could not face going back to fetch them. What if she ran into Karswell again in the bluish fluorescent glow, gliding up the hall six inches off the floor like the Prince of the Undead? Her rolled-up manuscript seemed to twist in her grip as if with a will of its own, and she clutched it tightly with both hands as she passed beneath the statue of Jim Bowie at the corner of the plaza. Usually he was silliest of the lot in his buckskin suit, with one hand cocked on his hip and the other holding his famous knife, erect and unsheathed. The age-old undergraduate legend had it that if a virgin was kissed under Bowie's statue, he'd drop the knife. But Virginia did not feel virginal today, and Bowie seemed to brandish the blade at her as she passed.

The heat began to warm her only when she left the campus and crossed Tejas Avenue. She walked through the whitish glare along the Strip, among undergraduates in shorts and T-shirts passing in and out of the Book Exchange, and past the slackers in torn jeans and filthy dreadlocks who sprawled along the baking wall of Charing Cross Records. One of the latter, older than the rest, with bleached, matted shoulder-length hair and a face as darkened and weathered as an old saddle, looked her up and down as she approached.

"It's my last day on the job, ma'am," he said. "Care to contribute to my retirement?"

"Fuck off," she said, marching past him toward her bus stop, and a chorus of "Whoa!" rose from the burnouts along the wall behind her.

Luckily, her bus arrived just then, and Virginia stepped up and showed her pass to the driver. He scarcely looked at it, slumped heavily over the wheel with his shirt open three buttons down his chest. The bus's air-conditioning was arctic, and Virginia sat next to the door, where at least she'd get a gust of warm air from time to time. Except for the driver and Virginia, the bus was empty, which struck Virginia as odd even for the middle of an August afternoon. The driver blew out a sigh and ground the gears, and the bus hissed and grumbled forward. He glanced at Virginia in the parabolic mirror over his seat.

"Sorry about the heat, darlin'," he drawled.

Virginia smiled back but said nothing. What was he talking about? The bus felt like a rolling meat locker. She leaned her temple against the window and watched the Strip slide by beyond the tinted glass, hugging herself against the chill and crushing her paper under her arm.

My Texas idyll is over, she thought. It's already lasted longer than an idyll has a right to.

At a stoplight she heard the driver sigh, and she looked up to see him sweating profusely, a thin stream running out of his hair and along his thick rockabilly sideburn. He glanced at her in the mirror.

"Wish I could at least get a breeze goin' for you, ma'am," he drawled, lifting his voice, "but it's a climate-controlled environment."

"Excuse me?" Virginia said.

"That's the fancy way of sayin' we can't open the windows," said the driver. The light changed, and he put the bus in gear.

"Ain't my fault the AC don't work," he said.

Virginia blinked at the man in disbelief. The bus was so cold she was getting goose bumps. The rolled-up paper pinned under her arm seemed to sting her a little, as though a corner of a page were stuck in her flesh. She shifted it under her other arm, but it seemed to scratch her there as well. At last the bus neared her stop on Crockett Avenue, and Virginia pressed the buzzer. The driver slowed the bus to the curb, and Virginia hurried down the steps, grateful for the blast of heat as she stepped outside. Another woman edged past her to get on the bus, and as Virginia stepped onto the sidewalk, her eye was caught by a vivid billboard on the side of the bus, a vast yellow rectangle with some rather small letters in blue at the middle of it, about halfway back. It was so bright she wondered why she hadn't noticed it getting on the bus. The lettering was much too small for anyone to see from any distance. You'd have to be standing right next to it to read it, she thought, not the most effective advertising technique for the side of a bus. She glanced up to see the driver and the new rider going through some sort of complicated transaction involving a transfer, and she walked back along the bus to read the sign. In discreet, dark blue letters against the sea of vivid yellow, the sign read:

In memory of John Harrington, A.B.D.
Providence, Rhode Island
Died Sept. 18th, 1989.
Three months were allowed.

That's weird, Virginia thought.

The door clattered shut, the brakes hissed, and without knowing why, Virginia banged on the side of the bus to keep the driver from pulling away. The bus sagged back on its haunches, and Virginia trotted up to the front, where the driver opened the door, looking annoyed.

"Do you know anything about the advertisement on the side of the bus?" she said.

"I just drive the goldang thing, darlin'," the driver said, reaching for the door handle. But Virginia put one foot up on the step.

"How can I find out about it?" she said. "Please."

"Call the Transit Authority, I reckon," he said. "Step back, please."

But Virginia was patting the pocket of her sundress unsuccessfully, and she cocked her head and gave the driver her sweetest smile.

"Say," she said, "you wouldn't happen to have a pen on you, would you? Just so I could jot it down."

The driver blew out a sigh and handed her down a well-chewed Bic from the litter on his dash.

"Thanks!" Virginia said brightly. "I'll just be a sec."

She walked back down the side of the bus, pulled her rolled-up manuscript out from under her arm, and uncapped the pen. She stopped before the sign, the ballpoint poised over the back of her paper.

The ad was gone.

Virginia stood blinking at the side of the bus. Her skin tightened with a chill that started up her spine and spread around her like a freezing embrace. The odd little message, blue letters on yellow, was no longer there. Instead there was a huge, garish picture of a local talk-radio DJ, his teeth the size of playing cards.

Virginia stepped back, looking sharply up and down the length of the bus. But the whole billboard was devoted to the DJ's morning show, displaying in huge orange letters the call letters of the station and an idiotic catchphrase. The traffic noise seemed to have stopped, and as if from a great distance Virginia heard a voice calling. She stepped farther back from the bus, as if the message she'd seen might resolve itself out of the grain of the huge photo, but it wasn't there.

The door clattered shut, the brakes hissed again, and the bus lumbered away from the curb. She glanced up, startled, and trotted after it, waving the pen in her hand. But the driver wasn't looking; he was watching the traffic in his side mirror and giving her the finger over his shoulder.

Virginia stood at the curb, the heat warming her shoulders, the noise of the avenue returning. She looked down at the pen in one hand and the manuscript in the other, and, before she forgot it, she wrote down the message from the disappearing sign on the side of the bus.

# four

VIRGINIA ARRIVED HOME PLEASANTLY SWEATY after the walk up the hill from the bus stop. The house, a little tin-roofed Texas bungalow, was stuffy, so she opened the windows and started the attic fan. She tossed the manuscript onto her desk and tried dialing Chip right away, but all she got was his friend Mel's answering machine—with Chip's voice on it, oddly enough—and she hung up without leaving a message. She sat down at her desk and picked up her manuscript, holding it loosely between her hands as if afraid she might damage it. It was creased down the middle where she had rolled it up and pinned it under her arm; the corner of one page was bent back, revealing a fragment of a word: -aim.

I ought to know what that word is without looking, she thought. I wrote this.

But it wouldn't come to her. She was frantic to know suddenly, as if it were somebody else's work, but she couldn't bring herself to turn the page. Claim? Proclaim? Maim? What was it? The sense of violation she'd felt in Karswell's office came back, making her shiver. The manuscript in her hands didn't even *feel* like her work anymore, as if she had no right to look at her own words. All she could do was gaze dully at the title page:

The Missionary Position: The Franciscan Construction of
Rapanui Gender, 1862–1936

by

Victor Karswell

Virginia dropped the paper as if it had stung her and jumped to
her feet, sending her creaky old office chair rumbling over the
hardwood floor. What's that say? she thought, and she leaned carefully over the desk and read the author's name again.

*Dunning*, it said. Virginia Dunning.

Virginia let out her breath and rubbed her eyes. In the dark behind her eyelids she saw the scene in Karswell's office again, saw
him jotting something in the margin of one of the pages just before he handed it back to her, and she opened her eyes and laid her
hand on the manuscript.

"No," she said definitively. The last thing she wanted to see
right now was Karswell's aggressively precise handwriting, let alone
whatever the note actually said, so she snatched up the paper,
yanked open the top drawer of her filing cabinet, dropped the
manuscript in, and slammed the drawer. She'd have to look at what
Karswell wrote eventually. But not this instant. Not right now.

Instead she pushed the cat off the sofa and stretched out with
the phone in her lap. She dialed her friend Elizabeth in Chicago,
praying that Lizzie was home. Elizabeth picked up the phone;
sometimes God answers even the prayers of Her postmodern children. Virginia related her story, stretched out flat on her long sofa,
a throw pillow pressed over her eyes.

But Elizabeth sounded distracted.

"I'm sorry, Ginny," she said, but her voice had the absentminded
timbre of someone holding the phone between her chin and clav-
icle as she did something else with her hands.

"What do you know about Karswell?" Virginia said. "Has he
done anything like this before?"

"Well, he's not in my field," Elizabeth began, and there was a
pause as Virginia heard the rustle of papers. Elizabeth had just got-

ten tenure in the English department at Chicago University, but she had problems of her own. Her commuter marriage to another English professor in Iowa had collapsed, and she was going through a bitter divorce.

"Yes, but didn't you have a friend who went to Providence?" Virginia said.

"Ginny, you've got me at a bad time," Elizabeth said. "I'm standing here looking at my divorce papers."

"Oh my God, I'm sorry," Virginia said. "Do you want me to call back later?"

A sigh came down the telephone line.

"Kah-lee," Elizabeth seemed to say.

"I'm sorry?" said Virginia, lifting the pillow off her forehead.

"At Providence, they used to call Karswell 'Kali.' "

Virginia heard the creak of the receiver being handled, and the timbre of Elizabeth's voice changed.

"Or Professor Kali. After the Hindu goddess of death. The joke was that he reclined upon the skulls of ruined graduate students. Most people at his level measure their success by the number of acolytes they place in good jobs somewhere. But Karswell, or so I heard, seemed to take a perverse pleasure in destroying careers before they even got started."

"Oh God," Virginia said.

"I also heard," Elizabeth said, warming to the subject, "that he tried his best to keep the department free of gender and cultural studies through sheer political clout, but that even he couldn't command the tide not to come in. Then I heard that he gave up on Pacific studies, underwent some sort of sudden conversion, and put out a theory-based book, very contemporary."

"Really," Virginia said. "Like, overnight?"

"Yeah, but the book was peculiar. It wasn't his usual topic. It was about sorcery in the Enlightenment or something like that. I forget what it was called. Some of it was actually quite good, very cutting-edge, or so I'm told. But most of it was just the same old stuff he'd always done, historiographically antique, the usual fussy, hyperfastidious exegesis of primary sources, only tarted up with a lot of pomo jargon. It was crap, basically."

"Is that why he had to leave Providence?"

Elizabeth laughed bitterly, more of a snort, really, which broke Virginia's heart a little. Lizzie had always been a first-rate intellect, but she hadn't always been so hard.

"Oh *please*, Ginny," she said. "He's a whimwit," she added, using their private term for White Man with Tenure. "He knows the secret handshake."

"So why *did* he leave?"

"Well, I don't *know*, Ginny, but I *heard* that after the book came out, he was accused of plagiarism by one of his grad students. By his only remaining grad student, in fact. Guy said that the more contemporary stuff in the book was his."

Virginia's heart began to race.

"What happened?" she said.

"Well, the case went unresolved, I guess. The guy killed himself."

"He *killed* himself?" Virginia put her hand to her throat.

"That's what I heard."

"And the university didn't pursue it?"

"They cut a deal with Karswell. They'd let him off the hook and seal the records if he'd leave the department quietly."

"What was the student's name?" Her pulse was pounding now.

"The grad student's? Oh God, I don't remember. Harrison? Harriman? Something like that."

Virginia sat upright on the couch. Her heart was hammering, and she tightened her voice to keep it from shaking.

"It wasn't Harrington, was it?" she said. "John Harrington?"

"Yes," said Elizabeth, brightening. "Yes, that was the guy." Then, a bit peevishly, "I thought you didn't know this story."

"How did he die?" Virginia whispered.

"Well, they ruled it was an accident, but there was something strange about it. He fell out of a tree just outside his own apartment. . . ."

Virginia stopped listening. The light in the room seemed to dim, and the breeze coming in the windows behind her felt almost autumnal, with a wintry bite to it, something from her Minnesota girlhood.

"But I have to go, Ginny, I'm sorry," Elizabeth was saying. "I have to see the lawyer in an hour."

"I'm sorry," Virginia said, forcing herself to concentrate. Certainly Lizzie's problems were as bad as hers at the moment. Maybe even worse.

"Look, I know it sucks, I know it's unfair." Elizabeth paused as if mustering her nerve. Then she said, all in a rush, "Hell, it's worse than unfair, it's criminal, it's fucking harassment. But if I were you, Ginny, honest to God, I'd give him what he wants. Let him put his fucking name on the paper. The cost of fighting him is worse than the humiliation of letting him get away with it. Anyway, you're going places, and he's not. When it's a chapter in your book, you can banish him to the acknowledgments. But for now, girl, you really don't have a choice."

Virginia was shaking so hard she scarcely heard what Elizabeth was saying to her. She knew she ought to ask about Lizzie's troubles, let her friend vent a little, but all she could think of was that disappearing yellow sign with the small blue letters. She remembered writing the message on the back of her paper, and involuntarily she glanced across the room at her filing cabinet. She could almost see the paper standing on edge in the drawer, and if she closed her eyes she could see the message in her own handwriting on the back page of her paper. *John Harrington*, it read. *Three months were allowed.*

"How's Charlotte?" she managed to say, forcing herself to concentrate. She didn't want to ask about Elizabeth's soon-to-be-ex-husband, a patronizing little weasel named Paul whom she'd never liked, so she asked instead after Elizabeth's beloved cat. But it was the wrong thing to say, apparently. Elizabeth sucked in her breath sharply, and Virginia thought for a moment that her friend was about to start weeping.

"It's still a man's world, Ginny," Elizabeth said bitterly, with a catch in her throat. "Damn them all to hell."

# five

THAT EVENING VIRGINIA ALLOWED HERSELF what her mother used to call a Scarlett O'Hara: she would not think about this today. She would think about it tomorrow.

"Because after all," she could hear her mother say, a native Minnesotan's rendition of Vivian Leigh's version of a Southern belle, "tomorrow is another day."

She went down to the Tex-Mex place at the foot of the hill for enchiladas, and back home she fed Sam, Chip's sweet-natured but not very smart Persian cat, and puttered about in shorts and a T-shirt, tidying up the house and soaking in the warmth of a Texas summer evening. Then she went to bed to watch television, sitting with her arms wrapped around a pillow, until she fell asleep watching a TV movie about campers terrorized by a pagan cult; the mother was played by the mother from some sitcom. Chip would know her name, she thought, cuddling the pillow, her eyes drifting shut.

She woke to the sight of Letterman leaning forward over his desk and putting his hands all over some nervously smiling young actress. Virginia sat bolt upright and groped for the remote.

"It's freezing in here," she said aloud, cutting off Dave in mid-fondle. She got up, clutching her elbows, and went around the house with Sam at her heels, turning off the fans and closing all the windows. A cold front must have come through, she thought, but glancing out the front window at Lamar's red-and-green skyline, she saw stars in a clear sky. No dark clouds, no flickers of light-ning, no rumbles of prairie thunder. She picked up the cat for warmth and carried him back into the bedroom, where he jumped to the floor and left the room again. Even with the windows closed, she was still chilly, so she put on leggings and a pair of socks and a long-sleeved T-shirt and got a blanket out of the chest at the end of the bed. She pulled the covers up to her chin and slept.

She was awakened again sometime later when something jumped on the bed and padded up the blanket in the dark toward her head. It was only Sam, doing what he always did, curling up next to her on Chip's pillow, but he startled her tonight, and she lifted her head to see the cat silhouetted against the glowing red numerals of the digital clock. It was one-thirty in the morning. She sighed and mur-mured Sam's name, drifting to sleep to the little rumble of his purr.

Only to awake again to the distinct sound of the drawer of her filing cabinet sliding shut. She was confused for a moment—had the noise waked her, or had she waked first and then heard the cabinet?—but the sound itself was unmistakable. The hollow rum-ble of the drawer on its track, then the thump as it slotted home and the click of the catch, and the briefest interval of metallic re-verberation. She sat right up in bed, instantly breathless, her heart racing. The dark was positively freezing. She glanced for the clock and saw nothing; the red numerals were out, the display was blank. The power's out, she thought. Which was not an unusual situation in central Texas in August—a storm might have knocked down a line or blown a transformer. But not all over the neighborhood: looking toward the bedroom door she saw a dim glow from the liv-ing room, where the streetlight shone through the front window.

Just my house, Virginia thought. She drew a deep breath and felt on the pillow beside her for Sam, and found him alert, his head lifted from his paws, his ears cocked. He'd heard something too.

Virginia listened hard. Her house was seventy years old—even the cat couldn't move across the uneven floor without making the boards creak—but she heard nothing, no footsteps, no rustle of clothing, no breathing in the other room. She gathered herself, then leaned abruptly over the side of the mattress and reached for the flashlight and the aluminum baseball bat she kept just under her side of the bed. Then she sat up and swung her stocking feet to the floor and stood, letting the sheet slide back to the bed. She stood next to the bed, taking deep breaths to calm herself, listening to the silence, hefting the bat in her right hand. It was a child's bat, cool and smooth and only a couple of feet long, but just the right length to do some damage one-handed. Virginia had decided long ago, even before Texas, that if someone ever broke into her home, she was damned if she was going to wait for him to come to her.

She stepped lightly through the dark to the doorway and slipped into the little hallway, with her back to the wall, where she could see into the kitchen and the living room at the same time. The little glowing clock had gone out on the stove, but through the side door she saw her neighbor's porch light shining.

Everybody's got power, she thought, but me.

She waited a moment, to see if her movement provoked a response, then she held the flashlight at arm's length away from her side and switched it on. The mottled, yellowish beam fell across the floor of the living room, and she swung it quickly past the front door, past her desk, past the sooty rectangle of the fireplace, and stopped it on her filing cabinet. There was no one there, and the cabinet looked undisturbed. Tightening her grip on the bat, she edged forward out of the hall, moving the beam farther around the room, across the sofa, the easy chair, one of the stereo speakers. Still she saw no one. The living room was empty.

She breathed a little easier and lowered the bat slightly. She shone the light into the kitchen, but she already suspected it was empty; anyone coming out of the living room into the kitchen made the glass in the side door rattle, and she hadn't heard it. She lowered the beam to the floor and stepped carefully into the living room, reassured by the creak of the floorboards under her bare feet. She glanced at the windows along the south and east sides of the house. They were still closed; through the front windows she saw the parti-colored lines and angles of the skyline downtown.

She tried the overhead light and a lamp, but nothing worked, and she crossed to the filing cabinet, glancing back once toward the hall before she laid the bat quietly on her desk. The handle of the top drawer of the filing cabinet was surprisingly cold to her touch, as cold as a can of soda just out of the fridge. She pulled the drawer open slowly, wondering as she did why she was trying to be quiet in her own house, but as she turned the flashlight beam down into the drawer, she was startled by a sharp, freezing wind blowing about her ankles. She slammed the drawer and snatched up the bat and whirled, sending the yellow beam glancing about the room. But there was no one there. Nothing moved. Bat in hand, she checked the front door and all the windows, looking for a draft, but everything was closed and locked tight.

She went back and opened the drawer. The handle was still cold, and a gust of dank air seemed to rise out of the drawer itself as she bent over it and shone the beam in. You're going crazy, she told herself. Her manuscript was undisturbed, just where she'd left it. She bit her lip, wondering at her own paranoia. Scarlett O'Hara notwithstanding, she'd gone to sleep brooding, no doubt, about Victor Karswell and had worked herself into such a state that she woke up thinking he was in the house, stealing her files.

"Calm down, kid," she murmured. If Karswell wanted her manuscript, he could have made a copy anytime over the last few months. Probably already had, in fact.

She closed the drawer and pushed in the lock, for good measure. Switching off the flashlight and picking up the bat, she padded back across the creaking floor toward the bedroom, letting the flashlight and the bat swing from the ends of her arms. Lizzie was probably right, she thought: the cost of incurring Karswell's wrath was probably higher than that of just letting him have his way. She came into the hallway, too relieved at the moment to work up any anger, and she heard something rustling in the bedroom.

She froze and lifted the bat again. Something was moving among her bedclothes. That's not possible, she thought. I would have heard someone coming into the bedroom.

She hesitated, balancing on the balls of her feet, tempted to turn and run out the front door, to go to the neighbor's and call the cops. But she edged forward into the little hall and peered through the bedroom door. The rustling was louder, something moving among the blankets, and Virginia blew out an audible sigh and stepped into the doorway.

"Sam," she said, "you goofball."

She lifted the flashlight and switched it on, and just then she heard the cat let out a long, bone-chilling hiss. The hair rose up on the back of her head and her skin tightened: the hiss had come from behind her, in the hallway. Sam was not in the bedroom. Something else was in the bed.

Virginia could hardly move, but she lifted the beam of light and saw the bedclothes rise straight up off the bed in a column of linen. She sucked in her breath, unable to scream. It looked like a person standing under the sheets and lifting his arms, but linens had lifted clear off the bed, dangling free. The figure swung slowly, from side to side, its head lowered, its arms groping, as if it were feeling for something. Virginia was scarcely able to breathe, but she managed to step back slowly out of the doorway. The floorboards creaked under her feet, the thing lifted its head suddenly into the beam of the flashlight, and Virginia caught a glimpse of her sheets crumpled into a sort of *face*, inhuman and malign.

With a sudden, smooth motion, it rushed at her, waving its drapery arms, and Virginia screamed and dropped the flashlight. The flashlight rolled in an arc along the floor, throwing its beam wildly, giving the scene a kaleidoscopic effect. In the flashing, mottled light the linen face thrust itself at Virginia, the arms groping. She hurled the baseball bat and heard it ringing against the floor. A corner of sheet dragged across her face, and she fell to the floor, speechless, and scrambled crabwise back away from it, down the hall. The light was still rolling. Now all she saw was a silhouette swaying above her, and she banged her head against the bathroom door. The cat crouched in the corner of the hall beside her, hissing and baring its fangs in the rolling light, and Virginia groped behind her for the bathroom doorknob, shoved open the door, and propelled herself backward onto the tile floor. The light rolled across the searcher in the hall, and as the bathroom door clattered against the wall, the thing swung toward Virginia, trailing its skirts along the floor with a hiss.

In a last burst of energy, Virginia lunged into the hall, snatched

up the snarling cat, and slammed the bathroom door. Sam shrieked
and scratched her and leaped into the bathtub, clawing his way
through the shower curtain. Virginia put her back against the door
and set her feet on the floor. But she couldn't get a purchase in her
socks, so she tore them off and flung herself back against the door,
gripping the clammy tile with her toes. Her heart was pounding,
her breath rasping, and she squeezed her eyes shut against the
dark and waited for an assault on the door. But nothing happened.
She held her breath, trying to listen over the pounding of her
heart. There was no sound from the hallway. She cracked an eye;
a little light from outside came through the pebbled glass of the
window. Nothing was moving in the hall. She released the tension
in her legs slightly and felt for the lock on the door, turning it as
slowly as she could until it clicked into place. Then she slipped
down the door to the floor, took a deep breath, and passed out.

VIRGINIA OPENED HER EYES THE FOLLOWING
morning to find herself nose to nose with the cat, who was croak-
ing pitifully at her from six inches away. At this distance, with her
cheek pressed against the clammy bathroom tile, Sam looked huge
and menacing—his eyes wide, his teeth long and sharp—and Virginia recoiled involuntarily, banging her head against the door. She
groaned and cursed and sat up stiffly, rubbing the back of her head.
Sam whined again, putting his front paws on her knee, and she
glanced up past the tub to see daylight through the window. Her
joints were sore, her neck stiff, her hip bruised from sleeping on
the tile. Then she remembered the night before and pulled herself to her feet by the towel rack.

But it was hard to stay frightened. The bathroom was already
warm from the morning light, and the cat was doing a furry figure
eight between her ankles. Virginia unlocked the door and peered
around the edge of it. Sam slipped through the crack into the hall,
and she watched as he paused to sniff the heap of linens on the hall
floor, then trotted nonchalantly around them toward his dish in the
kitchen, where he sat and looked back at her and whined some
more. She came into the hall herself and poked the sheets with her
big toe. The flashlight lay to one side of the hall, the battery dead.
The baseball bat had rolled into the living room.

"Okay," she said, half to herself, half to Sam. "Here I come."
And she bolted up the hall, leaped the bedclothes, and skidded

into the kitchen. By time she had fed Sam, picked up the bat and the flashlight, bathed herself, and eaten a bowl of cereal, it was nine o'clock. The sun poured in the window over her desk, and with each inch of light across the floorboards, the events of last night seemed more improbable. Finally she picked up the sheets from the hall floor and put them back on the bed. She tried calling Chip again in L.A. and got only Mel's machine, and she was sitting at her desk with the phone in her lap when it rang.

It was Elizabeth, speaking in a torrent.

"Look, Ginny, I don't have time to talk, but I just wanted to call and say I'm sorry if I was curt on the phone yesterday, I know just what you're going through and I sympathize, but I had a lot on my plate yesterday, and anyway I tracked down a number for you, someone you might want to call."

"Lizzie?" Virginia said.

"Have you got a pen?" Elizabeth said, scarcely breaking stride. "Write this down," and Virginia snatched up a pencil and wrote the number on her desk blotter.

"Her name is Beverly Harrington," Elizabeth was saying as Virginia sat blinking at the number. "She's John Harrington's wuh, wuh, wife."

Elizabeth paused for the first time and drew a breath.

"I mean widow," she said. "I was told she's a fount of information about Karswell, kind of more than you'd ever want to know, in fact. Ginny, I gotta go."

"Wait!" cried Virginia, waving the pencil. "Where does she live? You only gave me her local number. What's her area code?"

"Same as yours, Ginny," said Elizabeth. "She lives in Lamar now. Look, I *have* to go. Keep in touch."

Elizabeth hung up, leaving Virginia with the dial tone humming in her ear. She wrote down the woman's name next to the number, and held the phone in her lap, the eraser end of the pencil poised over the keypad. What did Lizzie mean, "more than you'd ever want to know" about Karswell? And why did this woman live in Lamar? There's something weird about that, Virginia thought. Why would she want to live in the same town as Karswell, after what happened to her husband?

Something stirred at the edge of her vision, and Virginia leaped up, the phone clutched to her chest, the pencil cocked in her fist like a dagger, eraser end down. But it was only Sam, jumping up into the patch of morning sun in the easy chair, settling in for his postprandial nap.

"Jesus," Virginia murmured, and she sat down again and punched in the number.

All she got, though, was a machine, and a woman's voice that did not give a name, but only the number and instructions to wait for the beep. Right away the voice on the machine annoyed Virginia: it was breathy and high-pitched, a baby-doll voice from a Betty Boop cartoon. Nobody's born talking like that, Virginia thought. There's no excuse for sounding like that in this day and age.

The tape beeped, catching Virginia off guard, before she'd thought of something to say.

"Hello, this is, uh . . ." she began. "Um, my name is Virginia Dunning, and I was given your number by Elizabeth . . . that is, a friend of mine gave me your number, I don't think you know her."

She caught her breath and thought, Why am I calling this woman, anyway?

"Anyway, my friend thought that you might be able to . . . that you know something about . . . well, it has to do with your husband . . . oh my God, I'm sorry, I didn't mean that . . ."

Virginia squeezed her eyes shut and sighed.

"I'm sorry," she said, "that was awkward. What I meant to say is, my name is Virginia Dunning, and I teach in the same department as Victor Karswell—"

The phone clicked and Virginia thought she'd used up the message tape, but then someone spoke.

"What did you say your name is?" said a voice, the same one as on the tape.

"Oh, hi," Virginia said. "I'm Virginia Dunning. Are you Beverly?"

"How do you know Victor Karswell?" the voice said. It was still small and breathy, but there was an edge to it live that didn't come through on tape.

"We're colleagues," Virginia said, wincing as she said it. "What I mean is, we're in the same department. At Longhorn State."

"What has he done to you?" said the voice.

Virginia caught her breath.

"I was told," she said, recovering, "that you might be able to tell me something about him."

"*What has he done?*" insisted the voice.

Virginia paused before answering.

"Look," she said, "I'm not sure I should say anything over the phone. Maybe we could meet for coffee."

"Where do you live?" said the voice.

"I'm sorry?"

"Your name is Virginia Dunning, isn't that what you said?" There was a definite edge to the voice that belied its Boopishness. "I have a university directory in front of me. I can just look it up if I have to."

"One-fifteen Whitman," Virginia said, surprising herself.

"Don't go anywhere," the voice said. "You need my help. I'll be there in fifteen minutes."

Before she could reply, Virginia found herself listening to the dial tone again.

Within fifteen minutes a ten-year-old Honda came buzzing up the street in front of her house, and as Virginia peered surreptitiously around the edge of her front window, the little gray car shuddered to a stop. A short, wide woman in a big tent of a blue denim dress pushed herself up out of the car and lifted a large leather purse over her shoulder. She glanced up the hill at the house, her round face framed in black bangs, and Virginia jerked back from the window. When she dared to look again, the woman was stumping up the front steps. Sam perked up his ears at the sound, and Virginia hovered at the center of the living room on the balls of her feet, giving serious thought to pretending she wasn't home. The bell rang, Sam bolted into the bedroom, and Virginia drew a breath and opened the door.

"I'm Beverly Harrington," said the fat woman, peering wide-eyed up at Virginia from under her black bangs.

Virginia managed a smile and beckoned her in, offering her hand. Beverly gave her a weak, damp grasp, then stood a bit breathlessly, looking around the room.

"It's Beverly, okay?" she said. "Not Bev. Don't call me Bev. I hate that."

"Of course," Virginia said. "Could I offer you . . ."

But Beverly had already let her purse slide down her arm and thump to the floor, and she walked slowly across the living room, the floorboards creaking. Some women are born big, others have bigness thrust upon them, and Beverly seemed to be one of the latter. She had small features that seemed to be sinking into the flesh of her face, and small hands at the ends of her meaty arms. She turned slowly as she went, breathing heavily, taking in everything about the room as if she were planning on buying the place.

"How did you know my husband's name?" she said, scanning Virginia's books.

"My friend Elizabeth told me," Virginia said, at her elbow. "She teaches at Chicago and told me about his . . . how he . . ."

"You didn't see it somewhere else?"

Beverly turned and directed her intent gaze at Virginia. She had a small nose and a narrow mouth and wide, lovely, violet eyes. In spite of herself, Virginia couldn't help thinking that a few years and seventy-five pounds ago, Beverly was probably very pretty. But now her face had a sickly sheen to it that came from something other than the heat, and her eyes were fierce and focused, even a little frightening.

"You wouldn't believe me if I told you," Virginia said. "I don't really believe it myself."

"Where did you see his name?" Beverly insisted.

"On the side of a bus," Virginia said, keeping her voice as steady as possible. "It said his name, a date, and the name of a city—Providence, I think—and then it said something like 'Three months were allowed.' "

Beverly nodded slowly at this, breathing hard through her nose.

"There was something else about it that was strange," Virginia went on. "When I went to write it down, it was gone. It had disappeared. In fact, it was like it had never been there at all."

Beverly smiled slightly, an overweight Mona Lisa.

"It's a good thing you called me," she said. "You might have a fighting chance."

"I beg your pardon?"

"Make us some coffee," Beverly said, turning away again. "No decaf. I only drink the real thing."

Virginia went into the kitchen to fire up her coffeemaker, and while filling the pot she peered back into the living room at Beverly stooped over her desk, reading the spines of the books across the back. Even in the kitchen, even with the water running, Virginia could hear the woman breathing, and she wondered how she could get rid of her, if it would be rude to offer her a cup of coffee and then ask her to leave.

When the coffee was ready, Beverly lumbered into the kitchen and pulled back a chair at the table, sitting with her knees apart and her arm on the tabletop.

"Black," she said before Virginia had a chance to ask. "No cream, no milk, no sugar. Just black. A bigger cup than that, too, if you have one."

Virginia put aside the first cup for herself and filled a soup mug with coffee for her guest. She sat as Beverly took an improbably huge gulp for a hot beverage, watching Virginia over the rim.

"Now," she said, setting the mug down. "Tell me everything. From the beginning."

"Well, I was coming home on the bus yesterday—"

"Before that," Beverly said, shaking her head.

"Okay," Virginia said evenly. "I left Professor Karswell's office yesterday—"

"Before that!" Beverly barked. "How do you expect me to help you if you don't tell me *everything?*"

After a couple more false starts, Virginia told her guest everything that had happened since she had submitted her paper to Karswell. Beverly interrupted a number of times, usually to bark a question—"Why'd you give the paper to him?"—or a demand—"I need some more coffee"—making Virginia increasingly frustrated, and making her wonder again if she shouldn't simply show Beverly the door. Some of the questions seemed picky and superfluous to her: "What exactly did Karswell say to you when he handed back your paper?" "Did he write something on the manuscript itself?" "Where is the paper now?"

"In my filing cabinet," Virginia said.

"Are you sure?"

"Yes," she said. "I saw it there last night, and then I locked the cabinet after . . ."

She paused to take a sip of coffee, using both hands to disguise the way they trembled.

"After what?"

"Well, something woke me last night, I'm not sure what, a noise . . ."

"Stop," said Beverly. "Back up. Start at the beginning."

Virginia sighed and looked away, and without meeting Beverly's chilly, wide-eyed gaze, she told the whole story. She started to fudge the details when she got to the part about the sheets rising off the bed, but Beverly clutched her wrist with her damp grip and made Virginia look at her and tell her everything, up to the point where she had locked herself in the bathroom. By the end of it Virginia was actually glad for this strange woman's touch on her arm; she was trembling in spite of herself, and feeling cold again for the first time this morning. When she finished she pulled her hand away and hugged herself. Neither woman said anything for a long moment.

"Okay," Beverly said. "I'm going to tell you a story now. Don't interrupt me. Just listen."

Virginia opened her mouth, and Beverly shushed her, a thick stubby finger before her lips.

"Just listen," she said.

seven

*I* WAS A HAPPY WOMAN ONCE, *BEVERLY SAID.* NOT like you see me now. I had a charming, ambitious husband who loved me. I was smart and ambitious myself, and I had some talent as a singer. Maybe not star quality, but I had a lovely soprano and good looks and some stage presence. Whether I sang professionally or became a teacher, I was looking forward to a career doing what I loved, and making a life with a wonderful man who adored me. Victor Karswell took that all away from me.

I met John Harrington when I was in the fine arts program at Providence. He came backstage after a student production of *La Bohème*, in which I sang the role of Mimi, and he gave me a single red rose. It's the sort of thing you hope will happen to you as a singer, eventually, but I didn't expect it to happen when I was still in graduate school. There aren't many men in their mid-twenties who fall for opera singers anymore. And John wasn't exactly my fantasy admirer—he was very thin and intense and nervous. He talked so fast that even after he handed me the rose I wasn't sure what was happening. I think he saw how confused I was, even made up like a consumptive, and he blushed and apologized and started to walk away. But even though I hadn't understood a word he'd said, my heart just filled, and I called after him. All I said was "Wait!" And he turned around. It was the most thrilling moment of my life.

We were married the following summer, and moved into an

apartment not far from campus, up among the treetops on the third floor of an old house. On warm days I would open the skylight and sing, and John would sit on the fire escape with his laptop and write. We got by on our graduate stipends, mostly. John did a little teaching, and I made a little money singing at weddings and anniversary parties. We were poor, of course, and struggling, but we were very, very happy. I'd already had a few auditions for some small companies, and a couple of important history departments had already expressed an interest in John, based on chapters from his thesis. We were going places, both of us.

John's work was very exciting and vital, an entirely fresh approach to the study of the occult in early modern Europe. John was not an immodest man, but he understood he was doing something new. He came home once and told me his chairman had said he was doing the most important work on the subject since Keith Thomas. I didn't know what that meant, exactly, but John walked on air for days afterward.

The only cloud on our horizon was John's dissertation committee. I don't understand all the politics of it, though God knows John explained it often enough. I was an artist, not a scholar. But I gather that a generational struggle was going on, even more than the usual one between professors and graduate students. And Victor Karswell was the most unpleasant of the older generation. He'd been a star himself once, but he had been in decline in recent years. His sort of history, John explained to me, was painstakingly archival and fastidiously limited in scope, and he had been bypassed by a younger generation that wrote in a larger context—gender historians and social historians and cultural historians, like John. Most doctoral candidates no longer needed his imprimatur to graduate from Providence, and eventually he had no grad students at all, and served on no one's committee.

The problem was that the early modern occult had recently become one of Karswell's topics. All he really was, John said, was a sort of archivist of the subject, just collating and translating all sorts of arcane primary sources. Odd sources, too, John said, insignificant writings that added nothing to the understanding of the period, or corrupted stuff that nobody took seriously anymore, writings of unreliable provenance. But even the chair couldn't keep him off of John's committee, not "in good conscience," he said. The spineless man.

So for a year, John's life, and therefore mine, was miserable. Karswell did everything he could to stand in his way, to trip him up. He subjected John's work to all sorts of useless tests, making him compile the sort of insanely detailed footnotes no one does anymore, challenging every statement that wasn't a mere statement of fact, and most of those that were. He tried to deny John grant money to go to Europe, he tried to stick John with teaching giant lecture courses, he tried to sabotage John's chances of getting chapters published in journals. Once a week he called John into his office and lectured him, John said, on "the futility and ideological mendacity of every historiographical method since Thomas Carlyle's." He asked for draft after draft of John's chapters, and never returned them.

And then, almost overnight, Karswell stopped. He asked to be taken off John's committee, to everyone's relief. Better still, from John's point of view, Karswell stopped speaking to him. It was as if we'd come out of a long, dark tunnel into the sunlight again. For another few months we were happy again, our lives were going forward.

Then Karswell's book came out. *A History of Early Modern Witchcraft*, it was called. No one knew he'd been working on it, he had presented no chapters in advance as articles or conference papers, and he had long since given up submitting his manuscripts to the major university presses. It came out with no fanfare at all, from some small university press that no one had ever heard of in western Massachusetts. It wasn't even stocked in the campus bookstore, with all the other faculty publications. John didn't know of it until he read a brief review in a journal, which savaged the book. I remember it vividly after all this time, almost word for word. It said the book was a mishmash of useless bibliographic detail, undigested postmodern theory, and split infinitives. There was an appendix to the book, the reviewer said, that gave English versions of old Northern European spells and curses, and the reviewer found it amusing that Professor Karswell thought it was necessary to reassure the reader in his introduction that none of these "recipes"—he called them recipes, not spells—that none of them would work in translation.

I thought it was funny that the nasty old bully had gotten his comeuppance, but John was queasy right from the start, especially at that phrase "undigested postmodern theory." It took him several days to track down a copy—none of the bookstores in Providence stocked it—and he came in the door that evening quaking with rage, nearly in tears, waving the book.

"Karswell's ripped me off!" was all he could say for half an hour.

But Karswell had done it cleverly, you see. Apart from a few terms or phrases here and there, he took nothing directly from John's work. But he'd stolen the heart of it, he had mimicked John's argument, and, worst of all, turned it into something bastardized and unconvincing, without any of John's passion or insight or subtlety. He even twisted the knife in John's reputation, by thanking him in the acknowledgments for John's help in compiling the bibliography. Anybody who read the book and who knew John's work could see what Karswell had taken and how he'd debased it, but he had laid his track carefully, he'd known just what he was doing by putting himself on John's committee for a year. Now he could simply say he'd thought of the argument first, that John's own work had been done under his direction and his influence, that John was, God help us, his acolyte. And no one could prove otherwise.

Though my John tried. I made him wait until he calmed down, but the next day he went to the department chair, he went to the dean, he even made an appointment with the president of the university. He retained a lawyer, and I took a part-time job to help pay the legal fees. And for a time it looked as though we might win. Everyone was sympathetic, and both the chair and the dean conceded in private that Karswell had stepped over the line. Our lawyer seemed to think we had a winnable court case, that we could even win damages from Karswell.

Then, one evening, three months to the day before John died, I gave a recital on campus. Very informal, just for fun, mostly for friends, some light classics and show tunes accompanied by a pianist friend of mine in a rehearsal room. Of course, John was there—he loved to hear me sing. And that night I was going to sing some of his favorites, a patter song from Gilbert and Sullivan, and "You'll Never Walk Alone." But when I came in and saw him in the front row, I was shocked to see my husband red-faced and glowering: Victor Karswell was sitting in the row behind him. Although I'd never met him, I knew it was Karswell, from John's description: small and sharp-featured, with an evil little smirk and frighteningly bright eyes. I remember him still, because it was summertime and everyone else was casually dressed, but Karswell wore a tweed suit with a waistcoat and a bow tie. He ought to have been sweating, but he was as cool and pale as a salamander, his eyes magnified by his pince-nez.

I'd been warming up, of course, but suddenly my throat was dry and tight. It was all I could do to get through the first selection, a medley from *Showboat*. John tried to smile at me, he applauded like mad after every piece, but I could see how upset he was. Karswell, I noticed, didn't look at me at all, but stared at the back of John's head the whole time. I was almost as upset as John. This was in July, and the room was air-conditioned, but it felt even colder than that, as if the room were refrigerated. My shoulders were bare, and I was shivering by the end of "Ol' Man River."

There was no intermission planned—I had only intended to sing for an hour—but after half an hour I suggested that people might like a chance to stretch their legs and warm up. Everyone rose, and I smiled at John, beckoning him over. But as he stood, Karswell tapped him on the shoulder. I didn't know why at the time, but my heart stopped when John turned to him. I started toward them both, to take John's arm and lead him away, but before I could get to him, Karswell offered John a copy of the program— just a little photocopied thing, I had designed it myself—and said, "May I give this to you? I have no further use for it."

I mean, it was insulting. I'm sure Karswell knew the performer that evening was John's wife. But there were other people around, and I was approaching, so John just took it and said, very coldly, "Yes. Thank you." His face turned very dark at that moment, and I was awfully afraid he was going to have a seizure of some sort. But I touched his arm just then and he turned away from Karswell.

Karswell said nothing more, did not even look at me, but just rose from his seat and left. He didn't even stay for the second half of the recital.

John could hardly speak. He folded the program Karswell had given him into quarters, very tightly, and stuck it in his jacket pocket, and I walked him up and down in the hall for a few minutes. Then it was all I could do to finish the program. It was hardly my finest evening. No one asked for an encore, and frankly, I didn't want to perform one. I only wanted to get John home again.

But it didn't get any better when we were alone. After he had heard me sing, John was usually very affectionate, very tender and loving, but that night he was restless and irritable and wouldn't let me touch him. When we got home I just laid my hand lightly on the small of his back in passing, and he jumped away from me and raised his hand. He nearly struck me. After that, preparing for bed, we were both upset, scarcely speaking. I heard him in the bathroom, brushing his teeth, running the water in the sink. Then he screamed suddenly, a horrible loud, piercing scream, the sort you hear in movies, the sort you hope never to hear in real life.

I was paralyzed at the sound. I sat bolt upright in bed, the covers clutched to my chest. The screaming stopped, something smashed in the bathroom, and I heard a sound I hope you never have to hear, Virginia, a more horrible, inhuman sound than I hope you can imagine: the sound of your loved one whimpering with terror, *keening* in fear like a trapped animal. The door rattled, the knob twisted, and I heard my darling John clawing at the door, trying to get out.

I couldn't stand it. I could hardly breathe. I don't know where I found the courage, but I leaped out of bed and across the room and grabbed the knob and opened the door. John was pushing from the other side, and he fell out, nearly on top of me, in a dead faint.

He didn't come around for ten minutes, and when he did I was on the verge of calling 911. His knuckles were bleeding, and I had put a pillow under his head and gone into the bathroom for a roll of gauze. The mirror was shattered, pieces of glass all over the floor. I bound up his hand, and as soon as he opened his eyes he tried to jump up, to flee from the bedroom, and I had to hold him by his shoulders and turn his face away from the bathroom door before he stopped struggling. I helped him into the living room, and he made me turn on all the lights in the apartment, but he wouldn't let me go into the bathroom again. It was some time before he could even speak, and then all he would say was that he'd seen something in the mirror, just over his shoulder, and that he had smashed the mirror with his fist. We stayed awake the rest of the night, holding each other on the sofa. He never would tell me what he saw in the mirror.

After that night, John was never at ease again. He constantly felt he was being followed, and even at home, with just the two of us, he felt as if someone were always watching him. My John was a nervous man to begin with, perhaps impressionable, but there was no accounting for this. He wouldn't go out after dark unless he absolutely had to, and even then he would drive where he used to walk, even to the convenience store down the block. At home he insisted that we keep the blinds always drawn, even during the day, and he shifted all his favorite places in the apartment—his chair at the table, his desk, his reading chair—so that he was always facing into the room. He shoved the bed into the corner of our bedroom and insisted we switch our regular places, so that he was sleeping next to the wall. He wouldn't let me touch him, but he wouldn't let me sleep in the other room, either. He began to tremble in bed at night, and say things, awful things, in his sleep. Please don't ask me what he said. I won't tell you.

Not long after this, one stifling evening in August, I was going through the pockets of John's jacket, the one he'd worn to the recital, getting ready to take it to the dry cleaner, and I came across the folded program that Karswell had given him. For some reason, I stood in the closet door with the jacket over my arm and unfolded the program. There seemed to be nothing remarkable about it at first—it was just a sheet of paper, folded in two—until I looked at the back page, which ought to have been blank. But written lengthwise along one edge, in red ink, was a row of odd-looking characters, very carefully done. I called for John and he took the program from me, looking at the markings.

"Where'd you get this?" he asked me.

"It was in your pocket," I said. "I think it's the recital program Karswell handed you." I looked over his shoulder at the markings. "Do you know what they are?"

"They look runic," John muttered, looking very upset.

"Could I see?" I said, but he whisked the program out of my reach.

"I'm calling Karswell," he said, very angry, and he marched out of the bedroom.

I followed him into the living room, trying to talk him out of it, but he wouldn't listen to me.

"That son of a bitch," he kept saying, and my John was not a vulgar man. He set the program down on the coffee table and held up his hand to silence me, something else he'd never done before. It angered me, in fact, and I was turning to leave the room when I heard John cry out and drop the phone.

It was a hot August night, as I said, not a breath of wind. The windows were all open, with no screens, because we were far enough off the ground not to be bothered by mosquitoes. It was almost too hot to move, but somehow a very chill wind was blowing through the living room, from the direction of the hall, where there was no window. When I turned, I saw John lunging across the coffee table for the recital program, which was being whisked by the wind across the room and out the window over the fire escape. There was a huge old oak tree just outside the window, hardly stirring, but its leaves began to rattle just then in the most alarming manner, almost as if a storm were passing, and the program shot up—not down, but *up*—into the tree and vanished into the shadows.

John was out the window in an instant, and I went after him. I had to clutch him by the arm to keep him from launching himself off the fire escape into the crown of the tree. John was very thin, and getting thinner, but even he wouldn't have been supported by the upper branches. We both went out to the yard below with flashlights and looked for the program, but we couldn't find it.

"It doesn't matter," I said. "I'm sure Karswell doesn't want it back."

And John blew up at me, in the yard, practically in public, with the neighbors' windows open all around. Even in the dark I could see the tendons of his neck tighten as he shouted at me.

"I don't know why you have to keep saying that!" he said, and when I protested I'd only said it once, he stalked away, not shouting anymore, but still angry.

"Oh yeah, right," he said. "More like *four times.*"

He went out again in the morning to look for the program, but we never saw it again. Meanwhile, the plagiarism case against Karswell, which had been going so well, with so much encouragement from everyone involved, slowed nearly to a standstill. The chair and the dean, who had been expediting things on our behalf, now hemmed and hawed and avoided John, and would not answer his phone calls. Karswell, it turned out, had not even retained a lawyer, and for some reason everyone was saying now that the situation was not so clear, that a result in John's favor was not so certain. Our lawyer took ill and removed herself from the case, and we could find no one else to take it on. A couple of John's friends even whispered to me—they wouldn't have dared to say it to his face—that he ought to drop the matter, to let it go and get on with his life.

Then, ten days before he died, I got my John back again. It was as though he had stepped back into the sunlight. He began to smile at me again. He put on a little weight. For weeks he'd been walking with his shoulders hunched, as if he expected to be struck from behind at any moment, and now he stood up straight once more, his shoulders squared, his head held high. He didn't want to give up his case against Karswell, but for the first time in months it wasn't the center of his life, and we talked about other things, about where we were going next, about starting a family. We began to make love again, but the sweetest of my memories is from the night before he died, when we went for a walk through our neighborhood—something he wouldn't have done under any circumstances a few days before—and we strolled easily in the dark under the trees, in the cool autumn air, and he held my hand.

Give me a moment. I miss him so.

On the last night, I was home alone. For the first time since all this had started, John wanted to work late at the library, and then walk home. It was late. I was in my nightgown already, reading a book on the sofa, when I heard my name being called. In fact, someone was screaming my name from outside, and I stood in the middle of the living room and listened. It was getting louder, coming closer, but it wasn't anyone I recognized, and I was afraid. I turned out the lights so that no one could see me from outside, and I went to the window by the fire escape. In the light from the streetlamp I saw that the leaves of the oak tree were shaking again, only this time as if someone were jerking them. The screaming was rising up out of the dark, where I couldn't see, and I was afraid to open the window and step out onto the fire escape. Whoever it was had screamed himself breathless. The branches of the tree continued to shake.

Then, in the dim light, I saw my husband's face rising out of the leaves of the tree. I'll never forget it. He was pale and wide-eyed with terror, and he was screaming my name, pulling himself up branch by branch in the tree as if his life depended on it. He was searching the windows with his eyes, I could tell, even in the dark, and he couldn't see me. I threw open the window and called to him, and he began to pull himself up even more frantically. He screamed my name again, begging me.

"Beverly!" he cried. "Help me!"

I crawled out onto the fire escape and called to him, I told him I was here. He was climbing desperately, grabbing each branch and pulling himself up without bothering to test it or see if there was another one above it. He never looked down.

"Open the window!" he was screaming. "Let me in!"

"It's open!" I called to him. "I'm right here!"

He was almost to the top, and I clung to the railing of the fire escape and reached out to him. I yelled for him to take my hand. He was trembling with the effort now, his face white, his eyes fixed on mine. He was only a few feet away from me, just beyond my reach, pushing himself up with both hands on a limb, when the leaves rattled all over the tree—not like a wind, but as if something were shaking the whole tree—and John was jerked downward, just as though someone had grabbed his ankle. He screamed my name one last time and threw out his hand to me, and then he fell.

The tree jerked horribly, for what seemed like the longest time.

I was breathless, I couldn't scream, I couldn't make a sound. Something hit the ground below with an awful, awful sound, and I ran from the apartment and flew down the stairs, scarcely noticing where I was going.

There's no point in dwelling on it further. I found several people in their nightclothes standing over something on the ground under the tree. It was John, all in a heap. He was dead, of course—his neck was snapped. He had the most dreadful face on him. I could only look at it once, but I'll never forget it.

I never found out what he was doing in the tree, why he didn't just come in the door and up the stairs. His briefcase was found a block away, on the sidewalk, and several people said they had heard or seen a man running frantically, cutting across lawns and down the middle of the street, just before John died.

His death seemed to put a little courage back into the university, and they persuaded Karswell to resign, by agreeing to drop John's case against him. I wasn't happy about it, as you might imagine, but there wasn't anything I could do. I think everyone was mainly relieved that it all went away. They were cowards, all of them.

Without my knowing about it, John had taken out a life insurance policy on himself, and so I was provided for. It's slim consolation, of course. I never got my degree. I haven't sung a note since he died. I put on fifty pounds.

Karswell found another position, of course. His sort always does. I followed him here, but I keep my distance, biding my time. He either doesn't know I'm here or, if he does, it doesn't matter to him. What can I do to him? I live very frugally, off the insurance money, and I wait. I am not idle, though. I devote myself to the study of Victor Karswell and his works. I am teaching myself. I want to know what he knows. I think by now that I know what he did to my husband and how he did it, but of course I can't prove anything. So I look for my opportunity and I keep him in my sights. And I wait.

# eight

I T WAS MIDMORNING BY TIME BEVERLY FINISHED.
The light had swung around the house from the front to the side
windows, and Sam had reemerged to stretch out in a patch of sun
on the sofa. Beverly had finished her coffee long since, and Virginia had let hers go cold in the cup. In fact, she felt cold again all
over, and sat in her chair hugging her elbow, her legs tightly
crossed, clutching the throat of her T-shirt in her fist. Beverly
gazed at her with her eyes wide, her skin shiny on her cheeks and
forehead.

"So," Virginia began meekly, trying to digest all she'd heard,
"you're saying Karswell wants to steal my work?"

Beverly closed her eyes and sighed.

"My dear," she said, opening her eyes, "Karswell wants you
dead."

Virginia let out a long, shuddering sigh which turned into laughter. She clapped her hand over her mouth, but she couldn't make
it stop.

"This is crazy," she managed to say. "I mean, I had a bad dream
last night, that's all."

"Have you seen his book?" Beverly said.

"His book?" Virginia clutched herself around her ribs, hoping
to make the laughter stop, but she couldn't.

Beverly pushed herself up with a grunt, retrieved her purse from
the living-room floor, and brought it back to the kitchen table. It

was a vast, bulging, black leather thing, but without rooting around in it she pulled out a little red-backed book and handed it to Virginia. It was the sort of cheap hardcover one saw from out-of-the-way university presses, with a pebbled leatherette cover, the title embossed in cheap gilt on the cover:

A HISTORY OF EARLY MODERN WITCHCRAFT

by

VICTOR KARSWELL, A.B., M.A. (Oxon.), Ph.D.

Virginia bit her lip to keep from laughing and opened the book. The paper was little better than pulp, the pages almost unreadably dense with Times Roman full of cracked type and smudges. She glanced at the title page; the publisher was Miskatonic University Press.

"Here," Beverly said, taking the volume out of Virginia's grasp. Without looking, she opened it to a page near the end of the book and held the volume up in both hands. Across the top of the recto page, Virginia read:

Appendix VII:
CASTING THE RUNES

Virginia felt breathless and weak, the way she used to as a girl after she'd been laughing uncontrollably.

"It's a do-it-yourself guide," Beverly said, glaring wide-eyed around the book at Virginia. "You cast the runes on people when you want to gain their affection—or get them out of the way. Especially the latter. This," she said, shaking the book at Virginia, "tells you how to do it. Everything you need to know, except the runes themselves. Karswell keeps that to himself."

She snapped the book shut and slapped it on the table. Virginia giggled weakly, and Beverly reached down, grabbed the edge of her own chair, and yanked it forward, until she was knee to knee with Virginia.

"If my husband," she said intensely, "had given that program back to Karswell, the one with the runes on it, and had gotten Karswell to take it back of his own free will, then John Harrington would be alive today."

She tried to catch Virginia's gaze in her own, from twelve inches away.

"Are you listening to me, Virginia?" she said loudly, and she grabbed Virginia's wrists and shook her.

"Where is the manuscript Karswell handed back to you?"

Virginia let herself be pulled to her feet, and she led Beverly numbly into the living room, where she unlocked the filing cabinet. As she started to pull the drawer open, Beverly, from behind her, slammed it shut.

"Are all your windows closed?" Beverly glanced about the room.

They checked all the windows in the house, and Beverly yanked on each one to make sure it was locked. Then Virginia followed Beverly back into the living room, and, as the cat watched curiously from the sofa, together they opened the top drawer of the cabinet and peered inside. Virginia half expected another gust of cold air, but it only smelled of manila folders and 3-In-One oil. She reached in for the paper, but Beverly batted her hand away and lifted it carefully herself, as if it were radioactive. For the first time, Beverly seemed nervous, her skin even shinier with perspiration, her breathing even more labored. She stood in the middle of the room with the manuscript trembling very slightly in her hands, and she lifted the sheets one at a time until she got to the last page. She breathed in a long hiss, a slow-motion gasp.

"Yesssss," she said. "I've got you now, Victor."

She looked up at Virginia, her eyes shining, and Virginia, hugging herself, edged up to Beverly and looked at the page. Written sideways along the margin of the last page was a row of angular runes in red ink, the lines and crossbars and serifs in broad, calligraphic strokes.

Virginia's skin tightened.

"What do they say?" she whispered.

Beverly glanced at her.

" 'Die, Virginia, die,' " she said.

Virginia gasped. Beverly rolled her eyes.

"Not really," she said. "How should I know?"

"Let me see it."

Irritated, Virginia reached for the paper. Beverly snatched it just out of her reach.

"You have to be very, very careful with this," she said, glaring at Virginia from under her bangs. "This is our only chance to stop Karswell."

"*My* only chance, you mean," Virginia said, and she took hold of one edge of the paper. The two of them pulled it tight between them, one to each side, standing shoulder to shoulder. Virginia twisted her head to look at the runes along the margin. She wondered which side of the runes was up, whether you read them left to right or right to left.

"If you ever lose this," Beverly said, "you're dead."

Behind them there was a papery rustle, and Virginia felt the hairs rise on the back of her neck. Sam crouched, alert, on the sofa. The two women glanced at each other, and then, still holding the manuscript between them, turned to the rustle behind them.

In two years in the house, Virginia and Chip had never used the fireplace, using the brick hearth as a place to stack old newspapers for recycling. Now the stack was stirring, as if in a gentle wind, and the top section of newspaper lifted and spread and began to peel slowly off into the air, sheet by sheet. The two women watched the sheets of newsprint spiral slowly about the room, and Virginia felt cold again, as if a draft were playing through the house.

"The flue," Beverly murmured.

Across the room from the fireplace, there was another papery rustle, and the women turned to see paper from the desk—check carbons, the phone bill, stray Post-its—lifting in a breeze. The pages of Virginia's book manuscript, in a loose stack on the corner of the desk, began to flick away into the air one at a time, slowly at first, then more quickly, as if someone were thumbing them off the pile. From the couch, the cat was growling.

Beverly tugged at the manuscript between them.

"I'd better hold on to this," she said.

"I got it," said Virginia, tugging back.

They both pulled. The manuscript slipped free. A freezing gust blew up from the floor between them, and the manuscript shot up into the air.

Suddenly the room was full of wind and paper, a whirling vortex of gray newsprint and white manuscript pages. Before she lost it, Virginia saw her festschrift paper spinning in the air, its pages fluttering like wings from the single hinge of its staple. She yelped and leaped for it and missed, and the manuscript disappeared in the blizzard of pages flying about the room. She shouted wordlessly, spinning with the wind, scarcely able to see to the walls of the room. She batted at the papers in the air with her hands, trying to claw her way through them to the pages that mattered. The edges of sheets scraped along her arms, their corners stung her face around her eyes. She couldn't see Beverly, but she could hear her roaring. The air beat with the flutter of paper, like a flock of birds. A sheet of newsprint plastered itself around her waist, and another one wrapped around her leg. Sam hunkered into the cushions of the couch and hissed.

"Where is it?" she cried. "I can't see it!"

"Don't let it leave the room!" cried Beverly, baby doll no more, her voice booming like a Valkyrie's.

For an instant Virginia thought she saw the manuscript, soaring near the ceiling in a wider and wider circle.

"I see it!" she cried, and a sheet of newspaper wrapped itself around her face, completely enclosing her head. She tried to scream but she couldn't, and she tore at the paper on her face, her nostrils full of ink and newsprint. But the sheet was slick and dry and wouldn't tear, and she lost her balance and fell to the floor. She heard the rattle of spinning paper, heard Sam crying in fear, heard Beverly stamping on the floor, not far away. Groping behind her head for the edge of the sheet, she thought of the face in the linen the night before and nearly passed out again, but she caught an edge of newsprint under her fingernail and pulled, yanking the sheet free of her face, gasping for breath.

The wind carried the sheet away, and Virginia looked up at the paper spinning above her. The space near the floor was clear, and in the eye of the storm she saw Beverly's solid legs a few feet away, her dress lifted like a bell, one leg coated in office paper, the other bare. Looking up at her from the floor, Beverly seemed to Virginia like a colossus, planted in one place, her arms wide and her massive legs set like a sumo wrestler's, her eyes fixed on one moving point in the storm. She moved only her head to follow it, her bangs lashing her face in the wind.

"Do you see it?" Virginia cried.

Suddenly the wind paused, and all the paper in the room hovered in the air, rustling quietly. Virginia followed Beverly's gaze to a point over her desk, where her manuscript seemed to hover like a seagull. Beverly said nothing, but hunkered down, spreading her hands, bending her knees, tensing her calves.

Then the wind began again, not in a circle this time, but a freezing stream, the airborne paper pouring across the room, into the open fireplace and up the chimney. Virginia shrieked, Sam howled. And Beverly leaped, propelling herself bodily into the air through the storm of paper and coming down flat on the hardwood floor with a sound like a feed sack tossed from a height, making the windows rattle and the floorboards shake.

The wind stopped. Sheets of newsprint caught in midair fluttered slowly to the floor, side to side. Office paper wafted down the chimney and piled like leaves on the grate. Virginia sat up and pressed her hands to her mouth. Beverly lay facedown on the floor, her hair spread over her face, her arms flung out to either side.

"Beverly?" Virginia whispered.

Beverly turned her head to face Virginia and blinked at her through a scrim of fine black hair.

"Close the flue," she gasped.

Virginia blinked, then scuttled forward on her hands and knees. She reached up into the dark of the chimney and yanked the flue shut with a clank. Soot fell in flakes along her arm and onto the pages in the grate. She turned and crawled back across the paper on the floor to Beverly, murmuring her name. But Beverly, with a grunt, rolled over heavily onto her back. Virginia's manuscript, on which she had landed, rolled with her, plastered to the front of her dress. Virginia fluttered her hands over Beverly, not certain if she should touch her. Paper was still drifting down like fallout, and she swept it away with her arm. Blinking up at the ceiling, Beverly peeled the paper off her chest with two fingers and handed it to Virginia.

"Take," she gasped. Her face was blotched with red.

Virginia took the paper with trembling hands, stood on quaking knees, and deposited it in the filing cabinet, locking the drawer. Then she turned to see Beverly levering herself up on her arms, in the middle of a floor carpeted with newspaper and the pages of her book, partially covered herself. Virginia bent to help, but Beverly waved her away, sitting up with her legs splayed, catching her breath. Virginia knelt before her.

"Oh my God, Beverly." She swallowed hard. "Are you all right?"

"Ten months out of the year," Beverly said breathlessly, "it's ninety degrees in this damn state. So why the hell does anybody in Texas need a damn fireplace?"

*B*EVERLY OFFERED TO STAY AND HELP CLEAN up the living room—"We need . . . to come up . . . with a plan," she said breathlessly—but on top of the events of the last twenty-four hours, this strange woman and her even stranger story made Virginia feel as though the walls were closing in. As politely as she could manage, she ushered Beverly to her feet, retrieved her book and her purse, and helped her down the steps and across the lawn toward her car. Lowering herself behind the wheel of her little Honda, Beverly tried to press Karswell's book into Virginia's hands.

"You'll need it," she gasped. "I have a box of them."

"Thanks for coming," Virginia said, closing the door of the car. But Beverly started the Honda and put it through a squealing U-turn, lurching to a stop in front of Virginia in the middle of the street, motor racing.

"You won't be able to sleep here tonight," Beverly snapped, her breath restored. "Call me." And she ground her gears and roared off.

Inside, surveying the snowfall of paper on her living-room floor, trying to keep from thinking about what had happened the night before, Virginia thought, She's right. I can't sleep here tonight. So she collected the papers on her floor and heaped them on her desk with no attempt to put them back in order, then threw some clothes in a duffel, asked her neighbor to feed the cat, and shut up the house. She stopped at an ATM on her way out of town, and headed west through the Hill Country in her truck. She picked up U.S. 10 across West Texas, and by nightfall she was in El Paso, where she stopped just long enough to have fajitas at a Taco Cabana and buy a packet of caffeine tablets at a TruckAmerica. Then, her nerves buzzing like an alarm, she drove all night, crossing New Mexico and Arizona in the dark at ninety miles an hour, the only civilian on the road, flying past the gliding geometric lights of long-distance truckers, her tires drumming on the road.

After dark she found herself reluctant to look in the mirrors, rearview or side, as if she expected to see something coming from behind. Finally, in the darkest hour of the night, bored by the twin cones of milky light ahead showing nothing but bleached pavement and the endless hyphens of the centerline, she looked once in the rearview mirror and saw only twin red taillights.

That wasn't so bad, she thought, and looked again. It took her a moment, but at last she realized that the taillights were in her lane, on *her* side of the median, and that they weren't going farther away, they were getting *closer*. Her foot fell on the gas and the speedometer needle quivered at 110, until her heart stopped pounding and she let up on the pedal. After that she didn't look in the mirrors again, afraid to look and afraid not to, too scared to stop but terrified she'd run out of gas and the advancing red lights would catch up with her, all alone, in the middle of the desert. Then, as she neared the California border, the mirrors began to fill with pinkish light and she made herself look, certain she was going to find something awful crouching in the truckbed and grinning at her through the rear window of the cab, but it was only the dawn painting the sky over the mountains behind her.

She arrived in L.A. by noon, and found the address of Chip's friend Mel without any trouble, a little courtyard apartment building four blocks off the Hollywood Freeway, under the lee of Griffith Park. The apartment door was open, and Virginia stood numbly in the bleaching California sun, her nerves singing with caffeine, her eyelids heavy with lack of sleep. She rapped on the screen door.

"C'mon in," called a woman, and Virginia walked in to find

Chip and a young woman with lank, dark hair sitting in a breakfast nook in matching terry-cloth bathrobes. As Virginia entered, they both froze in the act of eating bagels and cream cheese and reading the newspaper. They were so still Virginia wondered if she was experiencing another supernatural interlude. Perhaps time had stopped somehow and she was the only one moving. Which gave her momentarily the leisure to wonder why it had never occurred to her that Chip's friend Mel was a woman, why Chip hadn't told her this, and why they were sitting together in their bathrobes at noon on a weekday.

"Virginia?" Chip said, restarting the clock, his mouth full of bagel.

"Mel?" said Virginia.

"Ohmigod?" said Mel, with a rising inflection.

Everyone spoke at once. Chip asked Virginia was there anything wrong, Mel asked Chip what's *she* doing here, and Virginia asked Mel if she could use her toilet. In the little pink bathroom Virginia saw two toothbrushes and two types of shampoo in the shower, and across the back of the sink a neatly gendered division of territory, Barbasol and razor to the right, Clinique and cotton balls to the left. Through the flimsy door she listened to Mel and Chip hissing at each other—"Were you going to tell her?" "I was working up to it"—then she washed her hands, avoided looking in the mirror, and came out into the kitchen again.

"I'm going," Virginia said after another breathless moment, and Chip tried to extricate himself from the breakfast nook while Mel held him back by the skirt of his robe.

"And take your dog with you," Mel called out, propelling herself past Chip into the kitchen doorway and crossing her arms.

Virginia hesitated at the front door.

"What dog?" she said.

"You didn't bring Sam with you, did you?" Chip said hopefully, over Mel's shoulder.

"Who's Sam?" said Mel.

"You know," Chip said. "My cat."

"What dog?" Virginia said again. She stood with her back to the wall and glanced around Mel's small, untidy living room. There was nothing alive in it, not even a plant, only a large inflatable dinosaur in the corner, a big, green, cartoonlike *T. rex.*

"It wasn't a cat," Mel said. "It was a big black dog. It came in the door at her heels."

"I have to go," Virginia said, chilled suddenly, and she went out the door into the sun and marched down the courtyard to her truck, afraid to look behind her.

Once on the road, however, she didn't even think about the mirrors. The back of her neck burned with rage all the way back to Texas. As the sun went down behind her, halfway across Arizona, she turned off the AC, reached behind her without looking, and slid open the cab window, tunneling into the night with the desert breeze cooling her shoulders.

She arrived back in Lamar by twilight of the following day. Pulling into her driveway, drained and wound up like a clock, she contemplated not getting out of the truck but just sleeping where she was, behind the wheel. At last she stepped out onto the cracked concrete, barely able to stand, still wearing her sunglasses in spite of the gathering dark. She came around the house across the desiccated lawn and found Beverly seated on the front step reading an Anne Rice paperback in the crepuscular light, her purse a black lump at her feet. Beverly looked up as Virginia approached and held up a finger.

"Just a sec," she said, finishing the paragraph she was reading. Virginia stopped a few paces away, looking at Beverly through the added gloom of her tinted lenses. At last Beverly bent back the corner of the page, closed the book, and clutched it against her knees with both hands.

"What did I tell you?" Beverly said, looking up at Virginia. "You can run but you can't hide."

"Beat it," Virginia said.

Beverly blinked at her.

"I beg your pardon?"

"You heard me." Virginia stepped around her and up onto the porch. "Take a hike. Get out of here. Scram."

She stepped up to the door and discovered that she held her key ring in her hand. She flipped it over to single out her house key, and she aimed it at the lock.

"You only have three months, Virginia."

Behind her, Beverly had somehow sprung to her feet.

"That's how much time Karswell gave John," she was saying. "That means by the third week in November, you will be dead."

Virginia said nothing, loopy with fatigue. She was wondering if she could get the key in the lock on the first try. She wondered if she had the strength to turn the lock. It was like being drunk.

"Your only chance is to give the runes back to him." Beverly grasped Virginia by the arm and tried to turn her around. "And he has to take them, willingly."

Virginia inserted the key and turned the lock. She ignored the hand tugging at her arm until she had the door open, then struck it away, backhanded.

"Piss off," she said. "Go away."

"This is our only chance to get Karswell . . ." Beverly was saying, but Virginia whirled on her.

"I've had it with this shit," she said, distantly satisfied at the way Beverly stepped back. "I'm tired. I probably don't have a career anymore. I know I don't have a boyfriend. And now Victor fucking Karswell has me believing in voodoo."

"It's not voodoo," Beverly said. She lifted up her mammoth purse and begin to dig around inside it. "It's witchcraft," she said. "It's an entirely different tradition—"

"Shut. Up."

Virginia lifted her hand, silencing Beverly.

"Get over it, lady," she said. "I'm sorry about your husband, but get a life. Join the twentieth fucking century. I refuse to let that little asshole get to me like he's got to you. I had a bad dream one night, that's all, and now he's got me jumping at my own shadow. It's all suggestion. And all *you* did," she went on, raising her voice as Beverly tried to speak, "was make it worse. For all I know, you're in on it. How do I know he didn't send you over here to spook me?"

"Tell me this," Beverly said, crossing her arms. "Do you have windstorms in your living room on a regular basis?"

"This is Texas, honey," Virginia snapped. "We've got weather here like you wouldn't believe."

Beverly opened her mouth and closed it again. Virginia could hardly make out her expression in the double gloom of the twilight and her sunglasses, but it looked as if Beverly was trying to decide between disappointment and anger. She settled at last on a stony mask, her little features set as if in concrete in the slab of her face.

"What's that behind you?" she murmured.

Virginia jumped, the first spike in her brain waves in hours, and she whirled to look through the open doorway, into her shadowy living room. There was nothing there. She turned slowly back to Beverly.

"Get off my porch," she said. "Get out of my yard."

"You *will* call me." Beverly glowered up at Virginia from under her black bangs. "I'm your only chance."

Virginia turned and stepped inside the house and tried to close the door, but Beverly stopped it with the surprisingly firm pressure of her hand.

"Take this," she said, thrusting a copy of Karswell's book through the crack. "I don't care if you believe it or not, but you ought to know what *he* believes."

Virginia took the book, Beverly released the pressure, and the door slammed. Virginia heard Beverly's heavy tread across the porch and down the steps, heard her puffing down the hill toward her car.

She unlocked the filing cabinet and tossed the book in, on top of her paper, then closed the cabinet and locked it. She dropped her keys on her desk and took off her sunglasses. The disordered manuscript of her book lay like a pile of leaves on her desk. The blinds were still drawn. The house was quiet and dark and stuffy.

"To hell with it," she said, and staggered to her bedroom, too tired to undress, too tired even to consider what the blankets might be up to. Without pulling them back, she slid under the covers headfirst, pushing her hands ahead of her against the cool sheets like a diver. She stopped abruptly when she touched a mouth with sharp teeth and hair about it. It was alive, but it was not the mouth of a human being. She gasped and scuttled backward out of the bed, and she crouched against the wall, groping vainly about her for the baseball bat. The covers stirred, and something moved under the blanket, burrowing toward her. She was on the verge of bolting from the room when the edge of the blanket lifted and Sam stuck his little head out from under the covers. His eyes were wide with fright and loneliness, and he gave a piteous little cry. Virginia made a comparable sound, half laughter, half whimper of relief, and she knelt by the side of the bed and scratched Sam's head while he purred like a lawn mower.

"Aw, Sam," she said. "Oh honey."

OR THE NEXT WEEK, NOTHING OUT OF THE ordinary happened, no twisters in the living room, no linens with a will of their own, no freezing drafts in the Texas heat. A couple of times Virginia got the creeps of her own accord, and spent the night on the couch, with the windows closed and Sam purring beside her. But after a few days, she began to wonder if she'd imagined the entire thing. There was still Karswell's outrageous attempt to steal the credit for her paper—she hadn't imagined that—but going over the conversation in her mind, she couldn't remember him actually threatening her with anything other than removing the paper from the volume. After the term began, she'd call the press and find out what was going on.

In the meantime, Virginia had classes to prepare for the fall semester. One afternoon in late August, she went in to campus, telling herself that it was no big deal, while steeling herself for an accidental encounter with Karswell. She was determined not to show him any anxiety, but she didn't have to worry. Everyone had left town for the semester break; she was the only person in the building apart from a bored work/study student sorting the mail in the departmental office. In her own office, Virginia sat with the door closed for a while, typing her syllabi on her computer, and halfway through the first one, she got up and opened the door. She wasn't sure what made her more anxious—bracing herself for an encounter or pretending she didn't care—but either way, she couldn't bear to have the door closed. But with the blinds open to the late-August glare and the door open to the fluorescent lights of the hallway, soon her keyboard was clattering happily, and she found herself actually wishing that Karswell would walk past and see her in her shorts and sandals and T-shirt, fingers flying.

When the syllabi were finished, Virginia took them up to the department office to have them copied. The work/study student was hunched at the computer at the reception desk, nursing a Big Gulp and playing Doom. Virginia stood behind the girl and cleared her throat, but apparently the student couldn't hear her over the reverberating blast of gunfire and the squeals of dying aliens. Finally, as a hooved monster rushed the screen, hurling orange fireballs, Virginia tapped the girl on her tense shoulder, and she started violently in her chair, nearly overturning the Big Gulp in her lap.

"God!" she cried. "Don't do that!"

"I was only wondering," Virginia said, "if you could make copies of these."

"Right now?" the girl said. She didn't look at Virginia; she was trying to right her drink and save herself from the satyr, which was slashing at the screen with its claws.

"I'm already up to the toxin refinery," she added, glancing frantically over her shoulder at Virginia.

"Whenever," Virginia said.

As shotgun fire rang out and something inhuman shrieked, Virginia pulled her mail out of her box and left.

The sun felt good after the building's arctic AC, and a humid Gulf Coast breeze wrapped itself around her like steam. As she walked slowly across the plaza, Virginia sorted through her mail, sticking the items to keep under one arm and items to toss under the other. At the bottom of the stack were a letter and a colorful flier on blue paper, the sort faculty regularly got from local copy shops. As she recognized Chip's handwriting on the envelope, she broke stride, nearly stumbling, the loose toe of her sandal catching on a crack in the hot pavement. She stopped and held the letter for a moment, pursing her lips, then wedged it under her arm with the stuff to discard, and she started forward again toward the corner of the plaza, where she was about to pass under the knife-wielding statue of Jim Bowie.

"Asshole," she muttered.

Under the statue she slowed to toss Chip's letter and the other discards into a trash can, and she glanced at the copy-shop flier still in her hand. The half-sheet of blue paper was blank, so she turned it over to see what was on the other side.

Virginia froze. She glimpsed the name "John Harrington" and a date, and the light seemed to fade. She glanced up wildly, and above the looming figure of Jim Bowie, his knife poised to pierce the sky, she saw a single, gray-bottomed cloud floating before the sun, out of an otherwise flawlessly blue sky. A gray shadow slid over the campus, cutting the glare off the plaza and the stuccoed buildings all around and chilling Virginia, raising goose bumps off her bare arms.

"Such a tough lady," someone said.

Virginia looked down and sucked in her breath, and the leathery, sunbleached homeless guy who'd spoken to her on the street the week before stepped out from behind the statue and smiled at her. Instinctively she stepped back, and as she did, a hand—a hot, rough hand—snatched the blue flier out of her grasp from behind her.

"Hey!" she said, and whirled.

The plaza was empty; no one stood behind her. She whirled again, her heart pounding. She expected to see, in order, the grinning homeless guy, Beverly glowering at her from under her bangs, Karswell peering at her through his pince-nez. But the homeless guy was gone. There was no one in sight.

Virginia backed away from the statue, and she turned a complete circuit in short, frantic jerks, looking all around her, but there was no one else on the plaza, not another soul to be seen in any direction. She glanced down, hoping to see the flier scudding across the pavement like a leaf before the warm breeze, and then up, expecting to see it floating in the breeze above her. But it was nowhere to be seen. As she looked up, the cloud passed from before the sun, releasing the plaza from shadow. Jim Bowie was bathed in bright sunlight, making him gleam.

By the time she got home, she was furious. Her answering machine was blinking when she came in the door, and she hit the button, waiting impatiently as it rewound through five messages. The first one was Chip, and the first thing he said was "Good news, sweetheart, I sold the pilot." She cut him off and fast-forwarded to the next message, which was Beverly, in her breathy little voice, simply saying, "Please call me." The next three calls were from Beverly as well, each one an escalation of the previous message.

"You really should give me a call."

"Virginia, you *need* to call me."

"If you don't call me, I can't be responsible for the consequences."

Virginia turned to her desk and retrieved Beverly's number. Then she dialed it, getting only Beverly's machine. The beep seemed to take forever to come, and Sam wandered in while Virginia waited, stopping to sit at her feet and gaze up at her. Virginia clutched the phone tightly, tapping her feet.

"Listen, lady," Virginia said when the beep came at last, "I don't know who was responsible for that little stunt on the plaza this afternoon, whether it was Karswell or you or maybe even the two of you, but if you think you're going to scare me into joining your creepy little vendetta, lady, well, you've got . . . you've got a lot of fucking nerve is all I've got to say. Don't call me again. Don't show up on my doorstep anymore either. Don't leave me any books, don't send me postcards, don't e-mail me, don't send me any flowers or candygrams or singing gorillas. Just stay the hell away from me, because *I am tired of this shit!*"

Virginia slammed the phone down. She looked down at the cat, who crouched, ears back, ready to flee. The phone rang with her hand still on it, and she snatched it up and barked, "What?"

"Ginny?" Chip said.

"And the same goes for you too, jerk!" she shouted, and slammed the phone down again. Sam dashed from the room, diving around the corner toward the bedroom. Virginia unplugged the phone.

HE SEMESTER BEGAN, AND THE CAMPUS WAS crowded again with undergraduates. There were noontime rallies on the plaza, fraternities blasting classic rock out open windows, and every other Saturday, home games of the Fighting Longhorns. Virginia could hear the game from her front porch: the electronic crackle of the announcer, the tattoo of the marching band, and the Longhorn fans mooing at the opposing team, the whole stadium lowing like a stockyard.

For Virginia, there were classes to teach, meetings to attend, colleagues to run into at the copy machine. Virginia was a lively and popular teacher whose classes usually had a waiting list, and this semester she threw herself into teaching more vigorously than usual, taking extra care. Right up until the first day of class, she revised her lectures, adding new readings in the reserve room of the library. She had always taken a covert pleasure in the way her authority made her attractive, striding across the front of her classroom in cowboy boots and jeans, a dangling pair of earrings catching the light, and now she made an extra effort, wearing a little discreet makeup and a dash of perfume, doing a little gender construction of her own. Though she never encouraged it, she was not averse to one or two of her slacker undergraduates developing a harmless crush on her each semester. What was the harm in having some nineteen-year-old boy in baggy shorts and a baseball cap slouch diffidently in her office door, trying to think of questions to ask her?

But no matter what she did this semester, all of her students, women and men, slouched in their seats, doodled in their notebooks, propped their heads in their hands and dozed. No one asked any questions, no one volunteered any answers to hers. No one came to her office hours, no one turned papers in on time. She fought it for a few weeks, even to the point of scolding her students, but finally it became wearisome to struggle against their listlessness, and she began to answer her own questions, skip her office hours, let the paper deadlines slide. She reckoned it had to be one of those dud semesters she'd heard about from older professors, when nothing you did would rouse a class to interest.

And after a giddy week or two of reunions at the start of the semester, she found that her colleagues were not much more interested in her company than her students were. To begin with there were invitations to lunch, for drinks, to dinner, to parties, but in the end they never came about. On those rare occasions when she found herself with other people, over lunch or coffee, the conversation never seemed to include her, and at parties she found herself standing in the corner, drink in hand, alone. Some of this, she decided, was due to her friends' awkwardness over her situation. Surely everyone in the department knew that her tenuring was in doubt, and that she and Chip were no longer together. As far as they're concerned, she told herself, I'm just a lame duck with a broken heart. I am invisible.

And yet, in spite of her invisibility, she could not shake the feeling that she was being watched all the time. Even in class, when she *was* being watched, if listlessly, by her students, she had the feeling of someone or something just behind her, looking on intently, who was never there when she turned around. She moved through the halls of the history department half expecting a hand on her shoulder at any moment; she walked across the plaza with the feeling that someone was just about to tread on her heels. At home, she kept the lights on even during the day, buying lightbulbs by the boxful. She locked the bathroom door when she was in the shower, and never drew the shower curtain. She locked the bedroom door at night. To make sure she slept through the night, she put off going to bed until she could scarcely keep her eyes open, ending up asleep on the couch as often as she slept in her bed. Or she took a couple of sleeping pills, which left her feeling muzzy in the morning. At least with the pills she felt as though she could sleep through anything, that not even a grinning demon crouching on her chest could awaken her, but even so, she had bad dreams. Not nightmares, exactly, not enough to wake her in the middle of the night, but dreams that left her even more uneasy in the morning, dreams she could not remember.

In the evenings, she sat in her pajamas at her desk, before the glowing screen of her laptop, and tried to work on her book. But writing was turning out to be as difficult as teaching: she went through the motions, but her heart wasn't in it. Everything that came up on the little screen of her laptop seemed self-evident, unoriginal, useless. The insights that had struck her several months ago as groundbreaking now seemed like the self-important tautologies of an undergraduate. Again and again she typed a sentence, a paragraph, a page, only to read it through in disgust, select the entire passage with her trackball, and delete it with a savage stab of her thumb.

One night in September she sat before the little screen of the laptop, the room dark behind her; for once she had switched off all the lights. She had drawn all the shades but the one above her desk, so that she might refocus her eyes occasionally on the red and blue lights of the pomo skyscrapers downtown. The only light in the room was the purplish, subliminally pulsing glow of the screen, and Virginia lowered her head into her hands in frustration. Something vivid was present, just out of reach of her consciousness; it flitted across her mind, never quite taking shape. Something she thought she already knew, but couldn't remember, and it nagged at her, getting between her and the prose she was trying to write. It was giving her a headache. She sighed and lifted a hand to lower the screen of the laptop, and looked out the window.

A pale face looked back at her through the glass, not three feet away. Virginia yelped and gripped the edge of her desk. The face was oval and white and featureless, and it was worse than merely pale. It was a dead face, but with bright, living eyes that watched her without blinking out of the dark beyond the window.

Sam leaped up on the desk, growling at the face, and Virginia heaved herself back in her chair, rolling all the way across the living-room floor. She bolted into the bedroom, snatched up the aluminum bat, and dashed to the living room again, pulling up short a few feet from her desk, the bat cocked in both hands. The cat still crouched on the desk, his ears back. But now the eyes of the face in the window were dark. In fact, the eyes were gone: she could see the lights of the city skyline through them.

She flicked on the living-room light, turned on the porch light, and, mustering herself, yanked open the front door and stepped onto the porch in her pajamas. She lifted the bat chest high as if she were going to bunt, and glanced around her yard and down the street. But no one was there, only the porch lights and television glow of other houses, and the dappled shadows of the trees under the streetlight. She lowered the bat slightly and moved to the window. The face was a piece of cream-colored construction paper, a featureless oval, with eyeholes cut out of it. It was stuck to the glass simply by the humidity of the evening, and, glancing around once more, Virginia peeled it off the window. She looked on both sides for a message, but there was nothing, only the fibrous grain of the paper. She crumpled it in her fist and hurled it into the yard.

In the morning the crumpled paper was gone. After the bus had dropped Virginia at her stop on Tejas Avenue and she was striding along the Strip toward campus, she saw Beverly Harrington sitting in the front window of a café, her pudgy hands wrapped around a huge cup of coffee. Their eyes met for an instant, and Beverly stirred in her chair. But Virginia looked away and kept walking. From time to time Virginia had seen Beverly lurking about, watching from a distance. Sometimes Virginia saw her in the reference room of the grad library with books propped open all around her, sitting where she could see Virginia coming and going. Sometimes she haunted the history department building, sitting in the lobby and staring into space, or waddling through the press of students at class change, or, once, treading heavily past Virginia's open office door. Every time, Virginia had ignored her.

But now Beverly rapped on the café window as Virginia passed, and in spite of herself, Virginia turned to see Beverly risen half out of her seat, making the little round table wobble dangerously. She was pressing a hand-lettered cardboard sign to the glass. It read, in big, block letters, YOU'RE IN DENIAL.

Virginia stopped short and looked at the sign through the window, from six inches away. She was aware of passersby glancing at her and Beverly, and she felt the heat rising to her cheeks. She met Beverly's eyes, wide and bright, her eyebrows raised. Virginia held the other woman's gaze for a long moment: were these the eyes that had glittered at her through the mask the night before?

She turned abruptly away and marched into the café, into the air-conditioning and the smell of coffee and steamed milk. She stalked through the crowd of students and professors stoking up on caffeine for the morning, while next to the window Beverly busily cleared a space at her table for Virginia, lifting her purse off the other chair, mopping up with a paper napkin the coffee she'd spilled. A couple of students, a boy and a girl, shambled into Virginia's path, but the boy caught sight of her face and jumped back, pulling the girl out of the way. Beverly sat at her little table and beamed up at Virginia's approach, but Virginia reached past her, picked the sign up off the floor next to her chair, and tore it in half. She tossed it on the table before Beverly, and then turned on her heel and stalked out.

*"You need me!"* Beverly called, but Virginia was already swinging out the door, the back of her neck a flaming red.

She mentioned this incident to no one. In fact, she mentioned none of it to anyone. Who would care? Who would believe her? She scarcely believed it herself. For the next few weeks she continued to go through the motions, soldiering on through her own life as if playing a part: the committed teacher, the hardworking scholar, the casualty of love with a stiff upper lip. But privately she felt like some neurasthenic heroine from a nineteenth-century novel: *The Yellow Wallpaper,* starring Virginia Dunning. This is depression, she told herself, nothing more. I've lost my lover, I'm in danger of losing my job, and a powerful man has threatened my professional reputation, with or without the collusion of a crazy woman. That's enough to make anyone feel hunted, she thought, it's got nothing to do with the occult. She refused to give Karswell the satisfaction of believing that he'd put the whammy on her.

Another month passed. One cool afternoon in mid-October, Virginia came home to find a thick padded envelope on her porch, with a local postmark, addressed in block letters with a black felt-tip pen. It was the sort of envelope books come in, but squeezing it between both hands, it didn't feel like a book to Virginia. Rather, it was square, with sharp edges. For some reason, she didn't want to take it into the house, so she set down her briefcase and tore the envelope open on the porch, spilling gray padding on her shoes. It was a square block of pages, a word-a-day calendar for the current year. The first word, on January 1, was:

> **recalcitrant** (ri kal' si trent) *adj.*  **1** refusing to obey authority; stubbornly defiant  **2** hard to handle or deal with

Virginia flipped through the calendar with her thumb, wondering if Karswell was casting more runes on her, but there was nothing on each page but the date, the day of the week, and another word. She glimpsed words in passing—"mezzotint," "tractate," "antiquary"—and turned the calendar over in her hands. Oddly, some pages had been torn off already, not from the beginning of the calendar, but from the rear of it, at the end of the year. She peeled back the bottom page, and saw that the last date remaining was November 18, three months to the day from her last meeting with Karswell. The word for the day was:

> **moribund** (mor'i bund') *adj.*  **1** dying  **2** coming to an end  **3** having little or no vital force left

Everything after that was ripped out.

Virginia felt a twinge between her shoulder blades, as if someone were right behind her, and she turned abruptly. But there was no one, only that unshakable sense she carried with her always that she was being watched. The calendar wearied her more than it frightened her, though. There was no publishing information on any of the pages, and Virginia supposed that Karswell had had it printed up—"Victor Karswell's Satanic Word-a-Day Calendar." She stuffed it back in the padded envelope, carried it around to the side of her house by two fingers like a dead rat, and tossed it in the garbage. Then she marched back to the porch, picked up her brief-case, glanced once more up and down the street, and went inside, slamming the door behind her.

That night she hardly slept at all. Her heart began to pound whenever she closed her eyes. This whole situation was insane; she wasn't sure she could stand much more of it. Whether he had oc-cult powers or not, whether something spooky was going on or just a viciously sophisticated campaign of psychological warfare, Kars-well was getting to her. She lay with her head on the pillow and stared at the ceiling, and in spite of herself could not help but think of the calendar with the last month and a half of the year ripped out, the last date three months to the day from her meeting with Karswell. And of course that reminded her of the message she had seen on the side of the bus that very day: *John Harrington. Three months were allowed.* Which led her back to the strange story that his widow had told her.

If she is his widow, Virginia thought, thrashing about in her lonely bed. But then I called *her*, she thought, and only after Eliz-abeth gave me her number. So if Beverly is working with Karswell, then Elizabeth is working with them too, which means this whole thing could go back *as far as graduate school.* . . .

"This is nuts," she said aloud, clutching a pillow to her chest. I'm doing Karswell's work for him, she thought. This is what he wants me to think. He wants me to doubt everyone and everything. He wants to isolate me, to cut me off from the rest of the world.

She groaned in the dark. There was only one way out of this, only one way to make it all stop. Elizabeth had been right that first day: it was still a man's world, whether Virginia liked it or not. And in the end, she really had nothing to lose. Karswell, for all his in-fluence, was on his way down. And she was on her way up. Was one lousy paper worth all this anxiety and estrangement from everything she held dear? How much different was Karswell's suggestion, really, from an act of mentoring? Wasn't this the way the academic game was played?

She closed her eyes and breathed deeply. Sleep was coming now, she could feel it. She had decided: tomorrow she would go in to the department office and make an appointment to see Karswell. She was going to give him what he wanted.

## twelve

HE NEXT MORNING, VIRGINIA WENT IN TO campus in the longest skirt she owned, and she marched up to Karswell's office on the floor above hers and knocked on the door. But there was no answer, and the door was locked. She felt a chill at her ankles, and glanced down to see the hem of her skirt trembling in a cold draft blowing steadily out through the gap between the carpet and the bottom of Karswell's door. Some trick of the airflow sent the freezing draft up her skirt as far as her knees, and Virginia jumped back across the hall. Only then did she notice a neatly typed note on an index card, taped to the door.

"Professor Karswell is on sabbatical for the fall semester," it read. "All inquiries and correspondence to the department office."

"Did he leave a forwarding address?" Virginia asked the secretary in the department office, who pointed silently beyond her desk to a cardboard box along the wall, where Karswell's mail was piling up. Another neatly lettered sign taped to the box read, "Lufford Abbey, Warwickshire, UK."

"They keep sending it back," said the secretary, sounding pleased. "The post office in Warwick," she went on, fastidiously not pronouncing the second W, "says there's no such place."

"When's he coming back?" Virginia said, trying to sound casual.

"After Christmas," said the secretary, with a tone of secret satisfaction. "Not till winter term."

"I have to reach him," Virginia said. "It's vitally important."

"Mm." The secretary inclined her head and let her gaze wander. It was the look she used for all her professors, for whom every request was vitally important. "Of course it is. But *I* don't even know where he is. And I know where *everybody* is."

"Did everybody else know he was gone?" Virginia's knees were wobbling. "Why didn't anyone tell me?"

"I'm sure I don't know." The secretary twined her fingers and gave Virginia a look of wide-eyed sympathy, like a child from a Keane painting. "The fact is, not many people have been asking for him."

She glanced to either side and leaned forward.

"Just between you and me, Professor Dunning," she whispered, "Professor Karswell is not particularly well liked."

Virginia found herself in a daze for much of the day. If Karswell was gone, if he was not even in Texas, how could he have been orchestrating his campaign against her? Who had sent her the calendar if he wasn't here? And who had pasted the mask against her window? Whose eyes had looked through the mask at her? No doubt Beverly Harrington would have answers to all of these questions, but Virginia didn't want to hear them. She wasn't sure her nerves could take it. What had happened to Beverly was very sad, but grief had clearly driven the woman crazy, even crazier than Karswell. Virginia had no intention of joining them.

October turned into November. The days shortened, the nights grew longer, and even the Texas sky grew darker. More than two months had passed since Karswell had handed her manuscript back to her. Whoever or whatever was watching Virginia seemed to be coming closer. At times—alone at home, or crossing the plaza, or even standing before her class—she felt an icy breath at the back of her neck, or a stirring of the air just out of the corner of her eye, as if something had passed close by. Once, walking up the hall with her mail, she felt a touch on her shoulder, and she whirled to see no one. "Three months were allowed," the sign on the bus had said, and there were less than three weeks left. Until what? she wondered.

One evening in early November, Virginia stayed late in her campus office, long after classes had ended for the day. Seated before her desktop computer, she hadn't noticed that twilight had descended. A wedge of fluorescent light fell through her open door from the hallway, and the amber lamps around the plaza were just coming on, casting the gliding shadows of a few students on their way to the library and coloring the ceiling tiles above Virginia's head. Otherwise the office was lit only by the firefly glow of her computer screen. She had called up a chapter of her manuscript to pass the time during office hours, to which none of her students came any longer.

She'd been sitting without moving for a very long time, her fingers growing stiff on the keyboard. She could scarcely bring herself to read the chapter, let alone try to revise it. Looking up at last, she noticed the shadows gathering in the corners of her office, and she angled her watch into the glow of the screen. It was later than she'd thought. Everybody else on her hall had probably gone home a couple of hours ago. And not a single one, she thought, had stopped in the door to say good night.

She turned to the computer. No point in hanging around, she decided, and she reached for the mouse and closed down WordPerfect. She expected to see the program manager screen, but was surprised when a glossy black screen popped up instead, with the words "click here" highlighted in red at the center. Virginia lifted her finger off the mouse. She was looking at her Web browser, she realized, with its little perpetual rain of meteors in the corner. Somehow she had gotten online, which puzzled her; she got so little e-mail these days that she scarcely ever signed on. Moreover, she seemed to be connected already to someone's odd home page, though there was no Web address across the top.

Virginia slid the pointer to the words in red. The office was very quiet. No sound came from the hallway, or from the plaza outside. She sighed.

"Now what?" she said, and clicked on the words.

A black-and-white picture sprang into view, a full-screen image of an old woodcut, something (she guessed) from the seventeenth or eighteenth century. At the same moment her eye was distracted by two little red lights popping up to either side of the computer. The speakers had just switched on.

She reached for the mouse again, but moving it had no effect on the screen; the little pointer had disappeared. She clicked a couple of times and nothing happened, and she pursed her lips at the illustration on the screen. The woodcut was primitive but vivid, showing a woman in Puritan dress, with a little cap and buckled shoes and tightly laced doublet, walking down a shadowy lane on a moonless night. The woman, the dirt track, and the gnarled old trees along the lane were etched in blunt lines, while the darkness all around—the night sky, the gloom under the trees—was filled in with thin hatching. Yet even the woodcut's crude technique was able to evoke the strong emotion on the woman's face, her eyes wide, gazing straight ahead as if her life depended on it. There was something about the woman's expression that suggested that she didn't want to look back. Behind her, though, the road appeared to be empty.

A low hiss rose out of the speakers, sounding to Virginia like the wind in the trees at night.

"All right," she said, clicking the mouse again, "very funny."

She glanced over her shoulder at the open doorway, certain she was going to catch someone standing there—Beverly, perhaps, or the homeless guy, or even Karswell himself. But no one was there, and looking back at the screen she had the feeling that the picture had changed. She couldn't be sure, but the woman's head seemed to have turned. Now her eyes were swiveled to the side, glancing back over her shoulder. Something else seemed different behind the woman, a change in the shadow under one of the trees, but Virginia was even less sure of that. The hissing of the speakers seemed to swell and recede.

"That's enough," Virginia said.

Clicking rapidly didn't do anything, so she hunted up the escape key, pressing it firmly with her index finger. She looked at the screen. The woodcut was still there, but the image had changed again. The woman was looking forward once more, though perhaps her eyes were even wider than they had been. The shadow under the tree behind her seemed to have shifted again, somehow.

"Okay," she said loudly. "I get it. All right already."

She held the escape key down again, glancing back at the open door and then toward the amber glow out her window. The room seemed to fill with the soughing of leaves, and Virginia jumped up, sending her chair rolling back. She closed the office door and locked it, then bent over the desk while she hunted for the keys she wanted.

"Stop it," she said, her hands trembling over the keyboard. "Stop it, stop it, stop it."

She found the three keys she needed and pressed them all at once—Ctrl, Alt, Del—then released them and pressed them again. She glanced at the screen. The woman's head had turned once more, and this time she was looking directly out of the screen, her eyes round with terror, her mouth open as if she were beseeching Virginia. Behind her, stepping out into the lane from the darkness under the tree, a cloven hoof was just visible.

Virginia hit the computer's power button. But the hard drive continued to hum, the screen stayed lit, and out of the hissing speakers, a man's voice began to intone, rising above the leafy sibilance:

> Like one, that on a lonesome road,
> Doth walk in fear and dread . . .

Virginia jumped back, and the keyboard clattered off the desk, swinging by its cord. She dropped to her knees and dived under the desk, batting the keyboard aside and rooting in the dark with both hands, banging her head. The voice was filling the room.

> . . . And having once turned round walks on,
> And turns no more her head;
> Because she knows, a frightful fiend
> Doth close behind her tread.

Virginia found the plug and yanked it out with both hands. The voice stopped, and the light went out. Kneeling under the desk and clutching the cord, she heard the diminishing whine of the hard drive running down.

But the sound of the wind in the leaves remained. The space under the desk was too narrow to turn around in, but Virginia glanced from side to side. She could see nothing, not even the faintest glow of light from the plaza.

I've been staring at a screen, she told herself. My eyes need to adapt to the dark.

She dropped the cord and backed out from the under the desk, the tile cool and gritty under her palms. She felt the keyboard drag against her back, and she put her hands on the edge of the desk and stood. The soughing of the trees seemed to come from all around her now, and she felt a chill breeze blowing from behind, pressing her skirt against her calves. She turned from the desk to the window, but she still could see nothing. The darkness was absolute.

Power failure, she told herself. I must have pulled the plug on the entire university. She groped across the office toward the window, both her hands out in front of her. She walked carefully, afraid of tripping over her chair, but after a few steps she had not brushed into anything. She walked a few more steps, her heels clicking against the tile, extending her arms out as far as she could reach, but there was nothing there.

The wind was blowing from her left now, tightening the skin of her cheek. Over the wind she heard her own rapid breathing, and the deep pounding of her own pulse.

"Hello?" she called. "Who's there?" And was alarmed to hear her voice swallowed up in the darkness, with none of the flat reverb of her office walls. She might as well have been standing out of doors, in a vast, open space.

She turned and walked blindly back toward her desk, her chin lifted, patting the air before her with her palms. But she walked well past where the desk ought to have been, and decided to count her steps as a way to fight her panic. Counting only made it worse, though, and she got to thirty paces before she gave it up and broke into a trot, holding her arms up before her chest. Her steps sounded blunter now; she was no longer running on tile. The ground was rough and uneven, and her feet stumbled over lumps and hollows, threatening to twist her ankles. She started to run on the balls of her feet, to keep from catching her heels. A tiny, whimpering sound matched the frantic rhythm of her breath.

That's me, she thought. That's me making that sound.

The toe of Virginia's shoe caught on something yielding but tough, and she sprawled forward, landing on her face, knocking the breath out of her. The ground was cold and rough, and she gave herself a moment to catch her breath, then pushed herself up on her hands and knees. There was grass and dirt under her palms.

She pulled her legs under her, crouching, slapping the dirt off her hands. Her breath was shallow and rasping, and she glanced vainly about her, trying see something, anything, in the pitch darkness, if only the silhouette of a tree swaying against the sky. But there was nothing to see. There was only the wind blowing full in her face, and the rushing of the unseen branches.

Then there was a thump against the ground, some distance away in the windy darkness. Virginia held her breath and listened. It sounded like an apple falling. Then there was another thump, from the same direction. No, she thought, heavier than an apple, a stone maybe. Then another thump, and this time it didn't sound like something falling, but like a step, like something weighty but narrow hitting the ground. Like a hoof.

Virginia sucked in her breath and clapped her hand over her mouth. There were two more thumps, then another, getting closer, coming from the same direction as the wind. They sounded like the thudding footfalls of a horse, but the pace was wrong. They didn't move with the rhythm of four feet, but with the rhythm of two.

Virginia bit her lip to keep from crying out. Propping herself on the knuckles of one hand, she pulled off one shoe and then the other, clutching them together. The thumping footfalls came a little more steadily toward her, though still tentatively. Virginia hardly dared to breathe, though even now, a little voice wondered what "blacking out" would mean exactly in this situation. On the edge of hysteria, she giggled and caught her breath, and the hooves began to move faster in her direction.

Virginia shot to her feet and flung one shoe as hard as she could, off to her left, into the wind. She heard it thud against the ground, not as far away as she would have liked. But the hooves hesitated and then began to trot toward the sound of the shoe, *thump thump thump*. Virginia, still holding her other shoe and breathing silently through her open mouth, began to back slowly away in the other direction.

And froze again at a new sound, from the same direction as the hooves. The footfalls stopped, and she heard a long, deep hiss with something guttural to it, like a grunt. Virginia held her breath. Then the hooves started up again, coming downwind, toward Virginia. She flung the other shoe wildly, then yanked her skirt up to her waist in one fist and shot off in the opposite direction as fast as she could run.

The wind was at her back, breathing icily on the nape of her neck, and she ran with long strides, her heels pounding the ground, her elbow working. Her blood beat in her ears, her breath rasped even louder than the oceanic roar of the trees. For an instant she was exhilarated, as if she were running a race she could win, and she nearly shouted. But behind her she heard the narrow, thudding impact of hooves, two of them, coming down the wind, faster and faster. Their stride was not as long as hers, but they came very quickly, *thump thump thump thump*, gaining on her.

She lifted her knees and ran harder, pumping her elbows, pushing herself. Each impact of her heel against the ground jolted through her spine to the top of her head, and the soles of her feet stung with stones and twigs. The trees around her rushed like waves on the shore, and she thought, I'm going to catch myself on a root, I'm going to bang my head on a low branch.

The hooves behind her were very quick now, *thump thump thump thump thump*, getting closer. I can't run any faster, Virginia thought. This is as fast as I can go. Her heart hammered against her breastbone, a painful stitch stabbed between her ribs, her heels stung with sharp stones. Tears squeezed out of the corners of her eyes and whipped away into the dark. The hooves were just behind her now, taking longer strides. *Thump. Thump. Thump.* A current of disturbed air brushed her ear. She heard that awful grunt again, a deep expelling of air, just behind her head. She felt a hot breath on the back of her neck.

"Kuh," she said, or tried to. She hadn't the breath for speech, but she tried anyway.

"Kuh, Kuh, Karswell!" she rasped. "You son of a *bitch!*"

And then she slammed, at full speed, into a wall.

## thirteen

IRGINIA OPENED HER EYES TO THE FEATURE-
less silhouette of a man leaning toward her out of a vividly bright
light.

"Does this hurt?" the figure said, and touched her nose.

The pain was immense. Virginia screamed and passed out.

When she awoke again, she was on a gurney in the pastel hallway of an emergency room, her head throbbing. There was a weird
numbness at the center of her face, where her nose should have
been. She tried to sit up, and a hand on her shoulder steadied her,
helping her to sit with her legs dangling off the gurney.

"You're full of painkillers," said a small voice, breathy and high-
pitched. "Don't do anything stupid."

"Bevahly?" Virginia said. Her voice seemed to come from somewhere else.

The hand released her shoulder, and Beverly's large, round,
shiny face swung into view.

"*Now* will you listen to me?" she said.

"What happened?" Virginia said, but it came out, *Whuh hap ed?*

She felt as though she were peering out of a mask. She heard herself breathing through her mouth.

"A janitor found you on your office floor." Beverly narrowed her
eyes. She smiled. "Seems you ran into the door."

"I broke my nose?" *I bwoke by dose?*

"No, but you banged it up pretty badly."

Virginia lifted her hand to touch her face, and Beverly snatched her wrist.

"Don't touch it!" she snapped. "Are you nuts?"

The events of the evening were coming back to Virginia, and she was doing her best not to believe them. She pulled her wrist out of Beverly's grasp.

"How do you think that's possible?" Beverly said, her eyes alight. "That a person could get up enough speed in an eight-by-fifteen-foot office that she could knock herself senseless running into the door? You tell me."

Virginia looked away. She had an unavoidable urge to look in a mirror.

"That son of a bitch," she muttered. *Dat sud ob a bits.*

"I can't understand a word you're saying, dear," Beverly said, crossing her arms and smiling as she would at a willful child. "But last time we spoke on this subject, I believe you told me it was all the power of suggestion."

"That *bastard*," Virginia said, looking away.

"Well, what are you going to do about it?"

Virginia shot a glance at Beverly.

"I'll press charges," she snapped. "I'll report him to the dean."

"The deed?"

"The *dean.*" Virginia felt no pain, but her nose buzzed a little. "The dee-nah."

"And what are you going to tell him?" Beverly said, repressing a smile. "That Karswell made you walk into a wall? That he caused a cyclone in your living room? That he made your sheets attack you?"

Virginia glared at Beverly. Not only was Beverly treating her like a child, but she was beginning to feel like one, frustrated and ashamed. She wanted to smash something, but instead she gripped the edge of the gurney and squeezed. She could hear herself breathing through her mouth. She sounded like Darth Vader.

"What do *you* think I should do?"

Beverly beamed. Her face lost its sickly sheen, as if a spotlight had fallen on her. Her eyes shone. For an instant, she looked like the woman she claimed to have been before she had swollen up with grief and rage. Virginia was afraid she was going to start singing. Instead, she laid her hands on Virginia's shoulders, her lower lip trembling with emotion. There were tears in her eyes.

"All right." Virginia patted her hand. "It's all right."

Beverly sniffled and stepped away, and she lifted her immense bag off a chair along the wall, rooting in it until she came up with another copy of Karswell's history of witchcraft. The spine was broken, and little strips of paper stuck out of the top of the book.

"I don't suppose you ever looked at the copy I gave you," she said.

Her face looked thick and shiny again, and she peered at Virginia with a frightening intensity. Virginia shook her head.

"Well, I have," she said, opening the book to one of the strips of paper and clutching it to her ample bosom. "I know this monstrous little book by heart, but I won't bore you with the details. The upshot is, you have to give the runes back to him, and he has to take them willingly. You have to give them to him personally, on the same physical object that he gave to you. I can't give it to him for you. Nobody else can. He has to take it from your hand. You can't mail it to him, you can't photocopy it, you can't fax it or e-mail it or slip it under his door."

As Beverly went on, Virginia became aware for the first time that they were in a public place. She looked up the hall and saw a nurse and a doctor in green scrubs conferring over a clipboard. Beyond them she saw a long, brightly lit room partitioned off with curtains, and through the buzzing in her head she heard the incoherent chatter of a public address system.

"Beverly," she said, reaching out to touch Beverly's hand, interrupting her. "I'm not afraid."

"What?" Beverly said. "Are you listening to me?"

"No, really," insisted Virginia. "I don't feel afraid anymore."

She pushed herself off the gurney, forcing Beverly to back up. She was unsteady, but once she gripped the edge of the gurney she was able to stand. She looked up and down the hall, the sheer presence of the place and the vividness of her situation flooding in on her. She was in a public place with a huge bandage over her nose, blood on her sweater, and a fat woman staring at her from two feet away, but the feeling of being watched had vanished. A gasping, white-faced man swaddled in a wheelchair rolled by, pushed by a broad-shouldered orderly, and Virginia watched them pass without a trace of anxiety. Just hours before she would have been desperate to know why the man was gasping, wondering what had made him fight for breath, and she would have been certain that whatever the man had seen, it was standing right behind her, its predatory gaze focused at the tight spot between her shoulder blades. Perhaps it was the drugs they'd given her, but Virginia's back felt loose for the first time in months. Except for Beverly, no one was paying any attention to her. The shadow between her and the rest of the world had lifted.

"It's gone!" Virginia laughed, and she reached out and clutched the top of the book in Beverly's hands. "I'm not afraid!"

"Of course not!" hissed Beverly, jerking the book away from Virginia. "I *told* you this would happen. That was just how John felt in the last ten days before he died. The blackness lifts, you no longer feel hunted. And then, after ten days, you die."

"That's absurd," Virginia said, laughing. "That's just—"

"Paranoia?" Beverly stepped closer, only inches away. She was close enough to smell, if Virginia could have smelled anything.

"Think about what's happened to you in the last three months," she hissed. "Unless you think you've been hallucinating all this time, do you really think it can't start up again? Just like that?"

She snapped her fingers.

"Because even if you don't believe it," Beverly went on, "Karswell does. He knows exactly what he's done to you. As far as he's concerned, *you're already dead.*"

Beverly stepped back, clutching Karswell's little red-backed book to her bosom. Virginia's laughter died, and she watched her own thoughts as if they belonged to someone else. She was suddenly aware that her reason and her heart had changed places. For the last three months, her heart had told her she was in grave danger, while her head had told her it was all a bad dream. Now it was the

other way around. She sighed, her feeling of hopelessness returning.

"Karswell will never let me get near him," she said, her energy
draining away. "And even if I did, he'd never take anything from
me."

"Of course he won't," Beverly said. "Don't be stupid."

"So ten days from now," Virginia said wearily, "I'm going to fall
out of a tree and break my neck."

Even under the influence of drugs, Virginia regretted this last
remark, but Beverly didn't seem to have heard.

"None of these curses is ironclad," Beverly said, scowling at the
book. "There's always a way to reverse them, if you know what it
is."

Beverly gave a weird little smile.

"He has to take the runes from you," she whispered, "but *he
doesn't have to know it's you*, and *he doesn't have to know what you're
handing him.*"

"I don't understand."

"You'll have to disguise yourself."

Virginia groaned.

"Listen to me!" Beverly said gleefully. As she spoke, she stuffed
Karswell's book into her purse and dug for something else.

"You're tall and thin and slim-hipped," she went on, hauling out
a tape measure, "and your boobies aren't very big."

"My *boobies?*" said Virginia.

"Plus you've got sun damage on your face, some wrinkles around
the eyes which will come in very handy—"

"Wrinkles!" In spite of herself, Virginia lifted her hands to her
temples. "What wrinkles?"

"You could easily wear one of John's old suits," Beverly said, lifting Virginia's arm and taking its length as deftly as a tailor. "I'll have
to take in the cuffs a bit, but he had very narrow shoulders. . . ."

"You're not suggesting," Virginia said, "you don't seriously
think . . ."

Beverly dropped to her knees and started taking Virginia's outside leg.

"We'll dye your hair," she said. "A little spirit gum and a neatly trimmed beard . . ."

She lifted her moon face to Virginia.

"Raise your skirt, dear. I need to take your inseam."

Virginia jumped back, pulling her skirt tight against her calves.

"You're nuts!" she cried. "No one would believe me! Especially Karswell."

Beverly sat back on her knees, the tape in her lap.

"Not unless you *want* him to," she said, her eyes bright.

She lifted her eyes to the ceiling and quoted from memory.

" 'The notion that there is an 'innate' and 'natural' physicality to gender is fundamentally an essentialist notion. All categories of social order, be they class, race, or gender, are social constructions. All gender is performance.' "

She smiled wickedly.

"I've been reading your dissertation. Godawful prose, but I got the point."

"Now wait a minute," stammered Virginia. "Just hold on. You're oversimplifying a sophisticated theoretical position—"

"Oh, can it." Beverly flipped a hand dismissively. "Save it for your tenure committee. Where's my purse?"

Virginia nudged the black bag across the floor with her foot, careful to stay out of Beverly's reach.

"Beverly," Virginia said, speaking as slowly and clearly as she could, "it would never work. I don't even know where he is."

Beverly had plunged her arm into the bag up to the elbow and was rummaging with a rumbling and crunching sound, spilling pens and paper clips, a Chap Stick and crumpled tissues, a grease pencil.

"Ah, but I do!" she said, lifting her eyes to the ceiling and concentrating. "At least, I know where he's going to be. Ah *hah!*"

Beverly pulled her arm free, a postage stamp sticking to her skin. She dropped the purse. She held a little crumpled booklet.

"He'll be *here* in five days," she said, and she smoothed the booklet and handed it up to Virginia.

It was the program for an upcoming conference, glossy and expensive, with a graphic featuring an old engraving of a brutish

Hawaiian chieftain wielding a nasty wooden club, juxtaposed with a modern black-and-white photograph of a skull. The title page read:

"Captains" and "Cannibals": The Cultural Constructions
of the Death of Captain Cook
A conference at the University of the Midwest
Hamilton Groves, Minnesota
November 14–16, 199-

Virginia's heart sank: Midwestern was her alma mater.

"Now I'm sure it'll never work," she said. "I got my doctorate there. Half the history department knows what I look like."

"Not if you don't *want* them to," Beverly said. "Not if you're properly *motivated*. Help me up."

Virginia held out her hand and planted her feet and hauled Beverly upright. Beverly, panting, took the conference program and opened it.

"What you need," she said breathlessly, "is an incentive."

She held up the open program and pointed to one of the events on the schedule. Virginia peered at the page. Heat rose up the back of her neck. She took the program from Beverly and read the listing for one of the seminars on Saturday afternoon, the second day of the conference:

1–2:30 p.m.
Lecture Rm. A, Harbour Hall
"The Missionary Position: The Franciscan Construction of
    Rapanui Gender, 1862–1936," paper presented by Dr.
    Victor Karswell, Longhorn State University. Discussion.

For the first time a throbbing pain spread out from Virginia's nose and reached around her head, clasping her like a pair of giant hands. The words in the program listing seemed to burn as red as the runes on the draft of her paper. Which Karswell was about to give as his own, six days from now.

Virginia's hands shook. She looked up at Beverly, speechless.

"I told you," Beverly said. "As far as he's concerned, you're already dead."

Virginia drew a deep breath, and she let it out slowly. Then she lowered the program.

"What do I have to do?" she said.

# fourteen

AMILTON GROVES, MINNESOTA, WAS A
center of the universe, a station of the cross in the progress of
groovy academia. Two or three generations of scholars, stretching roughly from Marcuse to Foucault, all danced to more or less
the same tune—that the point is not simply to understand the
world, but to change it—the same people trading the same positions at the same institutions, moving from Madison to Berkeley
to Ann Arbor to Hamilton Groves in a game of musical chairs.
But over the years "the whole world is watching" had boiled down
to one's tenure committee, the cramped and filthy communal
kitchen had been privatized into a Williams-Sonoma showroom,
and the monthly anxiety of the Guaranteed Student Loan had ma-
tured into the padded comfort of TIAA-CREF. Still, walking
across the Quad at the center of Midwestern's campus, surrounded
by several generations of institutional architecture—forties colle-
giate gothic, sixties steel-and-glass Mondrian, nineties pomo pastiche—you could almost, if the wind was right, catch the whiff of
tear gas drifting through the maples, hear the furious chants of
"Attica! Attica!" from the steps of the grad library, or spy the devilish glow of a burning ROTC building against the dour Minnesota sky.

The sky today was especially grim, a sliding, slate-gray ceiling
driven by a freezing wind out of Manitoba, a sky that spat, in
stages, a needling rain, sleet, and finally snow the consistency of a

Slurpee. It was, noted the conference wags, just the weather required to make one long for the subtropical afternoon when Captain James Cook had been hacked to death by angry Hawaiians. One of the hottest controversies in the history and anthropology of the Pacific was the interpretation of that event: had Cook's attackers mistaken him for Lono, their god of renewal, as argued by Joseph "Joe" Brody, a blustering, profane old Irishman, the warhorse of Wisconsin State's famous anthropology department? Or was his death the justifiable response of a soon-to-be-colonial people to the first advance man of imperialism, as argued by Brody's former grad student, Stanley Tulafale, a dignified, eloquent, and massive Samoan, the force of whose intellect was matched only by the gentleness of his manner? Between them, these two men had turned the world of Pacific studies upside down. The Irishman accused the Samoan of ethnocentrism, for imputing to the Hawaiians a European bourgeois rationality, while the Samoan accused the Irishman of thinking like a "native," of a superstitious faith in the divinity of the Great White Father from Across the Water. This weekend they had been brought together for the first time since their days as mentor and student, to take each other on in open gladiatorial combat, face to face, *mano a mano*, before an audience of their peers and colleagues in Pacific studies. The conference was the work of Midwestern's star anthropologist, the boulevardier postmodernist Gregory Eyck, who had done everything from micromanaging the list of invited speakers to designing the poster. It bid fair to be the intellectual prizefight of the season, Pacific studies' own rumble in the jungle, its Thrilla in Manila. It had all the visceral appeal of a monster truck rally, and for many of the same reasons.

But the main event never took place. Like many a dilettante, Gregory Eyck had overestimated his talents in at least one area of the conference's preparation, namely that of graphic design. On the first morning of the conference, as he strode a fashionable ten minutes late into the packed lecture hall in the graduate school building, people's anticipation of a shindy had built to just short of the point where they might begin to flick their cigarette lighters in the air, chant like soccer hooligans, or body-surf over the heads of the crowd. They quieted a little as he stepped to the podium, tossed back his golden hair, adjusted the microphone, stroked his three careful days of stubble, and cleared his throat to read his witty and even-handed opening remarks. But before he could say a word, a dark-complected young woman with a mass of black hair coiled atop her head rose to her feet and in a very loud voice addressed a question to Professor Eyck about the politics of the conference poster. Why was the Hawaiian chieftain caricatured as a thick-lipped brute with a club, while Cook was represented by the starkly beautiful play of light and shadow on a white skull, a well-known metaphor for spiritual mystery and intellectual power?

The room was electric with silence. This promised to be even more entertaining than the scheduled event. Professor Eyck began to blink his blue eyes and stammer. The two contenders, seated at opposite ends of the dais, took note of this interruption each in his own way. Professor Brody's face turned even redder and more pugnacious than usual, giving him a startling resemblance to Spencer Tracy, and he cleared his throat repeatedly and tried to make eye contact with Professor Eyck, as if to say, "Let me handle this, young fella." Professor Tulafale, for his part, simply pursed his lips, folded his hands, and closed his eyes; let the white man dig himself out of this one. Meanwhile, Gregory Eyck invited the young woman to discuss the issue in one of the seminars later in the day. But she refused to sit down, proclaiming that the entire conference was entitled to an answer to her question. Like, right *now*.

Near the back of the lecture hall, Beverly dug her blunt fingers painfully into Virginia's arm. She had clung to Virginia all morning, in character as the faculty spouse from hell, tented in a green velvet dress and a cape with two armholes like some eccentric lady detective from Agatha Christie. The weight she'd put on since he last saw her was probably enough to disguise her from Karswell, but she had permed her hair and dyed it strawberry blond, just to make sure.

"What's going on?" she whispered.

Virginia opened her mouth, glanced nervously about her, and closed it again. So far her masquerade had required her only to glide as unobtrusively as possible across campus and through the lecture hall to her seat. Her hair was dyed dark brown and slicked back like a bond trader's, her feet wedged into a pair of men's black oxfords—size nine and a half—with newspaper stuffed into the toes. John Harrington's charcoal-gray pinstripe suit hung from her hips and her shoulders, and she wore a button-down shirt and a paisley tie knotted up to where an Adam's apple ought to have been. The clothes were loose—she could smell her sweat rising up out of her collar—but underneath she was bound up like a geisha, a sports bra a size too small crushing what she couldn't help thinking of now as her boobies. The bruising under her eyes had faded, but her nose was still tender and a bit swollen. The heat made her beard itch, and she worried about her sweat loosening the spirit gum, letting the mustache peel away like a caterpillar even before she knew it was gone. And carefully folded lengthwise in the inside pocket of her suit coat, pressed against her heart like a GI's pocket Bible, ready for her to pull out and thrust into his hands at the earliest opportunity, was her manuscript paper with Karswell's runic annotations, otherwise the instrument of her destruction in less than five days' time.

"Answer the question, Greg!" someone else called out from the audience to Professor Eyck, and Eyck mopped his forehead with a handkerchief.

"*What's going on?*" hissed Beverly, dragging on Virginia's arm.

Virginia slouched in her seat and ducked her head between her shoulders like a turtle. Midwestern was Virginia's graduate alma mater, and she was surrounded in the auditorium by people who knew her with varying degrees of intimacy. Luckily, most of her close friends had graduated and gone elsewhere, but her entire dissertation committee was present in separate regions of the auditorium; the chair of the department had walked right by her, scowling. She even knew Gregory Eyck, though she wasn't sure he'd remember her, and, at any rate, he had his hands full at the moment. The crowd was murmuring, though no one else had shouted out. The angry young woman was still standing, arms akimbo, stray hairs beginning to fly loose from her massive coiffure, as if she were charged with electricity.

"It?" called out another woman's voice, from the seat just behind Virginia's. Virginia stiffened at the sound.

"It?" said the woman again, loud enough to swivel the heads of the people sitting nearby. Beverly heaved around in her seat to look at her.

But Virginia kept her eyes front. Even on so small a word, she recognized the voice. Oh God, she thought, it's Vita.

"It, it, it?" stammered Vita Deonne loudly, drawing all eyes in the hall to her at last. "It's a good question."

There were murmurs of assent, and Virginia scrunched down farther in her seat. Vita's sitting *right behind me*, she thought.

"I, I, I," Vita went on, lurchingly, "I think you should answer it."

Vita Deonne was a junior professor in the English department, a pale, rounded young woman who dressed in drab, shapeless clothing and wore her colorless hair around her face like a wimple. Virginia had met her in an interdisciplinary women's reading group called the Ladies' Theory Circle, and for a few months she and Vita had become friends. When Virginia knew her, Vita had been a nervous bundle of contradictions: a rigorous feminist intellect who was also capable of a girlish sweetness, acutely aware of gender in every situation and circumstance, but also shy to the point of terror. The intellectual manifested herself in a finely focused rage and a stammering, censorious public persona, while the private Vita manifested herself in a peculiar fondness for Doris Day movies and, now and then, once she got to know you, an infectious giddiness. A misunderstanding of a personal nature had happened between Virginia and Vita, and to this day Virginia was sure she'd handled it badly.

Even from the rear of the hall, Gregory Eyck could be seen turning various shades of red, falling back desperately on his pixieish smile to bail him out. But calls of "Answer the question!" rose more frequently now from the audience, mostly in women's voices.

Vita stirred just behind Virginia, rising to her feet.

"I think, I think," she began, struggling unsuccessfully to be heard over the hubbub. Then she let it drop. Virginia knew from experience that Vita was caught now, afraid to compete with the louder voices in the hall, but afraid to draw attention to herself by sitting down. For once Virginia knew the feeling. She pushed herself as far down as she could go, the top of her head level with the back of her seat, her knees against the seat in front.

"Is this session going to follow the program?" A man's voice arose, high-pitched and as insistent as a mosquito. "If not, then perhaps I might be allowed to excuse myself."

Beverly heaved herself to her feet, rocking the whole row of seats, craning over the heads of the crowd. Someone else had stood up down front. Virginia inched up in her seat and stretched her neck out of her collar, and she caught a glimpse of a pale hand rising out of a tweed sleeve, waving a copy of the conference program. A whisper rippled over the crowd like a breeze on the surface of a pond.

*Karswell, Karswell, Karswell.*

"What rock did he crawl out from under?" said the woman in front of Virginia.

"I thought he was dead," said the man next to her.

"Karswell can't die," said Beverly, and the couple looked up at her. "Not unless you drive a stake through his heart."

The man and woman were half-smiling, expecting a witticism, but their faces froze when they saw the fierce light in Beverly's eye. Virginia reached up and tried to haul her back into her seat, but Beverly batted her hand away.

"Clearly this assembly has abandoned the rules of *civilized* conduct," Karswell declared, "and returned to the law of the jungle."

There were hisses, accompanied by a cry of "Sit down, Tarzan!" Someone hooted like an ape. There was a gust of laughter.

"Colleagues!" Gregory Eyck's voice boomed out of the public address. "Colleagues, please!"

"I see," Karswell said dryly, "that the inmates have taken over the asylum."

The crowd groaned, and there was more hissing. Beverly, still standing, reached behind her and grabbed Virginia's shoulder.

"He's collecting his things!" she hissed. "He's getting ready to leave!"

"Dow, dow, dow," stammered Vita. "Down in front!"

Beverly whirled, and Virginia threw her hands over her head.

"Hey!" Beverly barked at Vita like a drill sergeant. "What's your problem, lady?"

Without looking, Virginia could imagine Vita cringing and blushing a shade of red unknown outside of the rain forest.

"I don't, I didn't mean . . ." Vita's voice quavered.

If Karswell's curse doesn't kill me first, Virginia thought, I'll die of sheer embarrassment.

"I didn't mean yuh, yuh, you!" cried Vita. "I meant *him!*"

Virginia risked a glance back and saw Vita pointing across the audience at Karswell, who was sidling down his row toward the aisle. Beverly had already turned around and was gathering up her Miss Marple cloak and her purse.

"Let's go!" she said in an urgent sotto voce. "This is it!"

"You're free to leave, professor," the dark young woman who had started all this called out to Karswell, speaking in a posh, post-colonial accent. "Nobody's making you stay."

Cheers, applause. Something was going on at the podium that Virginia couldn't see. Someone's hand was over the microphone.

"Listen, I, I'm sorry." Vita was leaning over the back of Virginia's seat, speaking to Beverly. "I didn't mean . . ."

"Forget it," snapped Beverly.

She yanked on Virginia's arm.

"Move it, *dear*," she said through gritted teeth.

Virginia was furiously shaking her head and mouthing the words "I can't!" She rolled her eyes frantically at Vita, who was leaning between the seats.

"I hope you didn't misunderstand . . ." Vita insisted.

Beverly strong-armed Vita out of the way and hauled Virginia to her feet. Desperately, Virginia yanked her overcoat off the seat— John Harrington's old London Fog, in fact—and held it nearly over her head. Beverly gave her a push from behind, but Virginia dug in her heels. Karswell was marching briskly up the aisle, thrusting his arms into his own overcoat. The murmuring crowd was turning to watch him.

"I did not come here," he was saying loudly, "at considerable inconvenience and expense, in order to discuss matters of trivial and ephemeral ideological import."

"Good*bye*, Victor," said the dark-haired woman, to laughter.

Karswell stopped at the top of the aisle and turned.

"Allow me to say this, however," he cried, and the murmuring and laughter subsided. "This will *not* happen at my presentation tomorrow. We *will* discuss the scheduled topic, I can promise you that."

Beverly was pushing with both hands in the small of Virginia's back, hissing, "Go go go!"

Karswell marched to the door, and turned one more time.

"Saturday afternoon, at one P.M.!" he declaimed. "Harbour Hall, Lecture Room A!"

He pushed out the swinging door, which thumped back and forth behind him. There was a smattering of ironic applause, in appreciation of a dramatic exit. Virginia leaned back against Beverly's pressure, then suddenly it was gone, and she sprawled back across the two empty seats. Beverly was shouldering up the row toward the other aisle. People were heaving themselves out of her way.

"Are you okay?"

Vita was leaning over the seat, gazing wide-eyed at Virginia from twelve inches away. Their eyes met for an instant. Virginia's heart stopped.

"Honey!" Virginia cried, struggling to her feet in the narrow row. "Hang on! Wait for me!"

Virginia caught up to Beverly outside, on the steps of the building. Karswell was nowhere to be seen. The newly fallen snow was unmarked by footprints; it was as if Karswell had been lifted into the air. Beverly had flung her cape to the ground and was stamping her feet in a little circular dance of rage. She was cursing, her face flushed and shiny. When she saw Virginia, she gave a wordless cry and flung herself at the taller woman, her fists raised.

"*We lost him!*" she cried.

Virginia caught her by the wrists and held her back.

"Goddammit!" she shouted. "Calm down!"

"He's gone!" wailed Beverly. "We lost our chance!"

"Stop it!" Virginia shook Beverly hard. "*Stop it!*"

In their budget motel room, out by the freeway at the edge of town, Beverly had rehearsed Virginia far into the night, how to walk like a man, talk like a man, cross her legs like a man.

"Don't swagger," she'd said. "Don't puff your chest up. Don't pitch your voice lower. Cross your leg at the ankle. Speak in a monotone, through your nose. Just act like you belong wherever you are, like it's the most natural thing on earth."

Now Virginia gripped the wrists of her "wife" and barked in her face.

"This isn't the time!" she snapped. "His guard is up! He'd never let us near him!"

"Don't you *want* to live?" Beverly gasped. "Do you *want* to die a horrible, terrifying death?"

Virginia released her and stepped back and closed her eyes. She heard Beverly breathing a pace or two away. Virginia turned and opened her eyes, watching the silently falling snow across Midwestern's mall.

Beverly groaned and paced in a circle, panting and shaking her head.

"We had him," she said. "He was alone."

Virginia said nothing. She began buttoning her coat. She didn't tie the belt, for fear of giving away her waistline.

"What was that all about inside?" Beverly said, shaking her head and jerking her eyes up into her skull in imitation of Virginia.

"I know that woman," Virginia said. And, without thinking, added, "She kissed me once."

"She kissed you?"

"Well, yeah. We were in her apartment, and she just sort of . . . kissed me."

Beverly stooped to pick up her cape. A wet, heavy snow was falling all around.

"Look, it's not like I kissed her back," Virginia said. Then hastened to add, "Not that there'd be anything wrong with that."

"Kiss whoever you want. I don't care." Beverly flipped the cape over her head and dived expertly through the armholes. "Did she recognize you just now?"

"No. Well, I don't think so. We haven't seen each other in four years." She tried to catch Beverly's eye. "I'm sorry."

Beverly shook her head and flapped her hand.

"Look," she said. "You're probably right. Karswell just made himself the center of attention. Which means he couldn't be happier. But he also couldn't be more alert. His guard is up. He won't let anyone near him."

She turned to Virginia.

"If we'd offered him the runes now and he hadn't taken them, we'd have blown our cover, and we'd never get another chance."

The two women exchanged a look, and then each looked away, Virginia at her feet, Beverly across the snow-covered mall.

"All right, then." Beverly blew out a sigh. "Let's go find the little fucker."

Virginia stood up straight and adjusted her tie. She offered her arm to Beverly, and Beverly took it, and together they started down the steps, leaving two pairs of footprints in the snow.

# fifteen

THEY SPENT THE REST OF THE DAY TRACKING Karswell, but he was nowhere to be found. They consulted the program and covered all the scheduled events, making an appearance at each seminar room and classroom. But most of the events had been derailed by the blowup at the opening session. Some of the rooms were empty, the chairs in disarray as if a struggle had taken place. In others they found a heated debate going on over the conference poster, while the planned speaker and the discussants either joined in, looked on in dismay, or left, their useless presentations already shoved out of sight into their briefcases. Several professors whom Virginia knew quite well walked right past her, but no doubt that was as much an effect of the general excitement as of her disguise. Crossing the Quad, they passed Gregory Eyck himself at one point, trailing a little cloud of angry graduate students like a scandal-ridden politician hounded by reporters. All that was missing was the whirr of camera drives and the jousting of microphone booms. All the students were talking at once, and Eyck glided among them like a zombie, hollow-eyed and silent. The only student not talking was the black-haired young woman who had disrupted the opening session in the first place, and she guided the professor by the arm, like a proud guerrilla escorting a downed flier through a crowd of angry villagers.

In the last seminar room of the day they found a forlorn young physics professor waiting to give his paper on Hawaiian astronomy,

"Pleiades Rising: The Cosmic Bad Luck of Captain Cook," which his prospectus promised would provide the key to solving the controversy over the captain's death. He had come early to draw a complicated and elegant graphic representation of his theory on the blackboard, in chalk of many colors, showing the daily rising position of the Pleiades in relation to Mauna Loa for the entire month of November 1779. But by now he had given up hope, and sat on the edge of the table of the front of the room, his tie loosened, his shoulders slumped, his feet dangling. The only person waiting to hear his talk was an elderly woman in a vicuña coat in the front row, her handbag perched on her lap. When Virginia and Beverly came in, the man didn't even look up, but the old woman shifted in her chair and smiled warmly.

"Look, dear!" she said. "I told you someone would come!"

"Mother, please," said the professor, and Beverly and Virginia ducked out and hurried down the hall.

They left the campus finally and cruised the shops along Michigan Avenue, looking discreetly and unsuccessfully for Karswell in cafés, restaurants, and bars. They tried all the bookstores Virginia could remember, new and used; Beverly had an idea that they might come upon him buying a stack of books to ship back to Texas, that they could slip the runes into one of the volumes when he wasn't looking, and then hand him the book.

"I won't be happy until I put them right into that little bastard's hand," Virginia said. Together they squinted like trackers into the fluorescent glare of chain superstores and edged carefully around the book-crammed, makeshift shelves of used bookstores smelling of dust and mildew, peering into the dim light down the narrow aisles at furtive men in dark coats. But none of them was Victor Karswell.

By twilight they ended up at a book-signing party near the campus, at a handsome, well-lighted scholarly bookshop with a parquet floor and beautiful handmade shelves. Giddy conferees collected in knots in the aisles and crowded the nooks of the shop, recounting where they were and what they'd done that morning, like boomers recalling where they were when JFK was shot. As slack-key guitar music played over the sound system, they drank free wine by the bottle and snatched up crackers and Brie and carrot sticks, while the manager of the shop looked on, a ruddy, prematurely white-haired Canadian with a ponytail who was bemused by the gossip but secretly doleful at the thought that this crowd was not in a purchasing mood. At any rate, none of the authors had shown up, and the table heaped with their books—Brody's *The Barbecued God: Death of a Yorkshireman*, Tulafale's *Cooking the Captain: The Colonialist as Yorkshire Pudding*, and Gregory Eyck's latest volume, *(Re)visioning Resurrection: The Myth of Human Sacrifice*—the table stood abandoned, littered with wadded napkins, half-eaten crackers, and empty plastic cups.

Virginia and Beverly separated as soon as they determined that Karswell wasn't here either, each retreating to a quiet corner. Beverly sat with her boots off on a padded seat near the front of the store, a paper plate in her lap piled high with party food, and she made little sandwiches of Ritz crackers and Swiss cheese squares, dispatching each one in a single bite while she stared into the middle distance at nothing. At the other end of the store, across a murmuring, laughing crowd of enervated academics, Virginia leaned half out of sight in the store's film study section, her eyes drifting across the spines of classic screenplays, biographies of maverick directors, studies of slasher movies and revisionist westerns. She wished she could take her shoes off, too; her feet hurt from lifting the too-large shoes all afternoon. She must have looked like a circus clown walking in them, she decided, spreading her legs wide and lifting her knees to make sure she didn't trip on their enormous toes. But she didn't even unbutton her suit coat or loosen her tie, still afraid of giving herself away. Vita tended not to show up at functions like this, but Virginia couldn't be too careful. Even so, she was on her third glass of inexpensive wine, which was going straight to her head on an empty stomach, which was too tight with anxiety and frustration to eat.

"You're very tall," someone said, and it was a moment before Virginia realized that the person was speaking to her.

"I'm sorry?" she said.

"Do you work out? You're very lean."

A short, compact man with close-cropped hair and narrow eyes stood at the open end of the alcove, sipping his wine and watching her over the cup. He wore a snug pair of black jeans, motorcycle boots, and a leather jacket. He spoke with a British accent.

"I, uh, I," she stammered, pausing to reinstate her gender-obscuring monotone. "Well, no, actually. I, um, bike. I run, too. A little."

"Mm." The Englishman looked Virginia up and down in a way that alarmed her. He's checking me out, she thought, her pulse beginning to race. He's on to me. She stood up straight and squared her shoulders, clearing her throat in what she hoped was a masculine manner. She'd have stroked her beard if she hadn't been afraid that it would come away in her hand.

The Englishman smiled appreciatively.

"Well, it looks good on you," he said. "Is that suit a European cut?"

"The suit?" Virginia glanced down the front of her suit. Was her gender showing?

"I mean it as a compliment." The man smiled, showing uneven, tobacco-stained teeth. Definitely a Brit.

"Speaking as a European," he added. He offered his hand. "Martin Close. I'm with the BBC."

"Uh huh." Virginia squeezed his hand as hard as she could.

"And you are?"

Virginia blinked, unable to remember her *nom de guerre*, and afraid to glance at her own name badge.

"Younger," she blurted at last. "Cole Younger, Northfield State." She'd almost said "Jesse James."

"Aha." Martin nodded, trying to look impressed. "And you do?"

Virginia's mind ground its gears. She felt cornered. Do what? she wondered. Cross-dressing? Drag shows? Voguing?

"Do?" she said.

"History?" Martin said helpfully, looking bemused. "Anthro? I assume you're in Pacific studies, or you wouldn't be here."

"Yes!" cried Virginia. "Pacific studies! History!"

Please go away, she wanted to say. She felt paralyzed, unable to brush this guy off as effortlessly as she usually could have. He'd caught her in a lie, after all. All he had to do was turn around and say in a loud voice, Look over here, at the young lady with the fetching beard and mustache.

"Any particular region?" he said. "Or do you cover the whole of Polynesia?"

"Rapanui?" Virginia said, as querulously as an undergrad.

"Yes!" Martin brightened, looking genuinely interested for the first time. "I've been to Easter! Perhaps you've seen my film!"

Virginia's alarm mounted, her pulse racing. If he'd been to the island, he might have heard of her. Europeans with a professional interest in the island tended to know of each other. The fact that her book wasn't out yet, and that she hadn't even published a paper from it, did not reassure her. Virginia swallowed. Her head was getting light. Exposure of her charade was only moments away.

"Look, it's rather noisy in here," Martin said cheerfully, glancing back toward the door of the shop. "Would you like to go somewhere quiet and have a drink? I reckon we know some of the same people."

Virginia felt the heat rising from her collar. She was beginning to blush.

"Oh, well, I . . ."

"I don't think so," said another voice. "This bruiser's spoken for."

Beverly pushed her way past Martin into the alcove, and he danced nimbly to one side, lifting his cup of wine out of harm's way.

"I beg your pardon," he said, lifting his eyebrows in annoyance.

"Not necessary," Beverly said brightly, sliding in under Virginia's arm and wrapping her hands around Virginia's waist.

"This is, uh, this is . . ." Virginia said.

"Martin Close, BBC." He offered his hand.

"Oh!" cried Beverly. "A real Englishman!"

She just offered him the tips of her fingers, flashing a brilliant and insincere smile, a diva receiving an admirer.

"And *you* are?" Martin said.

"Mrs. Cole Younger!" she said, in the same swelling vibrato with which she might have said "Mrs. Norman Maine!"

Martin looked wide-eyed from Virginia to Beverly and back again. Beverly beamed with liquid eyes up at Virginia. Virginia looked into her plastic cup, blushing.

"Well, yes, I see," said Martin at last. "My mistake. I apologize. I didn't mean to cause any trouble."

"That's okay," Virginia said. "I mean, no harm done."

"Oh honey, don't you see?" Beverly beamed up at Virginia. "This man thinks you're gay."

There was a breathless moment as Virginia blushed even brighter, relieved and, in spite of her professional broadmindedness, even more alarmed than she'd been before.

"Oh," she said. "*Oh.*"

Martin repressed a smile at her embarrassment.

"You have a very good look," he said. "I just thought . . ."

Beverly threw her head back and shouted with laughter.

"Oh, that's my doing," she said loudly, drawing stares. She squeezed Virginia roughly around the waist, forcing all the air out of her lungs. "This big galoot couldn't match his socks without my help."

Martin laughed politely.

"He's *really* not your type," she added, with a conspiratorial wink.

"I can see that," Martin said, casting about. "I say, isn't that Gregory Eyck just coming in? The man of the hour, as it were. Will you excuse me?"

"Cheerio!" said Beverly brightly.

As he sidled out of the alcove into the crowd, Virginia let her breath out and sagged back against the bookcase. She might have slid farther if Beverly hadn't been still clasping her around the waist.

"*Ay caramba,*" murmured Virginia, closing her eyes. She felt a hand laid gently along her cheek, turning her head. She opened her eyes and saw Beverly beaming up at her, sincerely this time, her eyes sparkling, her cheeks a fulsome red. For an instant Virginia saw the hopeful young woman Beverly once had been, and she managed to smile. Beverly brushed Virginia's beard with her knuckles.

"John!" she said in an urgent, happy whisper. "It's working! We're fooling them!"

"John?" Virginia started to say, but Beverly took her face in both hands and kissed her tenderly on the lips. It was a long kiss, and Virginia could feel Beverly trembling. Her pity contended with her alarm, and she glanced past Beverly at the crowd of academics getting happily drunk on wine and scandal. No one was looking, and with Beverly's lips still pressed to hers, Virginia cast about with her plastic cup, setting it precariously on the edge of a shelf. Then she drew a breath and gently pulled away, taking Beverly's wrists and lifting her hands from her face.

"I'm not John," she said quietly, pressing Beverly's hands between her own.

Beverly slipped her hands out of Virginia's grasp and stepped back, fumbling behind her for a shelf to clutch. A chill tightened Virginia's skin. Of all the things she'd seen in the last few months, nothing frightened her quite as much as the sight of Beverly Harrington growing old before her eyes. The flush drained from Beverly's cheek, the light in her eyes turned cold. In a moment she had gone from Juliet to Medea, from the warmth of youthful passion to dark, stony rage. Beverly lifted her dead eyes, and the hair rose on the back of Virginia's neck.

"Tomorrow," Beverly said. "Tomorrow is the end of Victor Karswell."

*P*N THE MORNING, IN THEIR HOTEL ROOM AT THE edge of town, the two women prepared for the day like bullfighters, suiting up with a sense of foreboding and even some ceremony. Beverly dressed Virginia like a mannequin, tugging and cinching and arranging her, in order to fit her as convincingly as possible into a dead man's suit. Applying the beard and makeup, Beverly peered intently at Virginia from only inches away, but it was the gaze of the theater professional, gauging the effect and not the person behind it. When she was in costume, all but her shoes, Virginia lay back on her bed with her hands behind her head and watched Jenny Jones surprise her guests with their secret loves. Her draft paper, with the runes on the last page, was carefully folded inside the suit jacket.

Meanwhile Beverly dressed herself. Today she put on a dark cotton jumper with big side pockets, and while Virginia watched out of the corner of her eye, Beverly lifted a plastic Office Max bag out of her purse and pulled out a brand-new miniature stapler, a box of staples, and a little hinged, four-pronged staple remover. The end of Beverly's bed groaned as she sat, and she tore open the bubble wrap of the stapler with her teeth and loaded it with a line of staples. She clicked off a few staples to make sure it was working. Then she stood and tried various arrangements: the stapler in her right pocket, the staple remover in her left, then the stapler in her left pocket, remover in the right, then both of them in her left pocket. She faced herself in the mirror over the dresser, dropped her arms loosely to her sides, drew a breath and let it out, then jammed a hand into her pocket, pulling out the remover and then the stapler as fast as she could.

Virginia watched her openly now, the television droning on. Beverly did this several times, a little faster and a little more smoothly each time. Finally she just stood there, red-faced and breathing heavily. She caught Virginia's eye in the mirror. She turned.

"Let's go," she said.

"Why not?" said Virginia.

Friday's opening session was supposed to be the main event, the anthropological fight of the century, but instead an impromptu panel discussion was announced, on the subject of the conference poster, opening with a statement by Gregory Eyck. Today he was clean-shaven, his hair brushed neatly back, and he approached the microphone with his hands clasped and his brow furrowed. The crowd fell into a breathless silence, and he extemporized a passionate mea culpa for his thoughtlessness and Eurocentrism and latent racism, for all the world like a television preacher pleading forgiveness for having been caught in a motel room with a prostitute. But Virginia and Beverly didn't stay; indeed, they did not even take their seats. They had arrived before anyone else and posted themselves at opposite ends of the hall, watching to see if Karswell came in. When he didn't, their eyes met across the hall and they left.

They separated in order to cover more ground, each one dropping in on a scheduled event just long enough to look for Karswell. But Karswell did not appear at any of the seminars that morning, nor did he turn up at the luncheon in the faculty club. The meal was Hawaiian specialties, served buffet-style on steam tables, like a theme night in a dormitory cafeteria. Pineapple featured prominently in many of the dishes. Sharing a table with several conferees they didn't know, Virginia asked if anyone had seen Karswell since the donnybrook at the opening session yesterday.

"I heard he left," said an archaeologist from Duke named Montague, his face bronzed like a surfer's from years of sun and sea air in the Solomon Islands.

At this Beverly sucked in her breath, a forkful of pineapple pork chop halfway to her mouth. Virginia shot her a glance.

"I heard," said a small, sly, dapper historian from Harvard who did not have a name tag, "that some of the women at the conference hacked him to death with razor-sharp seashells."

"Then they boiled him down," said Professor Rhodes, a Margaret Meadish emeritus from UCLA, a pink-cheeked old woman in a flowery caftan.

"What's *in* poi, anyway?" said Montague the archaeologist, lifting a dab of it on his finger. Everyone laughed, except Beverly.

"Mmmpf." A gaunt postdoc from Berkeley, a very pale young man in jeans and a T-shirt, was putting away as much free pineapple shrimp as he could manage. His name tag said simply "James." Everyone turned to see him shaking his head, and they waited for him to finish chewing.

"I saw him this morning," James said, swallowing. "On the street. You'll never guess what he's wearing."

"What he's wearing?" said Virginia.

"A hard hat," said Rhodes the emeritus.

"A bulletproof vest," said the sly historian.

"A necklace of human ears," said Beverly.

The table fell silent, all eyes on Beverly. James the gaunt postdoc shook his head.

"Uh-uh," he said with his mouth full. "Knickers."

"Knickers?" chorused the table.

The postdoc swallowed.

"Whatever you call those things with the short pants and knee socks."

"Did he say where he was going?" Virginia said.

"Like I'd speak to him," said James. "Are you going to eat your shrimp?"

Virginia surrendered her untouched plate to the postdoc.

"Victor won't leave," said the Harvard historian. "Not if he's scheduled to speak. Demons from hell couldn't hold him back from presenting one of his, ah, little talks."

He smiled around the table.

"At any rate, I hope not. I'm due to introduce him . . ." He glanced at his watch. ". . . in about an hour. I don't want to have to face the crowd if he isn't there."

Beverly gazed with shining eyes at the historian.

"Do you think anyone will show up?" said Virginia.

"Oh, my dear, yes," said Professor Rhodes, rumbling with laughter, shaking the red blossoms on her caftan. Professor Montague was laughing as well, crinkling the leathery skin around his eyes.

"Mmmph," said the postdoc, choking.

The emeritus addressed Virginia like an aunt addressing her favorite nephew.

"Young man," she said, "all the women at this conference, and not a few of the men, would like a piece of Victor Karswell."

"I'll admit," said the historian, "Victor hasn't made many friends over the years."

"And after his remarks yesterday," Rhodes said, shaking her head, "at the opening session. 'Civilized,' indeed."

Montague held up two fingers like a pair of scissors.

"Snip, snip," he said.

The postdoc, his fork poised over a pineapple meatball, rolled it aside instead and went to work on his rice.

"Which puts me in a difficult position, rather," said the historian. "Two of my three discussants have dropped out."

"Indeed!" said Rhodes. "Who?"

"Mary and Ellen," said the historian, displaying his first-name acquaintanceship with two of the biggest names in gender studies. "They said they wanted to attend the extraordinary session on the conference poster instead. But I suspect that neither of them wanted to share a stage with Victor, especially after yesterday."

Virginia felt a sharp impact against her shin, the toe of a shoe. She moved her leg.

"Victor Karswell speaking on feminist theory," said Professor Rhodes, shuddering under her caftan. "The very thought."

"Yes." Montague's eyes sparkled. "It's like going to hear Dr. Mengele on oral hygiene."

The Harvard historian puckered his lips to keep from laughing.

"I suppose Karswell's pleased," said Montague. "He'll have the stage all to himself."

"Oh no," said the historian. "Victor enjoys the, how shall I put it? The cut and thrust?"

Someone kicked Virginia again, deliberately, and she saw Beverly lifting her eyebrows and jerking her head toward the historian.

"I was hoping," said the historian, smiling at Professor Rhodes, "that I could tempt you into joining us, my dear."

"Oh no," she said, laughing heartily. "I won't appear with Victor Karswell either."

Beverly waggled her eyebrows and jerked her head, and she began to make high-pitched little coughs into her palm, like the bark of a small dog.

"Then I may have to forgo the discussion of the paper altogether," said the historian.

Beverly kicked Virginia under the table hard enough to make Virginia gasp aloud. Everyone turned to her.

"My husband," Beverly said, "might be coaxed into joining your panel."

Virginia looked up from rubbing her shin.

"I don't think . . ." she began.

"What's your field?" said the historian, intrigued.

"Gender studies on . . . what's the name of your island again, dear?" said Beverly.

"Uh, I'm not really . . ."

"Professor . . . Younger?" The historian leaned across the table to read Virginia's name tag.

"It begins with an R," Beverly said, smiling sweetly around the table. "R something."

"Are you familiar with Victor's work?" said the historian, clearly interested now.

Montague, Rhodes, and James all turned to Virginia. She felt her cheek warming. The phrase "Victor's work" was like a slap across the face.

"Yes," she said after a moment. "As it happens, I am."

"Cole knows the field of gender studies *intimately,*" said Beverly, beaming. "Don't be modest, sweetheart."

"I can sense your reluctance, professor," said the historian, leaning forward and clasping his hands. "But when I was your age, this is just the sort of chance I'd have leaped at. The chance to go *mano a mano* with an old warhorse like Karswell."

Everyone at the table was looking at Virginia: the emeritus and the archaeologist with some bemusement; the postdoc somewhat jealously, his jaw working steadily; the historian with his eyes bright; and Beverly staring hard, willing Virginia forward. The thought terrified her, though. Meanwhile the draft of her paper, the one Karswell was to read as his own in less than an hour's time, pressed against her heart like a weight.

"All right," said Virginia.

## seventeen

T WAS JUST AS WELL THAT VIRGINIA HAD AGREED to join the panel; she might not have gotten a seat otherwise. Lecture Room A of Harbour Hall was large enough to accommodate eighty people, and there were already over a hundred there by the time Virginia and Beverly arrived with the Harvard historian, whose name was Professor Oppenheimer.

"No relation," he said with a wink, on the way across the Quad.

"No relation to whom?" Beverly whispered, tugging on Virginia's arm.

The lecture hall doubled as a film theater, and the seats were padded, rising gently in rows toward the back. Most of the audience were women of various ages and styles of dress and sexual preference, graduate students in jeans and work shirts cheek by jowl with tenured professors in tailored suits. The seating was purely democratic. Some grad students sat in the front rows while some tenured women stood along the back wall or hunkered down shoulder to shoulder in the aisle, their skirts pulled over their knees. Passing through the door behind Professor Oppenheimer, Virginia was met with a wave of heat and perspiration. The murmuring subsided somewhat as they came in, and she was keenly aware that every eye in the room followed her, the professor, and Beverly as they inched down the aisle.

"I see we're thick as thieves today," joked Professor Oppen-

heimer by way of apology as he squeezed through the women
seated in the aisle.

"Pardon me," mumbled Virginia, stepping high with her enormous shoes. "I'm really sorry."

Edging aside, the women in the aisle glanced up at her. She was
flushed already, and beginning to sweat, and she was acutely aware
of the underside of her jaw. Rather than holding her hands out for
balance as she teetered from one foot to another, she stuck them
in her trouser pockets to keep them from shaking. A whisper passed
like a breeze through the crowd.

"Who's he?" it said.

Across the front of the stage was a podium flanked by two long
folding tables. Karswell had not arrived yet, and the tables were
empty except for the other discussant, a pudgy, weary, middle-
aged white man in a misshapen off-the-rack suit, who sat hunched
forward, kneading his hands. He seemed to be searching the audience in vain for a friendly face. When he saw Oppenheimer and
Virginia coming down the aisle he sat up, smiling weakly.

Down front, Professor Oppenheimer managed to persuade the
women sitting on the floor at stage right to clear a space for Beverly, who perched sideways on the lowest of the steps leading to
the stage. Onstage the other discussant bounded to his feet a little
too enthusiastically and pumped Virginia's hand as Oppenheimer
introduced them.

"Bob Doe," he said, his eyes glistening. "Kansas State."

He leaned in, clutching Virginia's shoulder, and whispered
hoarsely in her ear.

"Buddy," he said, his breath hot and smelling of alcohol, "am I
glad to see *you.*"

Oppenheimer, however, looked perfectly collected, armored in
his snappy double-breasted jacket and his twinkling manner. The
murmuring was growing louder in the room, a susurrus of whispering. A hundred pairs of eyes were watching, and Oppenheimer
surveyed the crowd coolly.

"Well," he said, glancing at his watch, "where's our leading
man?"

"Here," said a precise, high-pitched voice, and Victor Karswell stepped through a low doorway at the back of the stage.

The hall fell silent, leaving only Karswell's footsteps as he crossed the hollow stage and set his briefcase on the table next to the podium. The latches of the case snapped like pistol shots as he undid them, and a smile played about his lips as he removed his paper. He looked exactly the same as he always did: the tweed suit and vest, the precise little gestures, the fussy Edwardian haircut. As the postdoc at lunch had reported, Karswell was wearing knickers, his short pants cinched just below the knee, his slender calves surprisingly sleek in woolen stockings. He looked as if he'd just returned from a walking tour of the Lake District, circa 1907.

Karswell placed his paper, a thin stack of pages stapled in the corner, on the podium and shut his briefcase with another pair of loud reports. He turned briskly on his toe to Oppenheimer, who stepped forward and murmured in Karswell's ear. Karswell nodded and said, "Yes, I see."

The audience seemed to be holding its collective breath. Virginia felt every pair of eyes on her like a navy searchlight. Even considering the number of out-of-town visitors, there must be any number of women in the audience who knew her, who could see past the dyed hair, the pasted-on beard, and the baggy suit to recognize the nervous young woman underneath. She glanced back at Beverly and saw her newly blond wife-for-a-day crouching on the bottom step with her hands on her knees, ready to spring. She watched Karswell with a gaze brighter than all the other gazes in the room combined.

"Professor Younger?" said Oppenheimer, and Virginia snapped her head around.

Oppenheimer was ushering her toward Karswell.

"This is Professor Younger," said Oppenheimer, "from Northfield State. He'll be joining our discussion today."

"Professor," said Karswell sharply, offering his hand.

Virginia's heart pounded, and she had some difficulty extricating her hand from her pocket. She had never actually touched Karswell before, and she was certain the moment she did, he'd know who she was. Oppenheimer pushed her gently forward, and she held out her hand as rigid as a board, locking her fingers as she met Karswell's palm. His hand was cold, frighteningly so, and he folded his short fingers around hers.

"Victor Karswell," he said, narrowing his eyes.

Someone in the audience hissed, and, to Virginia's relief, Karswell dropped her hand and turned to face the crowd, pursing his lips. Virginia exchanged a glance with Bob Doe, who stood near the back of the stage, sweating.

"Colleagues, please," said Oppenheimer, in a jocularly scolding tone. "No leaky tires, I beg you."

"Yes," said Karswell. "Please contain your expressions of contempt until after my paper."

There were gasps and even a little laughter. Oppenheimer turned to Virginia and Bob Doe and said, "Shall we?"

Everybody sat except Oppenheimer, who moved to the podium. Karswell and Bob Doe sat to the left of the podium, so Virginia moved to the right, sitting at the end of the table, as far away from Karswell as possible. Rather than face the audience and risk meeting the eye of someone she knew, she turned her chair slantwise to the table and crossed her legs—the way Beverly had taught her, ankle over knee, not knee over knee. She couldn't see Beverly from this position, but she was aware of the eyes of the audience, Beverly's in particular, burning toward Karswell like tracer bullets.

Oppenheimer pulled an index card out of his breast pocket and began a very diplomatic, bare-bones introduction of Karswell—no accolades or even pro forma expressions of collegiality, just his CV: his degrees, his publications, the positions he'd held. The closest he came to praise was a brief accounting of Karswell's research interests.

"And now he has surprised us all again," said Oppenheimer brightly, "with his paper this afternoon, which constitutes a return to his old stamping grounds—if one can be said to stamp in the South Pacific."

A pause for laughter, which did not come.

"It is, as well," Oppenheimer went on, like a trouper, with no sign of embarrassment, "a stimulating, if not to say exciting, intervention in the field of gender studies. Ladies and, ah, gentlemen, Professor Victor Karswell."

A single pair of hands began to applaud. Every gaze in the room swiveled to Bob Doe of Kansas State. His meaty, solitary, almost Zenlike handclaps slowed as he glanced about the room. The only other sound was the echo of his hands coming back to him, and he stopped. He lifted his gaze to the ceiling, licked his lips, and thrust his hands into his damp armpits.

Oppenheimer sat to the right of the podium, and Karswell stepped up.

"Thank you all for coming," he said, adjusting his manuscript.

A single hiss came from the back of the room, long and malignant, like a snake's. Karswell looked up. There was a long, breathless moment of silence. No one moved. Karswell did not even blink.

"I know what you all think of me," he said at last, barely repressing a smile. "I know you think that I am—how shall I put it? That my day is over? That I am yesterday's papers? That I should shrivel up and let the wind of postmodernism blow me and my kind away?"

"Works for me," said a voice from down front, and there was laughter, followed by an even tenser silence.

But Karswell smiled, and even from the side, from Virginia's vantage, it was a display as malignant as the sound of the hiss. He lifted his paper—*my* paper, Virginia thought—between his thumb and forefinger and displayed it to the silent crowd of women.

"I am here to *astonish* you," he whispered.

He drew a deep breath, and laid the paper flat and turned back the title page. He lifted his pince-nez out of his waistcoat and pinched it onto his nose.

But there was a rustling in the audience, a restless motion that caught his eye and caused him to look up. Virginia turned to look, too, and saw the faces of the women in the audience turning in a concentric ripple toward someone in the middle of the hall. Someone was rising to her feet, lifting her quavering hand in a series of tentative jerks. She was short and shapeless, wearing baggy slacks and a huge sweater, and her large glasses and colorless bangs framed her roundish face like a mask.

"Puh, Puh, Professor Karswell," stammered Vita Deonne. She flapped her hands, not knowing what to do with them.

Virginia nearly gasped aloud. The room spun, she saw stars. She snapped her gaze away from Vita and resisted the urge to look back at Beverly. She was certain what Vita was going to say next.

*Professor Karswell*, she would say, her voice quivering, her eyes shining with their peculiar light, *do you know that the gentleman two seats to your right is not a gentleman at all?*

The faces of the audience swiveled to catch Karswell's response.

"There will be time for questions afterward," Professor Oppenheimer said, lifting his voice.

"I, I, I," Vita insisted, raising her voice and clasping her hands before her like a novitiate, to keep them from shaking. "I'd like to know, why are there no women on your panel?"

The audience began to murmur again, and Virginia managed to breathe. She glanced at the back of Oppenheimer's head, then over her shoulder at Beverly, catching her eye. She raised her eyebrows, but Beverly gestured with her palms to stay put.

Karswell, however, was leaning jauntily against the podium, his pince-nez between his thumb and forefinger, his hand cocked back from his wrist.

"I see the natives are restless," he said. "No doubt after yesterday's ritual sacrifice they have developed the taste for human blood."

There was a chorus of hisses, and Oppenheimer rose to his feet.

"Professor, if I may," he said, authoritative but friendly. He turned to face Vita, who stood looking terrified, wringing her hands.

"That's a fair question, professor," Oppenheimer said, awarding the honorific on the benefit of the doubt, since he did not know Vita, "but I believe it would be more properly addressed in the question time after Professor Karswell's presentation."

Virginia licked her lips and shot a glance at the door at the rear of the stage. She could always feign illness and bolt, her hand over her mouth. An upset stomach—a piece of bad pineapple. Or cramps. But men didn't get cramps. Still afraid to look into the audience, she looked past Oppenheimer and Karswell to see Bob Doe at the far end of the other table, positively trembling in his chair. The sweat was pouring off him now, staining his shirt. Virginia's own smell was rising out of her collar. For the first time in her life, she knew just how a guy like Bob Doe felt. Her heart began to beat faster, and she risked a glance into the audience with her eyes lowered, just into the first row, and caught a whole line of riot grrls glaring at her, six young women with buzz cuts, torn jeans, leather jackets, and big black combat boots. They sat with their arms crossed and their knees spread wide, and one of them puckered up and blew Virginia a kiss with a snap of her wrist. Virginia whisked her gaze away. She knew just how they felt, too. This was an impossible situation.

"Wuh, wuh, with all due respect?" Vita was saying. "I'd like to know now."

There was a smattering of applause.

"Well, it's an unfortunate situation," said Oppenheimer, his knuckles brushing the table. "And I'd be happy to explain it—briefly—with Professor Karswell's permission . . ."

"Were no women available?" called out someone else from the audience.

"There are always women available," said Karswell, his eyes lifted to the ceiling.

The lecture hall filled with a swelling chorus of hissing.

"Very briefly," said Oppenheimer loudly, "a couple of our discussants had to cancel at the last minute—"

"And these two losers were the best you could do?" This from one of the riot grrls down front. Her compatriots rocked with laughter.

Virginia's breath came short, and her effort to breathe more deeply was hampered by the too-tight sports bra. Even over the hissing and laughter, she could hear from Bob Doe at the far end of the table a sigh of terror, like air being let out of an inflatable clown. His eyes rolled in his head. He looked like a terrified dog.

The hall filled with murmuring now, and Vita was stammering to be heard over it. Oppenheimer was holding up his hands, trying to quiet the crowd. Karswell rested his hands on the podium, the pince-nez propped between his fingers. He was smiling.

"Ladies and gentlemen," Oppenheimer called out. "Please."

"No gentlemen here," said a riot grrl, looking up and down the front row.

"No ladies either," said another.

Laughter washed over the stage. Virginia felt a prickling along the side of her head, and lifted her hand to brush away a trickle of sweat. But it wasn't sweat, it was her beard. The strip of it alongside her ear was beginning to peel away, drooping in a little sticky flap.

Virginia slapped the side of her head with her palm and glanced wildly back at Beverly. But Beverly was not looking at her, she was crouched on all fours on the steps to the stage, her shining gaze focused on Karswell. Virginia thought of turning around in her seat, so that the drooping sideburn would be upstage, but then she'd be facing the wall, away from the podium. She pressed the sideburn to her temple, hoping it would stay up, but when she pulled her hand away the beard stuck to her fingers instead, and she peeled another half inch of it off. She pressed her hand to her cheek again and rested her elbow on the table, glancing at the audience to see if anyone had noticed.

But everyone in the restless crowd, even in the front row, was watching the center of the stage. Women were talking freely now as if they were at a party. Oppenheimer lifted his voice in increments, asking for order. Bob Doe was gasping in the far chair, clutching himself under his arms. Virginia turned to Karswell, and her heart nearly stopped. He was looking directly at her, and, as their eyes met, he pulled his thin lips into an evil-looking smile.

He recognizes me, she thought. He saw the beard coming loose. It's too late.

But then Karswell slowly shook his head, and his smile broadened to include her, to make her complicit. You understand, don't you? his look said. You know where I'm coming from. Virginia was chilled to the bone. As the clamor from the audience mounted, Karswell mouthed a word to her, one man to another.

"Bitches," he said, without making a sound.

"Listen!" barked Oppenheimer, surprisingly like the top sergeant he'd once been in Korea. "Let me propose a solution."

The crowd quieted somewhat, and Vita swallowed what she was trying to say, in midsentence.

"Professor . . . ?" Oppenheimer offered his palm to Vita. "I'm very sorry, but I don't know your name."

"Vuh, Vuh, Vita . . ." she began, nearly squeaking in embarrassment.

"Well, Professor Vita," said Oppenheimer, "perhaps you would like to join us onstage."

"Me?" Vita pressed her hand to her throat. "I, I, I . . ."

"The ayes have it!" cried a riot grrl.

*Please don't bring her up here,* Virginia prayed, hunching closer to the table with her hand against her face. *Please don't make me shake her hand.*

"Or," Oppenheimer continued, gauging the exhaustion of Vita's courage and the level of her panic, "perhaps our assembled colleagues could choose a representative."

The crowd stirred, especially the riot grrls. With his eye on the front row, Oppenheimer raised his voice and added, "In an *orderly* and *reasonable* manner . . ."

"Orderly?" said a riot grrl, standing up.

"Reasonable?" said another, rising.

They were all standing now, stretching and rolling their shoulders.

"Say no more!"

"Did somebody call my name?"

"Over the top!"

Whooping happily, the young women from the front row took the stage, ignoring the steps and clambering straight up over the proscenium. The crowd surged forward, and for a moment Virginia thought they might rush the stage en masse, but they were only rising in their seats, craning to get a better look. The boots of the riot grrls thumped against the boards of the stage, and they popped up in front of the tables on either side of the podium, grinning like bikers swaggering into a PTA meeting. One of them, a tall young woman with a silver stud in her nose, popped up with a predatory smile right in front of the podium, within her arm's long reach of Karswell himself. Karswell was forced to look up to meet her gaze, but even so (Virginia saw) there was an eager light glowing in his eye.

"Colleagues, *please.*" Oppenheimer moved next to Karswell, as if to step between him and the grrl with the stud in her nose. But he managed to keep his voice level, sounding exasperated rather than alarmed.

"I rather hoped that we might have *one* or *two* representatives from the audience," he said, laying his arm across the top of the podium, in front of Karswell. "If you ladies would take your seats . . ."

It was the wrong word to use.

"*Ladies!*" cried Nose Stud, and on either side of the podium the riot grrls jumped up and slid over the table on their hips, one of them swinging her boots right over Virginia's head.

The audience gasped and many jumped to their feet. Oppenheimer threw his arm across Karswell's chest and held him back, while Karswell hissed like a cat at Nose Stud across the podium, who growled back at him and chattered her teeth. Bob Doe stood and was immediately confronted by a riot grrl on his side of the table, hitching up her jeans and straightening her leather jacket. He passed out with a groan, sagging to the stage like a sack of meal. Vita, meanwhile, was pushing down the aisle, heaving women out of the way like a bouncer and flapping her hands.

"No!" she cried. "That's not what was . . . ! That's not what I . . . !"

Virginia found herself on her feet, her hand still pressed to the side of her face. Next to her stood a bare-shouldered young woman in a leather vest, with pectorals like a middle linebacker.

"Hey there, Poindexter," she said. "Toothache?"

"Professor Younger!" Oppenheimer barked over his shoulder. "Would you see to Professor Doe?"

Virginia edged around the Linebacker, lowering her eyes and muttering, "Excuse me." And then froze, because Vita was stepping up onto the stage, her eyes wild, her hands frantic.

"Not like this!" she cried, stepping over the prone Bob Doe. Just at that moment the Kansan opened his eyes and lifted his head and saw Vita looming over him. His eyes rolled back in their sockets and he fainted again, cracking his head against the floor.

At the same time, the riot grrls surrounded Karswell and Oppenheimer at the podium, the tall one stooping under the table and emerging on the other side, looming over the two men from behind. Vita was jumping up and down, trying to push her way into the scrum around the podium, pushing brawny women aside with surprising force. Oppenheimer had both arms around Karswell, holding him back from a short, buxom young woman with a gold ring in the corner of her lip, who was trading invective and spittle with Karswell from a foot away. Everyone was shouting.

"I will have my say!" Karswell cried, waving his paper.

"Quit protecting him!" Nose Stud yelled, trying to peel Oppenheimer off Karswell.

"It's not *him* I'm trying to protect!" Oppenheimer called over his shoulder.

"You don't know who you're dealing with!" hissed Karswell.

"You want to deal with somebody, pindick?" The short riot grrl with the lip ring swaggered up to Karswell, chest to chest. "Deal with *me.*"

"Come on!" cried Karswell, in a voice not entirely his own, but deeper and rawer. "If you're man enough!"

His face had gone white, but it wasn't the fearful white of the unfortunate Bob Doe. Rather, it was as if every trace of humanity were draining from his skin, leaving only the monstrous apparition underneath. Lip Ring hesitated, backing up a half-step.

"Victor," Oppenheimer whispered, his lips at Karswell's ear, "don't do anything you'll regret."

For the first time Virginia detected a hint of fear in Oppenheimer's voice, and, as if to justify it, Karswell threw back his shoulders, shrugged out of Oppenheimer's grasp, and turned on him.

"You little man." Karswell's eyes glittered and he bared his teeth. "I regret *nothing,*" he said, and turned to the podium.

"I'll take you all on!" Karswell roared.

The room rang with his voice. But instead of shocked silence afterward, there was a rumbling throughout the lecture hall, a slow, inexorable shifting. Virginia, her heart pounding, turned to look for Beverly, but instead saw women from the audience moving up each row toward the aisles and streaming up the stage-right steps. She turned and saw that women were coming up on stage left as well. A couple of middle-aged women stooped over Bob Doe; one fanned his face with a conference program while the other checked his pulse with two fingers on his throat. All around the auditorium, in fact, women were streaming toward the stage in a slow-motion flood, with a clatter of seats and a swelling murmur of laughter and talk, filing onto the stage to the hollow thunder of Birkenstocks and Doc Martens, Reeboks and Ferragamos.

Indeed, the crowd was already closing around the knot of combatants at the podium, like an amoeba closing around its food. But there was nothing menacing about it; women were smiling and talking to each other. One of them winked at Virginia, and she blushed and looked away. By the podium, though, she saw that even Oppenheimer looked afraid, beads of sweat breaking out along his hairline. An image from a film popped into her head, some imperial epic Chip had talked her into watching once, Charlton Heston as Gordon of Khartoum, standing unarmed at the top of a flight of stone steps, facing down a crowd of angry Sudanese. Virginia felt the urge to laugh. Did Oppenheimer really think that the crowd was going to pierce him with spears and pitch him wriggling into the air?

But instead of escalating the tension, the women onstage filled every gap, surrounding the riot grrls, putting themselves between the young women and Karswell. The riot grrls, in turn, turned sullen, like children caught tormenting some small animal. Surrounded by older women, they all chewed their lips and looked at their feet, especially Nose Stud. The only exception was Lip Ring, who held her position in front of Karswell. She glared at him, her blood still high, ready for a dustup. One of the women in the crowd, a small, sharp-featured woman with close-cropped steel-gray hair, slipped through the crowd behind her and laid both hands gently on the shoulders of Lip Ring's jacket.

"Enough is enough," she said. "I don't like him either, but let's be civilized."

"Civilized?" Lip Ring spat the word out like an obscenity, without taking her eyes off Karswell. "*Civilized?*"

"You forget, my dear," said the steel-gray woman. "We *are* civilization." She smiled and glanced at the three men at the front of the stage, including Virginia. "All they've ever done is bring home the food."

Warm laughter washed over the stage, and with the steel-gray woman's hands on her shoulders, even Lip Ring laughed a little. Oppenheimer joined in too, dipping his head in deference. Virginia wished she could join in, wished she could peel off her beard and swing it around her head. But the manuscript inside her coat weighed against her heart.

But everyone had forgotten Karswell. He stood at the center of the crowd, sunk so far into himself his eyes were nearly shut, as if he were asleep. As the laughter subsided, he opened his eyes slowly and turned his pale face and icy gaze at the steel-gray woman.

"Slut," he said.

There was a moment of awful silence. Behind her Virginia heard the Linebacker's leather creaking as she tensed her pectorals. Even the crowd of women who had come up onstage to smother any trouble seemed to lean collectively an inch or two toward Karswell. No one spoke, no one breathed.

Then, everything happened at once, in slow motion. With a convulsive jerk, Nose Stud hurled chest first into Karswell from behind, ramming him. She looked as if she were falling, her eyes wide in surprise, her hands in the air. With admirable reflexes for the middle-aged, Oppenheimer lunged forward to thrust his arm between Nose Stud and Karswell, and the steel-gray professor yanked Lip Ring abruptly backward by her leather jacket, out of harm's way. Karswell, meanwhile, lurched forward to his knees, his hands flying upward, his pince-nez and his conference paper tossed involuntarily straight up into the air.

Shouts, gasps, chaos. Out of which Virginia heard her own name, in a penetrating hiss from somewhere near the floor. She glanced down.

Beverly lay on her chest under the table next to the podium, from where she had just this moment grasped Nose Stud's ankles and

jerked her off her feet, toppling her into Karswell. She was looking fiercely up at Virginia even as she let go of Nose Stud's boots.

"Grab the fucking paper!" she hissed.

Virginia lifted her gaze. The paper hung high above the heads
of the crowd, slowly flapping its pages like a pigeon. The pince-
nez spun in a stately manner, like some deep-space artifact in a
science-fiction film.

As graceful as Michael Jordan at the tip-off, like a wide receiver
vaulting for a pass at the last possible moment, Virginia leaped,
reaching with both hands. Below her the crowd seethed, slow as
lava. Oppenheimer and the steel-gray woman held back the crowd
with their arms spread wide, while Karswell, propped on one hand,
groped in the air with his other. Riot grrls were grasped by many
hands and hauled back from the center of the fray, even the Linebacker, several smaller women hanging from her massive biceps.

Virginia looked up again. She snagged the pince-nez with her
pinky finger. The paper rose, flapping, but she reached an inch
higher and caught it, bringing it down to her chest as she fell.

She landed hard, with a shock to her shins, and toppled sideways,
into Vita Deonne. Vita instinctively pushed back, pressing one
hand against Virginia's left breast. And immediately yanked her
hand away, as if she'd burned it there. Amid the shouts and uproar
all around, amid the crowd surging forward and back like football
fans, Vita and Virginia tottered together, nose to nose. Their gazes
locked.

Vita's eyes widened.

"Vir, Vir, Vir . . . ?" she stammered.

"Where's my manuscript?" Karswell yelled.

"I was tripped!" cried Nose Stud.

"Give me the paper!" Beverly hissed from near the floor.

"Virgih, Virgih, Virgih . . . ?" Vita said.

Virginia froze. She saw herself sitting on Vita's couch four years
ago, looking up as Vita stooped with her hand shaking, handing
Virginia a rattling cup of tea and trying to kiss her from the most
awkward angle imaginable.

"I will have my due!" Karswell cried.

"It was an accident, Victor," said Oppenheimer breathlessly.

"The paper!" rasped Beverly, yanking hard on Virginia's trouser leg.

Virginia dropped her hand with the paper in it without looking down, and Beverly snatched it away.

"Virgin, Virgin . . ." said Vita, and Virginia clapped her hand over Vita's mouth.

There was another violent tug on Virginia's trouser leg, and she glanced down to see Beverly's moonface, upside down and framed in strawberry blond ringlets, sticking out from under the table.

"Give me the other one!" she hissed.

"The other what?" said Virginia.

"The other paper, you idiot! The one with the runes on it!"

With one hand over Vita's mouth and the other holding the pince-nez, Virginia stuck the pince-nez in her own mouth, reached inside her coat, and yanked out her original copy of the paper. She dropped it to Beverly, and Beverly slid out of sight.

The crowd was swirling slowly to a stop, the riot grrls having been escorted to its fringes. Women were stepping back, giving Karswell room near the podium.

"*Where's my paper?*" Karswell was on his feet again, whirling in place, glaring murderously at the widening ring of women around him. "Where's my manuscript?"

Her hand still over Vita's mouth, Virginia plucked the pince-nez from between her teeth, thrust it inside her coat, and then fell to her knees, dragging Vita with her, out of sight behind the first rank of women.

"Don't say my name," she said, staring hard into Vita's eyes.

Vita stared back with the wide-eyed panic of a paralytic, and Virginia glanced to the side. Through the thicket of pantlegs and stockings and skirts she saw Beverly under the table, working with methodical fury, prying the staples off the two papers with the pronged staple remover, pulling off the last page of each version of the manuscript.

"Mmmph," Vita said, her mouth moist against Virginia's palm.

"Don't say my name," Virginia insisted, "and I'll take my hand away. All right?"

Vita nodded, and Virginia lifted her hand an inch, then pulled it away. There was the unmistakable click of a stapler.

"Here," hissed Beverly, thrusting a paper at Virginia through the crowd. She knelt amid a litter of loose pages. The crowd was thinning, and she glanced warily up at Karswell, standing a few feet away.

"Take it!" Beverly rattled the paper. "Give it to him!"

Virginia took the manuscript. Glancing at Vita, who was searching her face in astonishment, Virginia lifted the title page to look at the text. But it wasn't hers: that copy had been folded in her suit for two days and had a crease down the middle.

"This isn't it!" she whispered. "You mixed them up!"

"What have you done with my manuscript?" barked Karswell above.

"I switched the back pages, dammit," Beverly whispered hoarsely. *"Give it to him!"*

The crowd receded around Virginia and Vita, revealing them kneeling together in the middle of the stage. Violence averted, women were already trooping back down the steps. The riot grrls were being escorted away like defeated Little Leaguers, reassured from either side that playing fair was more important than winning. Nose Stud even kicked at the stage with her heel. Bob Doe, meanwhile, had been propped up in one of the seats in the front row, his hands crossed over his groin like a cadaver. Oppenheimer stood a few paces back from the podium, smoothing back his hair and trying to tug his double-breasted jacket back into line. Karswell gripped the sides of the podium with both hands and raged into the hall, at the backs of his audience, most of whom were gathering up their coats and purses and backpacks.

"No one leaves!" he cried. "Not until I get my paper back! Which one of you harpies has *stolen my work?*"

"Here," Virginia started to say, but Vita pressed her fingers against Virginia's lips. Their eyes met again, and Vita lifted her hand to Virginia's face and tenderly pressed the drooping sideburn back against her temple. Then, her eyes welling with tears, she pushed herself back, stood up, and disappeared into the crowd.

Virginia pushed herself to her feet, shooting her cuffs and straightening her suit coat. She reached into the coat and stepped up behind Karswell, the manuscript steady in her hand.

"Professor," she said, clearing her throat.

Karswell turned, his eyes aflame. She offered him his pince-nez.

"This is yours, I believe," she said.

Karswell, his face knotted in rage, blinked at her, then nodded, taking the little glasses.

"Thank you," he said in a strangled voice.

Virginia stepped closer.

"And may I give you this, Professor Karswell?" she said, her voice seeming to come from far away. "I believe it is yours."

Karswell reached for the paper and hesitated, glancing up from the title page to meet Virginia's eye. Her heart pounded, but she managed to hold her hand steady. Karswell looked down again, lifting the title page of the paper without taking it from her, and he read the first few lines. He smiled.

"Yes," he said, taking the paper from Virginia. "Yes it is. I am much obliged to you, professor."

He turned away, and as he lifted the paper to the podium, Virginia saw the red shadow of the runes on the back page, like a watermark bleeding through. She swallowed against a dry throat and stepped back.

Something shifted in the room. The hubbub of the departing crowd and the shuffle of feet faded. The light grew dimmer, and Karswell seemed to recede from Virginia. She glanced under the table. The litter of pages was still there, but Beverly was gone. Most of the audience had already left; only a few women remained out among the seats, collecting their things. Vita wasn't one of them, but before Virginia could look for her, Oppenheimer touched her elbow and murmured some apology, promising to make it up to her.

"Sure," she said, distracted. "No problem."

Oppenheimer turned away from her, and then stopped again.

"Who let that dog in here?" he said.

At the podium, Karswell whirled, glancing behind him. But there was nothing to see.

"What dog?" he said.

"I'm sorry," Oppenheimer said. "I thought I saw a black dog. All the excitement, I guess." He drew a breath and glanced out at the rows of empty seats. "Perhaps I can persuade some of them to stay. Shall we begin at last?"

But Karswell's face was red and he was breathing heavily. His eyes darted all about the stage. He whirled again, as if someone had touched him on the shoulder, and he gripped the sides of the podium to hold himself up. A little breeze, surprisingly cool in the overheated lecture hall, tickled the pages of the paper before him, lifting the title page, then the first page, then the next. Karswell banged his palm on top of it, pinning the paper to the top of the podium.

"I have to leave," he said, in a queer voice. "I'm not feeling at all well."

"Victor?" Oppenheimer said, stepping closer.

"I have to leave," Karswell said. He popped open his briefcase with shaking hands, stuffed the paper into it, and slammed it shut. He picked up the case and pressed it to his chest, glancing wildly out into the empty hall, where only Bob Doe remained, slumped in his seat. Then Karswell whirled and dashed for the back of the stage, brushing Oppenheimer aside. Virginia stepped back to let him pass, and Karswell hesitated, rocking on the balls of his feet. He shot a glance at her, looking her up and down, but without meeting her eyes. Then he bolted forward again, fumbled with the knob of the backstage door, wrenched it open, and plunged into the little hallway behind the stage. The last Virginia saw of him was the flash of his wool stockings fading rhythmically into the dark.

Oppenheimer sighed and jerked his tie loose. He lifted his arms and let them flop against his sides.

"Well," he said with a faint smile, "another profitable day in the marketplace of ideas."

Oppenheimer slouched down the steps and up the aisle, following the last of the audience out of the hall. Virginia closed the backstage door and crossed to stage right. Beverly sat at the foot of the steps, her face buried in her hands. Virginia came down and sat beside her. She peeled off her beard.

"You want this back?" she said.

Beverly lifted her face from her hands. Her cheeks were dry, her face pale, the light withdrawn from her eyes. She looked at the limp little strip of hair and shook her head. Virginia tossed it aside. They were the only ones left in the hall, except for Bob Doe twitching in his unconsciousness like a dreaming dog.

"May I ask you something?" Virginia said.

Beverly shrugged.

"Remember you told me how, not long before he died, your husband would talk in his sleep?"

Beverly nodded.

"What did he say?"

Beverly gave Virginia a long, searching look.

"Do you really want to know?"

"Yes."

Beverly looked away. She drew a breath and let it out. She started to repeat what her husband had said, but after a moment Virginia stopped her.

# eighteen

ERY LATE ON A COLD NOVEMBER NIGHT IN Texas—very early in the morning, in fact—a little man in a tweed suit, breathing hard and sweating heavily, trotted across the campus of Longhorn State University, muttering rapidly to himself in Latin, Old Norse, Sumerian. So far none of them were doing him any good, but he had not yet exhausted his alternatives; there were older, darker languages at his disposal. He tugged at his collar, trying to loosen his bow tie, but he was only pulling it tighter, making his face flush, making it even harder to breathe. He wore no overcoat, and he carried nothing in his hands. Indeed, his leather briefcase lay spilled on the asphalt in the middle of Tejas Avenue, under a traffic light that had switched to blinking yellow for the night. His cloth cap lay on the sidewalk not far behind him. He was making a beeline for the building that housed the history department, and he patted his pocket every few steps to make sure he had his keys, the building being locked at this hour of the morning. He trotted rather than ran because even in the echoing silence of the empty campus, as the only person moving under the yellowish security lights, he had no desire to call attention to himself. He did, however, glance over his shoulder frequently, wide-eyed, his lower lip trembling, looking back with particular attention at the shadows under the trees. He saw nothing, but he skipped a few steps faster as if he had, his heart leaping at the sight of the plaza ahead, and of the history building beyond, where lay—not his salvation, exactly, that's not the word—but at least the Latin originals of the recipes he had accumulated over the years. Meantime he was trying all the ones he had by memory, though none of them seemed to be working. Still, he had time yet, surely. No doubt he could find a loophole in the manuscript in his office. There was always an exception. You only had to know where to look.

The little man's footsteps as he entered the plaza attracted the attention of a young security guard named Hector Quiroga, who was having his dinner in the security office of the history building. Having clocked in at all his stations, he sat with his feet up on his battered metal desk, eating the sandwich he'd packed earlier and reading a paperback horror novel by the light of a single desk lamp. Hector aspired to being a horror novelist himself, and he sat with a No. 2 pencil stuck behind his ear, so that he could limn the passages he thought were particularly effective, in order to find them again for further study. This was the first book he had read by this particular author, a rising young Brit—"There's a new name for terror!" said Clive Barker on the cover—and the conceit of the novel was that an inexperienced occultist had accidentally opened a multidimensional portal and let Something through from Somewhere Else, which hadn't ought to be here. Hector was an experienced enough reader of the genre to recognize a ploy from Lovecraft when he saw it, but the book held his interest nevertheless with a new twist: The Something that had been Let In was behaving like a serial killer, and through some sort of multidimensional, topological hanky-panky was killing its victims by yanking them inside out like a glove. Better still, they didn't die right away, and there were loving descriptions of London bobbies throwing up all over their shoes at the sight of twitching skeletons hung like Christmas trees with glistening variety meats: pulsing brains and still-beating hearts and pink lungs that rose and fell like rubber bladders. Just now, the Other World beastie was stalking a pregnant woman, and Hector had put down his meat-loaf sandwich and was fumbling for the pencil behind his ear.

This is going to be good, he was thinking, when he heard footsteps on the plaza.

He looked up. The security office was in the half-basement of the building and possessed a wide window that started just at ground level. This meant that even tipped back in his creaking office chair, Hector had a striking, low-angle, CinemaScope view of the plaza, his eyeline just an inch or two above the pavement. Kitty-corner from the office, entering the plaza from the northwest corner, a man was running toward Hector in an odd sort of suit, with a vest, a coat, and short little pants that ended just below his knees, cinched around a pair of woolen stockings. The vest was heaving with the man's exertions, the tails of his suitcoat flying, and he was tugging hard at one wing of his bow tie. Even in the sickly yellow light of the sodium lamps, Hector could see that the man was flushed and breathless; damp patches had begun to bleed through his shirt front and under the arms of his suit. He was running hard, but he didn't seem to be making much progress toward Hector's window, and when the little man glanced back over his shoulder, Hector followed the glance and saw something that stopped his own breath.

Behind the man, quickly blotting out the stars, was the blackest ceiling of clouds Hector had ever seen, rising up the sky like a wall of darkness, dragging its shadow over the campus just behind the little man in tweed. Watching the man pump his legs furiously and make so little progress, Hector got the frightening feeling that the runner was *pulling* the darkness after him, like a man in a harness. The sight of it made Hector's skin tighten all over his body.

He leaned forward abruptly and shut off the desk lamp—all of a sudden he didn't want to be seen—and he rose slowly from his chair, putting his paperback facedown on the desk. The little man had reached the center of the plaza only after the most terrible exertion. He leaned forward like a polar explorer pulling a sledge, sweat staining his collar, his eyes bulging out of his head, his mouth working rapidly. Hector, his skin tingling, realized that the dark was gaining on the man, that no matter how hard he ran, he was only pulling the shadow *closer*.

The little man on the plaza was running in place now like a cartoon mouse with a grinning cat leaning on its tail. I should call somebody, Hector was thinking, when suddenly the man shot straight up into the air. Instinctively, Hector jumped to the window and looked up. Overhead, above the yellowish glow of the lamps, he saw the black storm front sliding over the pale stars like the lid of a box. But the little man was nowhere to be seen; it was as if he had been yanked straight up into the darkness by his invisible harness, by whatever huge load he was hauling. Hector inched a little closer to the glass without touching it, looking carefully from side to side for the man, seeing nothing.

A pair of legs swung suddenly out of nowhere and slammed into the window, fetching a long crack all the way across the pane, and sending Hector leaping backward into the dark office, toppling him over his chair to the floor. He scuttled to the rear wall and saw, through the wide window, the man flying away through the air, just a foot or so off the pavement. The little man was limp, as if he were being swung helplessly at the end of a line, and he flew in a wide circle around the plaza, screaming, with his chest forward and his useless arms and legs trailing after him. He was doing more than just screaming, he seemed to be saying something. The language was unfamiliar to Hector, but the tone was familiar: the little man was calling out with the last of his breath, beseeching someone.

"Thurisaz!" he seemed to be crying, or something like that.

The man swung around the plaza toward the window again, and Hector flinched, but now the man was spiraling upward as he went, and he passed the window above it, out of sight, his wordless scream dopplering past. Then Hector, rising to his feet, saw the man swinging around the far side of the plaza again, this time higher off the ground than a man could reach, and climbing.

He didn't know if it was because of his duty as a university employee or his curiosity as a budding writer—and afterward he tried not to think about it—but Hector snatched up his radio and dashed out of the office and up onto the plaza, ducking his head as he came out the door. A vicious, freezing wind pressed Hector's uniform to his legs and chest, while above him and all around the plaza the darkness closed in, cutting off the nighttime sky, obscuring even the buildings on the far side of the square. The yellow lights around the plaza flickered and dimmed, throwing the crazy shadows of the statues around the edge of the plaza forward and back and side to side.

And above it all, spinning higher and faster, in a tighter and tighter spiral, was the little screaming man in the tweed suit, his tiny voice barely audible above the arctic rush of the wind, calling out for help in a language the security guard could not identify. Hector clutched his radio to his chest with one hand and held his other up against the spiraling wind, squinting up at the little tweed speck that now rotated on its own axis, high above the center of the plaza.

"Blessed virgin protect me," Hector murmured, his words whipping away in the wind.

Then, as abruptly as if someone had shut it off, the wind stopped. His eyes still directed upward, Hector saw the little speck begin to fall, not straight down, but at an angle, rushing feet first toward the ground. The lights of the plaza flickered on and off and on again, and Hector backed against the wall of the building behind him and threw his hand up in front of his face, watching through his fingers as the little man came swooping down, with a last, long, descending howl of terror.

And collided with a sickening thump with one of the statues at the edge of the plaza. Hector winced and closed his eyes, but he cracked them open again, expecting to see the body bouncing back to the pavement, or at least sliding limp down the pedestal of the statue. But the man just hung there, from the statue, his head tipped back, his arms and legs dangling.

Hector started slowly across the plaza, fumbling at his radio with both hands. His legs trembled so badly he wasn't sure he could make it. As he walked, the dark around the plaza lifted and the pale stucco of the other buildings came into view. Overhead, the cloud was disintegrating before his eyes, tearing itself to shreds and letting through the stars and the velvety darkness of the sky.

"Plaza station, go ahead," barked the radio.

Hector found the speaker button.

"This is Hector," he breathed. "You better send somebody."

"Plaza station, do you need assistance?" said the dispatcher.

"Man, I'm not the one who needs it," whispered Hector, shutting off the radio. Coming to the edge of the plaza, he trod on something brittle, crunching it, and he stopped. He lifted his foot to see a pair of little lenses shattered under his boot. Then he looked up at the statue before him.

Victor Karswell hung from the statue of Jim Bowie, impaled on the upthrust knife of the hero of the Alamo. It was almost a sight out of Hector's dinnertime reading: Karswell hadn't exactly been turned inside out, but it was fair to say that he'd been gutted. The blade hadn't just penetrated him; it had slit him open from groin to collarbone. Steam rose from the cavity as from a goose just out of the oven, and his giblets hung in glistening loops in the lamp-light. Victor Karswell was making his own gravy. The bronze blade would have sliced him further, in fact, but for the stubborn knot of his bow tie. Now the professor hung limp by his neck, the tip of the Bowie knife pressed up under his chin, his head tipped back and his bulging, sightless gaze pointed up at the sky.

To keep himself from fainting, Hector Quiroga sank to his knees, and then sat cross-legged on the cold pavement. He closed his eyes and tried to draw deep breaths against a tightening diaphragm. He crossed himself, thinking that maybe horror novels weren't such a good idea. Perhaps he'd take up westerns instead.

## nineteen

IRGINIA DUNNING DID NOT HEAR OF KARS-
well's death the evening it happened. Instead of returning to Texas
after the conference, she made a surprise visit to her mother in
Bernt, Minnesota, where, after not quite convincing Mom that
everything was fine, she went to bed in her old room and slept for
eighteen hours straight. She did not hear of Karswell's death when
she woke up, did not hear of it, in fact until after dinner one night,
as she and her mother watched one of her mother's beloved tabloid
news shows. There, after the Duchess of York sucking on a fi-
nancier's toes in Monaco and a soap opera star's abduction by
aliens, was "The Gutted Professor: A Scholar's Mysterious Death
in the Lone Star State." There were teasing glimpses of the scene
of the accident from somebody's shaky home video—dangling
calves in wool stockings, a crushed pince-nez—but nothing was lin-
gered over.

"Did they say Lamar?" said Virginia's mom. "Isn't that where you
teach?"

"No, Mom," said Virginia. "I'm pretty sure they said College
Station. Nothing like that ever happens in Lamar."

Back in Texas, Virginia tried to call Beverly and got a recording
announcing that the number had been changed. A mechanical
voice read a new number, with an area code that Virginia did not
recognize. She thought she ought to write it down, but by time she
tracked down a pencil and a piece of paper, the number had slipped

her mind. She meant to dial the old number and try again, but she never did.

Karswell left no family, and no instructions to the department for the disposition of his papers. In the end, the university took possession of his books, absorbing some into the rare books collection, selling off the rest. When Virginia heard that the department was having difficulty finding someone willing to go through Karswell's papers on behalf of the university archives, to determine what was important and what was not, she offered her services. As a result, she spent much of her Christmas break that year sitting on the carpet of Karswell's office, going through boxes of files, sorting them by subject. Most of the books were gone by then, and only a few of Karswell's effects remained: his chair, his desk, the spike. Virginia pulled up the blinds and turned on the overhead lights, but even so, there was always a bit of gloom in the office.

On the last day of the year, as a dreary, dripping rain fell from a low gray sky, Virginia sat alone at Karswell's desk, sorting drafts of his manuscripts into piles on his desk. The last one she came to was an early draft for his last book, *A History of Early Modern Witchcraft*. Out of curiosity, she plucked down from the shelf a copy of the published version and spent a few minutes comparing the two, to see what changes the publication process had wrought. The prose was virtually the same; evidently the editor at the university press didn't care or had despaired of persuading Karswell to clean up his split infinitives. But the manuscript seemed much longer than the published book, and finally she turned to the end matter—the bibliography, the index, the appendices. There she discovered that the manuscript version contained not only the translations of the various "recipes," but the Latin originals as well. Karswell's little warning to the curious, that the recipes would not work in translation, was not present in the draft version.

Virginia turned to the appendix on casting the runes and saw that it was several pages longer than the published version; it included the runes themselves written directly into the manuscript in Karswell's hand. There was also a list in Latin, noting the various uses of each rune or combination of runes. Virginia did not read Latin, but turning back a page, she found the same list in English.

"To win the affection of another," said one. "To gain riches." "To win mastery over another."

Virginia smiled ruefully. Too bad there's not one for surviving your tenure review, she thought. After everything that had happened, she still faced the prospect of losing her job by the end of the school year. Professor LeFanu, her chair, had taken Virginia aside just before Christmas to commiserate with her recent bad luck, but he had also pointed out that having a paper accepted and then yanked from a festschrift volume, by an editor who had since died, was not going to do her any good.

"The clock is ticking, Virginia," said LeFanu, a little less Shelby Foote than usual. "If you don't come up with a publication this spring, I won't be able to do anything for you."

Virginia sighed and reassembled the pages of Karswell's manuscript. As she hefted it upright and rapped it against the desktop to straighten the pages, the overhead lights flickered and went out. Virginia caught her breath. Looking out the window, she saw that the rain had stopped. Lights still shone in the buildings across the plaza, and across the office Virginia saw the light from the hall shining under the door. She laid the manuscript down and switched on the desk lamp, which threw a yellowish glow across the title page:

A HISTORY OF EARLY MODERN WITCHCRAFT

by

VIRGINIA DUNNING

Virginia blinked, then read the author's name on the title page again. *Karswell*, it read. *Victor Karswell, A.B., M.A. (Oxon.), Ph.D.* She rubbed her eyes. This is nuts, she thought. Here she was fooling around with a dead man's manuscript when she still needed to publish her own. LeFanu was only telling her the truth: she might very well be looking for a job by the end of winter semester.

"I'll think about that tomorrow," Virginia said aloud, very definitively. She lifted the manuscript and lowered it into its cardboard box. Then she looked at the time and noted the gloom gathering outside the window. There was a New Year's Eve party to dress for, and a long walk home. Virginia stood, wrapped her scarf around her neck, and straightened the boxed manuscript, making it square with the edges of the desk. Then she buttoned up her coat, lifted her bag off the back of the chair, and paused to align the boxed manuscript again, which she must have knocked crooked putting on her coat. She shut off the lamp, and the shadows filled Karswell's office like a murmur. She could almost hear words in it, and Virginia sighed loudly to shut them out and crossed through the dark to the door.

As she touched the doorknob, she heard a thump on the carpet behind her. Virginia's skin tingled, and she hesitated before opening the door. Karswell still has my imagination working overtime, she thought. She turned slowly, and in the light from the corridor, she saw the manuscript of Karswell's last book lying in its box on the carpet in front of the desk.

I must have set it too close to the edge, she thought. I can't just leave it there—the janitor might toss it.

In the fan of light from the open doorway, her shadow creeping up the wall opposite, she went back and picked up the box and held it over the desk. The manuscript seemed to be lighter than it had been a moment ago.

I ought to lock it up in the desk, Virginia thought, or in the filing cabinet. But the keys were already tucked away in her bag, and she was late. Still, no uncatalogued manuscript was supposed to leave the office.

But I *am* the cataloguer, Virginia thought. I make the rules. I'll just take it home and bring it back after the turn of the year.

So she tucked the box into her bag, where it fit surprisingly well, and she carried it with her up the hall and down the stairs and out onto the twilight plaza, where the lights were just coming on and the pavement gleamed in the recent rain. The air was bracingly cold and wet, and Virginia walked with her long, confident rancher's stride. In the flickering light of the sodium lamps, she passed under the rain-wet statue of Jim Bowie, and she gave him a jaunty little two-fingered salute. She felt better than confident, she decided. For the first time in months she felt, well, empowered. She smiled to herself and passed into the welcoming shadows under the live oaks beyond the plaza. A chill winter wind began to blow from behind her, urging her along, but Virginia did not mind, because the wind was going in her direction, and the shadows reminded her of her gloomy childhood, growing up where the days were short, and the nights were long and cold and full of rich darkness. Indeed, the wind was like a mischievous old friend who teased her as she walked, playing about her ankles, tugging at her scarf, and whispering in her ear, all the way home.

# Author's Note

The third of these tales, "Casting the Runes," is a pastiche of the short story of the same name by M. R. James (1862–1936), the late Victorian academic and author of the greatest ghost stories in the English language. Aficionados will also recognize in my version the climactic moment from James's story "Oh Whistle and I'll Come to You, My Lad" and an idea from his essay "Stories I Have Tried to Write."

The debate over the death of Captain Cook is waged with considerable passion and wit in Ganneth Obeyesekere's *The Apotheosis of Captain Cook: European Mythmaking in the Pacific* (Princeton University Press, 1992) and Marshall Sahlin's *How "Natives" Think: About Captain Cook, for Example* (University of Chicago Press, 1995).

A number of good friends read these tales and gave advice and encouragement. Thanks and don't be afraid of the dark to: Margaret Wong and Ross Orr (formerly RotoBroil), Martin Lewis, Keith Taylor, John Marks, Gretchen Wahl, Becky McDermott, Dror Wahrman, Allan Gee, Debra Bloch, Tom Fricke and Chris Stier, Glendon and Mary Hynes, Laura Balbi and Mike Hynes, and everybody at Shaman Drum Bookshop in Ann Arbor. Thanks also to Bruce Willoughby and my brother Tom for helping me to keep my head above water. Thanks especially to Neil Olson, living proof that it's possible to be a great agent and good guy. Many thanks as well to the perspicacious George Witte, the hard-working Lauren

Sarat, and all the good folks at Picador USA. A melancholy farewell to the late Lee Goerner, who deserves to be somewhere pleasant, having a sherry and a laugh at my expense with Professor James. And thanks most of all to Mimi Mayer, for her love, her patience, and her unfailingly good advice.

Last but not least, thanks to Mr. Alp, Tiger Lily, and Sam, who take turns walking all over the desk when I'm trying to write, and who have forgiven me (I hope) for Charlotte.